S.D. MAYES

Letters TO THE Pianist

GELAN
Livonia, Michigan

Published by Gelan
an imprint of BHC Press

Library of Congress Control Number:
2017937916

ISBN-13: 978-1-946848-04-8
ISBN-10: 1-946848-04-2

Visit the publisher at:
www.bhcpress.com

Also available in ebook

ACKNOWLEDGMENTS

I am hugely grateful to the Fortnum and Mason historian who helped me out with some detailed research, and also the invaluable early readers of *Letters to the Pianist:* Kathryn Gross, Robert Zeffman, and John Darryl Winston, amongst many others, who helped give me clearer vision.

For my mother, Ruth

Letters

TO THE

Pianist

Prologue

Sunday, 3rd February 1946

Two hens erupted into the London sky, taking flight, their harsh *kawk, kawk, kawk* startling him. Pheasants. He hated the bloody things. The sight of them swamped his senses with the memory of their thick, pungent aroma, making his breath catch in his throat as the plump animals somehow managed to stay airborne. They'd lose the fight with gravity soon enough, return to their feeding ground and, although hunting season was months away, they'd still end up bagged and eaten by some wealthy landowner sooner or later.

'Stupid birds,' he muttered, squinting as they disappeared into the distance, the memory of gunshots exploding along with the frantic beating of their wings before they fell to the ground. He and they were the same in so many ways: victims of circumstance.

With whisky flowing through his veins, he shoved his shaking hands into the pockets of his tailored suit and strode unsteadily past the endless rows of Knightsbridge townhouses. God, how he'd come to despise their elegant white facades and black railings; just like posh prisons, concealing the worst type of sin.

1

He picked up his pace, shivering from the wintery chill, practically running by the time he reached his own imposing front door: midnight-black with a heavy brass knocker, shaped in the form of a lion's head, its jaws wide-open. Two Corinthian columns flanked the entrance.

Fumbling inside his jacket for the keys, he jabbed one into the lock, his heart racing as he twisted it open and almost lost his footing, lurching forward into the grand reception hall with white marble flooring, lit up by a dazzling Venetian chandelier.

Waiting, breathing heavily, he listened out for voices or suspicious sounds, wondering if he could still trust his beloved butler, Travers, or any of his supposedly loyal servants. Where were they and why was he not greeted in the usual manner? His eyes trailed the sweeping staircase that led up to eight en suite bedrooms, a library and a spacious ballroom. His stomach tightened—was there somebody up there lying in wait?

He gulped some air, feeling dizzy. He'd tried so hard to stay strong, bury his grief and regret, but an aching sadness overwhelmed him as he sank to the floor. *This was never my home,* he thought, recalling his gilded lifestyle inside the four-storey Edwardian property: endless deferential conversations over lavish society dinners honouring captains of industry, the landed gentry, and corrupt politicians bankrolled by titled millionaires. Everything, all of it, fuelled by artifice, like a rotting stench seeping through its impeccable grandeur. And there he was, stuck in the middle, acting out the most ridiculous role of his life, pretending to be one of them—but not anymore. He bowed his head, scraping his fingers through his hair. So what now? Would he ever find happiness? Would he ever play to a full house again, rise from the Steinway to thunderous applause and bask in the King of England's favour?

Footsteps rang out in the stillness. Someone was coming, but there was nowhere to run.

He slumped against the wall, feeling weary and broken, stuck on the recurring vision of that bloody mutilated corpse, whipped until flesh fell away from the bones, suspended upside down from a ceiling rafter, reminding him of hooked meat in a slaughterhouse. *I've done nothing wrong. I am a good man, worthy of a happy life,* he told himself, knowing there was only one path he could take if he didn't want to be next.

Chapter 1

Way back, in 1941, when I was still young and naive, in that twilight world of adolescent confusion, I could fritter away time daydreaming for hours. In truth, all three of us: the Goldberg children, escaped into a magical world, immersing ourselves in books like *The Secret Garden* and *Peter Pan,* or transforming into castaways wrapped up in old towels pretending we were on *Treasure Island* foraging for food. We grew to thrive on fantasy as if it were an energy fuel, always searching for a new diversion. Anything to block out the bitter reality of London life.

Our home was a red-brick terraced house on Sandringham Road in Hackney, known as the heart of the East End, a cosy haven despite the peeling paintwork and windows so thick with dust you couldn't see in or out.

There weren't many families like us that remained. Our once friendly neighbourhood, with the sound of children's laughter and neighbours chattering in the street, had long gone. It was now eerily quiet; the pavements strewn with rubble and a swamping sadness that hung in the air like the reek of burning flesh.

Most of my school friends had been evacuated, disappearing to the countryside without time for goodbyes, whilst others

5

were horribly maimed or killed in the blitz. But our daddy was adamant. 'We're not staying in a stinking shelter,' he'd say, 'home is our anchor and they can take me on bare knuckles an' all before I'd send you three away.' And I felt truly blessed that he kept us together despite the dangers.

At night, when darkness came along with the night raids, I often thought of my old friends as I tried to sleep, wondering if their spirits were rejoicing in heaven or aimlessly wandering the shadowlands of Sheol. I prepared to die so many times; the sirens screeching in my ears as I'd dive under the covers frantically reciting the Shema, trying to block out the grinding roar of planes overhead and the whistling bombs raining down, the deafening *boom, boom, boom* as they crashed into buildings and tore them apart. It all felt monstrously chilling, the cruelty of it all; in awe that our lives were so fragile, knowing we could be snuffed out in seconds and ready for a coffin.

In the morning, I'd clamber out of bed rubbing my gritty eyes, exhausted from lack of sleep, and walk straight into my warm fuzzy bubble, brushing away my worst fears as I awaited my handsome prince, hoping he would come and save us as promised in every happy ending.

That was all I had: pretence to help save my sanity and give me some kind of antidote to pain.

Until one day my bubble popped, bursting open.

And finally, I knew.

That dreams and wishes and fairy tales were like icing on a mouldy cake—they can't hide the truth—because when you take a proper bite, you choke.

Saturday morning, 8th March 1941

'I'm coming to get you,' I whispered in a sing-song voice. 'Something's going to bite you, rip you in two.' I leant across the breakfast table staring at my younger siblings menacingly as they ignored me, scraping up the rest of their porridge. I waited, ready to pounce. 'Last one out's a dead-un.' This was our favourite game; goading, teasing, scaring each other witless with our safe form of 'terror' until their spoons slammed down and in a shrieking mad scramble, we all hurtled outside like cannon balls ready to play.

I threw down a penny, hopping onto each numbered square, drawn out with chalk on the pavement a few yards from our house.

A stone skittered in front of me and I stumbled outside the chalky lines.

'Ha-ha you forfeit a point,' Gabi shouted, punching the air in victory.

'That's not fair, Gabi. You're cheating.'

'Boohoo,' he cried, wiping away fake tears as he broke into that big silly grin; so like our daddy's magnetic smile that could put a spell on you in a heartbeat and charm you into submission.

'Wow, see that?' squealed Hannah, interrupting our spat.

We spun round to look.

She pointed at the roadside, her blonde ringlets falling across her face as she crouched down scrutinising something that glittered on the kerb edge, near the drain that went down to the sewers. That was typical of her; she was such a magpie, always finding shiny things amongst the rubble, like marbles or bobby pins.

Gabi and I bent over, peering closely.

She took a breath and picked up a chain from the dirt and held it in the centre of her palm, wiping off some of the sludgy grime with the sleeve of her jumper. 'Woo, look at this little sparkler. I bet it's worth a fortune.' She draped it between her fingers and then glared at us. 'It's mine, all mine, do you hear? Finders keepers.'

I gazed at the gold chain with the Star of David dangling from it and instantly knew whom it belonged to. Looking back at the roadside, my heart raced as something caught my eye, lying in the kerb about a foot away. A bloody lump partly hidden under a heap of broken red bricks.

'What's wrong, Ruth?' asked Gabi.

I gulped. He must have noticed my fixed stare. 'Nothing,' I said, looking away.

'Have you seen an icky diseased rat scuttling about, because I've seen lots?' He laughed and pulled out a sticky humbug from his trouser pocket and popped it in his mouth making slurping noises.

'Yuck, rats,' said Hannah, wrinkling her nose.

'Can both of you cover your eyes, please?'

'Why? I don't want to.' Hannah stamped her foot in defiance. Gabi smirked.

'Do it! Or you might see something you really wished you hadn't.'

As with all our little scraps, they reluctantly obeyed, and I could breathe easier. Mama told me countless times, 'Ruth, get out of that pink fog!' She said being at war meant facing the ugly facts of life, especially now I was over fourteen and able to apply for work. Gabi was twelve and Hannah only ten and in my mind they were still the 'little ones' and I didn't want to give them nightmares.

Forcing myself to be brave, I leant forward, carefully moving the brick fragments out of the way.

I jumped back in fright.

A severed hand swarmed with maggots, one of the most disgusting insects of all time, and they were crawling everywhere, burrowing into the flesh. I covered my mouth to stop myself screaming, heaving at the sickening sight. Catching my breath, out of morbid curiosity I dared to look again, watching the maggots crawl around revealing patches of bloodstained skin.

Something seemed familiar: the glimpse of chipped nail polish and a pink Bakelite ring on the right forefinger. I looked down at my own matching ring.

This was my friend, Jane Beckerman's hand, discarded in the gutter like a piece of rubbish along with her necklace that she'd always treasured, a family heirloom her much-loved grandmother had passed down the family. I swatted away the swarm of flies that gathered from nowhere, flitting in circles, taunting me like a gang of bullies.

'Can I look now?' asked Hannah, the chain still draped across her fingers.

'No, not yet!'

'Hey, don't be mean!'

'Sorry, Hannah. Another minute, that's all.'

I scooped up rubble to re-cover Jane's rotting hand, ensuring it was completely camouflaged. 'I'm so sorry,' I whispered.

I turned to look at Gabi, the pupils in his eyes dilated with ghoulish fascination as he chewed on his plump bottom lip, the way he always did when he was nervous. Gorgeous Gabi we all called him, labelled 'pretty' ever since he was a baby, given his mop of wavy dark hair and those long feathery lashes that fanned his copper-coloured eyes.

'You saw, didn't you?'

He nodded.

'Well, I hope you don't get nightmares.'

'It's no big deal.' He leant forward so Hannah couldn't hear. 'I've seen worse collecting shrapnel off the bomb sites.' He tilted his head to one side as if monitoring my face for shock value. 'Once I tripped over a decapitated head.'

I sighed at his flippant bravado. He didn't know the hand belonged to my best friend and I felt it best to say nothing. It wasn't unusual for body parts to be torn off in explosions and fly into the air landing randomly. Usually, though, the relief workers cleared them away before you stumbled across them.

'You can look now, Hannah,' I said, my voice choked, 'but the necklace ... can I have it, please?'

She opened her eyes. 'Why? Might be worth a bob or two.'

'It belongs to Jane. She always wore it, remember?'

'Oh, yes, Jane, she gave me some liquorice.' She handed me the chain, pouting sulkily. 'Best give it back to her then.'

I cupped it in my hands as if it were a priceless treasure, placing it in the front pocket of my pinafore. It was all I had left of my best friend. We'd been close for years, more like sisters really; our arms always linked as we walked to the shops, giggling at any silly thing that caught our eye. This was all so unfair, a mockery of her life. Where was the rest of her body, I wondered. I pictured her gap-toothed smile and that frizz of ginger hair and my eyes filled with tears. It hit me hard. I'd miss her, really miss her, and now I'd never see her again.

I decided to sneak back later, wipe away the yucky maggots and put her abandoned hand in a shoebox along with her necklace. I would get daddy's trowel from the shed and dig a hole in our bomb-blasted back garden, in a private spot behind our leafless, charred apple tree. I'd recite a prayer and give her the humane burial she deserved. She was my friend and I had to make that count, because whatever they tell you, there are no gold stars for good behaviour; a perfect angel or a nasty monster, it's pot luck how you peg out.

Chapter 2

Over the next few weeks, I shuffled around in a daze, sobbing unexpectedly, trying to push Jane's broken body out of my mind. I was almost grateful to help Mama with the chores, so I didn't have time to think and she could teach me with her usual intolerance, 'wife skills' as she called them—how to cook, sew and knit. When I made my first apple cake, I was chuffed. It was a rare treat after Mama swopped our bacon vouchers for eggs and butter, and the aroma as it rose in the oven restored me, however briefly, to a sense of normality and wellbeing.

That evening, as the rain bucketed down, lashing against the windows on one of the wettest Aprils I'd ever known, we'd all eaten a slice after dinner, and everyone applauded my new found talent. 'Ruth, that's the stuff of dreams,' said Daddy with a grin, and even Mama nodded with approval. It was unimportant, silly really, but I felt a rush of happiness that I'd contributed something good.

Soon after, we all retired to the living room; my mother, Rose 'aged thirty-three and feeling fifty', she'd say, after managing our household budget on a shoestring was busily sewing up our clothes to make them last longer. She had what Daddy called a Rubenesque figure and wore her thick chestnut hair pinned up and curled into a victory roll at the front, revealing her rounded face and pursed thin lips.

In complete contrast, there was my beloved father, Joseph. Two years older than Mama, although everyone said he looked much younger, not surprising with his blessed genetics. Six feet tall and some might say dashing with his dancing eyes of cornflower blue and his thick, dark hair slicked back from his chiselled face with Brylcreem. But he had something else—something invisible that was nothing to do with good looks, and whatever it was, it made heads turn wherever we went. 'That voodoo magic,' Mama called it, 'something electric that heats you up.'

For my liking, we didn't see enough of him. He wasn't some big shot success, but he worked long hours in his own greengrocery store, Joe's Fruit and Veg. Relaxing for once in his favourite armchair, his head hidden behind the newspaper, occasionally he peeked above, pulling a funny face as we all stifled giggles. He was always the joker.

Hannah played with her favourite doll as Gabi teased me about wearing a brassiere, something he found rivetingly amusing, whilst I played solitaire on the small side table, pretending not to hear. We had to grow up early in those days and I certainly did, already developing an ample figure to rival my mother's.

It should have been the perfect end to a perfect day until Mama left the room and I heard the distinct sound of her court shoes pacing up and down the tiled kitchen floor.

'Ruth, come here,' she yelled.

'Yes, Mama,' I called back, wondering what I was in for this time as I hurried to see what she wanted.

She stood by the kitchen sink, studying me with her intense dark eyes.

I edged towards her. 'Is everything okay, Mama?'

She picked up a piece of paper from the kitchen top and waved it in front of my nose. 'See this. It's a bill from the coalman. Four months overdue.'

'Sorry, Mama. I'll look for work. I've been a bit distracted.'

'Distracted, huh,' she replied with a scowl, the deeply etched furrow between her brows deepening, 'Bone idle, more like.'

'No, Mama, that's not fair. I'm doing my chores.'

'Chores don't bring in wages,' she screeched, her brown eyes blazing with fury as she slapped me round the face before I saw it coming. I reeled back, wincing at the red hot sting on my cheek.

With her hands on her hips, her face flushed red. 'Why do you always talk back? I'd have been beaten by my parents for that kind of insolence. Money's tight and your father and I need a contribution. Now wash the floor before bed.'

With trembling hands I picked up the kettle and put it on the stove to boil water. I was baffled by my mother's changeable moods. She always picked on me whilst Gabi and Hannah got off scot-free. Did she hate me? I couldn't help but wonder.

Daddy peeped his head around the door. 'Everything all right?' he said in a hushed voice.

Mama nodded and waved him away. She was definitely the boss of our house, and he didn't like to tread on her toes when it came to discipline. I think he just wanted a peaceful life.

Finishing my kitchen duties, just before sunset, there was the usual flurry of activity as our parents scuttled around the house, drawing all the blackout curtains. Within half-an-hour, the day was over and we were all in our pyjamas waiting for them to say goodnight. We'd been sleeping downstairs in the living room for the last two years with mattresses on the floor, so there would be less danger if we did get bombed.

I still had the jitters when Mama came in, feeling a jealous pang when she kissed Gabi and Hannah goodnight. 'Sweet dreams, angels,' she said as they grinned broadly. She was never as warm with me. She pecked my cheek as I clung onto the smallest flicker of a smile, hoping, somehow, she might realise I was a good girl and love me too.

As usual, Daddy loved to play, crawling across the floor as he tickled each of us in turn and in response we wriggled about, chuckling, before Mama shouted, 'Come on, Joe.'

Daddy rolled his eyes and slowly got up. 'Night, night, remember to say your Shema,' he said as he switched off the lights.

'Night, night, love you,' we replied in unison.

We weren't brought up Orthodox like some of our friends, but these were scary times so we said our prayers no matter what. We listened for the door to click shut as they retreated upstairs and then covering both eyes with our right hand as scripture commanded, we recited the holy words.

'Hear O Israel, the Lord is our God, the Lord is One.'

We had one last thing to do before sleep, our secret ritual. Huddling close, we tapped our fingers together seven times for good luck, which we believed along with our Shema would surely grant us immunity from death.

It must have been only a few hours later when I awoke in the pitch dark, groggy, with a heavy weight crushing my chest. I gasped for air, swallowing grit that slid down my throat ... spluttering, choking ... praying this wasn't it, my last breath ... until I coughed ... a big throaty hacking cough, somehow managing to clear my airways. Dust fell from my hair like soot, going up my nose and stinging my eyes, making them trickle with water. I tried to move my hands to rub them, but I was stuck, buried up to my neck in rubble, unable to even move my head.

'GABI, HANNAH, CAN YOU HEAR ME? MAMA, DADDY?' I yelled, still muddled from sleep until the truth hit me like a brick in the face. *Oh God, we've been bombed! The sirens ... I must have slept through the sirens.*

I peered into the darkness, desperate to see some sign of life, but there was nothing, just black emptiness.

Where were they all, injured or dead?

Fear coursed through me, building like the sea at high tide. 'HELP! HELP!' I screamed over and over until my voice was hoarse. I had to escape, do something—clenching every muscle, pushing with my legs. But it was pointless: I was stuck, clamped tight.

Each moment felt endless; there was no sense of time in that black hole, only the ear-splitting sound of buildings crashing, glass shattering and objects colliding. Whimpers from a wounded animal came from somewhere until I realised it was me—whimpers that turned into howls, deep rasping howls that made my bruised chest ache.

And just when I'd lost all faith, I heard a faint voice calling back. 'We're coming.'

My eyes streamed with tears, blurring my vision. 'I'M HERE, I'M HERE,' I shouted, hoping they could gauge the direction from my voice.

'REMAIN STILL!' a man shouted back, 'IN CASE YOU'RE INJURED.'

At last I felt the rocks shift and I groaned with relief, finally able to free my arms and rub grit from my irritated eyes. I squinted as the torch light shone into my face and saw my saviour in front of me; his kind craggy face like something divine, a real life angel. 'Grab my hand', he said firmly as he hauled me out of the debris.

Clutching onto him, I staggered over tiles and shards of glass into the smoky air, spluttering from the toxic fumes still lingering from the explosives. I stared at our road in horror, trying to stay balanced as my legs almost gave way. Some houses got off lightly, but others were in ruins: smouldering wooden carcasses, half-demolished buildings revealing rooms with smashed furniture all higgledy-piggledy. I refused to look back at ours, turning away. I couldn't bear to see what had been lost.

'There'll be help arriving soon. Just wait here,' said my angel. He smiled reassuringly before rushing off to rescue others and I was left alone shivering in the darkness, unable to see clearly except for the blaze of orange and red flashing in the skyline like a vengeful sunset. For a few moments, I was transfixed. I'd seen plenty of big fires, but not like this; the horizon of an entire city lit up with flames.

The shadowy images of dazed survivors were all around me as I searched desperately for a familiar face. The heavy rain had stopped, but some were slumped on the flooded roadside sobbing, whilst others wandered around like lost souls through a wasteland littered with broken burnt remains. Then I heard Gabi's voice all rough and gravelly as he drifted forward.

'Hannah, Ruth ... where are you?'

'I'm here, Gabi,' I shouted, feeling elated. Somehow I'd cheated death and God had shown me I wasn't forsaken, that there was a loved one alive amongst the wreckage. We stumbled towards each other covered in filth, hugging tightly until the sound of sobbing distracted me. I spun round, looking everywhere, until I saw my Hannah curled up on the ground with smudges on her face, streaked with teardrops, her hair matted with dirt. I limped over, pulling her close as she fell into my arms like a floppy rag doll.

The blast from the bomb had thrown me into the centre of the house, Gabi into the front garden, and Hannah into the coal bunker. My head was all swimmy, but thankfully, none of us seemed seriously injured, just a bit battered with cuts and bruises.

'We haven't found any sign of your parents yet,' said a rescue worker appearing in front of us, covered in thick layers of soot, 'but we'll keep looking.' He smiled. 'Who's your next of kin?'

Next of kin? Unable to think clearly, I mumbled some names, before he scribbled on a docket and raced off.

We huddled together for warmth, and as we waited in the early morning light, barefoot like filthy street urchins in our tattered pyjamas, I dared to look back at our once cosy home, now just a desolate ruin along with the house next door where the bomb had landed between them.

It seemed surreal that hours earlier we had a family life like many others; warming our hands on our nightly cup of Ovaltine, although Daddy had his bottle of stout as we sat by the glowing flames of the fire listening to songs on the wireless. My father loved jazz numbers—songs by Louis Armstrong and Billie Holiday. 'You Made Me Love You' was one of his favourites, which he often sang to my mother in a soft, teasing voice.

'I didn't want to do it, I didn't want to do it, you made me love you,' he'd sing, pulling her up out of her chair for a slow dance, sometimes whistling the tune. She'd look all embarrassed if we were watching, but she couldn't help but break into a smile and when she did, goodness, she looked ten years younger.

It was taken for granted that the music would stop abruptly with a bleak newsflash:

'The bombing of London continues,' announced the newsreader. 'Over one million British homes destroyed and forty thousand civilians killed. And the death toll looks set to rise.'

Now we'd be part of those morbid statistics; I just never thought it would happen to us.

'Are Mummy and Daddy coming soon?' asked Hannah.

I looked at her and Gabi's tired faces, their eyes pleading for answers. But, of course, I didn't have any. In desperation, I prayed, 'Please God, keep them alive, don't let them leave us,' as a stream of salty tears ran down my cheeks, endlessly flowing until I couldn't see.

Sunday morning, 20th April 1941

'Where am I?' I mumbled, feeling dizzy as I struggled to open my eyes in the bright light.

'You're in the children's ward of the London Hospital, my love', replied what appeared to be the blurry image of a young nurse. 'You've been out of it for two days on and off, haemorrhaging blood. At first we thought you were pregnant or you had your menstrual cycle,' she continued, gabbling away in her cockney accent, 'but it just kept pouring out of you. Weren't sure if you were anaemic, what with the trauma and all ... thought you might be a dead-un, but seems it was just low blood sugar and shock.'

Pregnant! I was horrified. How could they think that? I was still a child, wasn't I?

The nurse handed me a welcome cup of strong, sweet tea which I took with shaky hands. And then I jerked forward, nearly knocking it flying when I heard the sound of shrieking and loud footsteps. She smiled and gave me a wink. 'Looks like you've got visitors, my love.' I grinned when I saw Hannah and Gabi run across the ward towards my bedside.

'Ruth, Ruth, we're so glad you're here. We thought you'd gone away and left us,' squealed Hannah. She looked completely unscathed after obviously having a good bath, her blonde hair hanging in loose ringlets around her heart-shaped face, making her look cherubic.

'As if I'd ever do that to the two of you.' I placed my teacup on the side cabinet and stretched my arms out to hug her, and she clung to me, nails digging into my skin.

Gabi looked well except for a big purple bruise on his forehead and his wrist was in a sling. He reached out his 'good hand'

and all three of us instinctively tapped each other's forefingers seven times for good luck—because, after all, we'd survived.

Aunt Fenella appeared by my bedside after talking to the matron. She was my mother's older, richer sister, having married a wealthy man. Well, the Rosenblums appeared to have more money than we did anyway.

'Hello, dear. Feeling better?'

My head throbbed, my throat hurt, but I didn't want to be a bother. 'Yes, thank you, Aunt Fenella,' I said, forcing a smile. I'd always admired her—in the same way you admire people who scare you a little. She reminded me of the actress, Katharine Hepburn: tall and slim with her greying auburn hair pinned up in a bun and gold spectacles on a chain that perched on the end of her long, thin nose.

'Rest assured, everything will be fine,' she continued, clasping her hands together. 'Once the rescue workers contacted us, I whizzed straight over. I'm taking you all to live with me.'

I sighed with relief. 'Thank you so much, Aunt Fenella. So, they didn't find Mummy and Daddy then?' I stammered, already sensing the awful truth.

'No, dear, I'm afraid your parent's bodies were never recovered.' She cleared her throat, avoiding my gaze. 'They are both presumed dead.'

My stomach churned as I looked at the floor. 'Oh, will there be a funeral?'

'A funeral during the war!' She patted my arm sympathetically. 'Not without a body and a coffin, my dear.'

My eyes welled up, ready to flow.

'Come along now, Ruth, don't cry,' she said, sharply. She pulled out a cotton hankie from her large leather handbag and handed it to me. 'Where's that British stiff upper lip? We're offering you a roof over your heads, so at least you can all be together.'

I nodded, wiping away tears. I knew I should be thankful, but I no longer knew what to say or what I felt, except clamp my hands over my mouth and stifle screams.

Chapter 3

Sunday morning, 20th April 1941

On the floor below, intensive care overflowed, littered with broken bodies sprawled across beds, trolleys and blankets, placed on any available floor space. A cacophony of tormented cries, groans and guttural rasps filled the air, melding together like a ghoulish orchestra, bouncing off the walls, echoing into the distance.

The ward sister steered a wheelchair around the casualties; another anonymous victim who winced with pain, his leg missing, bloodstained bandages covering his raw stump. 'Over eighty arrived this morning,' she called out to her staff, her strident voice piercing the thick atmosphere like a knife.

On the far side of the ward, the nurse shook her head sadly, tending to her patient drifting in and out of consciousness. 'Heavens above, where will we put them all?' She inspected the wound on the man's forehead and then checked his pulse and the saline drip.

'Good morning,' said the doctor as he strode towards the bed. He was a tall, lean man in his mid-thirties whose height completely dwarfed the short stature of the nurse. Despite his composed demeanour he had a weighted-down look, the patient thought, as if a lump of iron had been dumped across his shoulders.

The nurse quickly smoothed down her dress and white apron, her round face growing ruddy. She seemed anxious for some reason and he wished he could help. She'd been so kind to him, this sensitive, big-hearted woman, who had to suffer the indignity of a threadbare uniform that stretched so tight across her large breasts and hips, it looked like it might rip open at any moment.

'Good morning, Doctor Walters,' she replied with a frown.

The doctor looked at the notes on his clipboard, his round tortoiseshell glasses and Roman nose dominating his small face. 'So what's the history of this chap?'

The nurse brushed away some stray tendrils of hair hanging over her eyes, pushing them underneath her white starched cap. 'Well, this one's been a bit of a surprise. His body was dug out from under a heap of rubble and he was taken to the morgue with the rescuers thinking he was a stone cold corpse, and then he frightened everyone to death by letting out a long groan before collapsing again.' She gave a bemused smile. 'You should have seen him when he came in. He was so filthy we thought he was a vagrant.'

'Hmm,' said Dr Walters, scrutinising him, 'he still looks filthy ... tufts of hair clumped with dried blood and his jaw covered in thick unruly bristles. There's probably living creatures in there. A thorough scrub might be in order.'

Slumped against the pillow, the patient touched his hair, feeling self-conscious. It felt sticky and there was a distinct coppery smell. He peered down at himself. He appeared to be wearing a green hospital gown, his arms and legs splayed out over a bloodstained sheet. He looked pretty battered: bruises and cuts all over.

The nurse made a tsk sound under her breath and shrugged her shoulders. 'He needed to be assessed first, Doctor. He has been here for forty-eight hours!'

The patient watched the doctor glare at her, struck by the hazy images in front of him. Was this some kind of feverish hallucination or was it real? He shivered. Whatever it was, he felt sorry for the nice nurse. He wouldn't want to be given the evils like that.

'As you can see, nurse, we're packed to the rafters with injured survivors. I've been working around the clock. Now, what was his state on arrival?'

The nurse swallowed, clenching her hands together. 'Apologies, Doctor. He was confused and nauseous, complaining of a throbbing headache, all the symptoms of concussion. He was also dehydrated with a high temperature.' She pressed her hand against the patient's forehead and he released a deep-throated moan. It felt so good, so cool against the raging heat of his skin. 'He's stabilised these last few hours, although he seems to have no memory of anything, except a tune he tries to whistle. It's a miracle he's stirred back into consciousness.'

'Any idea of this poor man's name?'

'No idea, Doctor. All the records show is that he's a resident of the East London area.'

'Hmm, it's a sign of the times,' said Dr Walters, sighing, 'how can you identify someone when everything they own has been incinerated?'

Their voices felt sharp, back and forth, back and forth, like long pins jabbing through his brain. His head pounded with the constant buzz of the ward. He needed peace. He needed rest. His eyes half-closed drowsily as he felt the doctor's eyes bore into him. Now it was his turn to get the evils.

'Good morning, sir. I need to do a few routine checks.'

He winced with pain as the nurse helped him to sit up and adjusted the pillow behind his back. A torch shone into his eyes and he flinched, turning his face away.

The doctor placed his penlight back into the pocket of his white coat and held up one hand, his palm facing forward. 'How many fingers am I holding up?'

He leaned forward and coughed, his voice rasping. 'Four.'

'Good. And do you know your name, sir?'

He shook his head.

The doctor continued with his inspection; checking the patient's ears and listening to the sound of his heart and lungs with a stethoscope.

'You certainly have a strong, regular heartbeat. Are you married?'

He coughed, spluttering out words. 'I don't know.'

'Do you have children?'

'I don't know. I don't know, I don't know!' he snapped, his dark brows twisting into a frown. 'I don't remember anything.'

'I understand how you must feel, but I have to ask you these questions,' said Dr Walters. 'What's this tune you've been whistling?'

'I don't know.'

'Then why do you whistle it?'

'It's just a tune in my head. It distracts me from these blinding headaches.' He rubbed his forehead, 'and the boredom of just lying here. Please, Doc, understand ... I don't know who I am or where I am.'

Dr Walters smiled sympathetically. 'Well, just so you know, my good man, you're in the London Hospital on Whitechapel Road, a few miles from where they believe you were found.'

The patient remained silent, looking down at his hands.

'How often do you get the headaches?'

'They come and go.'

'That's understandable. From what nurse reports you've had a major blow to your head. I'll arrange for X-rays to determine if you have a brain injury.'

'Thanks,' he said, his head falling forward.

Dr Walters patted him on the back. 'Just remember, someone up there wants you here, matey. You literally came back from the dead!'

The patient looked up hearing footsteps and the doctor spun round. A luminous vision glided towards them. A young woman. She looked important somehow, graceful, as if she floated on fluffy clouds. Who was she? She was beautiful that was certain, and she caused quite a stir. Everyone's eyes hung out of their sockets, glued in her direction, except the half-dead patients and the nurse who rolled her eyes with irritation. What was that about?

'Hello, Dr Walters,' the beauty said with a smile. 'I've decided to offer my services today.' Before he could respond, she recoiled, covering her mouth with her hands. 'Sorry, Doctor, I felt quite light-headed just then.'

'Good morning, Lady Douglas-Scott,' replied Dr Walters, his floppy hair bouncing about as he talked. 'What an absolute pleasure. Are you okay?' He looked concerned as he reached over to take her gloved hand. 'I'm afraid it does take a while to adjust to the rich bouquet of antiseptic, sweat and decaying flesh, but such is the nature of hospital life.'

She laughed and held onto the doctor's hand as she regained her balance. 'I'm fine now, Doctor, thank you.'

'It's wonderful to see you again, Lady Douglas-Scott,' he continued, seemingly dazzled by her presence. 'You're a real blessing to us here in our hour of need.'

Her green eyes flashed with delight. 'Please, Dr Walters, call me Connie.'

The doctor smiled. 'Well, Connie, I must dash. There are simply not enough of us here to rally round and save lives.

Although, if you're in the mind for some charitable deeds, have a chat with this poor fellow.' He motioned to the patient gazing at them with watery eyes. 'I'm betting he needs some cheering up. Poor chap can't recall a thing about his past.'

'Oh, my goodness, of course, Doctor.'

Dr Walters said his goodbyes and dashed across the ward, leaving Connie standing there, gazing back. The patient watched her walk towards his bedside, the heels of her black buckled shoes making a tapping noise on the floor. His heartbeat quickened.

'So what's your name?' she asked.

He shrugged, gawping at the shimmering image in front of him, absorbing every detail of her heart-shaped face, cat-like eyes, and Cupid's bow lips surrounded by a mane of cascading chocolate waves. His eyes wandered down her slim figure encased in a tailored silk suit.

Her face reddened and she fidgeted, glancing around the ward before breaking the silence. 'Then I shall name you Edward, Eddie for short.'

'Thanks,' he said, feeling a surge of renewed energy. He lifted his bruised arm connected by a tube to the saline drip, extending a limp hand to shake hers as she perched on the end of his bed. 'It's nice to meet such a pretty lady.'

Connie leant forward and shook his hand with a coy smile. 'Thank you for the compliment. People say I look like Vivien Leigh. What do you think?' She tilted her head to one side and played with a lock of hair, twisting it around her fingers.

The newly named, Eddie, tapped his head, feeling confused. 'Vivien who?'

'Oh, yes, silly me, you have no memory. She starred in *Gone with the Wind* as Scarlett O'Hara and she's considered one of the most beautiful women of our time. Although I'm only twenty-four, so much, much younger.'

He grinned even though every muscle in his body ached. He couldn't help himself. 'I'm sure she's not as lovely as you.'

Connie looked down at her gloved hands and he felt a growing warmth towards this sparky, young woman. She seemed full of vibrancy and adventure. So at odds with his sluggish, trance-like state.

'You have a touch of Clark Gable about you,' she said, 'with a haircut and a shave, naturally.'

'Thank you, I think,' he replied with a chuckle. 'So what brings you here?'

'My father favours my charity work so I try to assist when I can. He says it's all about giving back. Papa is a great philanthropist.'

'How about that.'

Connie reached over and touched his hand. He sensed the nurse's disapproving glare, her face pinched as she looked up from tucking in fresh sheets on the bed next to them. He didn't like her intruding like this, not one bit. It wasn't right and it wasn't good manners.

'So, dear Eddie, I must now depart, but for my good deeds, I will endeavour to visit until you are better.'

He watched mesmerised as she pulled out a silky handkerchief from the handbag hanging on her arm. She continued to rummage inside the contents, taking out a bottle of perfume and twisting the lid open, shaking some scented droplets onto it.

'It's Chanel No. 5, something to remember me by,' she whispered, handing him the hankie. 'See you tomorrow.'

'I do hope so,' he murmured as he clutched it, wishing she could stay longer. He held the silky square over his face, inhaling the sweet fragrance as it transported him away from the decaying smell of the ward.

The nurse looked downwards through slitted eyes, giving the impression of a haughty sneer as she followed Connie's graceful wiggle through the exit.

'Did you see that, Sister?'

The ward sister walked over with a stoop, glowering as she held out a bottle of medication. 'I did, nurse. She's brazen that one! Throwing herself at him, so she was.'

'I think SLUT is the word,' replied the nurse, louder than necessary.

His eyes widened. *Slut?* Did he hear that right? How could she say that about such a lovely woman, an angel kind enough to give up her precious time to help the sick? He'd thought that nurse was nice, but she wasn't. His head might be buggered, but he knew the difference between right and wrong.

The nurse strode over to his bedside with his prescribed painkillers, opening the lid and shaking out two white tablets into her hand. 'Stick out your tongue, please, sir. They're for your migraine.' He opened his mouth as she popped the tablets inside and swallowed, pulling a face at the bitter aftertaste. God, how he craved some water to wash it away. He'd keep quiet, though. She might try to poison him.

'Word to the wise ... pay no heed to that young lady, mister.' She put her hands on her wide hips as if to suggest authority. 'A lot of these rich daddy's girls like to saunter in and play Florence Nightingale. They swan about with their noses in the air, doing their so-called charitable work because they don't need a wage like the rest of us. Her father is one of the richest men in Britain,' she snorted, 'so don't get your hopes up.'

He held onto the handkerchief as if it was a decadent luxury he couldn't bear to let go of. 'Hmm,' he murmured, 'but she's very pretty, and she did cheer me up.'

The nurse shook her head with disapproval, huffed and walked off.

He didn't care. He slumped back into his pillow feeling elated, savouring the moment of kindness the rich lady had shown him. 'Connie,' he mumbled, 'Connie Douglas-Scott ... I like that name.' He began whistling that familiar tune, embedded in his brain: 'You Made Me Love You.' If only he could remember where he knew it from.

Chapter 4

Sunday afternoon, 20th April 1941

Arriving at the Rosenblums it seemed things were looking up. We were on a posh road in North London, gazing at their grand Victorian house with swanky curtains, and we all skipped up the steps with excitement—but as the front door opened, I felt 'the tickle'—that nervous flutter in the pit of my stomach when something feels wrong.

'Hello, dearies.' He peered at us with two dark pebbles squashed into his doughy white face. 'Welcome to our humble abode.'

'Hello, Mr Rosenblum, sir,' I said, fidgeting.

'Hello, Mr Rosenblum,' echoed Gabi and Hannah.

'Oh, please, children, call me Uncle Harry,' he replied with a wide grin, revealing a set of yellowing crooked teeth. 'There's no need to stand on ceremony.'

I shuddered. There was something strange about his eyes and the way they lingered. I tugged Aunt Fenella's woollen coat around me to hide my donated hospital gown.

After being ushered into their elegant living room decorated in shades of pale green, my mood changed again as I stood in hushed reverence, witnessing something truly divine. There before us, was a long table set out in front of the bay window with the most mouth-watering display of food: platters of buttery smoked haddock and crispy potato cakes, bagels oozing with cream cheese, a dish of boiled eggs, a sponge cake trickled with honey, and my favourite, big round sugary doughnuts all set out on lace doilies. I was drooling, picturing the sweet jam exploding into my mouth.

'Wow, is that for us?' squealed Hannah, her curls bouncing up and down as she clapped her hands together.

It didn't look like anything solid had ever touched our Aunt's lips; whippet thin in her cream trouser suit, her grey eyes crinkled at the corners as she gave a wry smile. 'Of course, my hands are chafed to the bone.'

Gabi said nothing, his lanky frame swaying about as if in a trance.

I understood how he felt; all that food, when we'd been rationed, well, it was overwhelming, like being thrown a lifeline when you were nearly under, sinking in mud. The floodgates opened and I wept, sniffling as I wiped my damp face with my hands.

'What's wrong, dear?' said Aunt Fenella. She reached out to touch my arm. 'I did say no more tears.'

I could have done with a hug, but our family, with the exception of my father, had never been tactile. Thankfully, Hannah, the little sweetheart, wrapped her arms around my waist, looking up at me with big watery eyes.

'It's just so kind of you,' I stammered.

'Well, tuck in and try not to drop crumbs,' commanded Aunt Fenella, waving us towards the table. And like mad things we all rushed towards it, jostling against each other as we piled up our plates.

Now orphans, we'd arrived with nothing, so after our feast, Aunt Fenella directed Gabi and me to the upstairs landing so we could bring down two large sacks of clothes. 'You'll need something to wear,' she said, 'We've been given some charity donations, so pick out some hand-me-downs.'

'It feels like Hanukkah,' said Gabi with a grin as we staggered down the stairs, puffed out from the weight as we hauled the sacks into the living room. It was worth it though when we stuck our hands inside as if they were lucky dips, thrilled when we pulled out a pair of socks or a woolly jumper to see what would fit.

Thirty minutes later, Aunt Fenella beckoned us with a flourish of her hand to follow her on a tour around their four-bedroom property. With Uncle Harry's inheritance, we knew from Mama that they'd had renovation work done and we all gasped when we walked into a proper bathroom with a lavatory; something I thought only the toffs had. It was luxury compared to what we'd been used to: an outside toilet and a tin bath placed by the kitchen range.

And then we trailed into her walk-in pantry.

'How do you get all this on rations?' blurted Gabi. His eyes danced around the shelves crammed with tins of fruit, steamed cake and syrup alongside packs of cereal, biscuits and jars of jam.

Aunt Fenella toyed with the long pearl necklace that dangled down to her waist and replied, 'let's just say, we're rather fortunate. With attacks on food convoys, goods are being stockpiled and Harry, well,' she straightened her back, 'he was appointed by the Ministry of Food and made an Inspector of Stores.'

'So uncle gets special benefits?' I asked, feeling confused.

'Um, yes,' replied Aunt Fenella, looking away.

'No wonder he's got that big belly, 'I whispered to Hannah, 'but at least we'll get fed.' I don't know how he landed himself such a lucky job but Daddy always said Uncle Harry was a crafty old bugger.

As the days went by, we tried our best to settle in, but I often lay awake at night tormented by images of my parents abandoned corpses. *I should have helped find their bodies, they might still be alive.* Now I would never hear one of Daddy's silly jokes or taste one of Mama's delicious meals. She always knew how to throw scraps together and make something yummy with a sprinkle of spice or a dollop of cheese. I didn't think I'd miss her quick temper, but I missed every moment of our old life, good and bad.

Hannah often awoke shaking from nightmares as she tearfully clambered into my bed for a hug. Gabi wandered about with a dazed expression as if he were lost, and, of course, he was, we all were. He'd never admit to feeling weak so it was hard listening to his muffled sobs in the middle of the night, knowing he'd feel ashamed if I went to comfort him. Sometimes I wondered if his old chutzpah was buried somewhere along with Mum and Dad.

Like a sticking plaster our new luxuries eased our grief. We all loved having comfy bedrooms and treats from the pantry. Our Aunt and Uncle had no children of their own and I hoped we'd secure a space in their hearts as well as their home; that they'd fall in love with us and never let us go. Yet I felt increasingly uneasy about Uncle Harry as he hovered around me with his creepy stare.

'I am more than happy to help Ruth wash up,' he'd often say to my aunt after dinner as he'd hobble clumsily, because of his bad hip, to join me in the kitchen, brushing against me at any opportunity. Wherever I was in the house, he'd track me down, limping into the scullery when I was assigned the chore of putting washing through the mangle. When I saw it was him, my heart raced as I quickly looked away.

'You are nervy, aren't you, dearie?' he said, smirking.

Beads of sweat glistened on his thin top lip, and I gave a forced smile, continuing to turn the handle of the cast iron mangle as a wet jumper was squeezed through the rollers.

Shuffling towards me, he leant in close, whispering in my ear as I edged away. 'You know, you do look much older than fourteen.'

Shrinking back, I stared at him with disgust.

'You are a feisty one,' he said, stroking my hand with a chuckle, 'but perhaps you'll relax in time.'

I didn't have time to worry about what he was implying when I heard Aunt Fenella call out in her clipped high-pitched voice that she said was honed from her elocution lessons. 'Darlings, stop what you're doing and meet me in the living room. I need to speak to you all urgently.'

I heard Hannah and Gabi stomping down the stairs as I threw the jumper in a basket and raced out of the door, relieved to get away.

We waited anxiously as Aunt Fenella walked in and stood in front of us like a formal headmistress with her hands behind her back. 'After much thought,' she said, squinting above her half-moon spectacles at each of us, one by one, 'Uncle Harry and I have decided it would be best for all of you if Gabi and Hannah were evacuated to Dorset to stay with your Aunt Betty. I didn't realise what a handful you'd all be', she continued, 'plus the expense and, well, darlings, Harry and I simply can't cope.'

We looked at each other with confusion, not knowing what to say, except grab each other's hands, feeling terrified. All three of us had made a pact to help out as best we could so they didn't feel we were a burden and split us up. Housework proved the perfect antidote to heartache and we'd found joy in the grubbiest jobs, singing our favourite songs armed with sponges and a bucket of hot water, cleaning all the windows that were smeared with grime. We knew if we just kept busy, we'd make our Aunt happy and we wouldn't have time to think, and then missing our parents wouldn't be quite so painful. So why had this happened? Hadn't we done enough?

'The two of you, Gabi and Hannah, will be taken to Waterloo station tomorrow morning and Aunt Betty will meet you at the other end.'

'What about me?' I asked, my voice hoarse.

'You will stay here, Ruth.'

'But why? Isn't it safer for me to be evacuated too?'

'Come with me, dear,' said Aunt Fenella. She gestured for me to follow her into the kitchen as I trailed behind. 'I didn't want to embarrass you in front of your brother and sister,' she whispered, shutting the door, 'but you, Ruth, have a reputation for being the most rebellious and precocious of your siblings. Now you are a young woman, it is far better for your future if you remain here, under my roof, where Harry and I can give you the strict discipline you need to form a stable life.'

'But when will I see them again?'

'You see, there you go again. Always the outspoken one that asks too many questions. I know you think I'm cruel, but Ruth, we are at war with Germany. Your parents are dead and this is no time to be concerning yourself with thoughts of a future rendezvous.' She looked at me with a sympathetic smile. 'Sometimes, my dear, you have to accept your fate quietly and with good grace.'

'Thank you, Aunt Fenella,' is all I could mutter. I looked at the floor and gulped back tears. I felt pitiful, continually crying.

That night after putting all our pillows and blankets on the floor of the bedroom I shared with Hannah, we snuggled together in our cosy nest as I hugged my fretful siblings to sleep. I lay awake in the darkness for hours mulling over my Aunt's comments: *rebellious and precocious, where did that come from?* I knew I'd had my ups and downs with Mama, but had she discussed me with Aunt Fenella? Was I considered the black sheep of the family?

I looked at the clock on the wall. It was just after ten. Feeling restless, I crept downstairs to get a glass of water and heard muffled voices coming from the kitchen. I put my ear to the door and realised it was Uncle Harry talking to Aunt Fenella about me.

'As I've said before, she's impudent and greedy, always taking treats from the pantry. And I believe she stole a handful of coppers that I'd left on the kitchen sideboard. Before we know it she'll be off the rails and in the police station for petty theft.'

'Sadly, from what I heard, she's always been a thorn in her mother's side with her constant backchat. I'm glad I listened to you, Harry, about sending the younger two away. We had to stop her leading them astray.'

Unable to believe what I was hearing, I nearly tripped over as I strained to hear his response.

'It was definitely the right decision, darling. The trouble is, their father was an arrogant schmuck preferring to schmooze the ladies than concentrate on parenthood. It's time that she had more discipline from a strict paternal figure,' he continued as I blanched at his words. 'The more time I spend with her, the more she'll learn the value of respecting her elders.'

I clenched my fists. I wanted to hit him. I wanted to hit him right in his big doughy face ... if only I had the nerve. This was so unfair, the injustice. Now I knew why Aunt Fenella was sending the babies away—that man was making up stories that weren't true. And how dare he say that about my wonderful father when he was barely cold in his grave? He didn't schmooze women. He had a natural charm that put people at ease, something Uncle Harry could sorely benefit from. Now I really had lost everything; Mama and Daddy, and now Gabi and Hannah. 'Thanks, God, you've stripped me bare. There's nothing left,' I whispered sadly as I tiptoed back upstairs to bed.

After a few hours of broken sleep as the early morning light filtered through the window, I tried, for the sake of my sanity to look on the positive side. At least there are biscuits, the house is nice and Aunt Fenella has been kind, I told myself. Whatever life threw at me, I hoped that Mama and Daddy would watch over me from heaven.

Tuesday morning, 6th May 1941

I forced myself to be brave as we said our tearful goodbyes at Waterloo station.

'I'm going to miss you,' mumbled Hannah, wrapping her arms around my waist. 'We don't know Aunt Betty. She's a spinster so she doesn't know anything about children.'

It was true, Aunt Betty was the mysterious relative, considered to be the other black sheep of the Goldberg family, besides me. My mother often described her youngest sister—with more than a little bitterness—as headstrong and unlikely to ever find a husband with her spirited ways. I couldn't recall any of us ever meeting her.

'You'll be fine, I promise. I'll write whenever I can.'

She looked so sweet in her black beret. I stroked a blonde curl away from her face and did up some buttons on her tatty second-hand coat. And then I wrapped my arms around her, squeezing her with the biggest bear hug ever as she flopped against me.

Gabi stared at the ground and shuffled his feet, clothed in what could have been fancy dress; a tweed jacket two sizes too big and men's wide legged trousers that were turned up at the ankles and held on with braces. I tried my best to kiss him before he wriggled away, wiping his tears with his sleeve.

'Remember you two, secret ritual?' I ruffled Gabi's curly mop as we all huddled together and tapped out our special code, hoping once more it would keep us safe.

I watched them climb onto the packed train clutching a small case labelled with their names and future address in one hand and their gas masks in the other. They looked so small, weighed down with all their worldly belongings: identity cards, jam sandwiches and a small tin of nuts and raisins stuffed into the pockets of their coats. Their worried faces peeped through the window and as the train chugged away, leaving a gust of steam that filled the platform, I waved them goodbye, wondering with sadness if I'd ever see them again.

Chapter 5

Tuesday afternoon, 6th May 1941

Dr Walters wandered into the large untidy office clutching some X-rays. Stepping over boxes of files and medical journals, he noted his colleague remained oblivious to his arrival as he sat hunched over his desk. *What a mess*, he thought, *how can he work like this?* He coughed. 'Dr Jungston, if you have a moment. I've got the results on our amnesiac.'

The clinical psychologist spun round on his swivel chair and stood up, his bushy eyebrows raised in surprise. He was a short, stocky man with flattened down hair parted on the side, and as he smiled, his round cheeks bulged above his neatly trimmed beard and moustache. 'Ah, yes, Dr Walters. Please, I'm all ears.'

The doctor moistened his lips with his tongue. He felt anxious for some reason. The pressure of work was overwhelming and he was just about surviving on will power, adrenaline and extra-strong coffee, but he was a professional and there was no time for weakness. 'I've done extensive tests and our patients condition is stabilising, although he is still suffering from headaches and the occasional migraine—typical symptoms of post-concussion trauma.' He passed Dr Jungston the scanned images. 'And it appears there are no skull fractures or hematomas, just cerebral contusion to the temporal lobes, but like all bruising, that will heal in time.'

Dr Jungston glanced at the scans, hauled himself up from his chair and wandered over to the dusty sash window, holding them up to the light. Eminent in his field, he'd been recruited from one of the most advanced psychiatric clinics in Switzerland to help with the more serious cases of traumatised civilians. Dr Walters hoped he was worth the funding.

'Thank you for updating me,' he replied, with traces of an exotic European accent. 'It's certainly a favourable prognosis as far as his physical health is concerned.'

'Indeed! And he's a keen chap of good character but he's been here for weeks and there's an overflow of casualties baying for his bed. I'm hoping you've found some kind of resolution.'

'Well, it's good and bad news, I'm afraid.' Jungston pointed to the scans. 'As you can see there is damage to the hippocampus, the medial temporal lobe of the brain, and this explains his retrograde amnesia. Unfortunately, this can mean memory loss for one to two years, but if there is more undetermined damage, then I'm afraid, we're looking at fifteen to twenty years, or even longer.'

The doctor folded his arms and leant against the large oak desk piled high with clinical documents.

'In addition, he may also suffer from psychogenic amnesia which often occurs due to a traumatic experience that an individual wishes to consciously or unconsciously avoid. With this, the person forgets their entire history. The past is literally a blank!'

'Sounds like we have a rather broad diagnosis.'

'The treatment of neurological disorders is never an exact science,' Dr Jungston replied with a measured smile. 'Quite simply I've told him to keep a diary and write down anything, however odd, that springs to mind. If he can recall his own family name then we can try to locate his relatives.'

Dr Walters clenched his jaw, exasperated with the minimal conclusions. This was so typical of the mental health professionals. They were like wriggling fish always giving vague answers. Perhaps if he grabbed him by the collar of his crumpled suit and gave him a good shake, he might get somewhere. 'Anyway, you said there was good news?'

He took a deep breath, counting to ten as he watched Dr Jungston shuffle about, flopping the scans onto a filing cabinet in the corner of the room, taking his time, stroking his beard, staring into the distance. 'Yes, despite his memory loss he still has many functional aspects intact. A high intelligence, unaffected perceptual and linguistic skills, new short-term memory, excellent social skills and reasoning abilities. All of these things are necessary for everyday life and contribute to normal living.'

'Excellent. Let's discharge him then?'

'Not so hasty, Dr Walters,' he replied, flipping his chubby hands up in the air. 'He's still in shock and may relapse. Remember, he has nowhere to live and no one to care for him.' His face brightened. 'But I may have a potential diagnosis. I just need to monitor his progress for a while longer.'

The doctor checked his watch. Damn, he was late for his ward round. 'Fair enough, Dr Jungston. Let's reconvene in three weeks. That's the deadline!' He saluted him a goodbye and headed towards the door.

'Thank you for your patience,' Dr Jungston called after him. 'Good day.'

Dr Jungston stuffed his hands into his pockets and paced the worn carpeted floor, his mind in a whirl. He'd arrived in England over four months ago, and now hurtling towards his forties, he longed to prove himself, show what he was really made of. And by God, he loved a challenge, something to get stuck into and get those outstanding transformative results: a medical marvel that could be written up in journals and debated at international conferences with his name dancing on everyone's lips. This patient was exactly that: a rare breed ... too rare to let slip away. He hoped he could find a solution in time.

Chapter 6

Tuesday afternoon, 6th May 1941

Betty wandered up and down the railway platform peering at every child's face amidst the bustling crowds. She had an idea of what they looked like from old photos, but she was worried sick that she might collect the wrong ones and leave the poor souls abandoned. And then she spotted them clambering off the train with their luggage, looking around with worried faces.

She knew it was naughty, but she couldn't resist, so she crept up behind them and leant in close. 'Boo!' They spun round and stared at her, no doubt wondering who the blimmin' hell she was. 'Hello, you two. I'm your Aunt Betty, my new little chums.'

Hannah narrowed her eyes. 'You don't look much like Aunt Betty should. She's a spinster.' She hesitated and wrinkled her nose. 'You've got shiny red lips and blonde hair.'

'Shhh, Hannah, don't be rude,' said Gabi. 'Are you sure you're Aunt Betty?'

'Yes, I'm quite sure last time I checked,' she replied, taken aback. 'And, I do believe,' she continued with a wink at Hannah, 'that spinster aunts, if that's what I'm to be labelled, are allowed to wear lipstick too.'

Hannah's cheeks flushed pink and there was an awkward silence.

Betty wasn't quite sure how this would work, having never had any children of her own, but she was determined to make them feel welcome. As their eyes traced her from the feet up, she'd hoped she'd dressed appropriately for the occasion, something fun and not too formal. Black high heeled shoes, tan stockings and a lavender dress cinched in with a black belt. All complemented with a straw boater which she'd perched on her head at a jaunty angle.

'So, it's Gabi and Hannah, isn't it? Hungry are you?'

They both nodded, looking at her blankly.

Poor lambs, she thought, *they've suffered so much.* 'Well, you can't arrive in Bournemouth without having lunch by the seaside.' She gave them a big beaming smile and grabbed both their cases as they trailed behind her out of the station. Within twenty minutes they were gripping a warm parcel of cod and chips along with their gas masks, whilst she paid the kiosk man.

'Come on then, little ones.' Betty rushed ahead, quickly turning back to check that they were following her across the powdery sand, the scent of fried chips filling the air. Relieved when they found three empty deck chairs, they dumped all their belongings ready to eat.

'Ooh, it's a bit fresh for spring weather,' said Betty as the wind blew her hat off. She quickly grabbed it, stuffing it into her large embroidered handbag. 'So, children, I'm happy to have you stay,' she continued, reaching out a manicured hand and ruffling Hannah's hair, 'but I've got my own business and as the schools are all shut, you've both got to muck in.'

'No problem, Aunt Betty, 'we'll do whatever we can to help out,' said Gabi, briefly looking up from his food. He bit into a salty, fat chip, vinegar dripping through the newspaper onto his fingers, whilst Hannah nodded in agreement, wiping her greasy hands on her coat.

Grubby devils, she thought with a smile. She reached into her bag and handed them both a cotton handkerchief. She always had a pile for emergencies. They both eagerly took one, muttering thanks, and as the waves broke with a crash onto the shore, she was certain she saw a renewed sparkle in their eyes.

'Good old sea air,' she murmured to herself, 'a cure-all for the soul and mind.' And once they'd finished eating, she sprang up from the deck chair and brushed down her dress. 'So let me show you to your new home. It's only a hop, skip and a jump away.'

Arriving at her two-bedroom house in East Cliff, she opened the glossy blue front door, beckoning them inside, where an uplifting fragrance wafted through the air as they stepped into the hallway.

'What's that lovely smell?' asked Hannah.

'Ah, now that's the sweet scent of romance,' Betty replied with a giggle. She opened a door on the left and showed them into her cosy living room with a breathtaking view of the ocean shimmering in the distance through her two sash windows.

Hannah's eyes opened wide with wonder at all the vases of pink roses placed around the room. 'They're sooo beautiful, Aunt Betty.'

Betty gave her a warm smile. 'Thank you, Hannah. I pick them fresh from the garden. Roses always remind me of that poetic, soulful love we all secretly yearn for.'

They wandered around, gazing with fascination as if they were in a museum: the sumptuous chaise longue in a red velvet fabric with two matching chairs, a large gilt-framed mirror above the tiled fireplace, as well as numerous black and white photographs of Betty in elegant poses; one with a feather boa draped glamorously down her backless dress.

'It's like being in the home of a Hollywood starlet,' squealed Hannah excitedly as she nudged a dazed Gabi in the ribs.

'I'm sure you're dying to see your new bedroom,' said Betty, laughing at her comment. 'You'll have to share, though, so no squabbling.'

They followed her upstairs and into a large room at the back of the house with freshly painted white walls and a clean brown carpet. Two pine single beds were placed side by side with a cabinet in between. Against the opposite wall was an old chest of drawers made of plywood.

'Now, I know it's a bit sparse, but we can pick up more knick-knacks to pretty it up as we go. In the meantime, unpack your things, relax and breathe,' Betty said, touching her stomach as she inhaled deeply. 'And remember, you're safe now. It may take a while to adjust, but I hope you'll come to think of this as home.'

Hannah stood awkwardly by one of the beds, her bottom lip trembling as if she was struggling to hold back tears. 'Aunt Betty, um, well, do you think our sister, Ruth, will ever be able to live here too?'

Oh, goodness, what to say? Betty pursed her lips, trying to think. 'It would be a bit of a tight squeeze, Hannah. So, that would be rather unlikely. Sorry.'

Gabi's entire body seemed to crumple as he leant against the wall. 'Do you think we'll ever see her again?'

Betty smiled warmly and clasped her hands together. 'Why, yes, Gabi, of course you'll see her again.' She took a step towards them. 'Look, I know you'll miss her, and once things have calmed down and those nasty explosions stop going off, she'll be able to hop on a train and join us on the beach, and we'll all stuff ourselves silly with popcorn and ice cream.'

'Really?' asked Gabi, his eyes shining.

'Yes, really, Gabi. Every weekend if she likes.'

Hannah grinned widely and rushed towards her.

'Oh, sweetheart,' cried Betty as she opened her arms and scooped her up. 'I'm so happy to have you both here.'

Gabi stared at the floor.

Typical boy, Betty thought, *hugs equal embarrassment.*

'Now then, you two,' she said, still holding Hannah, 'I'll put the kettle on. So make yourselves comfy. We'll shop for essentials tomorrow.'

They chorused a thank you, threw off their coats and flopped down onto their beds, exhausted, but hopefully, finally feeling wanted. And Betty prayed that somehow, Dorset life would give them the healing they all so desperately needed.

Chapter 7

London: May 1941

After Gabi and Hannah had gone, the house was unbearably quiet without their noisy chatter to keep me in good cheer, and I quickly realised my new role: to become the Rosenblums' full-time skivvy.

Uncle Harry instantly took advantage, rubbing his hands with glee whenever Aunt Fenella left the house, knowing I was unable to do anything about his advances. And every moment I was awake became an ordeal. He'd 'accidentally' touch my breasts, lean in close and say, 'You are a big girl aren't you? They do get in the way,' enunciating his words, reminding me of a scaly lizard-like creature with his small darting eyes. He made my skin crawl and I wanted to shout, 'Uncle Harry, bugger off and leave me be,' but I was too worried about my Aunt's reaction. 'If you ever tell, I will have you kicked out and you'll be homeless,' he'd say, spraying spittle over me as he talked.

On Monday afternoon, six days after the little ones had gone, he ordered me to clean his car. I should have known better. As I washed the rear window with a soapy sponge, he snuck up behind me and shoved his hand up my dress. I felt him stroke my inner thigh and I trembled, my eyes widening in horror when he inserted a finger inside my knickers and slowly rubbed my privates up and down. My mouth fell open. I wanted to scream, yet no sound came out. He didn't feel human, more like a weird creature mauling me as I felt his hot breath on my neck, shocked that he could touch me somewhere, where only a husband should touch a wife. *Please, someone, stop him,* I prayed, gripping the sponge tightly, squeezing water down the front of my cotton dress, the thin material clinging to my skin. What must have been just a few minutes seemed like hours when I heard footsteps in the distance become louder—and then he stopped, pulling his hands away, whistling a tune, pretending nothing had happened.

Taking my chance, I ran inside the house and up the stairs, locking myself in the bathroom as I collapsed onto the toilet seat breathing heavily, no longer able to cry. I'd gone beyond tears, I just felt dirty, in fact dirtier than ever before in my life, even with the endless dust and grime that we lived with every day. I pulled off my sandals and tore off my dress and ankle socks, wanting to burn them, robotically putting the plug in the bath, turning on the taps, climbing in, listening to the glugging of the water as I felt a black despair fall over me like a suffocating cloak. My head throbbed as I grabbed the soap and nail brush and scrubbed and scrubbed at my skin until it was sore, and still I didn't feel clean. 'I can't do this anymore, live this life,' I said aloud, my voice cracking, knowing that no one was listening, that no one cared.

Hours later when Aunt Fenella called me down for dinner, I dreaded it, slowly plodding down each step of their steep stairway, desperate to avoid looking at him, that creature, as I shuffled in and sat down opposite him at the dining table. He smirked when I caught his eye and I felt sick with fear, quickly looking away. Was it my fault? From then on I would dress for camouflage, covering every inch of my body in baggy, shapeless, threadbare clothes—anything to keep him at bay.

The following night, I heard his footsteps on the stairs and I shook with nerves as my bedroom door creaked open.

'How are you sleeping, dearie?' he asked, peeking into my room without knocking as I quickly pulled the covers up to my face. He hovered over me as I avoided looking at him, focusing instead on the more harmless shadow he made on the wall of his short, plump body. I may have been a virgin but I knew how babies were made—and I knew I wasn't safe. Mama had drummed it into me, 'Don't let anyone touch your privates until you're married or you'll end up pregnant and shame the family.' Just the thought of him touching me again made me want to heave. His eyes traced the outline of my body under the sheets and I nearly wet myself with fear when he grunted and began rubbing his hand between his legs. *God help me*, I prayed, until suddenly, I remembered a way out.

'I'm cramping up, Uncle!' I clutched my stomach. 'I hope I don't ruin your sheets with blood.'

Unable to hide his disgust, he winced and dashed out the door.

I let out a long sigh, relieved he'd gone, but feeling utterly worthless as I lay there like dumped rubbish that no one wanted. Mama always called me her *Meeskait*, Yiddish for 'little ugly one'. 'You have the brains, Ruth, if only you would care to use them,' she'd say sternly. No one ever said I looked nice and why would they with that knobbly bump on the bridge of my nose and the spots on my forehead that sprouted when I hit my teens. I felt like the runt of the litter compared to my beautiful siblings.

I wanted to run away, but to where? Would Aunt Betty take me in? Without a penny to my name I couldn't buy a ticket to Bournemouth and even if I did, she would probably send me back to London saying there was no space, and I couldn't sleep on the filthy, dusty streets. I was trapped, at least until the war was over, whenever that would be.

Closing my eyes, I travelled back in time as comforting memories engulfed me like rays of warm sunshine. I missed Daddy so much it felt like a tug in my heart. There were so many happy times helping out at his greengrocer's. He could make me giggle for hours with his funny stories.

'The rationing don't matter, Ruthie. It may not be kosher to eat pork, but if you ever want a taste, we can make ham from hamsters,' he'd say with a grin, holding up my hamster, Dipsy, who we kept in a cage at the back of the shop.

'Don't be mean to Dipsy, Daddy, and you ham it up enough already,' I'd reply, pretending to be annoyed. We always found something to laugh at, and everybody loved him, everybody knew his name.

'Joe the Jokester' customers called him and how he lived up to it; juggling apples or whistling a tune before signing their ration books or bagging up their fruit and veg, and naturally, they'd chuckle or even give him a round of applause. In return, he'd beam happily and sometimes take a deep theatrical bow. Mama said Daddy missed his vocation and should have been on the stage basking in the spotlight. He was the instant pain relief in a time of despair when there was no future to look forward to and all you had was the moment you were in.

Sometimes, though, he would really embarrass me, especially when he gazed into one woman's eyes across the counter, crooning, 'You Made Me Love You.' Strangely, her eyes lit up and she gazed at him in a trance, looking quite giddy.

Oh, Daddy, that's Mama's song, I thought, pulling a face. It was times like that when I wanted the ground to swallow me up.

It was something I had to get used to, though. Daddy always said he liked nothing more than making a nice lady smile and I'd often hear a lot of the female customers saying, 'Your father is a good looking man and a charmer too,' and I must admit I was proud of him despite his 'moments'.

Then there was his reassuring wink across the dinner table whenever Mama got frazzled, or he'd make a funny noise when she nagged us from the kitchen. There he was, my ally.

Because Mama, well, once I turned twelve and got lumps and bumps as Daddy called them, we didn't get on. In fact, we fought all the time. I never did enough housework according to her. I should have brought coal in for the fire or cleaned the dishes or got the washing from the line. I shuddered, remembering when the top button of my school shirt had accidentally come undone.

'Look at you. You look like men's meat,' she'd screamed the instant I walked in from school. 'You're men's meat. Man bait. Is that what you want to be?'

I rushed upstairs, red with embarrassment, hating the fact that I had a womanly figure. The boys at school teased me enough, with their unwanted wolf-whistles. According to her, I was too plump and that's why my breasts grew so big so quick and how was that possible when we were rationed; that I must have stolen food, extra bread and dripping.

As I recalled her cutting words, I asked myself, *is that how Uncle Harry sees me—a big bag of woman meat—plump pink flesh that he can grab at?* I admit I was headstrong, the way I answered Mama back. My words, 'Shut up, leave me alone,' ringing in my ears, and, yes, we fought so much that in my guiltiest moments, dare I say, I wished her dead! Irrational thoughts whipped through my mind and I couldn't help but wonder—did my wishing kill her—accidentally kill them both?

How I yearned for my old life, to accept the rows and her criticism, just to have back the security of family; doing the chores, brushing our teeth, saying our prayers. All that mundane stuff seemed such a reassuring comfort now that my life was thrown up in the air and every day was a gamble as to how things would end.

We always hope we have an angel to watch over us, but we don't realise how our parents are the true guardian angels, for the good times and bad.

Chapter 8

Bournemouth: May 1941

Here we are,' said Betty, 'this is my precious baby.' She jangled a set of keys in her gloved hand as they stood outside a red-brick building in the middle of a row of shops. The name, Betty's Boutique, in black curly letters, sat above the eight-foot square window, displaying two mannequins in the latest 1940s designs.

'Is this all yours?' asked Gabi. He rubbed his nose, looking confused.

'Yes, all mine,' replied Betty, straightening her back. 'Built from scratch with a lot of grit and a lot of love.'

The children stood there silently dumbstruck. She knew they probably couldn't believe that a single woman like her could own a business as well as a house. Not many people did.

Betty marched forward to unlock the door as if she was preparing for combat. She was so ready for today, sassily dressed à la mode, her blonde bobbed hair softly curled around her face with a slick of scarlet lipstick to complete her war paint. 'Right then, bubbelahs,' she continued, 'onwards and upwards.'

'Remember, that's what grandma called us,' said Hannah. Gabi nodded as they both chuckled at their cute nickname.

Once they walked inside, Betty threw her shoulders back and took a breath. 'Welcome to Betty's Boutique, your new home from home,' she announced with a smile. 'So get acquainted, but please,' she gave them both a look, 'no grubby fingers on the fabric.'

Deeply proud of her little shop, she'd made it like a cosy den, packed with racks of colourful outfits, neatly displayed against two opposite walls with another rail down the centre. White wooden shelves with an assortment of sweaters and cotton tops filled the back of the shop and she'd draped some elegant silk scarves across the walls showing off their designs, along with a variety of berets, floppy felt hats and straw boaters.

Hannah gravitated towards the wooden counter to the right, where the cash till was, spying some shiny jewellery displayed on a metallic carousel. Gabi's eyes were everywhere as he wandered about.

After a few minutes, Betty stationed herself by a rack of dresses and gestured towards them. 'Children, huddle in because there's a lot to learn.' She had big plans in store, besides which, she always felt that throwing yourself into work was the perfect distraction for heartbreak. Lord knows she'd used that cure a thousand times.

'The Forties look is all about enhancing the hourglass figure,' she stated commandingly, pointing to herself. 'Look how I'm wearing a black pencil skirt, a classically cut blouse, a fitted jacket with padded shoulders, and a wide belt to emphasise my waist.' They both stepped closer, nodding appreciatively. 'And this all complements my red wedged shoes. So whatever age you are, it's about looking fabulously stylish and that starts with you two.'

Picking out some outfits from her small stock of children's clothes at the end of the rail, she held fabrics against them. 'You simply must look chic,' she stated earnestly as she knelt on the floor, pulling a tape measure out of her jacket pocket and wrapping it around their waist and hips.

'God, this is sooo boring,' mumbled Gabi.

Betty stood up, gave him one of her disapproving looks, before handing him an assortment of clothes. 'Here you are, grumpy. Now go get changed.'

Gabi scowled and mooched into the changing room hidden behind a red velvet curtain in the corner.

Waiting with anticipation outside, Betty sniggered quietly with Hannah as they listened to him scuffling about and tutting. As soon as he yelled 'ready', she pulled back the curtain and watched him saunter out, dressed in a brown wool suit, white shirt, blue silk tie, and a pair of shiny brown brogues.

'My, don't you look handsome, Gabi' she exclaimed with her hands on her hips. 'Fashion isn't just for girls you know.' She turned her gaze towards Hannah. 'Right, Missy, you're next.'

Ten minutes later, Hannah giggled as she twirled around in a floaty pink dress and a pair of white sandals.

Betty clasped her hands together with delight. 'Now then, how good do you both feel right now?'

'I feel pretty,' trilled Hannah with a grin.

'And Gabi?'

'I feel proper dapper.'

Betty laughed. 'Now, remember, every woman wants to leave this shop feeling as wonderful as you do.' She stretched her arms up to the ceiling as if she were flying, speaking with reverence to an invisible audience. 'A woman buys an outfit because she wants to feel transformed into a beautiful enchantress, just like the goddesses of the silver screen who can turn a man into quivering jelly. So from now on, you must think of this boutique as your stage and when a lady tries something on,' she clicked her fingers, 'remember to compliment, compliment, compliment.'

The children both nodded in agreement.

'Right, time for work. Gabi, help me dress the shop window and pin clothes on the mannequins. And Hannah, please check the rails for a size ten in the red sweetheart dress. A customer will be arriving to collect it soon.'

She was pleased to see them both jump to attention. An hour later, she sent Gabi off with a handful of wrapped dresses under his arms and a hand-drawn map, ready to deliver some local purchases by foot, whilst Hannah tied price tags onto colourful jumpsuits, scarves, and turbans. The shop had been quiet recently, but Betty sensed there could be big business in showing factory workers how to make the most of their looks, and later that day when a tired looking woman in dowdy brown overalls and a hairnet wandered in, she weaved her magic.

'You know, you're very pretty, and you could make a soldier smile if you bring out your beauty with a mascara wand and a shiny lipstick.'

The children watched the woman's face light up as Betty sat her down, tweaking her hair in front of a mirror and set to work, grabbing a bag of cosmetics from her handbag hidden behind the counter. Even though they were in short supply, she always had her pots of powder and rouge that she ritually used each morning, dabbing them onto the woman's pale skin with a large brush, applying eyeliner and mascara with skilful precision, and finishing off with her trademark red lipstick glossed onto her small rosebud lips. She sold her two brightly coloured turbans and a blue jumpsuit that day.

Over the next few days, word spread about her unique new service and the shop heaved with excitable women arriving with clothing coupons and cash. Betty ran around like a mad thing doing endless makeovers and taking payments, whilst Gabi and Hannah frantically searched for the right sized outfits.

By Saturday, she'd trebled her usual weekly takings and at 6 p.m. she locked up the boutique for the weekend. 'Well done, you two,' she said with a smile as they buttoned their coats. 'Now let's get you fed.' And just over an hour later they all staggered through her front door exhausted, carrying bags of shopping.

Betty knew they were starving and dashed into the kitchen to unpack the groceries, ready to prepare dinner as the children set the table. Buzzing with excitement and dancing about, she lit the stove and peeled some vegetables. Business was buoyant and the little ones seemed to be thriving, gazing back at her with electric eyes, inspired by their new work focus, she could tell, and looking *très chic* to boot.

She had to admit, she hadn't thought she could juggle the two, but things were going surprisingly well as a surrogate mum/business woman. She opened a few tins and threw everything into a pan to create a quick meal of corned beef hash with carrots and peas from her elderly neighbour's allotment. Nothing too clever, but simple and healthy. And after the children wolfed it down, they taught her to play their own versions of Whist and Gin Rummy, squabbling over scores, until they both trudged upstairs to sleep, barely able to keep their eyes open.

Once alone, Betty curled up in her velvet armchair, sipping a well-earned glass of chilled white wine. She was dressed for bed wearing some new silk pyjamas with a matching gown in rose pink, along with some white fluffy mules, similar to the night-wear Joan Crawford modelled in *Vogue*. The rare sample had just arrived at the shop and boy did they make her feel good; seductive and elegant.

Was she parenting them right, she wondered, telling them a stylish outfit equalled beauty and confidence. After all, it worked for her, hadn't it? Sparkles, rouge, and a figure hugging dress certainly helped weave some magic on that frosty bank manager to buy the shop, and got her discounts from gooey-eyed tradesman, so she had to teach them how crucial that was. And goodness, she adored having them around, snuggling up with them on the chaise longue as they listened to the wireless and telling them bedtime stories about the terrible fashion disasters she'd witnessed. This was new, these deep maternal feelings that warmed her heart; she'd been so busy working, she hadn't realised how lonely she'd been.

She wiped her face with her hand as a tear slid down her cheek. Her parents had been dead for nearly a decade, now joined in heaven by her sister, Rose. Not that they'd spoken much over the years. She'd kept her distance from both her older sisters. On the odd occasion she had heard from them, there was always a catty remark thrown in.

'Unmarried women that dolly themselves up often get an unfortunate reputation,' said Fenella, when she'd asked her to take on the children. 'So charitable deeds can cover the cracks.'

Despite Fenella having a dig as usual, more or less calling her a floozy, Betty kept quiet, not wanting a row.

She looked down at her ringless finger curled around her wine glass. Floozy, huh, that was the last thing she was. She'd been celibate for two years. Yes, she'd had a few dalliances, men she thought had loved her, but all of them had let her down, selfishly used her for their own ends. She'd been lied to so often, she'd given up ever finding a soul mate to love. Yet, somehow, despite her sadness, she knew if she could put on a little glitz and glamour, she could hold her head high whatever harsh obstacles lay in store. 'Onwards and upwards, Bet,' she told herself firmly. 'Don't look back.'

Chapter 9

Saturday afternoon, 28th June 1941

The sound of whooping and cheering reverberated along the labyrinthine corridors of the eighteenth-century hospital. Dr Walters pushed open the swing doors to the ward. 'What's all this commotion?' he asked brusquely, addressing a young man lying in bed, his plastered leg raised in traction.

'Look over there,' replied the man, pointing to the opposite end of the ward. 'Lucky Mr Edward's been sent more gifts.'

Patients leaned forward on their beds, hands clapping wildly as they stared, eyes agog at Edward. The doctor strolled over to his bedside and stood next to the young delivery boy, holding a Fortnum & Mason hamper.

'Thanks, lad. Put it here before you drop it,' Edward instructed the young boy in grey uniform. The boy nodded, bent his legs and heaved the wooden tea chest, bound with rope onto the bedside table, before bowing and leaving.

'Good day to you, Doc,' Edward said, looking up with a smile.

'Good day to you, Eddie. So what's all this? Christmas come early?'

'Your guess is as good as mine, Doc.' Edward untied the thick rope and prised open the wooden lid, his mouth dropping open.

'Blimey, there's enough food here to feed an entire family, grand-parents an' all.' He scanned some of the contents, picking them up one at a time: tinned quinces, fig rolls, oat cakes, tins of treacle sponge, and a packet of Darjeeling tea. 'I don't know what half this stuff is, but I certainly fancy a bit of cake.'

He clambered up and stood shakily on his bed, his arms outstretched. 'Hey, you lot,' he roared as every patient looked round. 'I'll be sharing all this grub out later. There's plenty here.'

There were more raucous whoops and cheers as he grinned, happy to put a smile on everyone's face before bouncing back down.

'Watch out, you'll be the Pied Piper of biscuits soon,' said Dr Walters, chuckling. He leaned over the tea chest to take a look. 'Hmm ... and I spy bottles of whisky, port, and gin. Do you think a certain someone's trying to get you merry?'

'Ha-ha, I should be so lucky.' He picked up the bottle of London Gin. 'Take this Doc. I daren't even sniff it.'

'Thank you kindly.' Dr Walters grasped the bottle, cradling it in his hands. 'A splash of the old firewater will be a great nightcap at the end of a long day.'

Edward leant back against his pillow. 'You know, I do feel spoilt, Doc, but I don't need all this. Just the scent of her perfume does me in.'

'Spoilt is the word! Haven't you already been sent some aftershave and scented soap?'

'Yep, along with a razor, some shaving foam and a brush. I took that as a strong hint. What do you think?' he said, stroking his jaw line.

The doctor laughed. 'Oh, yes, very smooth. Enjoy, dear Eddie. It's not often a titled lady indulges a gentleman with gifts.' He hesitated, tilting his head, the familiar clacking of high heels getting louder. 'And speaking of the delightful devil.'

They both turned to see Connie in the distance wearing a stylish black dress with a Chinchilla shrug around her shoulders, complemented by a red pillbox hat and matching clutch bag. They watched entranced. She seemed to glide through the ward, placing one strappy black shoe in front of the other as if she were walking along a tightrope.

'Good afternoon, Lady Douglas-Scott. How wonderful to see you again. You'll be taking up residency soon.'

She lifted her chin regally. 'Dr Walters, I did say to call me Connie, and, yes, I come, because someone has to care for this dear man.' She turned to Edward and gasped. 'Golly, look at that face. So there was a dashing gentleman inside that hairy monster.'

Edward grinned as she perched on the edge of his bed and peeled off her black lace gloves, placing them in her bag.

'Do excuse me.' Dr Walters bowed formally, clutching his bottle of gin as if it was fine china. 'No rest for us reprobates.'

''Bye, Doc,' said Edward with a wink.

Connie waved as the doctor marched off through the ward. 'Eddie, did I just spy Dr Walters hugging some liquor?' she whispered, leaning closer.

'Yes, and it's all your fault.'

She pursed her lips, looking puzzled.

'Those goodies you sent knocked me sideways, but you gave me a fair few bottles of the hard stuff and I can't drink in here.'

Connie chuckled. 'Well, drinkies aren't rationed, thankfully. I'm not sure what I'd do if I couldn't get a little squiffy now and then, but I'm sure there'll be a time when you and I can toast your full recovery.'

He smiled at her gaiety, taking in the sweep of her high cheekbones and her long graceful neck; the downy wisps of hair where it was pinned up loosely. She seemed to radiate sunshine along with an enchanting innocence underneath her glossy mask—the way she met his gaze and shyly looked away. 'It's good to see you again, young lady. Thanks for those delicious treats. I don't deserve it.'

'Oh, Eddie, of course you do. I mean, golly, the hospital food must be perfectly horrid.'

'I just don't want to be some charity case.'

'Goodness, you are silly. I've got an account at Fortnum's and I can't use food vouchers on dresses and hats.'

'So, I'm not taking up your time?'

'Heavens, no! Mummy's often at luncheons and Daddy's always in meetings with terribly important people. So actually,' she said, looking wistful, 'I do get rather lonely.'

'You ... lonely?' His thick dark eyebrows lifted in surprise. 'Surely a beauty like you must have a stream of admirers?'

Connie smoothed down her dress, eliminating creases that didn't exist. 'You're very kind, Eddie. And, yes, I was introduced to many eligible bachelors at my debutante ball, and I was all set to find a suitable husband.'

'Sounds grand.'

'I suppose.'

'You didn't fall in love then?'

'No. Mummy says I'm far too fussy.' She wrinkled her nose. 'Although there was one man I met. Very powerful he was too, but he was much older and ... he um ... well, he lives in Europe, so it wouldn't have worked ... but there's always some chap whisking me off to the races or taking me to dine at some official function.' She looked up at him with soft eyes. 'But I've discovered that one can be wined and dined by a perfect gentleman with a top-notch pedigree and still feel very much alone. Mummy would be livid if she heard me say this, but many of these men are terribly dull and dare I say pompous, obsessed with their investments or chasing off on shooting jaunts to the country. They want the right sort of girl on their arm but they show little interest in the real me.'

Edward stared at her intently. 'So what do you want, Connie?'

Her eyelashes fluttered. 'Just a good man ... kind and loving. Someone I can talk to ... who listens, that's all. Am I asking too much?'

She reached out to touch his hand, sliding her fingers in between his, and as he felt the warmth of their palms pressed together, he wished he could take her in his arms and never let go. 'No, Connie, you're not asking too much. I could listen to you all day. You help me escape from the misery of all this.' He glanced around the ward as more wounded casualties were wheeled in. 'Everyone here's been ripped to shreds, their families and homes wiped out. It's torture the way they cry with pain. The nights are the worst.'

Connie wrinkled her forehead. 'Gosh, Eddie, that's frightful. I often feel such a fraud when so many are suffering. Mummy says I walk around in my own little bubble at times, wondering if I've chosen the right handbag or if my shoes are the right match. It's just that,' she took a breath. 'I can't bear to see it ... you know ... the ugliness.'

Edward hunched over, his eyes watering, 'I don't blame you, Connie. It's a harsh world out there ... but you,' he gazed at her, 'you show me how amazing life could be.'

The edges of her lips flicked up into a serene smile as he lifted her hand to his mouth and kissed it, smelling the sweet freshness of her skin. She seemed nervous when he let go, struggling to slide each finger into her lace gloves, grabbing her clutch bag and stumbling as she stood up. She turned to walk away and he was worried he'd upset her—until she looked back to wave goodbye, her eyes lingering for a few moments, searching his.

Chapter 10

Monday morning, 30th June 1941

D r Walters marched into the psychologist's office desperate for answers. He had grown rather fond of his patient, but the hospital was now so overcrowded there were makeshift beds in the corridors. And given his gruelling schedule, patience was no longer his strong point, especially with bumbling foreigners who thought they knew better. 'Dr Jungston, any updates for me?'

Dr Jungston emitted a deep, audible sigh as he looked up from his desk with strained eyes. 'Dr Walters, good to see you. And thank you for the extended time, but sadly our patient's neurological functioning has proved rather complex.'

'Complex!' Dr Walters's took a step back, the muscles in his face tightening. 'Sorry, but that's simply not good enough. We have patients with organ failure who are losing blood. As much as I like the man, this place is not a hotel!'

'I appreciate that Dr Walters and on reflection, I might have a solution.'

'Wonderful,' he replied, his head jerking forward. 'I'm all ears.'

Droplets of sweat appeared on the psychologist's forehead and trickled down his cheek. 'I've been thinking … if his memory remains elusive,' he paused and gulped, 'he can come and stay with me.'

'Stay with you! Why?'

'Well, he's a likeable chap,' he said, folding his arms defensively, his paunch protruding through his shirt. 'And with so many casualties we must work together to do what we can.'

'Hmm, do humour me,' replied Dr Walters as he took off his glasses and rubbed his eyes. 'There must be more to this than mere charitable favours if you are inviting a relative stranger to come and live in your home.'

He cleared his throat. 'It's just ... um, well, put it this way ... there's a significant discovery, which is rather exciting. And I want to keep him under observation.'

Dr Walters raised one eyebrow. He'd grown uncharacteristically cynical over the years. 'Goodness, do tell?'

Dr Jungston stood up and paced the room, his hands clenched behind his back. Usually, he lumbered about, but today he appeared to have a real bounce in his step that he couldn't seem to contain. 'I gave our patient some paper and a pen and asked him to mark down in images or words anything that came to mind. When he returned the paper I noticed he'd written down some extraordinarily complex bars of music.' He stopped pacing, his brow furrowing into deep lines. 'Naturally, I asked him where his creativity came from and he told me that he was making up melodies from patterns of black and white blocks that streamed across his brain.'

Dr Walters motioned for him to continue.

'I was so intrigued that I brought him to my house and asked him to play this orchestration for me on my beloved baby grand. And by Jove, Dr Walters,' he said, his voice rising higher as he waved his arms around expressively, 'I was witness to a virtuoso. His fingers glided across the keys like a good strong whisky glides down your throat, climbing in lyrical chains of triads, skipping across melodic intervals and arpeggios and then striking the keys majestically, building to a dramatic crescendo ... I tell you, this man is as gifted as any of the great maestro's and the music, it seems, is entirely from his own compositions.'

The doctor remained unusually silent, digesting his every word.

'He was either born a talented musician or he has acquired the effects of Savant Syndrome and unlocked an artistic brilliance as a result of his brain injury.'

'Savant Syndrome, but that's extremely rare?'

'Indeed, but when it does occur, either through illness or brain injury, it can rewire brain circuitry, creating artistry, musicality, and mathematical genius. Certainly, wherever his abilities came from, he is unique ... a rare faceted diamond!'

'Well, well, this is fascinating,' replied Dr Walters with a mystified grin as he put his glasses back on. 'And in view of the exceptional circumstances, I won't berate you for taking my patient out of the hospital without permission. From what you say I am truly intrigued and would very much like to hear him play.'

'And so you will,' Dr Jungston chuckled, looking distinctly relieved. 'You may also have back your priceless hospital bed. Sign his discharge form and he can stay with me from tonight. I plan to continue my research into this man's phenomenal talent.'

Chapter 11

Fourteen months later
Bournemouth: October 1942

Wolf-whistles always embarrassed Betty, but she was ever gracious, smiling coyly. She was used to the attention. It came with the territory if you had your glad rags on. Besides it was a small town and everyone knew she was single, so she had her admirers. The children sniggered when yet another nervous suitor arrived in the shop, stuttering as they made any excuse to talk to her, but she politely brushed them all aside, until someone unexpectedly caught her eye.

'Oh, gosh, it's him again,' said Betty, feeling flustered. She craned her neck to sneak a look out of the shop window.

Hannah and Gabi peered through the glass and saw a soldier in khaki uniform ambling along the road. Nudging each other, they stifled giggles.

'Aunt Betty's got a crush?' teased Gabi.

A smile danced across her glossy lips. 'Well, you know, children, a girl can dream.'

'Didn't he come in the other day to browse?' asked Hannah.

Betty sighed. 'Yes, he did. And I saw him right up close and let me tell you,' she said, gazing into space, 'he's every girl's dream with that American accent and those puppy-dog eyes. And those muscular arms of his,' she bit her bottom lip, 'they could wrap right around you, so you'd always feel safe.'

'Ooh, look, he's heading this way ... he's gonna come in,' shrieked Hannah as she jumped about.

'Oh, dear God,' Betty muttered, not daring to look again. She quickly smoothed down her black pencil skirt, glancing at herself in a mirror as she fluffed up her hair with her fingers, swivelling around when the door clicked open.

'Good afternoon, ma'am.' The soldier saluted, cleaning his combat boots on the doormat before walking in.

'Good afternoon, sir, browsing for gifts again?' replied Betty, tilting her head to one side.

'Yes, ma'am. I had my eye on something.' He walked over to a rack on the wall with scarves hanging from it. 'May I ask what you think of this?' he asked, sliding the blue silk fabric between his fingers.

'Well, I may be biased but that's a much sought after Jacqmar scarf, the design is simply breathtaking. They're a rare find since the war started.' Betty played with the silver locket on her necklace. 'Is it for a fiancée?'

'No, I don't have anyone special,' he answered in his southern drawl. 'This is for my mom'. He stroked the material again. 'I don't know much about silk, but it sure feels good.'

'How lovely, what's the occasion?'

'It's for Christmas, ma'am.'

Betty laughed. 'You're ahead of yourself. That's two months away.'

'That's army life, ma'am. I'm away for so long that time disappears in a heartbeat.' He hesitated as if reflecting on past memories.

'I want to post this soon so Ma gets it in time. She's been on her own since Pa died.'

'Oh, sorry, to hear that. Where does your mother live?' She couldn't help but notice his engaging smile: pearly white teeth, straight out of a toothpaste advert.

'She's from the Deep South, born and bred in Alabama. Parcels take a good long while to get there. So I'll take it, ma'am. How much is it?'

'Of course, that will be two and six,' said Betty taking the scarf from him. 'I'll gift-wrap it for you.'

'Thank you, ma'am.' The soldier stood there watching her fold the crisp brown paper around the scarf as if he was mesmerised. She passed the package to him and he held it in his hands before taking a deep breath. 'I'd like to introduce myself properly, ma'am. I'm Sergeant James Cooper, but you can call me Jim. I wonder,' he added, his voice breaking, 'if you'd care to go out for dinner with me tonight?'

Aunt Betty didn't hesitate, the words tumbling out of her mouth before she could think. 'Why, I'd be delighted, Jim. Meet me here at eight.'

After he left the shop, the children gave Betty the thumbs up.

'He seems like the bee's knees,' said Hannah.

Betty giggled, brushing a blonde curl out of her eyes. 'Yes, Hannah, he does.'

After that first date with Jim, Betty arrived home on a 'high', after having dinner with him at the grand Metropole Hotel in the Lansdowne Circle. From then on they snatched any time together they could, grabbing an early morning pot of tea in the café next door to the boutique, or taking a quick stroll on the seafront and bringing back ice creams for them all to eat.

The children seemed to love having Jim around. Whenever he popped by the shop, they'd badger him with endless questions about the wild desert country of the Deep South with its cowboys and Indians and dangerous snakes just like they'd seen at the cinema. And Jim would chuckle, happy to oblige, regaling them with crazy stories that Betty knew he'd probably made up.

Things were officially serious three weeks later when Betty invited him home for dinner. It would be the first time he'd stepped over the threshold into her cherished sanctum and she felt quite flustered about presenting the perfect meal.

'This pot roast has got to taste good,' she said, studying the small joint of beef on the kitchen top with a frown. 'I've queued at the butchers, saved up coupons, and paid one and six, and it will probably end up ruined.'

'It probably will too,' whispered Hannah to Gabi. 'She might be pretty and clever but when she cooks it's usually half-burnt.'

'Cheeky devil,' said Betty, overhearing. She wagged a playful finger at her.

Gabi stepped forward with a smile. 'I can help if you'd like, Aunty. It was my favourite hobby watching our mama cook.'

Betty looked at him hopefully. 'Could you really, bubbeleh? I'd be ever so grateful.'

'Of course, I'll get cracking.'

'Big head,' Hannah muttered with a sulky pout.

Betty grabbed an apron that was hanging on the door and tied it around his waist, clapping her hands together excitedly. She watched as Gabi rolled up his shirt sleeves, grabbed a sharp knife from the cutlery drawer, sliced off some lard from a large block and threw a lump into the frying pan.

'I'll get the matches,' she said, rushing over to ignite the gas ring.

Placing the beef joint in the hot pan, they heard a loud sizzle. 'Hear that ladies? First, you must brown the meat to hear it sing.'

'And what then, Mr Know-It-All?' asked Hannah, goading him. She sat on a stool in her red pinafore dress, swinging her legs until a sandal fell off.

'It can make whoopee in a casserole dish with its old friends, stock, vegetables, and seasoning,' he said with a smirk.

'Gabi!' giggled Betty, 'you're such fun.'

Hannah rolled her eyes and then stared at the floor with her arms folded.

Several hours later, just before seven o' clock, Gabi placed the piping hot pot roast in the centre of the table, already laid out with Betty's lace table mats, expensive silverware, and crystal cut glasses.

Unable to wait any longer, Betty bent over and lifted up the lid, closing her eyes as she breathed in the aroma. 'Yum, that smells so good, Gabi. You really are the cat's pyjamas.'

Gabi grinned and wiped his brow with his sleeve.

Betty grabbed Hannah's hand and squeezed it, not wanting her to feel left out after her little huff, feeling cheered when the little one smiled and squeezed her hand back. Betty didn't want either of them to feel sad.

Jim arrived a few minutes later to a nervous anxiety in the air, everyone on tenterhooks, wanting to please him. He ambled in, winking at Gabi and Hannah, pausing to give Betty an affectionate peck on the lips. 'I've been dreaming of this all day,' he said with a grin as they all sat down to eat. After he'd swallowed a few mouthsful, they all waited for his verdict, with relief all round when he wiped his mouth with his napkin and said in his southern drawl, 'Guys, this is as good as my mom's home-cooking.'

Afterwards, he dug around in his denim jacket pocket. 'Hmm, what have I got here?' he said, pulling out two bars of Active Service chocolate. He waved them in the air and then handed them a slab each. Gabi and Hannah were speechless, taking the chocolate from him tentatively, as if they couldn't believe it was real.

'Oh, Jim, you are a sweetheart,' said Betty. She leant over and kissed him on the cheek. 'They haven't seen that good stuff in a long while.' She nudged his arm, both of them chuckling at the sight of their mesmerised stares, unwrapping the candy as if it were a prized delicacy.

Later that evening when Betty followed Jim outside to say good-bye, their figures silhouetted in the moonlight, the children watched, leaning out of an upstairs window.

'Do you see Gabi, the way they look at each other, the way they touch hands and kiss? I think they're falling in love.'

'Yep,' said Gabi with a wistful smile. 'It's definitely love all right.'

Chapter 12

North London: October 1942

Every month I received letters from Gabi and Hannah, stuffed into the same envelope. I kept all their scribblings buried underneath my underwear in the top of my chest of drawers, hidden from prying eyes, to keep something sacred, just for me. They told me all about their idyllic lives by the sea, having adventures with glamorous Aunt Betty and in return, I wrote back, telling them a bunch of big fat lies. I invented a new existence, stating that Aunt Fenella and Uncle Harry were loving and kind, taking me on historic excursions all around London and giving me their undivided attention. I couldn't upset them by letting them know the truth; that I was moping about, doing endless chores and jumping at the smallest creak in the floorboards.

Uncle Harry was no longer a scaly lizard, but a carnivorous vulture always hovering, ready to swoop, trying to find ways to molest me, often right under Aunt Fenella's nose.

God knows, the countless times I tried to catch her eye, praying that she'd see what was happening and intervene, tell him to leave and never come back—but she seemed to be clueless, focused intently on her crochet or reading a book. Perhaps it suited her not to. She might be modern enough to wear trousers, but she never challenged him about anything. And why rock the boat when you had a live-in skivvy to clean the toilets?

One night he'd pounced as soon as she'd retired to bed, lunging at me in the hallway. 'Come on little girl, kiss your daddy,' he squawked in his high-pitched nasal voice. Before I could think he'd grabbed my arms and held them tightly against the wall. I struggled against him, recoiling in disgust from the stench of his stale tobacco breath as he tried to force his tongue into my mouth. Summoning all my strength, I shoved him away and watched him fall backwards against the wall wincing in pain.

Every part of me shook as tears streamed down my face, but I was determined to fight my corner. So I threw my shoulders back, looked him right in the eye and said, 'Try that again, Uncle Harry, and I'll scream so loudly that everyone on this street will think I'm being murdered!' His doughy face twisted into a sneer as he flounced off, bitter at not getting his own way.

Craving privacy, the bathroom became my only sanctuary, soaking in a tub of warm suds until my skin went wrinkly, knowing I could lock the door. I'd avoided mirrors for over a year, hating the body my uncle lusted after, so it came as a shock when I dared to look down at my nakedness. There they were, those embarrassing large breasts of mine, along with those fleshy hips which had grown even wider, but thankfully, I appeared to have a more defined waist. And I'd grown several inches taller, my toes now easily touching the chrome faucet.

Taking a deep breath, I summoned the courage to look at my face. Reaching up with dripping hands, I grabbed a small mirror from the tiled window ledge and stared at my reflection, startled by the stranger staring back at me: eyes red-rimmed and too big for their sockets, cheekbones jutting out, and a mouth turned downwards in misery. I felt so sad; along with the puppy fat, the girlish innocence in me had long gone, left behind like burnt ashes. *At least my spots have cleared up,* I thought, *and my long hair detracts from that horrid nose.*

But private moments never lasted long and I jerked backwards, splashing water everywhere when I heard the dreaded banging on the door as the handle twisted back and forth.

'Let me in, I need the lavatory, right now,' he yelled.

My body stiffened, and I ignored him, hoping he'd disappear. It happened so often I no longer cared about the consequences. In a foggy daze, I blanked him out, trying to get through another day.

Thankfully, I'd found a part-time job which helped me stay sane; two days a week at the local estate agents on Golders Green Road. My aunt agreed it would be good for me to learn a profession. It was pretty humdrum: filing paperwork and making endless rounds of tea, but thankfully, I could share a joke with my new friends in the office. And after giving the Rosenblums half my wage, I hatched a plan for a 'freedom fund.' If I could save the rest, I could escape to Bournemouth and rent a room near my brother and sister. And then we could be a family again.

That small speck of hope kept me going—because most days I just wanted to die! I considered walking in front of a car, ingesting rat poison, cutting my wrists with the kitchen knife. But in the end, I couldn't do it. Because deep down I knew it took more gumption to stay alive. I'd survived this far, and I had to keep going. Something would change soon, wouldn't it? It had to.

Chapter 13

Central London: October 1942

On stage, illuminated by the spotlight, Edward bent over the imposing ebony Steinway, his fingers swift and sure, dancing lightly and then crashing across the ivories. He played Mozart's Overture from 'The Marriage of Figaro' with such ferocious passion, his body twisted and turned, his face contorted and his eyes rolled wildly. Then he eloquently changed key and with tender emotion played Liszt's, 'Dreams of Love', instinctively picking out exquisite harmonies that resonated around the Royal Albert Hall.

This was his first major concert in such an iconic London venue and his reputation as a modern-day Mozart was travelling like wildfire. People had booked for months in advance, queuing for half a mile down Prince Consort Road in South Kensington to see the celebrated pianist, Edward Chopard.

As his hands danced effortlessly across the keys, he looked out into an audience of over six thousand people. He was certain he had never felt such blissful joy as he witnessed a sea of faces so entranced by his music. The people he held dear watched from one of the exclusive boxes in the highly prized second tier of the auditorium; his beloved Connie with her serene smile and her parents, Lord and Lady Douglas-Scott.

His finale was the uplifting, 'Grande Valse Brillante' by Chopin. He finished to rapturous applause, stood up in his black tuxedo, out of breath and drenched in sweat, and bowed several times before leaving the stage, where he was met by his good friend, Dr Oliver Jungston.

'You were magnificent, Eddie. You transported us to another place in time,' declared Oliver, throwing his arm around Edward's shoulders.

'Thank you, Oli. I feel bloody euphoric,' said Edward with a wide grin, still panting for breath. 'Adrenaline is pumping through my veins.'

They both unashamedly hugged each other as they awaited the arrival backstage of the blue-bloods Edward now considered family.

Ever keen to keep his daughter happy, Lord Henry Douglas-Scott, the silver-haired, six feet two, multi-millionaire owner of one of most profitable city banks, had bankrolled Edward for all his venues. He'd also hired him a suite on the seventh floor of The Dorchester with sweeping views of Hyde Park. The hotel had a reputation for being 'bomb proof' because of its sturdy construction and he'd wanted to ensure the safekeeping of his new investment.

'Well done, dear chap,' bellowed Henry as he marched in, slapping Edward on the back. 'You can play the work of any composer and that is true artistry.'

Connie's mother, Elizabeth, waltzed in behind her husband, giving Edward two air kisses. 'Yes, awfully good show, you darling boy.' She was a sophisticated woman wearing her dark hair in a pompadour style, pulled up at the sides with a mass of curls at the back which complemented her jade silk swirling gown.

'You are both too kind,' replied Edward with a smile. His head turned. 'My darling, you look divine.' Transfixed, he gazed at Connie's radiant appearance; her glossy brown hair tumbling down in waves over her red strapless dress that swept across the floor as she walked.

Oliver bowed and kissed Connie's hand. '*Oui, tres élégant, ma chère.*'

'Oh, stop, please, I don't deserve such praise,' replied Connie with a giggle. 'And you, my darling man, were wonderful tonight,' she whispered in Edward's ear. 'I am the luckiest girl in the world.'

Edward pulled her towards him, rustling the taffeta on her dress. 'And I am the luckiest man. You have breathed new life into me.' He helped Connie on with her sable fur coat as they all followed a security guard out of the back exit into the cool night air, momentarily blinded by flashbulbs exploding in their faces.

'Ah, the hyenas, always lying in wait', said Oliver. He put his hands up as a barrier to halt the photographers surging forward, desperate for close-ups. 'Please,' he stated firmly to audible groans, 'let him breathe.'

Oliver escorted them to their chauffeur-driven Rolls-Royce, jumping in behind as the driver followed her parents' car to Southampton Street in Covent Garden, to dine at one of the most exclusive restaurants in the capital, Le Boulestin.

'You will love this place, darling,' cooed Connie as she clutched Edward's hand. 'It's a favourite of mine. Fashion photographer, Cecil Beaton once described it as the prettiest restaurant in London.'

It was already 10 p.m. when they were seated at the large round table, joined soon after by a flustered Dr Walters, who'd only just left work, all chattering noisily as the wine flowed.

Edward had fast become accustomed to a lavish lifestyle. He was relieved his weekly elocution lessons were paying off, removing all traces of any London slang or aitch-*dropping*—an understandable request from Henry now he was meeting esteemed members of the aristocracy, and earning plaudits as a virtuoso all over England.

'Compliments from the owner, Marcel Boulestin,' announced an exotically accented waiter appearing with two bottles of Moët & Chandon.

'Wonderful, do send Mr Boulestin our most humble thanks,' replied Edward, bashfully.

'I heard a whisper tonight from some of our friends in Fleet Street,' said Elizabeth, 'that the glitterati were clamouring to see you backstage, but security stopped them, and there was a rather disappointed Gustave Charpentier, the French composer, who wanted desperately to congratulate you, but you had already vanished.'

'Oh, Lordy, I must make more time to meet my fans. I'm so unused to all this attention.'

Oliver pulled a sad face and wrung his hands together dramatically. 'Sorry, that's my fault. I should never have rushed you out.'

Dr John Walters laughed, bemused by his colleague's theatrical affectations. 'I must congratulate you, Eddie. It appears tonight was a truly remarkable success. So where to next?'

'Ah, we have great plans for next year, so many cities, worldwide,' interrupted Oliver. 'Fortunately, I speak six languages. Eddie has already been booked to play at the Royal Concertgebouw in Amsterdam and at Musikverein in Vienna. Thank goodness for the Douglas-Scott connections.' He lowered his voice and tapped the side of his nose. 'Henry promised he could secure us a military aircraft. Eddie better get used to being airborne.'

Henry nodded, pulling a fat cigar out of his jacket pocket. He clamped his plump lips around it, igniting it with a diamond encrusted lighter.

'That's fabulous, but let Eddie speak for himself, old chap,' said John, raising an eyebrow.

Oliver shrugged his shoulders and sipped some champagne as everyone laughed.

'So, Edward *Chopard*, such a dignified name. How on earth did you think of that?' continued John, playfully putting his hand over Oliver's mouth to stop him speaking.

Edward gently touched Connie's arm. 'Over to you, darling.'

'We'd been thinking of something for quite some time,' she replied with a smile. 'He needed something snazzy, with a certain ring to it.'

Both doctors appeared fascinated, listening attentively as her father leisurely sucked on his cigar.

'Do go on, my dear,' said John.

'Well, Daddy bought me an exquisite Chopard watch for my birthday last year.'

'Worth five thousand pounds and custom-made to the highest standards!' declared Henry.

'Daddy, don't be vulgar,' snapped Connie. 'Anyway, this beautiful watch was surrounded by a cluster of diamonds on Sapphire Crystal glass with eighteen-carat-gold and hidden in a lovely brooch, shaped like a swan. I love Chopard for all his elegance and suddenly it was like an erupting light bulb of inspiration and that's when I turned to my beloved Eddie and said—"That's it! That's your name! You will be Edward Chopard!"'

John's face lit up. 'Ingenious.'

'Naturally, I organised a solicitor to draw up the deed poll documents,' stated Henry, 'and bang on the dotted line, it was done.'

'I love it!' said Oliver. 'It has the air of the exotic as well as a wonderful *legato* tone.' He sipped some more champagne appearing to reflect on the evening's event. 'I must say I love being a psychologist, peeking underneath a person's mask, but it doesn't compare with seeing Eddie launched at the Royal

Albert Hall. Tonight has been truly a triumph. Let us raise a toast to Edward Chopard.'

'Hear, hear,' declared the entire table as they raised their glasses into the air.

'I'll drink to that,' said Henry. He quaffed his bubbly in seconds and then wiped his mouth vigorously with a napkin. 'He must be worth it—my daughter clung on to him with every one of her pearly talons.'

Connie gave Edward a sultry look as she toyed with her two-strand necklace made of the finest natural pearls. 'Yes, I declare my heart snapped in two when you disappeared, darling. It took months to track you down. And both of you, John and Oli,' she continued, staring at them, 'and those awful belligerent nurses were most unhelpful, keeping very tight-lipped. '

'We had to, my dear,' replied Oliver with a smile, 'for patient confidentiality. But your persistence was most impressive.'

'Why, thank you. I got hot on the trail after I heard a rumour from one of your patients, Oli, and followed you home in my little MG. Although it took patience and stealth. I should have been a spy for MI5, but once I'd watched Eddie come out of your house, I knew he was living there. Admittedly, I went a little crazy, though, didn't I, darling?' she said, looking at Edward with a giggle, 'writing you endless love notes. I've never chased a man before. I thought I'd end up a sad old crone with ten cats mourning unrequited love.'

Edward lifted her hand to his mouth, kissing it gently. 'I'm so glad you didn't give up on me, my dearest Connie.' He hesitated, swallowing as he tried to find the right words. 'You appeared in my life like a dazzling angel when I had nothing to live for. Your unswerving faith gives me hope that you will soon become my wife and the mother of what I know will be beautiful children.'

The table fell silent as everyone waited, anticipating what Edward would say next.

He pulled his chair out of the way and dropped onto one knee. 'So will you marry me, my darling, Connie?' He looked up at her, producing from his pocket an eleven-carat, pink diamond ring, set in platinum.

'Oh, my goodness,' said Connie, choked with emotion as a teardrop slid down her cheek. 'Yes, of course I'll marry you. I've wanted nothing more.' She extended a shaky hand, enabling him to slide the ring onto her manicured finger. 'Eddie, this must have cost a fortune. Look, it's perfect,' she gasped as everyone leaned forward. 'I will be blissfully happy to be called Mrs Chopard.'

'Squire!' shouted Henry to the waiter with his usual sardonic humour. 'Three more bottles of Moët for the rabble and delight us with some of that excellent 1869 Brandy you have on display.'

As the waiter rapidly produced more bottles along with their entrées, Henry raised his champagne coupe and yelled, 'To Eddie and Connie, the toast of elite London society.' Everyone cheered and clinked their glasses together.

Elizabeth put down her glass and turned towards her daughter with an ecstatic smile, hugging her tightly. 'You're so blessed, my darling,' she whispered, 'so blessed, to have someone like Eddie.'

Connie yielded to her mother's warm embrace, fizzing with happiness. 'I know, Mummy. I'm hoping he'll be as good a husband to me as Daddy is to you.'

Elizabeth stroked her daughter's hair and then broke away, her eyes filling with tears. Picking up the champagne bottle, she poured some more into her shallow glass, watching it froth over the top as she raised it to her lips and gulped it down. Quickly pouring herself another, she studied her husband warily from the corner of her eye.

'All went as planned then,' mumbled Henry with a wink.

Edward tilted his head towards him and beamed. 'As smooth as mulberry silk.'

'Well, for the ceremony,' continued Henry as he paused to take out another cigar from his jacket pocket, holding it between his long thick fingers, 'keeping it hush-hush, our country estate in Shropshire is available. It's a seventeenth-century monument to good taste with its own private chapel. The local vicar can easily be appointed. In fact, it will probably make his year. Poor chap must be bored silly watching village simpletons tie the knot.'

'Sounds perfect, Henry, and thank you so much for buying the ring. How can I ever repay you?'

'Ha-ha, you won't be able to afford that for a while, Eddie. Pink diamonds are a rare find. That one was sourced from Australia. It's worth thousands.' He paused, tapping the ash from his cigar. 'Just keep my daughter happy. That's all it takes.' He scanned the room, cautiously watchful like a tiger surveying his territory until he suddenly glared at Edward with a menacing glint in his eyes. 'Because, dear boy … if you don't keep her happy … you might find I could turn very, very nasty.' He leaned back in his chair, drawing deeply on his cigar, before easing it out of his mouth and exhaling a long stream of smoke.

Edward shuddered. As their dinner continued, he played with his food unable to eat, feeling the warming effects of the brandy mix with a chilling sense of fear.

At 3 a.m., the couple climbed back into their chauffeur-driven Rolls to head over to Edward's spacious suite at The Dorchester, where they often mingled with the many writers, actors and politicians that haunted it, before retiring for night-time trysts.

Giddy with champagne and excitement, Connie rested her head on Edward's shoulder with a deliriously happy smile on her face. Edward closed his eyes feeling an overwhelming exhaustion sweep over him. Rubbing his temples with both hands, he dropped his head forward, trying to relieve the onset of another migraine. He'd been given a millionaire's lifestyle and for that he was immensely grateful. He only prayed he could live up to what the complex tycoon wanted, and that whatever rules he played by, didn't suddenly change.

Chapter 14

Seven months later
Saturday, 15th May 1943

Jim was spending every free moment at Aunt Betty's. He loved to spoil them all and that weekend he'd planned a surprise, taking them to a local park where a jazz band performed for all the servicemen to boost morale. Amidst crowds of soldiers dancing with their girlfriends, he pulled Betty towards him. 'Watch us jive,' he said, showing Gabi and Hannah his moves as he twirled Betty around. 'You've got to get the hip swivel right'. They both joined in, spinning around, kicking their legs, laughing so much their faces ached.

A few hours later Jim and Gabi left the girls to relax in the late afternoon sun watching the last few songs from the band, whilst they did 'boys stuff' nearby, kicking a football Jim brought around the field. They played for ages, racing about, skidding over, and grappling for the ball until they both sprawled out on a park bench with sweat dripping off their faces.

'I shouldn't feel like this,' gasped Jim, breathing heavily, 'I'm a soldier! I should be fighting fit.'

'Must be the heat,' said Gabi, looking at him with a smirk.

'Must be,' he nodded. He stared at the muddy football on the grass and began rolling it around with his lace-up boot. 'So tell me, Gabi, if you don't mind me asking? Do you ever miss your ma and pa?'

Gabi gulped, caught off guard by the question. 'Yes,' he hesitated, 'I miss them so much it hurts. Sometimes I wonder if they're looking down on me, Hannah and Ruth from some big fluffy cloud, guiding us.'

'Sorry,' said Jim, wrinkling his brow. 'Who's Ruth?'

'My big sis. She's staying with family in London. We haven't seen her for nearly two years.'

Jim looked at him warmly. 'Wow, that must be tough for you all.' He hesitated for a moment as if thinking deeply. 'I miss my family too, but I love Betty with all my heart, and I want you to know that there'll always be a place for you and Hannah with us.'

Gabi choked up, his face straining, trying not to cry.

'Don't worry buddy,' said Jim, ruffling his hair. 'We're living in a time when death is always at your shoulder, but I have a feeling you'll be fine. We'll all be fine.' And they both sat together in a silent, comfortable acknowledgement.

They all stayed out late that evening, long past the children's bedtime, and after a takeaway meal of pie and chips, the siblings both lay in bed, tired but happy.

'Gabi,' whispered Hannah as she flipped onto her side to face him.

'What?' he said looking over.

'I know it's hard to say forever, because we've never had a forever, but I really hope Jim stays forever.'

'Me too,' said Gabi softly. 'Forever and ever and ever.'

Wednesday, 19th May 1943

Jim turned up at 7 p.m. ready to take Betty to dine at their regular haunt, the Metropole Hotel. They both looked the epitome of glamour and Gabi and Hannah gasped in admiration when they said their goodbyes: Aunt Betty stunningly elegant in a beaded black dress with a red fur stole draped around her shoulders, and a black beret with feathers on the side—and Jim dashingly handsome in a black tuxedo and Fedora hat.

They both sensed there was something different about their aunt when she returned that evening—the way she floated through the door, her eyes glistening with excitement, her cheeks flushed pink.

'Bubbelahs, I need to talk to you,' she said in a breathless voice. She motioned for them to join her on the chaise longue. 'I'm so happy. Jim got down on one knee and guess what ... he proposed.' She proudly extended her hand to reveal her engagement ring.

'Wow, is that a ruby?' asked Hannah excitedly.

Betty laughed. 'No, Hannah, it's a garnet. It belonged to Jim's mother. He brought it with him for good luck, intending to give it to the right woman ... and I know we only met a short while ago, but from the moment I saw him, I felt he was the one ... the big love I've been waiting for.'

Gabi glanced at Hannah, her eyes shining, mirroring his own. It was as if God had finally answered their prayers and given them a second chance of a stable family life.

'We're so happy for you, Aunt Betty,' he said with a huge grin. 'We think Jim is wonderful.'

'Yes, wonderful,' squealed Hannah, waving her hands in the air.

Aunt Betty wrapped her arms around them both, plastering their faces in kisses as Hannah wriggled about laughing. 'Thank you, children. And I think you're both wonderful.'

Gabi's heart swelled with joy; they were truly blessed. Betty wasn't a mother figure, but a friend, a sister, and something else that couldn't be voiced—a heavenly goddess, inspiring and guiding them. And now they had the amazing Jim as well.

Chapter 15

Sunday, 23rd May 1943

I t was noon. Betty had just said grace and the three of them were all ready to tuck into a rare treat of roast chicken with all the trimmings when the dreaded sirens went off.

They all froze with terror—that familiar whistling sound, followed by the roaring crash of explosions as the German bombs rained down. The two living room windows shattered, glass flying everywhere as they all dived onto the floor in panic, lying face down.

'Are you both all right?' asked Betty, after a few minutes. Gabi and Hannah voiced a shaky 'Yes,' as Betty stood up and brushed herself down. 'Well, that was unexpected. I guess nothing is predictable with this bloody war! You best help me clean up the mess.'

Hannah nodded silently, grabbing the dustpan and brush from the kitchen whilst Gabi knelt down and picked up the bigger shards of glass. Betty raced around the house, opening all her cupboards, searching for some thick material and a hammer and nails to cover the windows, hopeful that getting on with things would push away fears of something worse.

Jim was on duty that day. She was desperate to call him, but there was no way she could get outside to a phone box in the swirling smoke and dust. She switched on the wireless, twiddling the dials, frantic for news—but there was no reception, just a constant crackling sound. The wait was agonising.

Early that evening, two servicemen knocked at her door. Betty answered, recognising them as Jim's colleagues. They wandered inside, introducing themselves as Tony and Mike, taking off their caps and saluting.

'Ma'am, we have some news for you,' said Tony. 'Perhaps you should sit down.'

'I'm fine, please carry on,' she replied, her voice hoarse. She tried to stop her legs from shaking, terrified of what she might hear.

The soldier cleared his throat before speaking. 'I'm sorry to say ma'am, that our dear colleague, Jim Cooper ... well, ma'am, I'm sorry to say,' he hesitated and then gulped. 'He's been killed in action, ma'am.'

Betty stared at him blankly, as though he'd spoken a foreign language. 'What, my Jim?' She raised a hand to her forehead, trying to take things in.

'Yes, ma'am, he's dead. I'm so sorry.'

She didn't scream, although her mouth fell open as she took deep breaths, trying to suck in air, her eyes rolling backwards.

'Ma'am, are you all right?' asked Tony. 'You look pale.'

She couldn't answer, his words were like fog drifting over her ... the room spinning as she swayed from side-to-side, until she collapsed onto the floor with a thud.

Both men glanced at each other with panic as they rushed over, lifting up her limp body and carrying her to the chaise longue.

Gabi and Hannah, who had been quietly hovering, looked at each other, frantic, not knowing what to do.

'Best make tea,' said Gabi, switching onto autopilot. Hannah raced into the kitchen to put the kettle on, whilst he ran to the bathroom, wetting a towel with cold water to put on his Aunt's forehead. They were like coiled springs, primed for emergencies.

Gabi waited anxiously as the first officer crouched down and checked Betty's pulse whilst his colleague leaned in watching for a flicker of her eyelids. They must have been used to dealing with death and grief, but this was different—this was Aunt Betty—their good friend's woman, and they looked as helpless as he and Hannah did. They could only hope for the best, knowing there were no ambulances available with so many injured survivors.

After a few minutes, Betty came round. Tony felt her forehead, looking relieved. 'Are you okay, ma'am?'

'Are you sure he's really gone? How can you be sure?' pleaded Betty. She looked at him tearfully. 'There must be a mistake.'

'They found his body, ma'am. I'm so sorry.'

He turned to face Gabi and Hannah, who'd returned from the kitchen, placing a tray of brimming teacups onto the dining table. 'We'd advise you all to stay home for a few days. You can't breathe with the stench of smoke, and you wouldn't want to see what's out there ... the streets are strewn with body parts.' He gave an awkward smile. 'We'll return later with any provisions you might need.'

Aunt Betty wrung her hands, trying, it seemed, to swallow the lump in her throat. Gabi and Hannah watched her in disbelief, their old wounds reopened and salted, destroying their dreams of a hopeful future.

'How long will this war go on, Gabi?' Hannah whispered, her eyes, deep blue pools of pain. 'How many times will we go through this ... lose someone we love?'

Gabi reached out to touch her hand. 'I wish I knew, little sis. But it has to end soon. It has to.'

The soldier walked towards the door with his colleague, but before he left he looked back at Betty with a mournful expression. 'If it helps at all, we know that Jim loved you very much. He told us, you were the love of his life.'

Betty covered her face to hide her tears and nodded, murmuring in a soft voice that they could barely hear. 'I know ... and he was mine.'

The three of them remained holed up for over a week wandering aimlessly around in shock. Gabi did all he could to comfort Hannah, hugging her to sleep at night, before climbing back into his own bed—but their aunt was inconsolable—and the Boutique, which had once been her passion, remained closed.

They could only look on feeling powerless as she slumped around the house in her silk dressing gown looking like a restless ghost. Her bloodshot eyes appeared haunted and sunken in her pale face without any of her magical war paint to gloss over her torment. She'd occasionally appear, drifting into the kitchen for a glass of water before heading back to bed to cry some more.

How wrong he'd been about Aunt Betty. She wasn't a heavenly goddess after all. She was human, just like they were, now stripped bare by grief, with all of the heartwrenching pain that comes with losing someone you deeply loved. And once again, without her strength to anchor them, they both felt lost.

There was news from one of the servicemen that there would be a low-key memorial for all the dead soldiers. They never said where they found Jim's body, but with so many dying that day, they confirmed that there would be no individual burials. They all had an invitation but Betty refused to go.

'I want to remember Jim as he was,' she said softly, 'and not someone thrown into a grave without the honour or respect of a proper military funeral.'

The days meandered by, time creating a senseless calm as they all tried to get back to normal. The Boutique was, fortunately, unscathed and Betty was back to her professional best, not wanting to focus on what had happened.

'Onwards and upwards. Don't look back, that's always been my motto.'

Gabi tried his best to be the man of the house, getting in the shopping and cooking their meals, relieved that his aunt had found some composure and thrown herself back into work. And yet, she seemed almost too perfect, too groomed and too organised as she ordered the new season's stock and rearranged the shop window.

He could only hope that her stoic appearance would last.

Chapter 16

Thursday, 10th June 1943

It had been eighteen long days since we'd heard the terrifying news on the wireless and I was exhausted, lying awake every night into the early hours, praying they'd all survived. I still missed the little ones like mad and seeing their faces again was all I had to cling onto.

I pulled out some crumpled paper from the pocket of my apron with my list of chores and began mopping the kitchen floor.

'*Mazel Tov*', I heard Aunt Fenella yell out. '*B'ezrat Hashem.* Thank God.'

I stopped cleaning, placing the mop back in the bucket and leant against the kitchen top. She rushed in, waving some flowery notepaper in the air. 'Ruth, they're all right, everything's all right. I've just got word in the post.'

Before I could say anything, she took a deep breath and read out the note in a tremulous voice. '"Dear ones, Please don't worry. Bournemouth town centre lies in ruins, but we are all safe. Sending all our love. Betty and the Bubbelahs."'

She looked at me warmly. 'Wonderful news, isn't it, Ruthie?'

I nodded, my tummy doing somersaults. I was so relieved, I wanted to hug Aunt Fenella and dance around the room singing with joy, but just as I hoped she might reach out to me with affection, she slammed the door on me once more.

'Back to work then, my dear,' she said with a smile, 'that floor won't clean itself,' before she turned on her heels and breezed out of the room.

I felt so stupid, but what else did I expect? I was nothing more to them than a servant to be used and abused. And now I knew my siblings were safe, my happiness evaporated and I was left with a sulky feeling of resentment. Life was so unfair. Why did they get to be happy whilst I was left stranded with hateful people who didn't care?

The next day, I was summoned to see Aunt Fenella and Uncle Harry in their living room.

'Uncle Harry has some exciting news for you, Ruth, that will really cheer you up,' said Aunt Fenella. She stood in front of their tiled fireplace with her typical stern demeanour, observing me above her gold spectacles, as if she was about to issue me with a summons.

'Oh,' I replied, feeling hopeful, 'that's nice.'

'Yes, Ruth,' said Uncle Harry with slitted eyes. He cleared his throat. 'A vacancy has become available as my secretary at the Ministry of Food.'

'So how does that affect me?' I said, looking back and forth as they stared at me.

'Ruth, do you need to have it spelt out! You need to resign from your part-time job so you can start work with Uncle Harry.'

I felt my legs buckle underneath me. 'But why? I love my job at Ellis & Co. It makes me happy.'

'Ruth, you don't seem to understand,' snapped Aunt Fenella. 'Uncle Harry is offering you a full-time position as his secretary with a proper salary. It's a step up from doing menial office work. So show some manners and some gratitude.'

Uncle Harry fidgeted as he stood there awkwardly, his potbelly hanging over the belt of his trousers like a sloping hill.

I glared at him. I knew what he was up to—another opportunity for him to make his disgusting advances and I was sick of it, worn out from feeling permanently on guard. 'Thank you, Aunt Fenella and Uncle Harry for your kindness,' I hissed through gritted teeth, with words laced with so much spite I'm surprised I didn't choke on my own poisoned saliva.

'Finally, a thank you,' muttered Uncle Harry with a smirk. 'Small mercies, I suppose, small mercies.'

'Well then, Ruth, you will start work with Harry first thing Monday, so you can give your notice in this week. Now off you go to the kitchen and wash the dishes. You're dismissed,' she said, waving me away.

I sloped off, feeling powerless once more as I attended to my list of chores, my mind ticking over. Here I was: the outsider no one wanted, trying to be good and obedient, and where did it get me? Turning on the taps to fill the kitchen sink, I felt my eyes sting with hot tears as I rubbed them with the fists of my hands. I'd wrongly assumed that Aunt Fenella would show a little kindness, but no such luck. So from now on I would live up to my defiant reputation.

That night as I lay in bed, the repulsion I felt for Uncle Harry grabbed hold of me like a black one-eyed monster. I imagined sneaking into his bedroom with the large rusty hammer from the toolbox in his garage, lifting up my arms to bring them down with maximum force and whacking him sharply on the head in his sleep, cracking his skull open, and killing him outright.

Of course, I couldn't risk that in the real world. Aunt Fenella would wake up screaming in fright and I'd be carted off to an asylum or even prison and I didn't want to spend the rest of my life locked up. If I wanted to make him pay, I had to be crafty—perhaps sneaking chopped worms into his serving of hot pot, or toenail clippings into his steak and kidney pie, adding a drop of rat poison before the pastry was put on top. How I wanted him to suffer. I pictured him doubled up with painful stomach cramps as I drifted off to sleep with a contented smile, hopeful that justice might finally be served.

Fuelled with adrenaline, I jumped out of bed around six the next morning and got dressed. Before my aunt and uncle were awake, I crept downstairs to the kitchen with another fiendish plan. Taking the bottle of castor oil from the pantry, I snuck out of the front door, pulled out the cork and tipped most of the thick golden liquid onto their steep driveway. Now, when Uncle Harry hobbled out to climb into his car, I knew he could easily slip over with his bad hip, land flat on his face and hopefully end up bedridden for months with his broken legs in plaster. How delicious. I felt sinfully elated. But, as I crept back inside the house, picturing what other despicable things I could do, fate stepped in, changing everything.

Just as I placed the castor oil back on the pantry shelf where I'd found it, my stomach flipped when I heard the click of the letterbox. Hurrying back to the front door in anticipation of a possible letter from Gabi or Hannah, my heart sank when I saw a telegram lying on the doormat addressed to me. I was petrified. A telegram during the war meant one thing—bad news!

The Rosenblums were still asleep with only the resonant sound of Uncle Harry's snoring rumbling through the house. Tiptoeing upstairs to my bedroom, clutching the telegram, I opened it with trembling hands, feeling a chill run up my spine, unable to believe what I was reading. Sent from a solicitor in Bournemouth, the message was short and blunt:

YOUR AUNT BETTY BLUMENTHAL IS DEAD —(STOP)—
CONTACT US URGENTLY FOR MORE INFORMATION —(END)—

Bewildered, my mind raced with questions. Why was Aunt Betty dead? How did this happen? I couldn't grieve. I didn't know her. But I thought of my brother and sister, frightened and alone. They were my family and they needed me. Admittedly, I felt a sense of relief. Now I had the perfect excuse to claim my freedom, walk out of my aunt and uncle's home and never come back.

With no time to think, I grabbed a few items of clothing along with my gas mask and snuck back down to the pantry. Rummaging through the shelves crammed with food, I came across a large wicker basket hidden under endless tins of corned beef. It was perfect for my belongings, so I quickly moved all the tins and dragged it off the shelf, throwing everything in, along with some bread rolls, three apples, and two packets of digestive biscuits. Hauling it over my arm, I slipped into the hallway, pausing to check no one was coming before creeping out the front door.

Using some of my saved wages, I got a bus to Waterloo station and jumped on the first train to Bournemouth, stumbling down the aisle to find a seat. I sat down, placing my basket by my feet and looked out of the window feeling some much longed-for peace. *You made it, Ruth,* I told myself. *You've finally escaped that monster.* Now if he did fall and break his neck, I would be far away from the fallout and reunited with my family. A burst of energy erupted inside me and for a few moments, I felt I could shake off the strange, ugly, fat girl I'd always believed I was. 'I, Ruth, am courageous, adventurous, and uniquely beautiful, whatever anyone thinks of me,' I whispered. And somehow I knew if my life were to change, really change, I had to believe that with all my heart.

I thought back to my scribbled note to the Rosenblums that I'd left tucked underneath the tub of salt on the kitchen table.

Dearest Aunt Fenella and Uncle Harry,

Thank you for your kind hospitality over the last two years. Aunt Betty has been taken ill, so I've had to leave urgently for Dorset to look after the children. I will be in touch when I can.

Yours truly,
Ruth

I couldn't risk telling them the truth, that Aunt Betty was dead. They might stop us all being together, yet again.

Chapter 17

Saturday afternoon, 12th June 1943

The long awaited society wedding took place in the quaint chapel, tucked away within the grounds of the spectacular Mortis Hall. This was the Douglas-Scott's rambling stately mansion in the medieval town of Shrewsbury with its imposing Doric columns and long sweeping driveway. Set amidst ten thousand acres of lush Shropshire countryside near the River Severn, it overlooked a wooded hillside and had its own private shooting range and extensive stables.

It was a warm summer afternoon as Edward stood anxiously waiting at the altar with Oliver as his best man. The atmosphere of the historic chapel could not have been more charmingly romantic. Everywhere you looked, there were orchids, freesias and roses and their scent permeated the air, whilst the long wax candles attached to the walls cast a luminous glow.

'Someone to Watch Over Me' played in the background as Connie emerged through the chapel entrance. She glided along the aisle to audible gasps of wonderment from the guests, holding onto her proud father's arm, her face covered with a lace veil as she clutched her bouquet of sweet peas and freesias.

Edward was transfixed. He had never seen her look so radiant, taking in every detail of her dress: designed by Wallis Simpson's French-American couturier, Mainbocher, with its sweetheart neckline and floor-length skirt made of ivory beaded lace, sequins and pearls. The long silk train was held by her two little bridesmaids; anonymous nieces she barely knew, but who looked angelic.

Connie handed her bouquet to her maid of honour, who lifted up her veil, and stood next to her future husband. Impeccably handsome in his midnight blue suit, the couple looked the embodiment of perfection, their hair, eyes and skin appearing to sparkle as if they'd just been unwrapped.

Edward stroked away a tendril of hair that had fallen onto Connie's face, the rest of her glossy curls softly pinned with diamond jewellery that glittered in the light. Gazing into her emerald green eyes, he whispered, 'You look like a goddess.'

She smiled back at him, her eyes shining and full of love.

'Dearly beloved,' stated the vicar, addressing the packed congregation. 'We have come together in the presence of God to witness and bless the joining together of this man and this woman in holy matrimony.'

'Through marriage, Edward Chopard and Connie Jane Douglas-Scott make a commitment together to face their disappointments, embrace their dreams, realise their hopes and accept each other's failures ...'

Edward tried to focus, his heart pounding in his chest, the rest of the vicar's words blurring into white noise. Here he was, a man without a past, making a life-long commitment to a much-younger woman ... a woman, he felt, despite their eighteen month courtship, he still didn't know that well. Yes, he cared for her. Yes, he wanted, needed that loving bond of security. But what if this was a huge mistake. Was he doing the right thing?

He swallowed, his mouth dry, realising it was his turn to speak. 'I, Edward Chopard,' he stammered, 'take you, Connie Jane Douglas-Scott to be my beloved wife, to have and to hold from this day forward, for better, for worse, for richer—'

And then his thoughts froze, his head spinning, as an ethereal presence appeared before him. A woman with long blonde hair and the most mesmerising eyes he'd ever seen, shimmering like a cerulean sea as she smiled at him warmly, beckoning him towards her. As her image faded away, he lost all sense of where he was and why he was there.

'Darling, what's wrong?' Connie whispered. 'You look spooked!'

'I don't know', Edward mumbled, feeling unsteady. 'I blanked out.'

He felt Henry's steely eyes boring into his back as he heard the sound of collective murmurings, aware that over one hundred people, lords and ladies from an elite society set watched him intently.

Oliver looked puzzled. 'Are you all right?' he mouthed.

Edward nodded, taking a gulp of air. Squaring his shoulders, he smiled at Connie and continued his vows, emitting a long jittery sigh as he placed the platinum band onto his new bride's finger, and then kissed her tenderly in front of blinding flashbulbs from the society photographer.

Soon after, everyone trailed into the thirty-foot panelled dining room for their reception. Antique tapestries, several stags' heads and huge oil paintings of the Douglas-Scott ancestors adorned the walls.

The guests sat at long wooden tables set out in a U-shape, as maids in black dresses, white aprons and frilly caps bustled around serving food and pouring champagne under the direction of the resident butler.

Edward sat alongside a beaming Connie, watching the illustrious fat cats feasting on multiple courses of rich delicacies placed between the gold candelabra whilst he picked at his food, unsettled by the strange vision in the chapel. A rousing cheer urged the couple to stand up and cut the six-tier wedding cake. He attempted a smile, faintly registering the round of applause.

Thankfully, Oliver diverted his attention as he stood up, sheepishly ready to give his speech as best man. Dressed in a smart tuxedo and bow tie, somehow he still looked dishevelled, with a few buttons of his white shirt gaping open as the fabric stretched over his belly.

'My Lords, Ladies and Gentlemen, it's been two wonderful years since I met my dear friend, Eddie,' stated Oliver. 'I admit, initially, I was driven by ambition. I thought he'd be my *cause célèbre*, the breakthrough that would make my career, and in many ways he has ... but he was also a lost man with a special gift bestowed on him by some benevolent, divine plan.' He briefly looked heavenwards and placed his hands together. 'And soon I knew he'd come to mean so much more to me.' The room remained silent, every guest giving him their full attention. 'Having achieved huge acclaim as a celebrated pianist, he has come so very far along life's winding pathway.' He looked over to the couple with a smile. 'And above all, he has found a good-hearted woman in the bewitching Connie, who has given him both love and family. I am so proud. And I hope he considers me one of his most loyal allies.'

To resounding applause, Edward stood up, clapping enthusiastically. 'Absolutely, my old chum. You are indeed like a brother to me.'

'Hear, hear,' shouted Henry as all eyes swivelled towards him. He stood up, somewhat shaky, having already downed half a bottle of scotch. Pushing out his protruding gut, he stretched out the braces that held up the trousers of his custom-made suit, tailored to hide his rotundity. 'I too, have never been so proud,' he proclaimed, emitting fumes of alcohol with every breath. He paused to take a puff from one of his long, fat cigars that he'd been holding between his yellowing fingers. 'The fact that you are both so in love is a marvel, but I'll tell you now, it won't last.'

A ripple of nervous titters escaped from some of the guests; his wife, Elizabeth, wearily shook her head, her face growing pale.

'Love will fade, just like the setting sun,' he continued, slurring his words, 'but money and what it can buy, will always bring you comfort.'

'Daddy, really!' snapped Connie.

Henry pulled out an envelope from his jacket pocket, flicking cigar ash all over the table as he swayed unsteadily. 'This, my dear friends, is a telegram from a rather brave comrade of mine, Mr Adolf Hitler.'

Many of the illustrious guests' eyes widened, their bodies stiffening as the room became completely still.

'He says,' he cleared his throat. '"I wish Mr and Mrs Chopard my congratulations on their marital bond. My dream is now theirs. My warmest wishes from Berlin and I deeply regret that I cannot be there with you all. Let us dine together soon."'

Henry looked around with a smirk. 'What a kind and decent chap.'

Some of the guests clapped, hesitantly, whilst many others shifted around in their seats.

'Is this a joke?' muttered Edward.

'Oh, that's Daddy all over,' replied Connie. 'He's a terrible tease.'

'Churchill, on the other hand, says he couldn't give a stuff,' bellowed Henry. He guffawed with laughter, his face getting redder and more swollen as awkward sniggers rippled around the room.

'Shhh,' continued Henry. He placed his finger over his lips as he stuffed the telegram back into his pocket and pulled out three bunches of keys, dangling them like puppets. 'What are these?'

he asked, scanning the room. 'Hmm, well, let's just say that my daughter and son-in-law are now the official owners of an eight-bedroom townhouse in the exclusive district of Knightsbridge.' He threw the keys over to Edward where they landed in the middle of a plate of caviar.

Edward and Connie looked at each other with surprise, before joining in with another burst of applause.

Henry coughed loudly. 'And there are more keys here.' He swung them around on one finger. 'One set for you, Eddie, my boy, to open the doors of a shiny blue Bentley, and,' he winked at Connie, 'the other for my precious princess ... a canary yellow Mercedes.'

Everyone stood up, cheering loudly as Henry flopped shakily into his chair and hiccupped.

Connie leant over and kissed him on the cheek. 'Thank you, Daddy. You old drunkard.'

'How lucky are we?' She turned to Edward. 'Daddy has surpassed himself.'

'He certainly has, my darling.' Edward jumped up, straightening his tie. 'My Lord,' he said, addressing his father-in-law. 'Your generosity of spirit is overwhelming, and I would like to raise a toast.' He lifted his champagne coupe into the air. 'Let us elevate our glasses to the magnificent Lord and Lady Douglas-Scott for their open hearts and for allowing myself and my dear Connie to be married on their resplendent country estate.'

'Hear, hear' shouted the roomful of guests before chanting, 'For he's a jolly good fellow.'

All except for Connie's mother, Elizabeth, who appeared to have vanished.

As daylight faded into dusk, all the guests flowed into the magnificent eighty-foot ballroom, and Connie reappeared, having taken a leisurely break to change into something more comfortable. To a roar of cheers, she smiled demurely, gliding elegantly towards the jazz band waiting to perform, the bottom of her rose silk dress trailing across the white marble floor until she stopped to whisper to the dark-skinned singer.

'May I have your attention,' sang the middle-aged crooner into his microphone. All eyes turned to the stocky figure in his white suit and bow tie, as he added with a wink, 'Here's something special for our bride and groom's first dance.'

Edward looked at Connie with surprise. Wandering towards her, his eyes welled up as he swept his new bride into his arms, waltzing her around to the song, 'You Made Me Love You'. 'Thank you, darling, this means so much,' he said, nuzzling her neck, relieved, after his fleeting concerns, that this beautiful, caring woman was now his wife.

As other couples danced alongside them, he noticed over Connie's shoulder that her mother, Elizabeth had returned, her hair somewhat dishevelled. He wondered where she'd been for the last few hours.

Around 2 a.m., the resident butler, Cranford, dressed in his black uniform of waistcoat and tailcoat, led the newlyweds back along the winding hallways of the eighty-room mansion. He opened the door for them as they held hands, wandering into the privacy of their bridal suite with its soft lighting and majestic four-poster bed, draped with orange and gold curtains.

Connie slipped off her high heels, her feet sinking into the plush cream carpet as she padded across to the dressing table. She sat down in front of the mirror and carefully removed her jewellery, beginning with her sapphire and diamond drop earrings.

Edward collapsed onto the gold satin chaise longue, yawning with sleepy eyes.

'Tired, darling?'

'I just need a soak in the bath, my angel. It's been a wonderful but exhausting day.'

'Yes, it has.' She smiled, jumping up and sashaying towards him. She wriggled onto his knee and ran her fingers through his hair. 'You know this place has been known to be haunted?' She reached up and tugged on the tasselled bell pull hanging from the ceiling to summon one of the maids. 'Maybe, you did see a ghost earlier. They probably thought you were too handsome to be taken just yet.'

'Maybe, my darling, that is exactly what happened', he replied with a grin.

Minutes later, a knock on the door interrupted their embrace.

'Enter,' commanded Connie.

The door opened and the maid curtseyed. 'You called, m'lady.'

Connie stood up. 'Evans. Would you kindly draw Mr Chopard a bath, please?'

'Yes, m'lady.' The maid walked into their ensuite bathroom and turned on the gold taps. She poured in some scented bath oils and laid out their towels, before curtseying again and leaving.

Most of the guests had left for home and the house seemed eerily silent until Edward heard the engine roar of a car pulling up outside the house. He looked through the window with intrigue. The car headlamps illuminated his mother-in-law's face as she talked with one of the male guests. He peered closer and saw them embrace, kissing feverishly as if they were old lovers. Startled, he quickly closed the curtains.

'What was that?' said Connie.

'Nothing, darling, just some last minute stragglers.'

He didn't intend upsetting his wife on their wedding night. What right did he have to expose her mother's secrets and deny her some sort of happiness? He'd often sensed her loneliness at being married to a driven workaholic. Henry's life revolved around money, status and alcohol in that order. Everything else came under his list of possessions and she was merely another, trapped in a mink-lined dungeon. He only hoped for her sake that her tryst wasn't discovered.

Padding into the bathroom, he undressed and climbed into the porcelain bathtub, lying back in the scented water. He rubbed his forehead to ease his anxiety, hoping the throbbing in his brow wasn't the beginnings of another stabbing migraine. He felt incredibly grateful to his father-in-law, but Henry's ostentatious generosity and strange humour made him increasingly uneasy. That joke telegram from Hitler—was that really supposed to be funny in the middle of a war? Perhaps Henry assumed he could buy anything or anyone. It was what he might want as payback that worried him.

Connie wandered into the bathroom, jolting him from his meandering thoughts. She gazed at him with smouldering eyes and slid out of her silk bathrobe. 'Do you mind if I join you?'

He studied her naked, lithe body and smiled in apprecia-tion. 'Please do.' Watching her gracefully climb in, he sighed as she lay back against him. 'You are so delicious,' he murmured, wrapping his arms around her, squeezing her breasts, both of them submerged under the frothy bubbles. Reaching forward, he slid his hand slowly over her stomach and hips, stroking between her thighs, and slipped his fingers inside her as she moaned with pleasure.

'Mmmm,' she murmured, wriggling against his hand. 'Now we're legal, you know you can ask me for *anything* you want.'

'Is that so,' he said, his voice husky. He lovingly nibbled her neck and then bit into the flesh with so much ardour that he nearly drew blood as she squealed, and arched her back, stretching out her long legs, sending ripples through the water; the ache in his brow melting away.

'Right, this means business,' he said firmly. He climbed out and wrapped a towel around his waist before reaching into the water and lifting Connie's dripping body out of the bath. Carrying her to their bed, he dried her slowly with a soft pink towel as she giggled. He picked up her hand, gently removing her wedding ring. 'Read this,' he said, showing her the engraving inside the gold band.

Una in Perpetuum. Amor Sempiternus.

'Sounds romantic, darling. What does it mean?'

'It's Latin for *Together Forever. Eternal Love.*'

Connie rolled forward and kissed him, the strands of her dark lustrous hair falling onto his face. 'Oh, Eddie, what beautiful words. You have no regrets, do you?'

'No regrets, my angel ... only ecstatic happiness.'

Kissing her passionately, their tongues touching, he pinned her down so she couldn't move. He was happy to let all his worries fade away, absorbed in his wife's body; licking and sucking her small round breasts until she screamed with pleasure, lifting her hips, pulling her against him as he thrust deeply inside her, their arms and legs entwined in a rhythmic dance.

An hour later with a naked Connie contentedly asleep beside him, his mind was free to wander, recalling the mysterious blonde. A vivid memory surfaced of frenzied lovemaking: licking, biting, grabbing voluptuous flesh as she dug her nails into his back, climaxing noisily. Waves of guilty pleasure swept over him as he squirmed under the bedclothes, trying not to touch himself, struggling to push away the erotic images. Who was she? A lover or wife from his forgotten past, or wedding day jitters playing tricks with his mind? He just wished the distraction would fade away.

Sleep eluding him, he crept out of bed, tiptoeing to the desk in the corner of the room. He sat down and picked up his fountain pen to unburden his confused feelings in the diary Oliver had given him. And as the ink flowed, he was grateful the diary was one he could lock.

Chapter 18

Saturday afternoon, 12th June 1943

An elderly lady answered the door, stooping over as she stared at me, the skin on her face like thin parchment, crisscrossed with hundreds of fine lines.

'Ah, you must be Ruth,' she said with a shaky voice. 'I'm Mrs Mary Sullivan from next door. I've been keeping an eye on the children until someone came.'

'Yes, I'm Ruth. Thank you,' I replied as she beckoned me into the hallway.

'I'm so sorry to hear about the tragic news,' she continued, limping as she walked. 'Betty was a lovely young woman.'

Trailing after her into the kitchen I saw them both slumped over the table. I breathed deeply, steadying my nerves, worried about how they'd react after so long. They gazed up at me with watery eyes.

'Ruth, is that you?' said Gabi, peering at me.

'Of course it's me, Gabi.'

'Blimey, you look different. You're taller and thinner ... and, well, I hope you don't mind me saying, but you look just like Mum.'

I flinched at his words. "Course I don't mind. She did give birth to me after all.' I walked towards them, digesting every new change the years had given us. 'My goodness, don't you both look grown-up.'

Gabi, now fourteen, looked quite the dandy in his striped trousers, white shirt and knitted waistcoat that hugged his muscular physique. And that face: washed out with worry but so handsome with those coppery eyes and chiselled jaw, just like Daddy's.

Hannah, bless her, still a wide-eyed innocent with a head of tumbling curls, looked so frail in her flowery dress and ankle socks, she could have blown away in the wind. 'You need feeding up, young lady,' I said, looking at her. And with their initial shock over they both shouted 'Ruth' in unison, nearly knocking me flying as they wrapped their arms around me.

'I'll make a brew, kettle's already boiled,' said Mary. She shuffled around the kitchen in her pink slippers, getting teacups.

And just like that, we were a family once more as we sat around the table sipping our tea. We'd been apart for so long, it felt like a lifetime and I couldn't wait to share stories and discover what really happened to Aunt Betty.

I was thankful to Mary but she showed no signs of leaving, resolutely stationed at the kitchen table like a protective guard dog as she slowly slurped on her last dregs.

'You can go now, Mrs Sullivan, if that's okay.'

'Are you sure, dear?' Her crinkly eyes trailed across Gabi and Hannah's faces as if awaiting their permission.

'Yes, I'm sure. What do you say ... Gabi, Hannah?'

'Thank you so much, Mrs Sullivan, for all your help,' added Gabi, reaching out to shake her hand.

'Thank you, Mrs Sullivan' said Hannah, waving her goodbye.

'Well, I'm only next door if you need me, my dears.' She hauled herself up from the chair, puffing out her cheeks as she clutched her back. 'I can bring you round some gingerbread, if you'd like.'

I stood up, offering her my arm, which she gripped as I lead her to the door. 'That would be lovely, Mrs Sullivan, but another time perhaps. We have a lot to catch up on.'

Once they felt free to talk, I put my past troubles aside and sat between the two of them on their uncomfortable chaise longue and did what anyone in pain would want me to do—just be there and listen—and that's what I did, over endless cups of hot, sweet tea. And boy, were they upset.

Gabi mumbled incoherently in a rasping voice I could barely hear. 'She's dead, she's really dead,' his face full of torment.

'We don't understand why,' Hannah spluttered as she gulped back tears.

'It's all right, I'm here now,' I said softly, pulling them both towards me. 'Now, take a deep breath and tell me what happened.'

'We came home from playing tag in the park,' said Gabi. 'There was no answer when we knocked, even though we banged and banged. Both of us panicked, so we climbed through an open window, knocking all her ornaments flying. We called out again, "Aunt Betty, Aunt Betty", as we raced from room to room—until we opened the bathroom door.' He covered his face with his hands. 'And saw her.'

'Saw what?'

Hannah started sobbing, burying her face into my jumper as I rocked her back and forth.

'Aunt Betty had hung herself from the light fitting and was dangling from the ceiling.'

'Oh,' I gasped. 'I'm so sorry. That must have been terrifying.'

I could see him struggling to hold back tears, before looking back at me with red-rimmed eyes. 'We both ran out screaming hysterically.'

'And then what happened?'

'Our neighbours, Jack and Mary, banged at the door. We answered but we couldn't speak—just pointed them to the bathroom. They called the police and her body was taken away.'

I watched as Gabi got up and walked over to the side cabinet, picking up a letter, his hands shaking as he handed it to me. I swallowed every word, rereading it, trying to take it all in.

My dear, sweet bubbelahs,

What a true blessing you have been to me in these recent years. I'm so sorry to say goodbye like this, but without my beloved Jim, my life has lost all meaning. Please, don't be sad, for I know that he and I will be reunited again in heaven.

Knowing you would be homeless, I have drawn up a will. My house and boutique have been bequeathed to all you children. I have trained you to a standard that I know will help you run the Boutique with your delightful enthusiasm and panache.

Ruth can finally join you as I have requested with my lawyer that now she is seventeen, she can officially become your legal guardian. Please contact the solicitors on the card with this letter.

With all my endless love,
Betty

I looked at Hannah and Gabi in bewilderment. It appeared that our aunt, even in her death note, was loving but business-like to a fault.

'What does she mean?' asked Gabi. 'Can we really stay living here?'

'I guess we'll have to see what the solicitor tells us, Gabi. But we better not get our hopes up. There might be a catch.'

Betty's words held so much promise, and we'd all suffered for so long. Was the pain really over? I didn't dare believe that our wishes might come true.

The first few days back with my siblings were challenging. It was agreed that I would sleep in Aunt Betty's former bedroom, so we cleared it out, painstakingly going through all her precious mementoes and donating most of her clothes to the Red Cross, except for a few select items.

Hannah beamed as she tried on some of her skirts and dresses in front of the mirror. They hung loosely on her slender frame, but she raked them in with a wide belt. 'I feel like she's hugging me when I'm wearing these,' she said, spinning around, 'and I'll grow into them.'

'Don't you think it's ghoulish?' asked Gabi, looking at me strangely, 'sleeping in her room.'

'I have no choice, there's no other bedroom here,' I replied, noting his troubled expression. 'But remember, it's not so strange for me. I didn't know her like you both did.'

Secretly, I was thrilled to have my aunt's bedroom. It was decorated like a French boudoir: sophisticated and feminine with rose silk curtains and expensive white bed linen with a lingering scent of French perfume—but I understood only too well how they felt, because we'd all been through this desperate grief before. Even now, the loss of our parents still felt raw. I could only be there for them until somehow they found a way to heal the void she'd left in their lives.

'We thought she'd found some peace,' said Gabi, trying to find answers. 'We even visited the cemetery with her and put some flowers on Jim's grave, although she was shocked when she saw his name listed on the communal headstone:

James Cooper—RIP 16th April 1919—23rd May 1943
WWII US Camp—16th Infantry Regiment.

'She realised he was only twenty-four. I remember her saying, 'Oh Lord, he was just a boy!''

'She felt a bit of a cradle snatcher, coz he was six years younger than her,' Hannah added, 'but they were so in love, they never talked about age.'

'True love has no barriers,' I said, hoping my words rang true. 'But I'm surprised. You never mentioned this Jim in your letters.'

Gabi looked at me sheepishly. 'She asked us not to. She thought if Aunt Fenella and Uncle Harry heard, they might judge her and stir the pot.'

I gulped, feeling my throat tighten. 'I would never have spoken to them about your life. I barely spoke with them at all.'

'Sorry, Ruth,' said Gabi, reaching out to touch my hand. 'Don't take it so personal.'

Chapter 19

Tuesday afternoon, 15th June 1943

Aunt Betty's funeral was held in our local synagogue in East Cliff, packed with locals who had read her obituary in the local press. According to Jewish custom, the dead are buried within a day, but traditions faded away like dispersing fog during the war as everyone did what they could. We felt blessed to find a temple still standing intact.

After the service, many stopped to pay their respects, wanting to say a few words of kindness. I ended up as spokesperson: Gabi and Hannah were cemented in the pews, too distressed to speak.

A lanky man appeared before me, a camera hanging around his neck and a notepad stuffed into the pocket of his brown corduroy jacket, along with some long sticks of liquorice. 'Good afternoon,' he said, shaking my hand as I wondered if he were another guest offering their condolences. 'I'm Tommy Jones, a reporter from the *Bournemouth Echo*. Is it possible to interview you about your famous aunt? She was well thought of locally.'

I frowned. 'I see, er, I'll have to discuss it with my brother and sister. Leave your details and I'll get in touch.'

He tossed back his head, flicking his floppy fringe out of his eyes. 'Apparently, it was a tragic love story with one of the US servicemen based here?'

'Look,' I said with a sigh, 'I know you're looking for some tittle-tattle for your rag, but as you can see my brother and sister are too upset to speak at the moment.' I pointed towards the wooden benches.

The reporter looked over at Hannah, quietly weeping, whilst Gabi, with his head tilted forward, stared solemnly at the wooden casket in front of them.

'I'm so sorry.' He turned back to face me. 'They look devastated, but I can assure you, I'd only write something positive. It would put all the controversy to rest, you know, about what happened.'

He handed me his business card and I took it with a forced smile. I had no intention of calling him. The last thing we wanted was our aunt's private life exposed in the press for locals to read about over their tea and toast. If people wanted to speculate and gossip then that was their problem.

After everyone had left, the three of us wanted to mourn in private as we once more breached tradition and gazed into the open casket. Aunt Betty lay there, perfectly made up with her powdered face and trademark scarlet lipstick, dressed in a red silk suit, arms folded as if in some kind of eternal prayer. Apart from old childhood photographs, this was the first time I'd ever seen her—and it felt tragic that I was staring at her corpse—that I never got to meet the stylish woman who made such an impact on my brother and sister. 'From one black sheep to another, I hope heaven is good to you,' I whispered, feeling somehow that she and I might have got on well as the unconventional outsiders. I prayed that this moment would bring healing for Gabi and Hannah, seeing her lying there peacefully, blotting out their last traumatic memory.

But prayers along with hope and faith are often misplaced and life was never going to be that simple. Nighttimes were the worst, for all of us. I would jolt in my sleep at the slightest noise, forgetting where I was—frightened that Uncle Harry was waiting to pounce. Hannah woke with night terrors, climbing into my bed, shaky and tearful just like before, whilst Gabi often wandered aimlessly about the house, too restless to sleep. It would take a long time before we all recovered.

Monday morning, 21ˢᵗ June 1943

We felt like proper grown-ups when we attended our appointment at Bradshaw & Sons to sign the legal documents that could change our lives.

The solicitor, Mr Billingsgate, bald and bespectacled, looked at me across his big oak desk as he passed me the paperwork. 'So, Ms Goldberg, just to be clear, special provisions have been made by your Aunt Betty, prior to her death.

'What does 'special provisions' mean?' I asked, biting one of my nails.

'It means that because of the exceptional wartime circumstances, and given your ability to generate an income, we have been able to cut through any red tape regarding your age that might prevent you becoming a legal guardian to your siblings. With her written consent, you are able to take control of her assets, that being the house and her business, Betty's Boutique.' The solicitor stared at me awaiting a response. 'Do you understand?'

I looked at the paperwork and nodded, crossing my legs in the only tailored suit I could find in Aunt Betty's wardrobe that would fit. 'That's clear, thank you, but may I ask you something, perhaps out of kilter, Mr Billingsgate?'

'Yes, of course, Ms Goldberg.'

'Did you never question why my aunt organised her will so suddenly?'

'Indeed, I did, Ms Goldberg. I'm afraid,' he paused, examining his wide stumpy hands as if to avoid eye contact, 'she told me she was dying from a terminal illness.'

The room fell silent as all three of us looked at each other with sadness.

'You do know it was suicide, Mr Billingsgate?'

'Yes, Ms Goldberg. I did hear about her untimely death. It was tragic, simply tragic.'

Yet, as his words filtered into my mind, I realised, in a way, it was terminal; her broken heart led her to do the unthinkable—cut short her life and leave the children abandoned once more.

As I signed my name on the paperwork, my hands shook with nerves.

'What about me and Hannah?' said Gabi. 'Do we sign?'

'Yes, Master Goldberg, you will all sign.' Mr Billingsgate handed him the document. 'You all have a legal share in the house and the business as stated here in Paragraph IV.' He pointed at the wording with his fountain pen.

Gabi stared blankly at the paperwork, looking baffled, as Hannah glanced around the room with a bored expression.

'But everything will remain under the control of your sister, Ruth Goldberg, until you both come of age.'

'Gabi, don't worry, I'm not gonna rob you. I love you.'

Gabi rolled up the sleeves of his striped shirt. 'I know, sis. I just don't understand all this stuff.'

'Oh, and another thing,' said Mr Billingsgate, peering at some more paperwork. 'You have also been left the sum of five hundred pounds.'

'What!' I yelled, my heart racing. 'Five hundred pounds! Oh, golly.' I clutched my head, trying to digest what I was hearing.

'That's like zillions!' squealed Hannah, her oversized skirt left by Aunt Betty swirling around her waist.

'We're rich, we're rich, we're crazy, crazy rich,' crowed Gabi in a sing-song voice, leaping up from his chair and jumping around. I grinned. It was heartening to see my pensive teenage brother regress to being so childishly silly.

'May I suggest,' said Mr Billingsgate soberly, 'that you use this inheritance wisely. You will have stock to buy for the boutique and there'll be bills to pay. It may seem like a lot of money, but it will disappear as fast as it came if you are not careful.'

I nodded in agreement. 'True, but we can still celebrate with some chips and a milkshake. I'm starving.'

'Hooray,' shouted Gabi and Hannah, waving their arms in the air.

'Can we go to Molly's on the seafront?' asked Hannah, her saucer eyes pleading with me. 'They serve the most delicious knickerbocker glories.'

'Of course we can. We can go wherever you want, but remember, I don't know Bournemouth like you both do.'

'Whoopee, follow us,' beckoned Hannah.

I stuffed the paperwork into my handbag and shook hands with Mr Billingsgate before rushing outside, ready for our new beginning.

That afternoon after finishing our lunch, we all ambled onto the beach and sat down on the damp sand looking out to an infinite ocean of blue as we breathed in the fresh sea air. A flock of seagulls flew overhead and I wondered if they were one big family too. I looked over at Gabi and Hannah and smiled. 'I think this might be a good time to give thanks to Aunt Betty, don't you?'

They both nodded, closing their eyes in remembrance as I reflected on what to say.

'Dear Aunt Betty, wherever you are, we love you. In your death, you have given us a life beyond our craziest, maddest, most glorious dreams. For that, we thank you.'

'Thank you, Aunt Betty,' chorused Gabi and Hannah with choked voices.

Right at that moment, a seagull cawed loudly and we all gazed at each other in silence, praying that this was a sign Aunt Betty was with us? We certainly hoped she was.

Chapter 20

Three months later
Thursday, 16th September 1943

Edward parked his Bentley in a side street near the London Hospital, hoping a stroll through the East End might trigger something about his past. 'You don't mind, do you, darling?' he asked, holding the car door open for his new wife. 'It just seems opportune as we're meeting John for lunch.'

Connie smoothed down her raw silk suit and elegantly climbed out, shivering in the cold breeze. Edward grabbed her sable from the back seat of the car and helped her on with it. 'Not at all, Eddie, I could do with some fresh air, although this place is such a slum.' She wrinkled her nose, staring at the dusty street. 'I shall just have to gaze at you.'

Edward laughed. He had to agree that the area did look rather ramshackle.

Holding hands they ambled along the rubble-strewn Whitechapel Road passing endless rows of boarded up shops and demolished buildings, occasionally stopping to kiss, still cocooned in the warm bubble of their honeymoon bliss, until Edward heard someone yelling.

'Joe! Joe! Is that you?'

They both spun round and saw a woman walking towards them, pulling her woollen trench coat around her for warmth. She stared directly at Edward, her mouth falling open as if in shock.

'Sorry, madam, do I know you?' asked Edward.

The woman stopped in front of them, raising her thin, arched eyebrows in surprise. 'Of course, you know me, Joe. It's me, Emma. I can't believe it's really you. I've missed you.' She smiled at him. 'Have you missed me?'

Edward's breath caught in his throat and his eyes widened. Was this woman a precious link to his past? Was he Joe?

He gazed at her curiously: her copper-coloured hair curled into a victory roll at the front and pinned back at the sides, revealing a pale face with tired, bloodshot eyes.

How should he handle this—ask for more information without giving too much away? After all, she may have mistaken him for someone else. He took an eager step towards her. 'I'm sorry, um, I'm afraid I can't quite recall you. How did we meet?'

'You can't recall me,' the woman gasped, her voice choked with emotion. Ignoring Connie, she reached out to grab his hand, squeezing it. 'That's typical. I've been through hell, grieving for so long, I thought you were dead! And that's all you can say?' Her eyes filled with tears. 'It's me, your little darlin'. You must remember?'

This was more than he bargained for. He pulled his hand away, mindful of Connie's presence, shaking his head to indicate a 'No'.

'Joe, please,' cried the woman, her body trembling.

'Excuse me!' snapped Connie. She peered at the woman from underneath the black mesh of her fascinator, the edges of her fur coat flapping in the wind. 'You're mistaken, my dear. Now run along.'

The woman continued to stare at him, swallowing every detail of his face. 'I'm not mistaken,' she said. 'I mean, you might look a bit fancier,' her eyes followed the cut of his black Crombie overcoat, 'but I'd know my Joe anywhere ... those blue eyes ... that smile ... even the way you walk,' she continued, looking wistful, 'those long strides with that slight bounce in your step, it's the same.'

Connie's face reddened with fury as she glared at her. 'Really, is that right? And who exactly are you?'

'I'm Emma Cohen. I live around here, always have done and always will,' she replied, looking Connie up and down with an indignant expression, 'but perhaps I should be asking, who are you? Or are you another one of his floozies?'

Edward was stumped, not knowing what else to say, as he watched Connie rear forward on her high buckled shoes like a cobra rising up, ready to strike.

'Excuse me, how dare you! Let me point out to you, Ms Cohen, that this is not your Joe. This is Edward Chopard, the famous pianist. I'm sure you must have seen his photo in the papers or heard his classical compositions on the wireless?'

Edward felt deeply sorry for the woman. She looked bewildered, staring into space.

'A pianist? Um, well, I haven't read the papers for a long time. There's too much sad news.'

'Then let me formerly introduce you, dear,' stated Connie drily as she extended a black gloved hand to touch Edward's arm. 'This is Edward Chopard and he is a pianist! A famous virtuoso! And I am his wife. And it is quite evident to me that you have never mixed in our elite circles.'

'Oh, then, maybe I am mistaken.' She gazed back at Edward with sadness. 'You have such a likeness for my Joe, that's all. Seeing you, well, it quite knocked me sideways. He was the love of my life. I'm sorry. I'm so terribly sorry,' she stammered as she turned and briskly walked off.

Edward stood in silence next to Connie watching the woman disappear into the distance. *Love of my life*, he thought. He so wanted to grab this Emma by the arm, talk to her alone, find out more, but didn't dare having witnessed Connie's virulent green-eyed rage. He took a deep breath. 'Well, that was awkward.'

'Awkward isn't the word. Can you believe that? Why, the audacity!'

'Hmm, although I felt you were a little hard on the woman.'

'Hard on the woman. Really, Eddie?' Connie's face darkened as she glowered at him.

'Don't worry, darling.' He reached out to grab her hand, gently pulling her across the road to head back to the hospital. 'There's no harm done. It was just a simple misunderstanding.'

Connie remained quiet and he felt deeply frustrated; his young wife was upset with him and yet he'd done nothing wrong except witness a stranger's overly emotional reaction. Whoever this Emma was, he hadn't felt a flicker of recognition. But what if she had known him? What if they had once been lovers? Surely he had a right to uncover his past without judgement?

They walked into the entrance of the London Hospital and sat down on the row of chairs in the busy reception packed with injured survivors as they waited for Dr John Walters to finish his ward round.

It was rare that Connie mixed with 'the natives' these days, as she and her father called them, and she hated it. She covered her nose with her gloved hands attempting to block out the over-whelming stench of sweat and winced at the sound of an old lady spluttering and wheezing. Yet even the unsavoury lower classes couldn't distract her from their earlier encounter; the words swirling around her mind. 'Are you another one of his floozies?' What on earth had she meant by that? Was that skinny commoner, Eddie's former lover? Was he some kind of heartless rake?

She couldn't stem the force of her angst any longer as the words burst out. 'Is she your type then, that redhead?'

Edward looked baffled, turning to face her. 'What! Why do you ask that?'

'Well, is she?' she asked, looking down at the floor.

He reached out to touch her thigh, gently stroking it through the fabric of her suit. 'Don't be silly. She's a vulnerable stranger who believed she knew me ... but whoever she was, I have eyes for only one lady, and that's you.'

Connie sighed and smiled at him. 'I'm sorry, Eddie. Seeing that woman ... it's put my mind in quite a spin.'

'I understand. The incident shook us both up, darling. If I did know her, I'm sure I would have remembered something. Besides,' he said, squeezing her hand, 'whilst I'm curious about my past, it's the here and now that I'm focused on. The rest is history.'

Connie leant forward, brushing her lips against his and then grabbed Edwards face with both hands and kissed him passionately.

The patients all nudged each other, murmuring, their eyes riveted on the couple and their unchecked intimacy.

'Oh, Eddie,' gasped Connie, gazing at him. 'You've got me all giddy.'

John suddenly emerged, striding towards them with a big grin. 'Well, hello, you two love birds.'

Connie smiled, brushing some hair away from her face as they both stood up. 'Hello, John, I must be blushing furiously right now. My dear husband has a way of sweeping me off my feet.'

'Not at all, glad to see you both so in love.' He took Connie's hand, bowed his head and kissed it.

'Good to see you again, old sport,' said Edward with a wide grin.

'And you, my good man.' They shook hands. 'I hope you're both hungry. I've booked us a table at The Halal Restaurant just around the corner. It won't be quite the style that you're used to Connie, but it's a favourite of mine. They serve excellent Asian cuisine.'

Connie winked at him. 'Wonderful, John. I'm getting used to slumming it.'

The aroma of cumin, coriander and chilli spices filled the air as they all sat around the large round table in the spacious Indian restaurant. The waiter brought over their chosen bottle of Château La Tour Blanche and poured some wine into their glasses.

'None for me,' said Connie to the waiter. She flicked her eyes around the room, unable to relax as she tapped her manicured nails on the table.

'Are you all right, Connie?' asked John. 'Can I pour you some wine? It's an excellent vintage, a 1928 Sauternes.'

Connie squirmed in her seat. 'No, thank you, John. I'm feeling a bit out of sorts after our strange encounter.'

'Strange encounter ... do tell?'

Connie relayed the event whilst playing with a lock of her hair.

John sat forward, pausing to reflect. 'I can see how it's disturbed you, Connie, but do have some sympathy. From what you've said about this poor woman, it's rather tragic. It sounds like she lost the man she loves and thought it might be you, Eddie.'

Edward nodded and sipped some wine. 'Indeed. The poor thing looked quite overcome.'

'Yes, but she was still rather rude approaching Eddie as if I didn't exist. I mean she must have known he was Edward

Chopard. He's famous for Lord's sake. She might have been one of those fortune hunters.'

'To be fair on the poor woman, Connie, she wouldn't know who Eddie was unless she loved classical music and attended the Proms. He's hardly a household name, not yet anyway. No offence, Eddie.'

Edward sighed and chuckled. 'None taken, my friend.'

Connie looked thoughtful. 'I suppose, although I am rather curious about my Eddie's past.' She patted her stomach with a wry smile. 'I definitely want to know more about your gene pool.'

She excused herself from the table and disappeared off to the powder room just as the waiter arrived with two trays of curried dishes. He placed them down on the table, picked up their bottle of wine and refilled their glasses.

John leant in towards Edward. 'You know, old chum, it's quite possible that woman did know you. You threw away a big chance there to discover who you once were.'

'Yes, I know.' Edward looked down at his hands. 'But she came out of left field and I was totally thrown, especially with Connie getting so defensive. It was all rather awkward.'

'Well, do let me know if you have any other occurrences. I'll support you all I can.'

'Of course, John, and thank you.' He sank into his chair feeling a deep sense of sadness, grieving for a lost past and missed opportunities, his secret burdens weighing heavily in the air. He daren't tell his friend about the blonde vision at his wedding. He wasn't ready to discuss that, certainly not over lunch when Connie was due back any moment.

'Anyway,' added John, 'let's sample some of this delicious food. I'm famished'

They both sat in silence for several minutes, serving themselves some of the spiced dishes, meditating on the aroma as they waited for Connie to return so they could commence eating.

John drank some more wine and then looked around as if to check that Connie wasn't hovering in the background. 'May I say, Eddie, the atmosphere seems, er, a little strained between you both.'

'Hmm, well between you and me,' Edward whispered, 'she appears to have got herself all worked up. I think it's the hormones.'

'Hormones?'

'Yes, she's pregnant, John. Nearly three months. We're both delighted, but so far we've only told her parents. We don't want to jinx anything.'

The doctor beamed with surprise, raising his wine glass. 'That's fantastic news, Eddie. Let me be the first to congratulate you.'

Chapter 21

Friday, 15th October 1943

E dward's butler, Travers, had just finished packing his
suitcases for Paris. His glowing press reviews had spun a
golden publicity trail leading to a six-week tour throughout Europe as well a finale in New York, returning him home in
time for a succession of pre-Christmas galas.

He was sad to be leaving Connie in her condition and frustrated that he'd been persuaded to spend his last precious night
with Henry and his upper-class cronies. 'You must come and
meet the boys,' Henry had said. 'I absolutely insist. I simply won't
hear the word no.'

Given that his father-in-law was bankrolling him as well
organising his overseas flights, Edward felt he couldn't deny him.
He was under no illusions that their relationship was based on
an unspoken pact: Henry accorded him a gilded lifestyle and in
return, he danced attendance like a marionette for his puppe-
teer. So despite his reservations, he found himself standing in
the panelled bar room of the Mayfair Club right in the heart of
privileged London.

The private club was a selective bolthole for the aristocracy,
the landed gentry and the super-rich investment kings who were

part of a gilt-edged society set, so wealthy that the world was truly their oyster. Invisible to anyone who wasn't a member and situated in the basement of a four-storey Georgian townhouse in Clifford Street, Henry's eccentric cousin, Lord Benson owned the club. The old man, now in his seventies, resembled a bizarre Albert Einstein figure, shuffling about as he welcomed all the arrivals with his shock of white hair that stood up on end as if he'd just been electrocuted.

Edward waited to be served a glass of scotch by the resident barman, Bob, a chirpy character with a toothy smile set in concrete on his chubby face. The pungent cigar smoke furled around him like coiled letters as he attempted to take in the political and financial banter. Try as he might, he couldn't digest a word any of them were saying; their collective yah-yah nasal tones merging into a monotonous hum of white noise.

'How's your lovely wife, Mr Chopard, and your dear mother-in-law?' asked the barman. He filled a glass with some ice and poured in the spicy golden liquid.

'Very well, my good man, but glad to be with the boys,' interrupted Henry as he suddenly appeared, swigging the whisky straight back so Edward had to be poured another. 'The women are where they should be, at home mastering the rules of the kitchen and the bedroom, ha-ha. Mind you, both of those wenches don't need to cook, do they, Eddie? So we left them to gossip, a hobby most women are experts at.'

Edward looked at the floor bemused as the barman smirked.

Henry spun round to face everyone in the room, his jowly face wobbling as he extended his arm towards Edward. 'Welcome, my Right Honourable Lords, Gentleman and Scoundrels,' he bellowed. 'I'd like to introduce you all to my delightful son-in-law, Edward Chopard, the virtuoso pianist, no less. Let's raise our glasses and celebrate his initiation into the Mayfair Club.'

'Hear, hear,' shouted the room full of impeccably groomed men, all dressed in Savile Row suits of pinstripe, black silk and wool herringbone, accessorised with brightly coloured cravats. They raised their glasses and Edward smiled sheepishly, raising his glass of scotch in response.

'Castlebury, old chap, any more on that bloody man, Sachs?' yelled Henry to a banking colleague on the other side of the room. He lit another of his habitual cigars. 'I'd love to bring that sullied *ikey* down.'

'Ah, yes, the owner of Sachs & Sons,' replied Richard Castlebury, walking over. 'As always he's up to his ears in moneyed clients. Bloody Jews, they think they can take over the entire financial community. They come from peasant stock most of them. They should be stoned, never mind gassed. Don't you agree, Edward?'

Taken aback, Edward had no idea how to respond. It seemed strange that someone would be so outspoken and offensive. 'Um, I don't really have an opinion to be honest.' He picked up his glass, rattling the ice and taking a sip. 'I haven't met any of these Jews you speak of.'

'No opinion! Don't be spineless, stand up and be counted, Eddie.' Henry slapped him on the back as the barman placed yet another whisky on the bar. 'Now swig that back, it will put some bloody hairs on your chest.'

'You may think you haven't met any, but they are crafty and come in many forms, sneaking up on you like the very devil himself,' said Lord Becket, owner of the stately Becket Hall. He bent his knees, his hands claw-like in front of him, pretending to pounce as sniggers rippled around the room.

Henry swept his hands through his thick silver hair. 'And you don't have to know them to bloody hate them! You only have to look at the banking, fashion and film industry and see how they've infiltrated it. Cocky upstarts! Snatching work from under our very noses.'

'I agree,' said Richard Castlebury, his lips shrinking into his mouth. 'I can't bear the sight of them. Keep them out of the country I say and out of our business.'

'Well, put it this way,' continued Henry, leaning against the bar. 'If I knew any of my employees had even a thimble of Jewish blood in them, I'd not only sack them, but I'd have them beaten to a pulp for the indignity of being born.'

Edward squirmed, gulping all his whisky down in one go.

Lord Becket dressed in a too-tight tweed jacket reclined in a large leather chair with his glass of brandy, looking smug. 'All I can say is thank the Lord for Hitler. At least he weeded out some of the lower life forms. I'm sure Edward would agree.'

But Edward wasn't listening, distracted as a film played out in his mind of a fresh-faced young boy wearing a skullcap, reading intently from a scroll, trying to memorise the words. The image lasted only seconds, disappearing as fast as it came, yet the impact left him unnerved. He stared into space.

'Eddie!' shouted Henry, 'come on boy, give us your opinion.'

Feeling disorientated, Edward looked around the room and saw a sea of tense, belligerent faces waiting for his response.

'Sorry, would you mind repeating that?' asked Edward quietly. He loosened the red silk tie around his neck.

'Perhaps you don't care for our ethics?' snapped stockbroker Douglas Hetherington-Jones. He was a tall beanpole of a man, dressed in a check wool suit with a waistcoat and black bow tie. Somehow he reminded Edward of the grim reaper; his gaunt face revealed the angular definition of his skull and his large hooked nose protruded like an eagle's beak.

'Er, I simply prefer not to judge, without knowing more about the facts.'

Douglas pulled out a chained monocle from his waistcoat pocket, placing it over his right eye and peered at Edward through it. 'We all judge, Mr Chopard,' he said, pouncing on the impartial comment with gusto, 'however much of a moral high ground you wish to take.'

Edward glanced around the room, steeling himself. 'I guess I've always believed in the philosophy of live and let live.'

Swigging back his brandy, Douglas slammed the empty glass back down on the bar. 'Goodness, you really are left wing aren't you, Mr Liberal! Just remember the next time you have a choice between a pretty girl or an ugly one, or a joint of beef and a tin of spam—tell me then that your choice isn't about judgement or prejudice. That damning seed exists in every one of us,' he continued, his eyes flashing, 'but remember, one day you'll meet someone like Sachs who'll inveigle your clients and beat you to a deal and that seed will take root and grow faster and stronger than you realise. Maybe then you will finally be on the same page as us.'

Edward sighed. It was evident they all wanted to spar with him to validate their judgements, yet he baulked at the absurdity of what he'd heard. In not knowing his own ancestry, he couldn't understand the point of prejudice. And he wasn't going to bow to pressure for anyone.

'Get off your soap box, Dougie, and give the man a break,' boomed Henry. 'The poor chap lost his memory. We think Eddie was once a pampered posh boy who doesn't know his arse from his elbow—but trust me—it won't be long before he joins us all for tea with Hitler in Berlin.'

'Tea with Hitler,' Edward blurted out, feeling confused, 'but he's England's adversary!'

Henry smirked. 'So he's finally found his voice. Well, to us, he's an old comrade and proud to say it. We've all dined on Bavarian sausage and sauerkraut with him, haven't we boys?' There was a collective nod as Henry guffawed with laughter, the rest of his colleagues joining in.

Edward shivered, unable to comprehend his father-in-law's behaviour. As soon as he thought he had a handle on him, he slithered out of his grasp like a wriggling fish. And that's what worried him. Feeling weary he decided he'd had enough of their strange madness for one night. He stood up, grabbing his hat from the table and strode towards the door.

'By Jove, that was a flying visit,' yelled Lord Becket sardonically from his comfortable chair.

'I'm afraid duty calls. But it's been an absolute pleasure.' Edward quickly waved goodbye and sped out of the basement and up the steep flight of stairs, along the winding hallway towards the front door, desperate to escape the polluted atmosphere as fast as possible. He looked back anxiously, hearing footsteps, waiting when he saw Henry's heavyset frame lumber after him.

Henry stooped over, red-faced and panting. 'Good Lord, Eddie, when you move, you move fast. I'm an old man you know.'

Edward gritted his teeth with measured politeness. 'Sorry, Henry. I didn't realise we needed to speak again.'

'Merely confirming that a chauffeur will collect you and Oliver at eight tomorrow morning to take you to a location in Surrey.'

'Yes, of course. What's the address?'

'Don't worry about minor details, Eddie. It's a field somewhere. The chauffeur will know. It's wonderful the good doctor has managed to take a sabbatical.'

'Yes, I'm eternally grateful to him, as I am to you, although, I'm a little uneasy, having never flown before.'

'Oh, relax. You will be met by Air Commodore, Gus Hofmann who will introduce you to a very experienced pilot.' He smiled widely. 'Not too bad, is it, being given your own six-seater military aircraft?'

'Indeed, I can't thank you enough.'

'You're welcome, dear boy. Luckily, I've always got plenty of favours to call in.'

Henry grinned as he pulled him into a bear hug. 'Apologies if the boys gave you a rough ride tonight. They always test the club virgins, but I know you're made of sterner stuff.'

Edward looked away. 'Yes, I wasn't prepared for that.'

'Consider it a baptism of fire,' Henry said with a wink. 'Enjoy your tour. I know you will have sensational reviews and Lizzy and I will miss you as much as our darling daughter.'

They shook hands as Edward gazed into Henry's hawkish eyes wondering if they glinted with ruthless cunning or just a well-honed roguish humour. 'Thank you, Henry. That means a lot.'

Stepping into the cold night air, he felt strangely troubled, as if he were treading in black treacle. Whilst grateful for Henry's patronage, there were so many unanswered questions. How did he secure an aircraft when military resources were already tightly stretched? Why was the location a secret and how could they ensure a clear flight path during a war? That night, for many reasons, had unnerved him far more than he dared admit.

'How was your night with Daddy?' Connie asked sleepily as she lay curled up on their four-poster bed.

'Let's just say, I've had better evenings.'

She rolled onto her side, her silk negligee hanging off one shoulder as she screwed up her eyes in the light of the table lamp. 'Why, what happened?'

'Put it this way, as grateful as I am to your father, I'm surprised that he and his favoured colleagues don't have swastikas printed on their foreheads and carry a German flag.'

'What do you mean?'

'I didn't realise they all had such a vehement dislike of the Jews, ranting on about how they've infiltrated society. I felt under attack to join in. And if that wasn't enough they all seem to enjoy fraternising with Hitler.' He sat down on the edge of the bed feeling his head throb.

Connie leant towards him nuzzling his neck. 'Darling, you know Daddy is all bluff and bluster. Mummy said earlier that he'd had a few run-ins with a Jewish banker. His nose is a little out of joint that's all.'

'Well, I need a nightcap.' He leant forward and grabbed a bottle of brandy from his side cabinet, pouring a double measure into a glass. 'That doesn't explain his comment about dining with Hitler.'

'Oh, darling, I told you. Daddy's a tease. He doesn't mean anything by it.'

He rubbed his eyes. 'It just wasn't a pleasant evening.'

'Just relax. None of this has anything to do with us,' murmured Connie in a soft, seductive voice. She began massaging his shoulders, kneading into the muscles with her fingers as he took a deep breath, feeling a release of tension. 'Besides, he's always far worse when he's with his fellow financiers and he's got his chieftain hat on. That lot are known to whine and carp like a load of old fishwives when they get together.'

He laughed. 'You're so right. They are like old fishwives. I am probably being far too sensitive.'

'And didn't Daddy organise a plane for you tomorrow?'

'Yes, he did.'

'Well, then, he's not such a bad egg is he?'

'No, I guess not. Maybe I just need some sleep.'

'Just focus on the important things, darling. Remember I'm the mother of your baby and I love you,' she said, stroking his face. 'Me and bump will be missing you, Daddykins, so don't flirt with any pretty ladies.' She bit her lip and looked down at the floor.

Perhaps she's still worried about that girl, Emma, he thought. Wanting to reassure her, he leant over and planted a kiss on her slightly swollen belly. 'Connie, you are the only woman I want.' He looked at her warmly. 'Your absence will only tweak my imagination, making me hunger for you even more.'

'Oh, Eddie,' I do love you,' she whispered. She loosened his tie, grabbed his hand and pulled him onto the bed.

Chapter 22

Friday, 15th October 1943

How could you disappear like that? I've been going out of my mind with worry.' Aunt Fenella's voice screeched down the phone. 'I've had enough on my plate with poor Harry and yet all my letters go unanswered. Did you not think I would hear on the grapevine about Betty's untimely death? She was my sister and I have the right to grieve properly.'

She continued in high-pitched hysteria, without pausing for breath. Closing the stock room door for privacy, I held the phone away from my ear; her words a muddled mess in my head. 'Aunt Fenella!' I shouted, interrupting her rant. 'I'm sorry. I didn't think. It's been a madhouse here—but tell me—what's happened to Uncle Harry?'

'Well,' she said quietly, 'I found him lying on the driveway groaning in pain not long after you left. We think he slipped over. Anyway, the poor love was taken to hospital with a fractured hip and now he's back home, I'm still having to nurse him. That silly old bone just won't heal.'

'Oh, I'm so sorry, Aunt Fenella, that's awful news.' I smirked, trying to stifle a giggle, savouring the image of Mr Dough Face bedridden and helpless. It felt good to see him punished. Would I go to hell for hating a nasty old man, I wondered.

'Anyway, that's another burden to bear! It would have been nice to have been invited to my sister's funeral and be informed of her will.'

'Sorry, Aunt Fenella. I didn't think.'

'You didn't think, you didn't think. Goodness me, young Ruth, has your brain frozen over?'

I felt a rush of anger, feeling chastised, just like the old days. I took a breath, trying to stay calm. 'I'm sure you'll be pleased to know that Aunt Betty left everything to us, and as you can tell, we're here, answering the phone, running her boutique.'

An awkward silence followed. She replied, her voice wooden. 'She left everything ... to you three?'

'Yes, the shop, the house, and some money.'

'Hmm, and not a penny to the rest of us. Typical Betty! I suppose she didn't want to see you youngsters out on the streets after she'd killed herself. It's a sin, you know, Ruth, to take your own life, especially in wartime when staying alive is a blessing.'

'I suppose.'

'Well, well' she sighed, 'a little extra would have come in handy.'

I remained silent at her clumsy hint. They were rich enough already. And I wasn't going to budge an inch.

'Anyway,' she continued, 'I've posted you off some family photos. They were lying in a dusty box in the attic. Did you get them?'

I felt a warm glow inside; the thought of seeing old snaps, knowing our own treasured mementos had been destroyed. 'Oh, yes, thank you, Aunt Fenella.' I didn't dare admit I hadn't seen them—quickly remembering our heaps of unopened post.

'Well, dear, remember we're still family, even if you did leave without a proper goodbye. You must all come for tea when Harry's better.'

I flinched. Over my dead body. In her own way, she'd been as bad as him. She must have known what he was like, the way he stalked and tormented me, yet she turned a blind eye. 'We'd love to Aunt Fenella,' I muttered through gritted teeth. 'And thanks again for the photos.' Truthfully, I hoped that was the last we would ever hear from the Rosenblums.

Once home, whilst the youngsters raided the kitchen for treats, I rifled through all our post that we'd dumped in a cupboard in the hallway and found the package, carefully opening it, and taking out the packs of sepia images as if they were fragile works of art. I stared joyously at the first picture I found: Mama and Daddy in their wedding outfits, drinking from each other's wine glasses, gazing into each other's eyes. They looked so in love back then. Another showed all three of us holidaying on the beach in South-end-on-Sea, proudly standing with our spades having buried Daddy up to his neck in sand. I chuckled at the memory.

Wanting some alone time, I ran upstairs to my bedroom, and lay down on my bed, leafing through the rest until I couldn't bear to look anymore. Somehow those nostalgic reminders made me feel lonelier than ever, hammering home the truth that our parents were dead and we were orphaned.

Don't misunderstand, the three of us being reunited was wonderful, the anchor we all needed—but it wasn't the same. I never realised how tough the adult world would be: shopping on rations, paying bills and working full-time. It wasn't easy selling clothes in wartime; we were lucky if we got three customers a day. And our five hundred pounds was now just under four hundred, and dwindling away fast. I felt worried sick, holding up the roof, but I had no other choice—who could I depend on?'

We'd all settled into a routine. Gabi and Hannah perfected their sales patter whilst I was officially 'manager' handling all the boring stuff like ordering stock and bookkeeping (being good at school arithmetic paid off, and I worked things out from Betty's accounting records)—except Gabi turned into a right bossy boots believing he was top dog and nothing I did was ever right. One afternoon, he actually told me with a snotty air that I didn't have the right look for fashion.

'S'pose my figure don't suit the clothes in 'ere,' I said with my hands on my hips. 'Am I not slender enough for your discerning tastes?'

Gabi was examining a rack of clothes for any imperfections, pausing to look me up and down. 'It's not about my personal taste, Ruth. It's about how the clothes hang on you. It's not a judgement, it's a science. Aunt Betty didn't order in anything above a size twelve and that size is too tight on you. It ruins the look.'

'Whoa, Gabi, you are becoming a real dictator. Hitler would be proud of you.'

Gabi shook his head as if I was an irritant. 'Sorry, Ruth, but you don't understand fashion. Aunt Betty trained Hannah and me to the highest standard. You have to know what looks right so the customers trust your judgement.'

I wanted to shout, 'Don't talk to me like that, you uppity idiot,' when a customer walked in. For the survival of the boutique, I had to bite my tongue.

But Gabi's criticisms had riled me. I wasn't known as the rebellious black sheep for nothing. I had a point to prove and money to make, so days later, when a factory manager said they were too busy to fast track orders, I discreetly dialled *The Lady* magazine to advertise for local dressmakers.

Ten days later, I received only one reply by post, but one was all I needed. I raced down to the haberdashery department at Beales department store and bought four rolls of linen and then walked along to the dressmaker's house in Bentley Road, twenty minutes away, holding them in my arms, along with a ripped article from the *Picture Post* on the latest must-haves.

A small, thin lady in her forties opened the door, her brown hair covered in pink rollers.

'Hello. Is this Ann Taylor's house?'

'That's right,' she said, looking puzzled.

'I'm Ruth Goldberg. You answered my ad in *The Lady*.'

'Oh, yes,' she said, staring at me.

'Well, I've bought you some fabric in red and cream and I know I'm asking a lot as I don't have sewing patterns,' I continued, the words tumbling out of my mouth, 'but could you copy the design of these two dresses in the picture and make up samples of each in fourteens and sixteens?'

Her face remained blank.

'I'll give you two shillings for every dress you make. If they sell, I'll order more.'

Her expression transformed into a beaming smile as she lifted the rolls of material from my arms. 'Oh, thank you so much, Miss Goldberg. I'll have them done in a jiffy. You won't regret this.'

True to her word, a week later, the dresses with padded shoulders and a peplum skirt arrived freshly pressed and I hung them proudly on the rails.

'What the hell are these?' asked Gabi as he picked up a dress from the rail and looked at the size.

'I've ordered them in!'

He stared me at me with an incredulous sneer as if I was a complete fool. 'Why? This is a size sixteen! They won't sell. You've just wasted money.'

I stared back at him, determined to hold his gaze to show who was boss. 'There are plenty of women my size and proud of it. If Rita Hayworth is celebrated for being voluptuous, then why can't the rest of us rejoice in our curves?'

Gabi rolled his eyes. 'There's being voluptuous, Ruth, and then there's plain chubby. Fashion is for those who can pull it off. It's about glamour!'

Hannah wandered out of the stockroom, pursing her lips. 'Gabi, that's rude. Apologise to Ruth.'

'No,' said Gabi, ever blunt 'I won't.'

'Well, sorry, little brother, but fashion is for everyone. It's about that stamp of individual style that is unique only to you. I have control of the cash and I'm in charge of ordering the stock, so stick that up your jumper.'

Gabi glared at me, grabbed his coat and stormed out of the door in a huff.

Livid with his attitude, I opened the door and called after him. 'We are, whether you like it or not, pleasing larger ladies in this boutique. We can't all be skinny minnies like Hannah and Aunt Betty.'

As I turned around, Hannah grinned, pleased with herself no doubt that she could gobble all the cake she wanted and never put on an ounce.

And that brings me on to the little Miss. Whilst Gabi acted like our lord and master, Hannah was nicknamed 'the snail', leaving a trail of mess in her wake as well as thinking she was on a permanent shopping spree.

'We'll all be bankrupt at this rate if you carry on,' I told her repeatedly. 'You can't keep taking your pick of dresses from the shop. Besides, it's illegal. You're supposed to stick to your statutory clothing coupons.'

'Aunt Betty let me do it,' she'd whine and stomp off, sometimes throwing in, 'you're as mean as Mama was!' That remark cut me to the quick and I admit, I gave in, knowing she'd reward me with a big hug. Although I didn't want to lose my rag like

Mama used to, I was being pushed to the brink, and it made me question whether I ever wanted children of my own.

The truth was I'd become their annoying surrogate mother; they resented my authority, sensed my weak spots and manipulated to get their own way. How I longed to be their big sister again, the one they used to laugh, play and scrap with, but I knew without doubt that if I stopped setting boundaries, our family life and our business would quickly collapse like a fragile house of cards.

If it wasn't for the local schools being bombed, the discipline of a decent education might have helped their attitude. Perhaps they were still grieving for Aunt Betty. The boutique had always been about the three of them. In many ways, I was a reminder of her absence and it hurt to feel that I might be a sorry replacement. She'd always be special to them, but I did feel frustrated when they spoke about her as if she was a heavenly angel that could do no wrong. After all, she'd topped herself, abandoned them to fate—but death, it seems, so often sanitises human frailties.

Somehow, miraculously, we got through each day without killing each other, and I prayed for a time when war would be over, so we could start to focus on the future and not the past; maybe then, everyone's spirits would be lifted.

Chapter 23

Saturday, 20th November 1943

Edward awoke from a fitful sleep in the middle of the night, the howling wind rattling the windows and tearing through the branches of the trees, baffled by the image of the young boy stuck in his head. Moonlight seeped into the room creating an eerie half-light and he jumped out of bed with that familiar sense of urgency; something he always felt when the creative waves surged within. It was as if his mind, struggling to find answers, found release through sound only as melodies filtered into his consciousness. Grabbing a pen from the bedside cabinet, he opened up his diary and scribbled down the musical notes.

He ambled out of the bedroom in his silk pyjamas and over to the piano positioned in the corner of his spacious penthouse suite at the Ritz-Carlton. Sitting down, he lifted up the mahogany lid and, his fingers gliding over the keys, brought forth a haunting rhapsody he called, 'Sonnet of Disguise'.

Hearing the poignant melody resonate through the walls, Oliver pottered into the lounge bleary-eyed, wearing his old wool dressing gown and slippers. He sat down on an armchair, captivated, watching Edward play with so much passion his eyes filled with tears. 'Bravo, Eddie,' he exclaimed, applauding once he'd finished. 'You must play this composition tonight at your New York debut. It's incredible. It touches the very depths of the soul.'

'Thank you, it was born out of painful confusion,' Edward said, looking up from the keyboard, his eyes full of sadness.

'Hmm, and isn't it that internal struggle that often leads to the exquisite finale of artistry?'

Edward stood up from his stool and walked towards the large square window, gazing at the glowing half-moon surrounded by a sky full of shimmering stars. 'So true, in the process of creativity, there is always a sense that you are somehow healing the maelstrom within.'

Oliver ran his fingers over his beard. 'Indeed, can you believe we're on the last leg of the tour and you are playing at Carnegie Hall, one of the most significant venues in the world, to an audience of over two thousand people?'

'Yes, it is truly inspiring. New York is glorious and it does make me feel very humbled.'

'And the audience, in turn, will be humbled by your extraordinary gift.'

'By the grace of God,' he said, his eyes watering.

Oliver leant forward, feeling confused. 'What's up, Eddie? You don't look happy. You should be feeling like you're king of the world. I mean, look at your good fortune ... a new baby on the way, incredible concert reviews, and a pilot flying us around the globe. There's a lot to be thankful for. Your musicality is turning everything to gold.'

Edward stretched out his back and let out a long sigh. 'Believe me, I know I'm blessed. I just have this constant nagging feeling. Right here in my gut,' he said, patting his stomach, 'that something isn't right.'

'Then unburden yourself,' replied Oliver with a smile, 'I'm a doctor.'

Edward laughed. 'Well, Doctor, I have a recurring vision of the same thing, of a young boy wearing a skullcap. He seems perplexed, trying to understand the meaning of words from a scroll. And it's written in a foreign language he struggles to interpret.'

'Intriguing. So the boy of your visions wears a skullcap, which usually indicates the Jewish faith?'

'Yes, and it frightens me.' He gulped. 'It happens so often, I'm scared I've lost it ... you know ... my mind.'

Oliver peered at him. 'How so?'

'I often wake up wondering where I am and it takes me several minutes to adjust.' He paused, his forehead furrowing into deep lines. 'I worry that the damage to my brain has messed me up, making me conjure things up that aren't real.'

'But why would you conjure up a young Jewish boy?'

He looked down at the floor. 'Perhaps because there's so much vitriol against the Jews? Many in my current circles appear to detest them as much as the Nazis and their collective enmity is frankly unnerving. Maybe I'm, you know, blurring the lines somehow, through fear?'

'Ah, so you mean visions induced by paranoia! Hmm, I suppose it isn't beyond the realms of possibility. You have no history of your own and fear is a powerful emotion that could incite an illusionary perception. It could also be a symbolic metaphor from your subconscious, that you are coming into a new phase of wisdom, because of the scroll.' He took a breath. 'But we must also consider that there may be another, more plausible option.'

Edward's eyes lit up. 'What's that?'

'That you may be recalling your own past!'

'Recalling my ...!' Edward squirmed in his chair as if the thought irritated every inch of his skin. 'Are you saying I might be a Jew? Someone my peers would abhor.'

'Well, yes, you could be.'

'But surely if I were a Jew, I would have dark curly hair and olive skin.'

'Eddie, you are stereotyping. The Jewish race come from all over the world. Some are fair-skinned and even blond.' He hesitated. 'Perhaps you are finding arguments to avoid what could be a worrying truth, and this truth will nudge away at your psyche until you accept it.'

'And how do you know so much about this, Oli?'

Oliver tightened the thick cord around his dressing gown. 'Because, Eddie, I am a Jew.'

'What!' said Edward, sinking into a chair nearby, 'with a name like Jungston?'

Oliver leant over and poured himself a glass of water from a carafe on the coffee table nearby, the early morning light filtering into the room. 'I am a Russian Jew! Back in 1921, my father, Isaak, fled our hometown of Yaroslav to escape the bloodshed and famine. We arrived in London when I was eight.'

'But you came to England from Switzerland?'

'Indeed, I lectured all over the world, doing some of my greatest work at the Burgholzli Clinic in Zurich where psychology was more advanced.'

'So why don't you have a Jewish surname?'

'My father was a clever man, a chartered surveyor who had a sixth sense on how to make money, so he built up a business in the city. He wanted me and my mother to have a good life, but with a name like Abramovich, he knew we would suffer discrimination.' He took a glug of water, leant back into his chair and crossed his legs. 'Father was a great admirer of the Swiss psychoanalyst, Carl Jung, believing his work on the collective unconscious would have a momentous impact on generations to come.'

Edward remained silent, listening intently.

'He felt the name might be fortuitous, making it easier for me to break into the medical profession, and so our family name became Jungston.'

'So he believed that good fortune would come from the name, Jungston. Isn't that a bit of a wing and prayer?'

Oliver fixed his dark brown eyes on Edward. 'One day, my friend, you will see that it is *belief* that transforms destiny. Father was eager for me to become a psychologist, as was I. He *believed* the name would help me achieve that goal and he passed that energising conviction onto me. His philosophy was simple—that by serving others you create positive energy—reaping rewards in the physical and the unseen world.'

'Goodness, what fascinating history. I admire your father's strength in fleeing to another country and building up a company from scratch.'

'Yes, I admire him too, but really he had no choice. It was merely survival.'

Edward took a breath. 'At least you have a history. It's lonely knowing my life had no beginning until the day I regained consciousness.'

'In some ways, you are fortunate, Eddie. There is a free-dom in living only in the moment. Many of my patients have wasted valuable time obsessing about the past or fantasising about the future.'

'That's true, but I would love the choice,' he said, pausing as if to reflect. 'There are some other strange events that I can't make sense of.'

'Like what?'

'Do you remember when I blanked out on my wedding day?'

'Yes, I assumed it was nerves.'

'Well, whatever it was, I nearly keeled over. A woman appeared in front of me, almost like an apparition.'

'What did she look like?'

'She had long blonde hair and the most exquisite eyes I've ever seen. And she seemed to know me very well. Naturally, I daren't tell Connie that another woman entered my mind when making my most sacred vows to her.' He looked down at his hands. 'Once again, I'm stuck, unsure whether she's a ghost from my past or my crazy imagination playing tricks.'

'Has she come into your mind since?'

'Yes, especially these last few months, whilst I've been sleeping alone.'

'I see ... so why didn't you tell me all this before?' said Oliver, scratching his head.

'I apologise. I haven't found the right moment and trust me it's been tough not having anyone to share it with.' He paused. 'There's something else I haven't mentioned.'

A frisson of anticipation ran through Oliver's body.

'A woman approached me, two months ago, whilst out strolling with Connie. She thought she knew me ... that I was her lost love ... but no memories emerged, despite her striking titian hair.'

'And where was this?'

'Around the corner from the London Hospital. We were meeting John for lunch.'

'This is all very significant,' said Oliver, his voice peaking with excitement.

'What do you mean?'

'These connections ... the young boy, the blonde, the London Hospital, your lunch with John, the chance meeting with the redhead, even our conversation right now—they are known as *meaningful synchronicities.*'

Edward looked baffled, rubbing his chin.

'To explain, Jung's philosophy is based on the principle that life is not a series of random events, but rather an expression of a deeper order, referred to as *Unus mundus,* Latin for *one world* or *one energy.* A meaningful coincidence occurs from a conscious or unconscious need, want or desire, that draws the observer and the connected phenomenon together through *Unus mundus.* Listen to me, Eddie,' he said, standing up and waving his arms around like a conductor of an orchestra, 'it's all good.'

'So you don't think I'm slowly going insane?'

'Not at all. These coincidences reveal a deeper realisation that something more powerful is at work. In short, the *unconscious you,* has brought about a chain of events so that you can rediscover your past. Your soul is pushing you to confront your emotional history.'

'Hmm, sounds a bit mystical.'

'Well, in a way it is. Jung believes these meaningful synchronicities direct us back to our spiritual nature.' Oliver gazed into the distance. 'There are links in every living thing. We magnetise them to us. There are no accidents.'

Edward sat quietly, appearing to digest his words. 'That does make sense. I've felt so lost, getting flashes of information that I can't tie together. They're like single frames of a film that make no sense when you don't see the rest of the story.'

'I understand. Your brain cannot make the cognitive leap to connect everything. Amnesia is a subject we don't fully comprehend. We try to give it medical terms, but it can last years and often we don't know what we're dealing with.'

He wandered over to Edward and patted him gently on the back. 'I suggest after the tour we get to the root of all this. I can put you into a safe hypnotic trance to see if we can find the connectors that give you some kind of psychological framework as to what you are seeing.'

A slow anxious smile flickered across Edward's face. 'Well, I can't say I'm not nervous, but thank you. I feel it's time.'

'Good, good. In the meantime,' said Oliver, grabbing the telephone, 'let's order some fresh coffee and smoked kippers for breakfast and then focus on your concert. You mustn't let anything disturb tonight's performance.'

Chapter 24

Friday, 10th December 1943

Connie sat at her dressing table in her negligee gazing at the exquisite pair of diamond earrings Edward had brought back from New York. Edward knew she would love them: three-carat, high-quality D grade, set in gold. She clipped them onto her ear lobes, admiring how they sparkled in the mirror.

'Darling, thank you. You have flawless taste,' she said unscrewing a pot of expensive face cream, scooping some out with her finger and smoothing it over her skin.

She caught his reflection in the mirror as he watched her, still naked between their rose silk bedclothes, enjoying some much needed rest. 'You're welcome, my darling. You deserve only the best.'

Heavily pregnant, Connie heaved herself out of the chair and padded towards him, her legs still retaining their elegant shape and only her feet and ankles showing signs of being uncomfortably swollen. 'I'm so glad you're home, Eddie. I nearly went out of my mind, longing for your touch, worried that you'd forgotten about me.'

'I missed you too, desperately,' he said, reaching out to grab her hand as she sat on the edge of the bed. 'And you must never worry about being forgotten, my angel.' He leant towards her, brushing against her expanding belly, nuzzling her neck. 'When we married, I committed myself before God, body and soul.'

She smiled, snuggling into him and he felt so happy to be back, witnessing her in all her blossoming glory. She was due to give birth in just under a month and yet as her silk gown gaped open, she looked more beautiful than ever now that he saw her as a mother as well as a wife. He breathed in the sweet scent of her perfume, noticing that everything about her was rounder, softer and more sensual: the plumpness of her lips, the fullness of her breasts, her once lithe body transformed into cushiony voluptuousness.

'By the way, we're invited to Mummy and Daddy's for dinner,' Connie murmured, breaking the silence. 'They're both dying to see you.'

'Hmm, can't wait,' he replied drily. Dinner with her parents felt akin to being on stage in many ways: wearing the smart tuxedo, performing the art of rapt listener and laughing at Henry's grandiose banter. Yet despite their differences, he'd grown deeply fond of his in-laws, even missing them whilst he was away. *Besides,* he thought, *they're the only family I have.*

Later that evening, they attended the Douglas-Scott's stately Georgian property in Richmond, overlooking a picturesque view of the Thames.

Seated at the dining table, piled high with a veritable feast, Edward was certain that he'd never seen such a grotesque display of extravagance: platters of every kind of meat and fish as well as a vast selection of multicoloured vegetables. He knew pheasants and turkeys were reared on Henry's own land but he did wonder how he acquired the rest of the produce without breaching rationing laws, and if the rumours were true about many of the blue-bloods—that they paid a hardboiled criminal to obtain whatever they desired from the black market.

The butler appeared, wandering around the table, filling up their tulip-shaped glasses with a rare vintage wine, one of several bottles that Henry had brought upstairs from his cherished collection. Entry to his wine cellar was strictly forbidden and he kept the keys with him at all times, paranoid that someone might steal away with a much-prized 1893 Château La Mission Haut-Brion or a 1923 Château Fortia Châteauneuf du Pape.

'Bon appetite, or as I prefer to say, nose in the trough,' yelled Henry.

Everyone raised their glasses and laughed.

'Chin-chin, darlings,' said Elizabeth. She met Edward's eyes and clinked her glass with his.

'Chin-chin,' Edward replied, gazing at her. Ever since he'd witnessed her illicit kiss on his wedding night, he saw her in a completely different light. She was no longer just Connie's mother but a beautiful woman, looking much younger than her fifty-something years with her sculpted bone structure, clear unlined skin, and those unusual green eyes that had a touch of wild panther about them. Connie had inherited her good looks. *If she ages like her mother, I'll be very happy,* he thought. He didn't blame her in the slightest for her dalliance, he just wished he hadn't witnessed it. The last thing he needed was to be the holder of yet more secrets; he dared not imagine Henry's explosive wrath should he ever find out.

'Eddie, come and join me for a glass of port on the Veranda,' Henry commanded in his Sgt Major clipped accent after they'd finished dinner.

'Of course, Henry.' Edward jumped up from the dining table and followed him outside.

'So how was the tour?' Henry's silver hair shimmered in the moonlight.

'It was a great success, thank you. We couldn't have asked for more.' Edward leant against one of the thick wooden posts holding up the slatted porch roof and looked out at the large central waterfall set amidst luxuriant grounds which sloped down towards the river.

'Good, I expected nothing less with your outstanding talent. We certainly all missed you, back in Blighty.'

Henry's butler, Rutherford, appeared holding a silver tray with a port bottle and poured them both a glass.

'That's very kind, Henry.' Edward took the port from the tray and sipped it.

Henry peered at him with a strange look in his eyes. 'As you know, Eddie, I'm a straight-talking man. So let's get to the nub of things.'

Edward flinched.

'Connie tells me that our club night unnerved you?'

'Did she?' He gulped, glancing around, distracted by high-pitched howls.

'Ha-ha, don't worry, it's the sound of those bloody foxes calling out to each other, rampaging for food. They are annoying bloody vermin.' Henry stepped forward, leaning closer. 'You know, you really are a sensitive man, Eddie, and that's a remarkable virtue, but may I say, you do take things to heart. We're just a crowd of black-humoured bankers who love to mock and taunt each other. It's part of the culture.'

'Oh, that's absolutely fine,' replied Edward with a nervous laugh, 'I'd forgotten ... it's a while ago now.'

Henry knocked his drink back in one swig. 'Rutherford,' he yelled, 'fill her up.' He held up his glass as his butler walked over, pouring in some more of the sweet dessert wine. 'I'm a man who likes to settle old scores ... or concerns, Eddie', he said with a smile, 'past or present.'

'I see, um, well, I didn't realise I was in the middle of a hate campaign against the Jews.'

'Oh, Eddie, come on, let's not kid ourselves. Many people hate the Jews, not just us, along with all the other immigrants who flock here for a safe haven. I only have contempt for the cut-throat Hebrews in the banking industry that make my life difficult. But be realistic, much of society also hates the rich, the monarchy and bankers for the fact that we make such enviable profits.' He cleared his throat and they both sipped their drinks, looking out onto the tranquil view of the Thames in the distance as a row of swans glided by. 'Society feeds on hatred and judgement. It gives them a channel for all their pent-up frustrations about the misery of their sad existence. You and I can't change that.'

'I understand we all make judgements, Henry,' replied Edward, lowering his voice. 'It was just a little intimidating.'

Henry pulled out one of his cigars from inside his jacket pocket, lighting and then sucking on it as if his life force depended on the burnt tobacco. Edward waited for a response as Henry blew out rings of smoke and watched them float away.

'Yes, you're right. I put it all down to Eton. It all starts with the public school initiation of pushing each other's heads down the toilet. We've never stopped competing for the top-dog pecking order. That's our excuse anyway.'

Edward laughed. 'I can see how influential that could be. Your chums were certainly on a mission to convert me to their views.'

'You know, Eddie, the Mayfair Club is about relaxing and letting off steam, saying what you think. At heart, they are a likeable bunch. Laugh it all off, my boy. Opinions are like a pair of men's balls. We all have them. But some are bigger than others.'

He smirked at Henry's typical audaciousness wondering if this was the right moment to discover the truth. 'So, um, are you good chums with Hitler then?'

'Oh, Eddie,' Henry replied, dabbing beads of sweat off his brow with a handkerchief. 'You are naive at times. Hitler's far too busy bombing us senseless to be engaging in tittle-tattle with the likes of me.' He threw his arm around Edward, pulling him closer. 'Forget all that silly speculation and remember I'm a family man at heart. We know you don't have loved ones, so embrace Lizzie and me as your refuge. I've always wanted a son. It's been my dearest wish.'

Edward relaxed, his hunched shoulders dropping. 'Thank you, Henry. That means everything to me. And you're right ... perhaps I am a little oversensitive.'

'Splendid, you and Connie must join me in Shrewsbury soon. We'll get out the big guns and shoot some game. It's a wonderful way to unwind.'

'Thank you, Henry. I would be delighted.'

'*Prost!*' shouted Henry as they clinked their glasses together. 'Whoops, sorry, Eddie, wrong language,' he chuckled. 'Cheers—to a very long life.'

Back home in the privacy of their bedroom, Edward loosened his tie and walked over to the window. 'Connie, darling, can we talk?'

'Of course, Eddie. ' She wandered over, wrapping her arms around him.

Edward ran his fingers through her thick chestnut hair. 'Your father and I had a chat tonight about the Mayfair Club.'

'Oh, good, everything all right?'

'Yes, fine, but darling, why did you feel it necessary to share my concerns?'

Connie looked up at him with wide-eyed innocence, pouting her lips. 'Eddie, I know how Daddy can be. He gets carried away. I wanted him to know he'd upset you. Please, don't be angry with me.'

'I'm not angry,' he said, kissing her forehead, 'but if I wanted you to fight my battles, I would have asked.'

'No, you wouldn't, you're too proud,' replied Connie, pulling away.

Edward pulled her back towards him and gripped her face with both hands. 'Connie, I need to know that what goes on between you and me must remain confidential, otherwise, you are breaching the trust we have together.'

Connie unbuttoned his shirt, stroking his chest. 'I understand, darling, but you are being so terribly serious and I haven't seen you properly for so long.' She ran a long fingernail down his spine. 'It won't happen again, I promise.' She unzipped his trousers and slid her hand down, teasing him with her fingers as he groaned with pleasure. 'Now, come and make love to me.'

She grabbed his hand, leading him over to their bed, his worries melting away as he surrendered to her sensual embrace. As they lay there naked, Connie on her side, pressing her back into his chest, her pregnant belly protruding under the sheets, Edward's mind wandered. You are a fool, he told himself, she's your wife, the one person, the only person, you should completely trust.

Chapter 25

Seventeen months later
Tuesday, 8th May 1945

It was the moment we'd all waited for: Churchill officially announced the war was over. As soon as we heard his speech on the wireless, we threw our arms around each other, locked up the boutique and raced outside to join in the celebrations.

Everything that day felt magical; our seaside town had been festooned in red, white and blue bunting, church bells rang out and planes roared overhead, doing victory rolls in a clear blue sky.

We arrived for our street party fuelled with excitement, barely able to move as we squeezed our way through the crowds. The atmosphere buzzed with feel-good energy as people waved flags, shook hands or hugged each other in a show of camaraderie. It felt like one huge happy family rejoicing together in the name of freedom.

All three of us stood transfixed as we watched couples jiving on the beach to the sound of a live band. We latched onto one of the conga lines that snaked around them, giggling as we collided with a group of tipsy soldiers who were raucously singing.

Amidst all the noisy festivities I suddenly heard my name called. Gabi and Hannah jumped around wildly to the music as I stared into a sea of smiling faces, wondering where on earth the voice came from. 'Miss Goldberg. Miss Ruth Goldberg. How are you?' I spun round, recognising him as the lanky, pale reporter with floppy brown hair from Aunt Betty's funeral. It was nearly two years ago, but as we gazed at each other, I remembered, there was something about him, a naughty twinkle in his eyes that I'd liked.

'You never did get on the blower,' he yelled. He manoeuvred his way towards me, his camera dangling around his neck.

'That's right, I didn't, because I don't care to speak to pushy reporters.'

He flushed bright red, which I found quite endearing, somehow managing to squeeze into a space right in front of me. 'Sorry, I was only doing my job. Your Aunt was a fascinating woman.'

'Yes, she was, but the Goldberg family don't air their dirty laundry in public.'

'Quite right, too. So let me reintroduce myself. I'm Tommy Jones,' he said with a cheeky grin. He reached out and shook my hand.

'Good to meet you again, Tommy Jones.' I said, feeling a little giddy.

'How long you been partying?'

'A few hours.'

'Well, can I interview you about something else?' He pulled out a notepad and pen from his jacket pocket. 'I need a happy story for VE day.'

'Sure. If we can have some publicity for our business?' I winked, trying to keep my balance, jostled by endless people pushing past.

'Gladly, let's do it!'

I shouted to Gabi and Hannah to follow and we all wriggled, pushed and apologised our way back through the swarms of people, feeling quite out of breath in the heat of the sunshine.

Back in Poole Road, I stood proudly outside our little boutique. 'Well, Mr Jones, here we are.'

'Looks proper classy,' said Tommy staring through his camera. 'Right then, huddle together and I'll take some pics.'

'What's this all for?' muttered Gabi. He looked bored as he stretched out his arms and yawned, whilst Hannah gazed at her reflection in the shop window.

'Come and stand either side of me.' I snapped, waving them over. 'And make an effort to smile.'

This was my big moment, so I thought of my idol, Betty Grable, and tried to remember how she posed for photos. I tilted my head to the side, angled my hips and pointed one leg forward. Gabi and Hannah squashed in either side, copying by sticking one leg out.

'Beautiful, beautiful, show a little more leg, Ruth,' he yelled, clicking away. 'Toss your hair back and laugh, all of you.'

I giggled. 'What else do you want us to do, cartwheels?'

'Cartwheels are good,' he said with a grin. 'Okay, throw me some lines?'

I squeezed my eyes shut trying to think of something sharp. 'How about, "Whatever size you are—slim, hourglass or extra curvy—you'll leave Betty's Boutique feeling like a hotsy-totsy glamour puss"'. I smirked, noticing Gabi's dismissive look, but I felt so proud, putting Betty's Boutique firmly on the map. We might even get more custom.

Tommy scribbled down my words. 'Perfect. Anything else you might want to say?' His voice trailed off as he stared at me.

'No, that's it.' I extended my hand to shake his, meeting his gaze. 'But thank you, Tommy, this means a lot.'

He shook my hand with a slight tremble and then stuffed his hands into his trouser pockets and looked at the ground.

'Are you all right?' I wondered why he was acting so strange.

'Um,' he mumbled, looking at me with soft brown eyes. 'Fancy watching the fireworks? There's a big display around eight.'

I was speechless. Here was I, nearly nineteen and I'd never been asked out before. In fact, I didn't think I ever would, accepting my fate as the plump, plain girl no one would fancy.

Tommy shuffled about, continuing to stare at the ground as he waited for my response.

'I'd love to, Tommy.'

He looked at me with a relieved smile. 'Great, I'll meet you back here at seven-thirty.'

I felt on such a high, I could have floated right up into the sky, past the clouds and into infinity. Life was getting better and better; the war was over, we were running a business and now I'd been asked out on a proper date!

But later that evening, my chutzpah vanished as I spent hours wriggling into different outfits only to discard them, because frustratingly, they were too tight. With clothes strewn all over the floor, I finally chose a blue halterneck swing dress. And then I sat in front of the dressing table mirror using curling irons to twist my hair into rolls and pin them up, copying a picture I had of Betty Grable.

'You look really pretty, Ruthie,' yelled Hannah as I left the house, which made me smile, and even Gabi yelled out, 'Enjoy yourself.' It was nice to see my arch-tormenter off his high horse for once.

My tummy felt like a warm ball of fuzz when I saw Tommy walk towards me, his floppy hair slicked back with gel and dressed in one of those swanky zoot suits I'd seen on Frank Sinatra in magazines.

Holy Mackerel he looks rather dishy, I thought, wondering how a proper lady should behave. Should I listen attentively, giggle a lot, and what if he kisses me? Oh golly, does a lady kiss a fellow on a first date?

Thankfully, we just smiled at each other and linked arms, chatting away like old pals who'd known each other forever, whilst we strolled along the coastline listening to the roar of the ocean merging into an explosion of pops and bangs.

When we passed a chippy, Tommy gallantly rushed in and bought us some, handing me the warm parcel as we sat down on a stone wall looking out to sea.

I munched through all my chips, gazing at the orange and gold sunset thinking how lovely it was, and was about to screw the greasy newspaper into a ball, when I looked down and froze, spotting a familiar face amidst the print.

'Hang on a minute, Tommy,' I said, standing up. I walked towards the glow of a street lamp, smoothing out the sheet of paper, not daring to believe what I saw.

'What's wrong?' asked Tommy, jumping off the wall to join me.

'You see this picture?' I said, pointing to it.

'Yes, I see it.'

I tried to breathe slowly to calm myself down. 'That's my dad. I'm certain of it.'

Tommy scratched his head looking puzzled. 'Hang on. I thought your name was Ruth Goldberg?'

'It is!'

'Well, I don't want to state the obvious, but that's the famous pianist, Edward Chopard. He's appearing at the Proms in a few months. My father's a big fan.'

I felt my face drop. 'But I swear this man is the double of him.'

'I'm confused,' he said with a frown. 'What happened to your father?'

'Um, he was presumed dead,' I stammered, feeling my hands shake as old memories flooded through me. 'Our house was bombed. They never found his body.'

'Oh God, I'm so sorry, Ruth. You must miss him?'

I nodded as a tear trickled down my cheek.

'Grief … it does funny things to us sometimes,' he said softly. Gently taking the newspaper from my hands, he folded it neatly and handed it back. 'Perhaps you should keep this for now.' He kissed the top of my head and put a protective arm around my shoulders as we continued to walk along the beach watching the fireworks, until, like a gentleman, he walked me home.

Wednesday, 9th May 1945

Restlessness consumed me, and I wanted answers, only Hannah and Gabi lazed around the house, under my feet, bickering constantly.

'Don't I get a minute's peace? Go out for a bike ride and enjoy the light evenings.'

Hannah narrowed her eyes. 'Why, you trying to get rid of us?'

'She wants to bring her new fellow back, that's why,' said Gabi with a snigger.

I rolled my eyes. 'You've got a filthy mind, Gabi, and I don't mind saying it.'

Thankfully, they agreed to run some errands for me, if I gave them pocket money. And once the door slammed shut and I had the house to myself, I rushed to dig out photos of Dad and compare them with the pianist in the paper.

As I held them in my trembling hands, my stomach flipped. The images on the black and white print were identical to his angular face and deep-set eyes. Surely there couldn't be an exact double of my father? My brain was like a ticking bomb. If I could somehow locate where this pianist lived, I could jump on a train the very next day, knock on his door and ask him outright, 'Are you my dad?'

Hang on, calm your horses, Ruth, I told myself. He might think you're crazy—besides you'll never get past the servants.

There was only one way to discover the truth.

The newspaper stated that he'd play Beethoven at the Proms for one night only. I could attend his concert on the twenty-fourth of August, pay one guinea for the ticket and somehow sneak backstage—and once I stood in front of him, if he really was my father, he would recognise me for certain, we'd hug each other tightly, and I'd discover where he'd been all these missing years.

It was three months away, but I'd just have to wait and be patient, which was hard knowing he might be alive, just a train ride away, out of my reach.

Closing my eyes, I travelled back to the old days when we'd turn on the wireless and have family sing-along's to tunes like 'Roll out the Barrel' and 'Two Lovely Black Eyes'. We'd collapse into giggles when Daddy imitated Bing Crosby, crooning tunelessly in a deep baritone. I chuckled at the memory when the front door clicked open and I heard the youngsters arrive back, stomping up the stairs. Panicking, I shoved the newspaper under the bed. It wouldn't be fair to upset them with false promises, build up their hopes, only to have them dashed. I needed to find out more.

Thursday, 10th May 1945

Still drifting off into nostalgic daydreams as we arrived for work early the next morning, something else diverted my attention. A long queue of women all patiently waiting for the Boutique to open.

'What's the big urgency?' I asked.

'You mean, you don't know?' said one woman I recognised as a cashier from our local Woolworths.

All three of us looked at each other with baffled expressions.

'It's that wonderful article in this morning's *Bournemouth Echo*, my dear,' said Doris, a regular customer in her fifties, standing at the front. She reached into her bag and handed me a rolled up copy. 'I can't wait to pick out a size sixteen dress for our Ellen's wedding. I've only ever bought a handbag or scarf.'

'Not before I do,' interrupted another woman as she flexed the muscles in her arm.

I unfurled it, and looked at the front page. *The Bournemouth Echo*. Of course. Tommy's article. I fished the shop keys out of my handbag, desperate to see what he'd written.

After they all funnelled into the shop, we could barely move as we sorted out dress sizes and payments whilst a continual stream of women arrived from all over town. Our cash till had never been so full.

I felt vindicated. The larger sizes were selling like hot cakes and I did nothing to hide the smug look on my face when I asked Gabi to cycle up to Ann, the dressmaker's house so she could make up some more.

We were wrung out when we stopped for lunch at three and put the closed sign on the door. Gabi sat in the stock room saying his feet hurt whilst Hannah joined him, sprawled out on the floor like a starfish, complaining her tummy was growling.

I looked at them both and laughed. 'Well, how about a hot dog, chips and a milkshake to cheer us up?'

Without saying a word, they both jumped up and stared at me with a manic glint in their eyes.

Scooping out a handful of coppers from the till, I dropped them into Gabi's jacket pocket and they both raced out of the door fuelled by hunger. I could finally snatch some time, sit behind the counter with a cuppa and read the paper. And boy did I get a thrill when I saw the headline.

WARTIME ORPHANS MAKE BETTY'S BOUTIQUE BOOM

Women everywhere can throw off their overalls and put on their dancing shoes, the war is over. But where do you go to get your glad rags for that special occasion?

When Betty Blumenthal passed away, her pretty and determined niece, Ruth Goldberg, along with her industrious siblings, Gabi and Hannah, channelled their grief by breathing new life into Betty's Boutique. And now they're launching their new season of summer outfits.

Their stylish dresses, jackets and skirts come in all sizes for all shapes.

"Whether you're slim, hourglass, or extra curvy, we want you to come out of Betty's looking like a glamorous starlet," says the charming, Ruth Goldberg.

Next to the editorial was a photo of us Goldbergs, proudly standing in front of the shop window.

I was floating again, sailing through the sky, every inch of my skin tingling as I obsessively reread the words.

Once Gabi and Hannah arrived back and handed out supplies, they squashed onto the same chair, next to mine, where they both skilfully stuffed half of their hot dog into their mouths, devouring it in seconds.

'Let's have a look,' said Hannah, tugging the paper away from me, the pair of them eyes down, poring over the page.

'That reporter must have the hots for you,' Gabi added, moments later.

'He called me pretty.' I stared into space dreamily. 'I want to hug him so hard I might actually squeeze the life out of him.'

'Ha be careful or he might break wind!' laughed Gabi.

'You are disgusting, Gabi.'

'All boys are,' said Hannah, grimacing.

And before we could finish our chips, a tapping on the door announced another crowd of eager customers.

'I cannot believe our trade today. We were rushed off our feet,' I said excitedly. I sat opposite Tommy in our local pub, the Black Bear, after inviting him out for pie and mash that evening to say thank you. And I must admit I felt quite saucy as I leant over the table and gave him a blatant kiss on the cheek.

His eyes crinkled at the corners as he broke into his gap-toothed smile. 'Aww, thanks, Ruth. Hopefully, now, you won't think all us hacks are just after a scandal.'

'I don't. You're truly the cat's meow.' I glanced at my hands, feeling awkward, 'and by the way ...'

'Yes, Ruth.'

'Do you really think I'm pretty?'

Tommy winked. 'Sure do. I'd liked to have said more, but I think our readers might suspect, quite rightly, that I had a thing for you.'

I looked down at my glass of cider, my face burning hot. No boy had ever paid me a compliment before.

He leant forward and grabbed one of my hands. 'In fact, tonight, you look so radiantly happy, you've become quite a beauty.'

Suddenly, I had no control over my facial muscles; my mouth stretched into a huge beaming grin right across my face. I now knew this Tommy thing wasn't just a crush, it was something much, much more; a warm, squashy, glowing explosion within that made me want to dance, sing and feel happy just to be alive. For want of a better word, I'd call it love.

By the end of the month, I wasn't just beaming, I was bouncing off the ceiling. We'd made a killing, enough to put some money aside for savings, and Tommy had become my steady boyfriend, taking me out three or four times a week. I couldn't believe things could change this fast, so along with my good fortune came a renewed faith in love and life and I was determined to meet the pianist now more than ever. Problem was, I didn't fancy heading up to the big smoke on my own.

'I've always loved Beethoven,' I said to Tommy when he popped into the shop after work. 'There's something magical about a symphony.'

Tommy laughed and grabbed my hand, pulling me into the stock room for some privacy. 'You just want to check out this Chopard bloke close-up, don't you?'

I nodded, biting my lip.

'Well, classical music isn't really my thing, but father thinks the man's a genius. In fact, he was only talking about getting tick-ets the other night.' He led me to a corner where we were hidden behind two racks of dresses as he kissed me. 'And I guess we could always stay somewhere overnight, make a weekend of it?'

Bubbles of excitement fizzed up inside me. 'Tommy, is that an invitation?'

'Might be,' he said with a wink.

'So does this mean ...?'

He grinned, wrapping his arms around me. 'Yep, we're going to the Proms. Dad's organised it. We've got the best seats in the house and we're spending the night in a posh hotel.'

'Oh, Tommy, you are a darlin'.' I felt a rush of euphoria as I stood on my tiptoes, smothering him with sloppy kisses.

'More, more,' he yelled. We both giggled and fell onto the floor in crazy, blissful madness.

Now, all I needed was a spectacular dress to wear—because this grand event would be a landmark in time—discovering if my beloved father was really alive!

Chapter 26

Friday, 24th August 1945

I woke up that morning with the heebie-jeebies. Three months
had whizzed by and the big day had arrived. As I clambered
out of bed, my legs were like jelly and I felt so queasy that I
almost talked myself out of going.

What's the worst that could happen? I reasoned as I brushed
my hair. Even if you discover the pianist is just an eerie doppel-
ganger, life will continue on as before. Realistically, there was
nothing to lose.

But that was my logic talking. Who was I kidding? I couldn't
bear to think Mr Chopard might not be my father.

Needing a distraction, I booked myself an early appointment
at Maggie's, the local hairdressers. When I arrived home, two hours
later, Hannah, who was curled up in one of the armchairs, looked
over at me and gasped when she saw my new blonde bob.

'Wow, you look so different, Ruth. It suits you.'

'Thanks, Hannah. It was a shock—they lightened it and
lopped off four inches.' I bounced over to the mirror above the
fireplace and stared at my reflection, feeling thrilled; my hair was
just like Jean Harlow's.

It was blazing sunshine and I had to get ready fast, so I ran upstairs to my bedroom and slipped on a canary yellow halter-neck dress that I'd had my eye on for ages in the Boutique. I hated my stomach, hips and thighs, but the fitted waist and flowing skirt flattered me, making me look as though I had the perfect hour-glass figure. To complete my look, I strapped on some black high-heeled sandals and wore a black beret, tilted slightly on one side, à la Marlene Dietrich.

Gabi walked in on my posing. 'Whoa. I never thought you could turn leather into silk, but you pulled it off.'

I gave him a withering look. 'Cheers, Gabi.'

He grinned as he leant against the doorway. 'Why are you going to the boring Proms anyway? It's for fuddy-duddy's.'

I avoided his eyes, feeling a tad guilty that I was hiding such a colossal secret. 'I've already told you, Gabi, it's Tommy's father's treat. We'll be away for the whole weekend, so you two get the house to yourselves.'

Hannah let out a long groan, overhearing our conversation as she walked upstairs. 'Great,' she yelled, 'I'll just have to sit there squeezing my eyes shut whilst Gabi and his girlfriend smooch in front of me, eww.'

'Don't look then,' he shouted back with his usual diplomacy.

Gabi, now seventeen had just begun dating a local girl he'd recently brought round for supper. Of course, with his aesthetic tastes, she was a natural beauty: tall and slender with long blonde hair. She made me feel like a waddling hippo every time I looked at her.

I heard a car horn signalling Tommy's arrival and rushed to grab my black cape from the hallway as they both followed me downstairs. I glared at Gabi before opening the front door. 'Keep your eye on your little sister and that's an order.'

Gabi nodded and they both kissed me on the cheek, dutifully waiting on the doorstep, ready to wave me goodbye.

Tommy jumped out of his father's Austin 10 Saloon to greet me, giving one of his characteristic winks. 'Wow, you look ritzy. Check out that new hair!'

'You don't look so bad yourself.' I smiled approvingly at his smart grey suit.

He opened the car door for me and I slipped into the back seat next to his mother Frances, a slim pretty woman with a short elfin hairdo. 'You look lovely, dear,' she said, putting me at ease.

'Thank you, Mrs Jones, and so do you.'

His father, Gerry, turned his head towards me from the driver's seat and gave me a grin. 'Good to see you again, Ruth.'

He looked so distinguished with his salt and pepper hair and bow tie. 'Likewise, Mr Jones, and thank you for your hospitality.'

'You're welcome, dear, and please, just call us, Gerry and Frances.'

I smiled happily. Tommy's so lucky to have such lovely parents, I thought.

Finally, we were all set for the three-hour drive to London. Tommy sat in the front, ready to navigate, peering at a map that was on his lap as his father started up the engine. I waved goodbye through the window to Gabi and Hannah feeling another flutter of nerves.

A few hours later, an usher guided us to our seats in front of the spectacular stage at the Royal Albert Hall.

'Wow, look at little old me living it up,' I said to Tommy with a grin. I took off my cloak and looked around the arena watching all the thousands of devoted fans milling around like giant ants as they filled up every possible space. It seemed incredible to me that this Edward Chopard had the confidence to perform to such a huge audience knowing all eyes would be on him, especially when Tommy whispered to me that this night was extra special.

We heard a ripple of applause as everyone stood up.

'Look up there,' Tommy said. He pointed to one of the exclusive boxes, to the right side of the auditorium.

I gazed up and saw two people, dressed all glitzy.

'That's his Royal Highness, King George VI with his missus, Queen Elizabeth.'

My mouth dropped open. I couldn't believe it, royalty were watching. 'Gosh, Tommy, this is amazing. I mean, front row seats too. Can your Dad afford all this?'

He looked at me with a wry smile. 'Oh, don't worry about that. They're free.'

I stared at him. 'How come?'

'Because Dad's a journo like me, only he writes for *The Times*, so he gets press passes. Didn't mention it before, but he's been ringing round, desperate to get an interview with Mr Chopard.'

I saw Tommy's father wave at a silver-haired man sitting in one of the posh boxes and he, in turn, saluted back.

Tommy followed my gaze. 'Now, that's Lord Douglas-Scott, and a little birdie has told me that he's the man responsible for our complimentary seats and our stay at the Savoy.'

'The Savoy!'

'Yep, that's where we're staying later.'

'Ooh, blimey! The blimmin' Savoy! Why would he do that, though?'

Tommy gave me a cheeky wink. 'Dad says he's a keen patron of the arts. Mr Chopard is his protégé and he wants him to have the right kind of press coverage.'

'A bit like bribery then?'

'Shhh,' he said, placing his finger over his lips, 'don't let Dad hear you say that. It's more a case of you scratch my back and I'll scratch yours.'

I sat back in my chair, tingling all over. Everything was falling into place, and I had plans. If there was any mutual scratching going on, I wanted to be first in the queue.

Resounding applause broke out as Edward Chopard walked onto the stage, and my heart drummed so loudly, I thought the entire auditorium would hear. The atmosphere was electric and I clasped Tommy's hand as he gave me a reassuring wink. Mr Chopard took his seat at the grand piano and I squinted to see more clearly. There was no doubt that this man was the double of my father.

I knew nothing about classical music but as he played the haunting, 'Adagio un Poco Mosso', a silence descended on the auditorium, and I was in a bubble of peaceful tranquillity. Then he changed harmonies flowing into 'Moonlight Sonata' and something deep inside me stirred, wanting to rise, fall, and merge with the melody.

At the finale, the audience were in a frenzy, applauding and cheering as Mr Chopard stood up, bowed and left the stage.

'That was magnificent. What a talent. What showmanship!' exclaimed Gerry, clapping wildly.

'Absolutely delightful,' said Frances. Her eyes glistened as she dabbed at them with a hankie.

I sat quietly, strange feelings whirling inside me.

We all stood up to leave, but I had to see this man backstage, I had to, and thankfully, Tommy's father answered my silent prayer.

'Follow me,' he whispered, gesturing with his hand.

I watched him give the young usher a tip as Tommy and I trailed behind his parents to the exit at the back of the hall. The usher spoke to a security guard who led us along winding corridors until he stopped and knocked on a door.

We all waited as he walked in. 'Excuse me, Mr Chopard, there is a member of the press here with his family who have a prior arrangement to see you.'

'Which newspaper? I won't talk to the tabloids,' said the muffled voice.

'It's Mr Gerry Jones from *The Times* newspaper, sir. It was organised by Lord Douglas-Scott for a prospective interview.'

'Oh, right, then yes, absolutely.'

We all funnelled into the room as Mr Chopard sat at a desk surrounded by bouquets of flowers and bottles of champagne with good luck cards pinned on the wall.

Gerry shook his hand, introducing himself as I gazed at the pianist mesmerised, praying no one in the room could hear the sound of my rapid breathing as I wondered if this man really could be my father.

I gulped when Gerry introduced me. 'Mr Chopard, this is Miss Ruth Goldberg.'

Mr Chopard looked at me, and I held his gaze, feeling so jittery my legs nearly gave way. He extended his hand to shake mine and I reached out, clasping it, holding on for dear life. He tugged it away from my grip and then shook Frances's hand, and then Tommy's, but my eyes were soldered to his hand and with good reason.

Along the tendons of his fingers, near his wrist, was a red, raised scar about two-inches long, identical to the one my father had. The memory flashed back: the blazing bonfire in our back garden, his burning skin, the pain on his face. I now knew, deep in my bones, that whatever he called himself and wherever his talent came from, this man was undoubtedly my father, Joseph Goldberg.

As this certainty sank into my consciousness, I hoped he'd glance back at me with a reciprocal double take. *He must know it's me.* He always told me how much I was wanted, that I was premature, weighed only four pounds, and how he and Mama prayed that I'd survive. We had such a strong bond. Yet there wasn't even a flicker of curiosity. I wanted to shout out, 'Daddy! It's me, Ruth!' knowing if I did, they would all think I'd lost my marbles.

Tommy elbowed me in the arm. 'Ruth, stop staring!' And I quickly looked away.

'Apologies, Mr Chopard we're all so overwhelmed by your glorious talent. Would you mind if we got your autograph?' asked Tommy. He offered him our programme leaflets. He was so good at ladling on the charm.

'Of course, be happy to.' Mr Chopard smiled, signed our leaflets and handed them back to him.

Before I knew it, the encounter was over and Tommy was practically dragging me out of the door, my mind a blur, except for my father's face and that scar.

'My dear girl, are you all right?' asked Frances as we ambled out of the back exit and along Kensington Road, heading toward an Italian restaurant for dinner.

I nodded, remaining silent. I didn't want to talk.

Gerry pushed open the heavy door of the restaurant where a waiter appeared and ushered us to a large round table.

I remained quiet throughout most of the meal, fidgeting in my seat, whilst Tommy poured me a glass of white wine and asked if I wanted black pepper on my spaghetti.

'Are you all right, Ruth?' asked Frances once again. 'Don't be embarrassed. We've all felt a little star-struck in our time.'

'I'm fine, just a bit tired,' I mumbled.

The truth was I felt worse now than ever, knowing my father was alive but hadn't recognised me. And I had no idea how I'd ever see him again or get the answers I so desperately needed. I mean, it was all so weird. Why could he play the piano? Why did he never try to find us? Why did he have a different name?'

'Well, I am exhilarated and not just with tonight's performance,' said Gerry. He sipped some wine. 'I was handed a note as we left and it seems I have managed to secure an interview with Edward Chopard at his Knightsbridge townhouse in the next few weeks, where I believe I will meet his lovely wife and baby son.'

'His wife and baby,' I spluttered, almost choking on a mouthful of pasta as they all stared at me.

'Yes, that's right' replied Gerry, with the perplexed expression of someone who's concerned about your sanity.

I spent the rest of the meal in a daze, my head reeling.

That night I lay sprawled on the king-sized bed in my luxurious hotel room with Tommy lying next to me. We were at the Savoy, one of the poshest places in London with rooms next to each other, but I just felt miserable.

Tommy stroked my hair. 'What's wrong, honey? You haven't seemed right since the concert.'

I couldn't help it, everything poured out, my chest heaving with broken words and wracking sobs.

Tommy waited for my tears to subside, and then planted a kiss on my cheek. 'Okay, let's say for argument's sake that he is your dad.'

'He is!' I cried. I pushed my face into the pillow.

'Well, look at it this way, you were nearly fifteen when he died and you're now nineteen. You've also cut and bleached your hair, and even I was thrown when I saw you this morning—you look gorgeous, but very different.' Tommy grabbed my hand as I flopped around to look at him. 'He's met you completely out of context. He might be thinking of you right now, wondering why you seem familiar, just as you are about him.'

'You're right, maybe, I expected too much.' I stroked his cheek. 'Promise you won't tell your parents about this? They'll think I'm nuts.'

'I promise.' He smiled and gently kissed my lips.

And I trusted him because I knew he wasn't convinced either. He'd listened and agreed, because he loved me, but he didn't believe me, I could tell. I mean, how could he accept something so outlandish? How could anyone? It was laughable really; that I was the long lost daughter of a famous pianist who didn't know who I was.

The next day on our journey home, I felt desperate, daring myself to ask Tommy's father if I could attend the interview with him, but I realised it would seem odd, especially after my outburst. And what would I say if I were there—meeting Daddy again with his new wife and baby? It made me quite sick, the thought of it; us three orphans fending for ourselves and yet he had a whole new family to love and cherish. A baby son!

It made no sense, none of it. Yet, somehow, someway, I was determined to get to the bottom of this crazy, confusing riddle.

Chapter 27

Saturday, 6th October 1945

Edward gazed lovingly at his son, Alfie, now twenty-months-old and an energetic toddler happily trotting up and down the living room of the Douglas-Scott's Shrewsbury residence. In the distance, he heard the traditional morning ritual: the sound of the hunting horn, riders galloping on their trusty steeds and the hounds running ahead, hungry for the scent of fox.

An hour later, Henry staggered back, breathless and drenched in sweat. Dressed in his full riding regalia, he bulged out of his scarlet tailcoat and white breeches, his face blotchy and red. 'That was exhilarating,' he trilled, still on a high and exuding a strange feral aroma. 'There's nothing better than a good hunt.'

Knowing that Henry's banking cronies would all be there, Edward felt relieved that he'd avoided the chase, happy to spend his time playing with his son, tickling him as he wriggled around chuckling.

'Well, I've never seen anything like it,' said Henry. He watched him with a bemused expression. 'A man entertaining a child, whatever next!'

Edward ruffled Alfie's soft downy hair. He was a smaller version of himself with bright blue eyes and an impish smile showing his two front baby teeth. 'This little chap is everything to me, although the rascal has run me ragged all morning.'

'Ha, you've more patience than I,' muttered Henry. He sank into a stately Edwardian armchair, hand carved from walnut.

Connie wandered over to her husband and kissed him on the lips. 'Eddie's been truly marvellous with Alfie today. Nanny Pickford can count her lucky stars she got an unexpected morning off.'

'Yes, my darling son-in-law is a fine example of a sensitive man,' said Elizabeth. She was repositioning some exotic flowers and foliage in a vase, frowning at the florist's arrangement. 'He doesn't want to be a husband and father just as a charade, do you, Eddie?'

Henry glared at his wife. 'Oh, is that right, Lizzy? Perhaps you live in a fog, because most men born into aristocracy laze about, unlike me, running around like a ruddy moron overseeing the financial infrastructure at my bank. I, like my father before me, am a worker!' He glanced over at his father's eight-foot, gilt-framed portrait on the wall. 'It wasn't ever my desire to hang around the house making silly gaga noises to infants.'

Elizabeth remained silent, continuing to rearrange the flowers.

'Anyhow, I'm off to get changed out of these clammy clothes.' He hauled himself out of the chair and strode out of the room.

Edward was astonished Elizabeth had spoken up. She rarely revealed her opinions, appearing so often to be in the backdrop of family life as if she was some kind of ghostly presence. She spent less time at home, making excuses that she needed to visit her mother or support wartime charitable events. 'I don't understand where Mummy disappears to,' Connie would say. 'I'm always trying to track her down.' Edward knew the truth: that Elizabeth's heart lay with her lover.

Could Henry not see his wife slipping away, recoiling when she was anywhere near him? He vowed to treasure his family, loving Connie even more after the trauma she'd endured, giving birth to their son a month early. He'd been in agony waiting outside the maternity suite, hearing his elegant wife morphing into a wounded animal. As her tormented moans grew louder, he knew then he'd been a father in the past—seeing himself pace a hospital corridor, too frightened to sit down, waiting to hear whether his premature daughter would live or die. The images felt so real, he shed a tear as he recalled them. *Where are my wife and daughter now? Did she die in infancy? How many other children do I have?* He gazed down at his son drifting off to sleep in his arms, his lips curved into a blissful smile. *I'm so very blessed,* he thought.

'The press coverage from the Proms was fantastic. Did you see it?' Henry asked Edward after they'd finished luncheon around the dining table.

'I don't believe I have,' he replied, wiping his mouth with a napkin.

He passed Edward the *Times* article, headlined: **CHOPARD PLAYS HIS BEETHOVEN BEST**. 'It's very complimentary,' he continued as Edward peered at the black and white print. 'It says Connie has a luminous beauty and that with your brooding looks, you make a striking couple.'

'How very flattering,' replied Edward. 'More importantly, I've read that I play the piano like a man possessed, with gusto and eloquence, a rare mixture apparently.' He laughed, folding up the newspaper and placed it on a side cabinet to peruse later.

'Yes, he's a good writer that Gerry Jones.'

'Hmm, he's certainly a pleasant chap with a wide knowledge of classical music. I briefly met his wife and son backstage, along with another young lady, who stared at me rather strangely. I felt quite awkward.'

Connie smiled at Edward lovingly. 'She was probably in awe of you, darling, as so many of your admirers are.'

'Indeed,' agreed Elizabeth. She sipped some tea.

'How do you know him, Henry?' asked Edward, fidgeting in his chair. He'd never felt comfortable with flattery.

The butler brought in a tray of cheese and biscuits, tea and port.

Henry picked up his glass of port and drank it back in one gulp. 'Oh, I'm in touch with a coterie of writers I know will give the right kind of publicity. We don't want any of those cynical hacks throwing a spanner in the works in the so-called name of journalism. Lord knows, I've had my share.' He heaved his heavy frame up from the table with a grunt. 'Anyway, my boy, time to get ready. No wriggling out of this one.'

Edward nodded. He had never handled a gun before and he hated the thought of killing anything, but he knew the shoot was another rural custom and it would be considered bad form to keep making excuses.

Edward wandered outside amidst the red and gold autumn leaves that had fallen onto the lush green fields, part of Henry's ten thousand acres of land. It seemed a perfect day; the warmth of the dappled sunshine penetrating through his tweed jacket and jodhpurs. He took a breath, inhaling the fresh air deeply into his lungs and for a few moments he felt completely at peace, until he found himself surrounded by the Mayfair Club members: Richard Castlebury, Douglas Hetherington-Jones and Lord Becket, as well as a mysterious stranger.

'Eddie, let me introduce you,' said Henry. 'This is my brave chum of old, Archibald Ramsay, a former conservative politician who tried to put England back into the forefront of political power and got pounded for it.'

Ramsay said hello and Edward shook his hand energetically.

'He's also a Mayfair Club member. So next time you join us, there will be another recognisable face.'

Over my rotting corpse. He had no intention of attending that Club ever again.

'Absolutely, the Mayfair Club keeps us going,' said Ramsay, a stern looking man with a receding hairline and a bushy moustache that completely concealed his top lip. 'Let's hope it doesn't get shut down. We need it to remain our secret bolt-hole.'

Henry sucked on his teeth. 'Indeed, I will ensure it keeps its veneer of respectability.'

Edward studied them, curiously. Why did they need to maintain respectability? Had they broken rules of some kind?

Henry, immaculately dressed for the shoot in his tweed cap and herringbone jacket, chatted to his gamekeeper overseeing the event. He pointed out the 'beaters,' the young boys who would be driving the game over to the party so they could take aim.

'There's a choice of two guns,' said the craggy-faced gamekeeper to Edward. He held them in his rough, outstretched hands. 'A .22 Rimfire which has low noise and minimal recoil, or the one on my right, a .410, ideal for a novice shooter, sir, such as yourself.'

'Thank you,' said Edward. He looked at each gun in turn, deciding he could handle the Rimfire, picking it up awkwardly.

'Show us your balls then, boy,' shouted Henry.

Edward took a deep breath, staring up at the sky and took aim, firing in succession at several flying birds. 'Damn!' he groaned with exasperation, missing every time.

'You'll get the knack eventually, Eddie. Persistence is the key.' Henry picked up his double-barrel shotgun, admiring it. 'I adore this Magnum. It really hammers them from the sky, but by God, it weighs a ton.' His eyes narrowed as he pulled back the trigger, aiming it at a pheasant frantically flapping its wings. A loud gunshot followed, the bird falling to the ground. Henry clenched his hand into a victory fist. 'Yet another delicious feast to be prepped by the chef,' he bellowed.

Edward grimaced, watching a young boy run over to pick up the dead bird, holding it by the legs, its body dangling. 'Are we going to eat that?'

Henry snorted with laughter. 'We won't be eating today's quarry. They need to be hung for a while to ferment and develop that sublime tangy flavour, but we'll certainly be tucking into some game from the last kill.'

Edward blanched.

'It's the law of the countryside, Eddie. You should never shoot anything you aren't going to devour,' stated Henry with a wide grin. 'Although with the sub-humans, it's a different story. Killing for the mere pleasure can be fun.' He caught Ramsay's eye and they both chuckled.

'Ha-ha, I agree,' said Douglas. He aimed his gun at a plump bird. 'This is exactly what I'd like to do to that Jew boy, Sachs.' He shot at the pheasant, hitting it straight on as it dropped to the ground with a thud.

'Now don't chastise us later for our remarks, will you, Eddie?' Henry winked. 'It's just a bit of fun.' He glanced around. 'He's a sensitive chap you know.'

The group of men all looked away with expressions of intolerant bemusement.

Edward took aim again and finally nailed one of the pheasants.

'Well done, Eddie. You see, handling a firearm takes practice, like anything. The more you use it, the better you'll get. I personally adore the velocity of my Magnum.'

Lord Becket pointed at Henry's rifle and sniggered. 'Can you believe Henry is using a gun designed to stop a six-ton bull elephant in its tracks? Only Henry could go so overboard on a bloody pheasant.'

Henry smirked. 'It's an upgraded replica, Becket, of the one used by Prince Maximillian, the German explorer over one hundred years ago. He's a great hero of mine.'

'Yes, but he used his rifle for safari expeditions to Brazil. You don't need a gun that powerful for local game. You're just showing off.'

'You seem to know your guns rather well,' said Edward.

Henry squared his shoulders, posing regally, placing the gun across his chest. 'That's because I am a show off, Becket, and yes, I do know my guns well, Eddie. When you spend time in the sticks and you have a lot of land, you need a firearm for every type of animal and occasion.'

'And intruders, Henry, don't forget them. There've been a few that have needed to be kept in line,' said Douglas, with a wink. 'Why do you think he keeps his cellar keys with him all the time? I'm often curious what else might be lurking down there, apart from his prized vintage collection.'

Edward noticed Henry glare at Douglas, wondering if this was another of their in-jokes until he was distracted by shouting as Richard aimed his gun. 'Come on, birdie. This one's for Sachs too.'

'That's right, kill him,' shouted Henry, jumping about, suddenly animated again. 'Shoot him right between the eyes.'

Edward watched as lost in their own world, they blasted bird after bird, shouting out Jewish names, their growing vitriol spewing out with every word. He caught sight of Henry's sneering face and shuddered, seeing bloodlust in his eyes as each shot was fired.

That night at dinner, wine was decanted and several pheasants presented to the table, cooked to perfection by Henry's personal chef, the bullets still embedded in their guts. Edward sat quietly as slivers of the bird were placed onto his plate by Cranford, the butler.

'Tender cocks slaughtered last weekend by yours truly and friends,' announced Henry. 'Enjoy.' He placed his face close to his plate and breathed in the pungent aroma, looking up as if in ecstasy. 'Delicious,' he said, smacking his lips together.

Douglas poked at his gums with a toothpick. 'Absolutely, they died with blasts of fascist venom.'

'And there is always more where that came from,' agreed Ramsay, his eyes slitted. 'Let us raise a toast to the former King of Fascism. It's the end of an era.'

Edward watched as everyone raised their glasses of claret, shouting, 'Heil Hitler!'—including his wife Connie, her glass lifted, her other hand raised in victorious salute, eyes flashing as if remembering an inspired mentor. He stared down at his plate feeling puzzled, stabbing his fork into the white flesh when he inhaled a gamey stench that made him retch. Overcome with nausea he covered his mouth with his hand as he stood up and staggered towards the door.

'Are you all right, darling?' called out Connie as she got up to follow him.

'Leave him, dear. Some of us have weak stomachs,' said Henry with a chuckle. He forked some game into his mouth, pounding it with his teeth.

Stumbling into their bedroom, Edward flopped down onto the four-poster bed. Connie swept through the door after him, her signature Chanel permeating the air like a scented breeze. Sitting on the edge of the bed, he felt her stroke his forehead, feeling the coolness of her fingers contrast with the heat emanating from his brow.

'How are you, darling?'

He wrinkled his forehead. 'I don't feel well.'

'But you must eat, Eddie. Are you going to join us later?'

He groaned. 'I've got one of those awful migraines. Do apologise for me.'

Connie leant over and kissed him on the lips, stroking his cheek as he turned his face away.

'Is everything all right, darling?'

'I just didn't think you were an Adolf fan?'

Connie pouted and folded her arms. 'Oh, so that's what this is about. Honestly, Eddie, you are being silly. I merely raised an innocent glass of claret to a dead man. We must all learn forgiveness for the damned, and I can't sit there like a party pooper. Daddy would have thought me terribly improper for disrespecting his comrades.'

'Forgiveness,' said Edward, staring at her blankly.

'Yes, Daddy's philosophy has always been to raise a toast and bless your enemies. It's a family superstition ... in case you meet them in hell.' Connie giggled.

He closed his eyes, feeling more confused than ever.

'Do come down when you're hungry, darling.' She stood up and smoothed down her dress. 'I can tell chef to fix you something light, perhaps some scrambled eggs and smoked salmon?'

'Thank you,' he said wearily. He waited for the door to shut, relieved to be left alone. Family superstition. Could that really be true? Despite the many times he tried to whitewash it, there was something about Henry's nature that was deeply disturbing.

It was like hearing a violinist play a rapturous melody that lifted your spirits until, without warning, there was that one shrill, discordant note, so unbearably, piercingly out of tune, that it made you want to scream for it to stop.

Henry was undeniably a ringleader to these boorish buffoons and they looked to him for direction, yet it was a direction that led to only dark, festering enmity. Despite having all the trappings of fame and wealth, he wondered if he'd somehow sold his soul to darker forces. What price would he have to pay for his hallowed lifestyle, allowing this strange man to become the patron of his musical career?

He mulled over his recent hypnosis sessions with Oliver. A potent memory had finally surfaced; all sensual curves and porcelain skin, she lay naked between white cotton sheets, her blonde hair loose and wavy like an image from a pre-Raphaelite painting. How happy they'd been, wrapped in each other's arms, tenderly kissing as she whispered, 'I love you.' He even had a name for her: Rachel. 'I loved that woman deeply. I know it in my bones,' he'd said to Oliver, certain she'd been his wife. 'I wish I knew where she was. I miss her.'

He yearned for answers, yet he was grateful for his dear Connie who had given him a sense of family. She was a good woman, a kind woman, despite her odd behaviour that evening, but thankfully that was a rare occurrence.

Sunday morning, 7ᵗʰ October 1945

Feeling rested after a good sleep, Edward collected their belongings ready for them to be chauffeured back to London. Whilst Connie was downstairs with her mother and their son, Alfie, he knocked at Henry's office door to say goodbye. Usually it was locked, but when there was no answer he turned the handle and wandered in.

In front of him on Henry's desk was a large red file with the words 'Serpentem Corde' written across it.

Serpentem Corde. What on earth is that?

Fuelled by intrigue, he peered out of the window and saw that Henry was near the stables talking to a groomsman. He opened the file, stuffed with letters. A telegram fell out. He picked it up— the date: June 12th 1943, struck a chord instantly. It was from Hitler, sending congratulations on his wedding day.

So Hitler's gesture of goodwill wasn't one of Henry's pranks.

Double-checking Henry's location, he grabbed one of the letters from inside the file, his heart racing as he took it out of the envelope and unfolded it. Written in German, he couldn't decipher the words, but saw the signature—Hitler. Slick with sweat, he slipped the letter into his jacket pocket, and closed the file, placing it back in the same position on Henry's desk.

As he left the room, he saw a large framed quotation sewn onto silk in italics, discreetly placed on the wall behind the door.

> *Make the lie big, make it simple, keep saying it,*
> *and eventually they will believe it.*
> *Adolf Hitler*

Chapter 28

Sunday afternoon, 7ᵗʰ October 1945

By the time Edward arrived back at his London townhouse, panic had set in, knowing he had stolen political intelligence from a man who could be a frightening tyrant. His hands trembled as his butler, Travers, took his coat, welcoming the family back into their marble reception hall, along with Connie's personal ladies maid, Miss Jackson, and Nanny Pickford.

'Is everything all right, darling?' asked Connie. She stared at him with concern. 'You do seem rather on edge.'

He gave Connie a quick peck on the cheek. 'I'm fine, angel. I've just got some urgent work to attend to. I'll see you later.'

He sprinted into his office-cum-music room, one of the many rooms situated off the main hall. It was a huge, light-filled space that he considered his private haven where he kept his personal documents, an inbuilt safe on the wall for valuables and his opulent custom-made Steinway to play at his leisure, along with shelves of sheet music from all the great maestros.

Shutting the door behind him he took out the crumpled letter from his pocket and placed it onto his desk. *Thank God, I'm seeing Oli in a few days. Perhaps he can translate?* His dear friend was the only person he could trust to read the contents without tipping off the press.

He jolted when he heard a loud knock at his door. Flustered, he leapt up to place the letter in his safe, turning the combination lock as he heard yet another insistent knock.

'Who is it?' he called out, feeling blood rush to his face.

'It's Travers. I have some correspondence for you, sir.'

'Oh, Travers!' said Edward, feeling relieved. 'Please, do come in.'

His butler entered carrying a silver tray with a handwritten envelope.

Edward took the letter and peered at the writing to see if he recognised who it was from. 'Thank you, Travers. You may go now.'

'Very good, sir.' Travers bowed and left the room whilst Edward waited until the door had shut before slitting open the envelope with his ornate letter opener, shaped like a ceremonial sword. As he read the short note inside, his chest tightened.

1st October 1945

Dear Mr Chopard,

I'm sorry for intruding on your privacy, but I may as well get down to brass tacks. You may recall that I met you backstage after your recent concert along with Mr Gerry Jones and his family. I have good reason to believe you are my father, Joseph Goldberg, who I thought had died when our house was bombed, four years ago, on April 18th 1941.

Please, Mr Chopard, could we meet? I can tell you more face-to-face. I run a shop in Bournemouth called, Betty's Boutique, and you can contact me

*via the address or phone number at the top of this
notepaper.*

Kindest wishes,
Ruth Goldberg

Reading the letter several times, he paced the room. Ruth Goldberg, backstage with the journalist. Yes, of course he remembered. She was the blonde girl who kept staring. Could she really be his long-lost daughter? She called him Joseph. That redhead called him Joe. Had he finally been guided to his true identity?

He wandered over to his drinks cabinet to pour himself a glass of neat whisky, needing something to steady his nerves. Swigging the scotch straight back he shuddered, feeling the burning aftertaste in his throat. Were the questions that plagued him, he wondered, like lost prayers that he'd now been granted answers to? But as he turned things over in his mind, doubt crept in. What if this girl was a fortune hunter or a crazed fan obsessed with his music? Either way, one thing was certain, he had to find out sooner rather than later.

He knew Connie would be devastated if she discovered he had a child. Breaking his marital vows of trust and honesty, he would have to keep this a secret. He steeled himself, picking up the phone on his desk, hoping to verify if the shop actually existed.

'Betty's Boutique, how can we help you?' answered the soft, lilting voice. He slammed it down. He wasn't ready to speak, not yet anyway.

His diary was packed with appointments, but sitting down at his desk, he decided to write a letter instead, asking if they could meet in Bournemouth in just over a week's time on Tuesday, 16th October at one o'clock in the afternoon. Driving there to see her would be far more respectful than making her travel to London. He would ring on arrival from a phone box and they could arrange to lunch somewhere nearby—and then, perhaps, he might gain some answers about the man he once was.

Wednesday, 10th October 1945

Edward arrived at Oliver's house in Fulham, his stomach in knots. The explosive missives like dynamite waiting to go off, weighed heavily on his mind. A dour-looking girl with dark bobbed hair and black-rimmed glasses opened the door. *Who is she? A secretary, a maid, a lady friend?* He didn't like to ask. After they exchanged mutual hellos, she led him into the eclectic living room which the psychologist often used for his therapeutic sessions and then disappeared in the direction of the kitchen.

Edward scanned the room and smiled when he saw the baby grand in the corner. He had fond memories of joyously playing his own sonata's to Oliver's rapt attention when he first came here from the London Hospital. Shelves lined every wall, stuffed with books on philosophy, psychology and anthropology and a few others, he noticed as he moved closer to inspect them, on regional cookery and wildlife.

Oliver wandered in and motioned for Edward to have a seat. 'Good afternoon, Eddie. You may have wondered why I asked you here?'

Edward laughed. 'I merely presumed you were being a good sport and would offer me a glass of port for my sins.' He sank into a worn leather armchair.

'We can most certainly enjoy a glass later if you so wish, Eddie. Depending, of course, on how you might feel at that time.'

'What do you mean?'

'Well, because we have struggled to gain access to crucial aspects of your history with conventional methods, I'd like to try out a new technique. It's a powerful herbal infusion that I discovered on a recent trip to Kenya that can aid a more deeply relaxed state.'

'Really, you are an intriguing fellow, Oli. Why on earth were you there?'

'Ah, now that is a story,' said Oliver. He took a seat on the sofa opposite Edward. 'I was invited to stay with an American friend of mine, Susan, on her ranch. She'd poured all her family inheritance into her big passion, to open a wildlife sanctuary. It was a safari adventure I'll never forget, seeing all the big cats up close, rolling around, playful and free.'

'Fascinating, do go on?'

'It was there that I met a lady called Mawusi. She was a handsome Kikuyu woman with a mahogany complexion and the whitest teeth I have ever seen. Susan found her lying by the side of a desolate road, bruised and weak from lack of food after a beating from her husband. My friend was so shocked by her condition, she brought the woman back to live at the ranch and she became the resident cook, serving up the most delicious African food you have ever tasted. As we got to know her, we realised Mawusi was highly intuitive with an innate understanding of herbal medicine. It was there that she shared the recipe of a unique concoction that I tried myself, to induce deep trance. And this potion is guaranteed to unlock the memories buried deep in your subconscious.'

'She sounds fascinating, but if you don't mind me asking, what exactly is in this potion?'

Oliver pulled out a beaten-up notebook from his trouser pocket, peering at a page. 'There are two crucial ingredients. The root of the *Kava Kava* plant, a sedative, along with the herb, *Artemisia Absinthum,* which has a powerful psychoactive effect, influencing the central nervous system. And a sprinkle of chamomile and patchouli for flavour.'

Edward remained silent, pursing his lips.

'Don't look so worried, Eddie. These herbs could alleviate those terrible migraines of yours. They're known to reduce stimulation of the cerebral cortex.'

'Sounds almost too good to be true.'

Oliver got up and went to the kitchen, rushing back with a cup that he passed to him. 'The herbs have been infused in boiling water and left to cool.'

Edward sniffed at the contents, trying to work out the confusing aroma. 'Good job 1 trust you, Oli. Only you could get me to drink some yellowy-green muck.'

Oliver chuckled and placed a carriage clock onto the coffee table in front of him and sat back down. 'Now, simply sip the liquid as you listen to the sound of the ticking clock.'

Edward put the cup to his lips and swallowed, pulling a face at the bitter taste. 'Oh, God, that's awful.'

'Hold your nose if it helps.'

'Ha-ha, thanks, 1 will.'

After Edward drank the infusion, he felt somewhat dizzy ... the colours in the room leaping out at him, becoming more vivid.

'How are you feeling?' asked Oliver, monitoring Edward's expression.

'Um, well, 1 feel like I'm floating ... as if my brain is being slowly dissolved. Hopefully, it isn't!'

'Good, good, don't worry, it's only temporary. Now, Eddie,' said Oliver speaking in a deep, soft voice, 'listen to the rhythmic sound of the clock and allow your breathing to become in tune with the tick, tick, ticking. Feel your eyelids become heavy, weighted down. You're walking down steps ... count down with me ... twenty, nineteen, eighteen, feeling sleepier and sleepier.'

Edward's head fell forward as he sank into a well of darkness within, the herbal concoction taking greater effect, his breathing pattern becoming slower and deeper as he heard Oliver's voice in the background ... like a whisper echoing down a tunnel, soothing and guiding him.

'Tell me everything that floats into your mind?'

'I'm in a place of worship, wearing a white shawl over my head and I have black binding on my left arm.'

'What's it called?'

'A synagogue. I'm reading Hebrew from a scroll but I'm struggling ... I'm struggling to understand.'

'What is this scroll?'

'It's the Torah.'

'And what's your name?'

'My name is ... Joseph Goldberg.'

'How old are you?'

'I'm thirteen and this is my special day. It's the day I become a man!' His eyes rolled around under his eyelids from left to right, witnessing an array of hazy images floating into view.

'What are you seeing now, Joseph?'

'I'm at a wedding ceremony. I'm twenty years old and I'm giving a dark-haired woman a ring.'

'What's her name?'

'Rose. She has been chosen for me. I can't see her face. It's hidden by a veil. And now I'm breaking a wine glass covered with a cloth. I have to stamp on it, to crush it with my right foot.'

'And then what happens?'

'Everyone, all the guests, are shouting, *Mazal Tov*.'

Memories flicked through his mind like disjointed frames from a film as he saw himself throwing wood onto a bonfire, the sound of screams, his red blistered hand and then a river of rubble hammering down on him so vividly that he raised his arms in the air desperate to protect himself. 'No, No, No,' he shouted, his eyes staring wildly, beads of perspiration dripping from his forehead and cheeks.

'Eddie, you look frightened. What did you see?'

His heart banged in his chest as the room began to spin. Slamming his hands over his ears, he attempted to stop the unbearable popping sensation. 'Sorry, I couldn't go on,' he said in breathless spurts. 'I was being burned and then buried in rocks.'

'Hmm, it appears that your conscious mind has finally allowed you to see a harrowing memory of how you ended up in hospital, but it was still too distressing.'

Edward sat hunched over, staring at the floor, trying to calm his breathing.

'Don't worry. The sedative effects will wear off. And I must say, well done.' said Oliver, his voice heightened with excitement. 'We bloody well got there!'

'But it was over in a flash.'

'Perhaps, but you have now thrown light on some crucial memories—the one that's haunted you for so long—as a thirteen-year-old boy where you were reading the Torah, a scripture written in Hebrew ... hence the struggle. It can take years to master the Torah.'

Edward nodded, digesting the information.

'You mentioned it was the day you became a man. It appears, this was your Bar Mitzvah, a coming of age ceremony when you take responsibility for your own actions, ethically and morally. Maybe that's why it was troubling you.'

'So what was the white shawl for and the binding on my arm?'

'Ah, now,' said Oliver, putting his forefinger up as if to mark his recall, 'the white shawl is called a *Tallit* and is used during morning prayers, along with the black binding, *Tefillin*, small leather boxes linked together, inscribed with verses from the Torah. But more importantly, you've discovered something pivotal—that you were married, reliving your wedding day to Rose in a traditional Jewish ceremony. You said she was 'chosen for you'. You were probably introduced through *Shidduch*.'

'*Shidduch?*'

'Yes, it's a Jewish system of matchmaking. You also broke a glass with your foot, such a cultural part of the Judaic marriage ritual.'

'But my wife was a brunette. So who is Rachel, the beautiful blonde? I thought she was my wife?'

'Maybe you were married twice?'

'Anything's possible, I guess,' said Edward, reflectively. 'Or is Rachel a lover with some kind of hold on my heart? And then there's ...'

Oliver shifted onto the edge of his seat. 'What Eddie?'

'The redhead,' he continued, feeling more confused than ever.

Oliver looked at him sympathetically. 'You are on a journey with many mysteries to unravel, but I'm certain you will find the answers in time. At least we now have the key to who you really are—your identity. Your name is Joseph Goldberg ... and you, my dear friend, are most definitely a Jew!'

The furrow between Edward's brows deepened as he focused on the name—Goldberg, Goldberg—the fog in his head suddenly clearing—the letter received from Ruth Goldberg a few days ago. *She really is my daughter,* confirmed beyond all doubt. He remained quiet, not wanting to tell his trusted confidant anything just yet. Not until he knew more.

'Eddie! Eddie!' The doctor tapped his knuckles hard on the table to attract his attention.

Edward jumped at the sound.

'You drifted off. Where did you go?'

The colour drained from his face. 'Sorry.'

'Aren't you happy? The speculation is over.' Oliver walked over to him patting him on the back. 'As a fellow Jew, I can now officially call you brother.'

'No!' said Edward. He leant forward, his head heavy like concrete. 'This is not good.'

'But surely this is what you've been waiting for? Now you can start to understand where you came from.'

'Don't you remember,' Edward said, looking up sadly. 'Henry and his society cronies hate the Jews. If they knew the truth, they'd shoot us both like dogs in the street.'

'Steady. Hate is a strong word. Although I don't advertise my history, you should be proud of your bloodline. I am sure in giving Henry a much-loved grandchild, that all your family will love you unconditionally, whatever your ancestry.'

'I do hope so.'

'Have faith, Eddie. A shot of caffeine will bring you round. You still look a little dazed.'

'Anna! Coffee please!' yelled Oliver, sitting back down.

'Coming now,' Anna called out from the kitchen with a strong Russian accent.

Five minutes later, they heard the sound of rattling as Anna carried in the cafetiere, milk and sugar on a silver tray and placed it down on the coffee table.

She looks like an upmarket maid, Edward thought, noting her black fitted dress with a frilly apron tied around her waist.

'Bolshoe Spasibo.'

'Pozhaluysta' she replied. She walked back out of the room and quietly shut the door.

'You're speaking in your native Russian, Oli?'

'Yes, apologies. Anna doesn't speak much English. I found her crying in the hospital corridor after losing her job as a cleaner, poor thing.'

'So you employed her?'

'Only for three days a week. And she cleans, cooks, gets in the shopping. You have to give people a chance and it's good to talk in my native tongue. She's become a good ally.'

'Hmm, I did wonder who she was. Thought you'd found yourself a filly, old sport,' said Edward with a wink.

Oliver laughed and shifted about, his face reddening. 'Not with my crazy workload.'

Edward sipped the strong Kenyan brew, relieved to eliminate the taste of bitter herbs and be roused from his grogginess. He hesitated, feeling anxious. 'Oli, would you possibly grant me a small favour before I depart?'

'Of course.'

'I have a letter here, written in German.' He pulled out an envelope from his jacket pocket. 'Would you be able to translate it?'

'Absolutely, I speak German fluently.'

'I knew you'd be able to help,' he said with a sigh, 'but promise that whatever you discover will go no further than this room?'

Oliver stared at him intently. 'Eddie, you know we have a bond of trust. We are like family.'

'Thank you, dear friend.' Edward handed him the letter and waited with anticipation.

Oliver read the crumpled missive, a bewildered look on his face. 'Is everything all right? Is it translatable?'

'Uh, yes ... but this is quite shocking. Where did you find it?'

'In Henry's office.'

'So you stole it?'

'Yes.'

'You are brave, Eddie, given what I see here.'

Edward's stomach churned. 'Please, do go on.'

15th March 1942

Dear Heinrich,

Thank you so much for the thirty thousand pounds you have kindly bestowed to the Nazi Party. With your help, we can work on advancing our military technology and removing Churchill from his seat of power. You would make a wonderful prime

*minister. Serpentem Corde will multiply and rise up
in mighty fury.*

Oliver went quiet for a few moments, before whispering the words, *'Entfernung der Juden.'*

'Pardon,' said Edward, leaning forward.

'It's German for *removal of Jews.'*

'Meaning?'

He swallowed, continuing to read.

> *As we both passionately agree, the removal of the Jews must be the government's final goal. Judaism is a race, not a religion, which has been preserved through a thousand years of inbreeding and is only concerned with the pursuit of money and power.*
>
> *I look forward to you joining me on my birthday on April 20th in Berlin.*

Yours faithfully,
Your true comrade,
Adolf

Oliver continued to stare at the letter, his face growing paler by the second. 'Well, this funding certainly explains something.'

'What?' asked Edward, feeling confused.

'Why the Luftwaffe had a never-ending supply of ammunition allowing the war to go on for so long.' He paused, taking a breath. 'Your father-in-law funded a mass murderer to destroy his own country. So I take back what I said earlier. You married into a family who are your worst enemies.'

Edward shook his head sadly. 'And they hoped to eliminate Churchill so Henry could become Prime Minister?'

'Seems that way.'

'Ha, that is so typical of Henry's megalomania.'

'But Eddie, this was written three years ago and nothing happened! Becoming Prime Minister is probably the fantasy of many a man. It sounds like Hitler may have been fanning the flames of Henry's ego, perhaps to secure more finance.'

Edward sat in silence, not knowing what to think.

'Perhaps, some solace is that now Hitler is dead, Henry and his aristocratic circle may think differently.'

'Not if you'd seen them at a pheasant shoot recently.'

'What do you mean?'

He emitted a long sigh. 'Let's just say the collective anti-Semitism is as strong as ever. And what on earth is Serpentem Corde?'

'I was thinking the same. I've never heard of it. All this madness may explain why your memories took so long to resurface. Your instincts were protecting you from a difficult truth.'

Edward flopped forward, dropping his head into his hands. 'Oh Lord, I wish I could just run away.'

'What!' Oliver jumped up. He grabbed Edward by the arm, pulling him off his chair to hug him. 'Now you listen to me ... you don't go anywhere. And do you know why?'

'Why?' he said, his voice choked.

'Because, dear chap, you have everything to live for.' Oliver opened his arms wide as if to signify abundance. 'An incredible career as a celebrated pianist and marriage to a beautiful woman who has given you a perfect son. Connie's still your loving wife. She is not your enemy.'

'Yes, but I have to be careful what I say to her.'

'Agreed, I would be careful too because blood is thick and blue blood even thicker. But she is your family! All you need do is pretend today never happened. Play your part as you unknowingly always have done, as a gentile.'

'But how can I pretend? Now I know who I am. I can't live a lie.'

Oliver pressed his hands together, interlinking his fingers. 'Listen to me, having amnesia so far has served you well and given you a good life. We think that our bloodline is what makes us who we are, but that is not the nub of what really defines us. Treating people with kindness and embracing the moment you are in is, in truth, what really counts. So, be the best actor you can be, because as God is my judge, your ancestry needs to be the biggest secret you will ever keep.'

That night Edward lay in bed gazing at his sleeping wife in the darkness, watching her chest rise and fall with the rhythmic sound of her breathing. How he wished he could turn to her for comfort and unburden his fears, but he daren't. Everything had changed and he felt like a lost soul stumbling forward into a place far worse than death, a place of sickness with no release. He closed his eyes. *Remember, you have a daughter, someone else to love; you don't have to feel alone. You're not alone.*

Chapter 29

Tuesday, 16th October 1945

My stomach flipped over. There he was standing in front of Harry Ramsden's fish and chip restaurant in his swanky charcoal suit, red tie and Homburg hat, looking so dapper he could have stepped out from the pages of *Harper's Bazaar*. He appeared to be daydreaming, gazing into space, until he saw me and broke into that memorable grin.

'I'm so pleased to meet you, Ruth.' He reached out to shake my hand and I clasped it tightly.

'Hello, Mr Chopard,' I mumbled. 'Thank you for driving all this way to meet me.'

'Not at all. It's a small price to pay.'

I nodded not knowing what else to say, my heart pounding. I pulled my coat around me, the cold wind blowing my hair across my face.

'So let's get you in the warmth and have some lunch, I'm ravenous,' he said. He touched the small of my back and ushered me inside the long narrow room full of chattering customers.

We sat down on opposite sides of a wooden table, next to a window overlooking the beach. I took off my coat, fumbling with the buttons and turned to face him. An awkward silence hung between us as we gazed at each other. I longed to throw my inhibitions aside, reach across and hug him, but I couldn't. There was a stiff formality, a line we couldn't cross.

'Can I take your order please?' asked the waitress, holding her pad and pen, breaking the tension.

'Absolutely, now what would you like to eat, Ruth?'

'Cod and chips, please.'

'Good idea. That's cod and chips twice please, with an espresso for me and ...'

'A strawberry milkshake, please,' I replied, feeling like a kid again.

The young girl nodded and dashed off, ready to serve more customers who had just piled in.

I gulped and dug up some courage. 'So, do you recognise me, Mr Chopard?'

He gave me a wink. 'Please, Ruth, call me, Eddie.'

'Okay ... Eddie,' I replied quietly.

He pursed his lips, studying my face. 'You do look familiar.'

So he did remember me. I sat up straight, feeling a rush of energy.

'From your visit backstage at the Proms.'

I crumpled, slouching back into my chair.

'You reminded me in your letter that you were with the journalist, Mr Jones and his family.'

'Yes. He's my boyfriend Tommy's father.'

'Ah, I see.'

'So you don't remember anything else?' I felt a lump in my throat. *Don't cry, Ruth. Don't cry.*

He leant forward, clasping his hands together. 'If it helps, Ruth, my memory hasn't been working too well.' He touched my arm gently, looking into my eyes. I think he noticed they were watering.

'Your memory?' I repeated, trying to understand.

'That's right, but the date of the bombing made perfect sense to me, and that's why I wanted to meet you. Apparently, I was taken into hospital on Friday, April 18th, 1941, with severe concussion and amnesia. And there's still so much I don't know about my past.'

I took a breath. A ton of weight had been lifted. Now I understood why he hadn't recognised me. 'That must have been tough?'

He raised his eyebrows, his forehead contorting into deep lines as he grasped for words. 'Yes, it was, but I stumbled ahead, rather clumsily perhaps, trying to feel my way forward.' He paused whilst the waitress brought our drinks. 'Can I ask you something, Ruth?'

'Of course.'

'What made you so certain I was your father?'

'It's that scar,' I said, my eyes widening. 'The one on your right hand!'

He glanced at the long red mark. 'Oh, that ugly thing. I've often wondered how it got there.'

'I remember, clear as day,' I continued. 'It was Guy Fawkes and we were all in the back garden. I was only six. You were throwing wood on the bonfire, the flames getting higher and higher. I was so excited, chanting "More wood, Daddy. More wood, Daddy." You always said that old apple tree needed cutting back. Then a long branch fell onto the fire ...' I stopped, choked up. 'It bounced across your hand, burning your skin—you were so brave, but I'll always remember your face. You must have been in so much pain. Thankfully, Mama didn't waste time. The nearest phone box was ten minutes up the road, so she flew outside in her slippers to call an ambulance. And after a long wait, you were whisked off to hospital.'

His eyes were focused, listening, taking everything in. 'Funny, I have memories of a fire and the pain. It's good to know how things piece together.'

I felt comforted that something made sense. We stopped talking whilst our fish and chips arrived at the table. I picked up my fork, my stomach churning, too anxious to eat.

Catching a whiff of cologne, I looked at his hands as he held his cutlery. How things had changed. Back then he always smelt earthy with rough worker's hands from digging up muddy vegetables straight from the ground. Now he spoke all posh, smelt expensive and his nails were clean and perfectly shaped.

He paused between mouthfuls. 'So tell me more about our history?'

I played with my food, cutting up chips, shoving them around the plate. 'Gosh, where, do I start? Um, well, your name is Joseph Goldberg.'

'That's right.' He smiled. 'I recalled my name under hypnosis. We're Jewish, aren't we?'

I nodded. 'Before I forget, I've brought you something.' I reached into my handbag, pulled out two photographs and handed them to him.

He looked at the first one, his eyes lighting up: all of us celebrating Hanukkah in 1940, a year before the bombing. He was pulling one of his silly cross-eyed expressions as we all laughed hysterically. 'Ha-ha, I can still see it's you,' he muttered, soaking up every detail, 'even though you're now a sophisticated blonde. And these other two children ... I'm guessing they're mine too?'

'Gabi and Hannah. Yes, they work at the boutique with me.'

'How wonderful,' he murmured, continuing to gaze at their faces.

'We've all changed a lot since then. We're teenagers now.'

'And do they know about me?'

'No, nothing. I've lied actually ... about meeting you today ... only little white lies, but I wanted to wait until I knew more.'

'Very wise.' He studied the second photo of our mother, Rose, on their wedding day, dressed in her lace bridal gown, smiling happily for the camera. 'And this lady was, my wife?'

'Yes, that's Rose.'

'Goodness,' he said, holding it up to the light, 'you are so like your mother.' He continued to stare at the picture, his eyes shadowed, questing.

What was he seeing, wondering, doubting? Was it something bad?

'Tell me, Ruth.' He looked directly into my eyes. 'Has anyone tried to hurt you, because you're a Jew?'

His words threw me as I stared at him blankly, trying to think. 'Gosh, I've never been asked that before.' I looked at my plate: a pile of mushed-up food like a carcass scavenged by vultures. 'No, I mean, sometimes kids at school would call us names, but then kids call everyone names. But no one's singled us out since.'

'I'm relieved to hear that,' he said with a hint of sadness. He breathed deeply, pushing the remainder of his food away, looking at the photo of my mother once more. 'So what happened to Rose?'

'She died when our house was bombed, just as we believed you had.' I paused, feeling upset. 'Yet here you are.'

He smiled. 'Yes, here I am. I guess I got lucky.'

Time seemed to fly and thankfully he didn't mention his wife and son and I daren't ask. I had no interest in his new family, not when I'd only just found him again. But I was desperate to know one thing: about his miraculous ability to play the piano—a gift he presumed he was born with until I told him differently. A talent that came as naturally as breathing this post-war dusty air.

'A good friend of mine, a doctor, thinks my brain injury might have caused it,' he said, 'but, of course, we'll never know for sure.'

My head felt foggy as I tried to make sense of things, except nothing made sense. Could a brain injury really magic up musical talent from nowhere, or had he been touched by something divine; an angel on the brink of death that bestowed him with an extraordinary gift?

I caught sight of the clock on the wall. It was five o'clock! I jumped up, grabbing my coat and bag. 'Sorry, I must dash. I've left Gabi and Hannah back at the shop. They'll have a search party out soon.'

He got up to follow me. 'I completely understand, but can I ask you one more thing before you go?'

'Yes.' My heart fluttered.

He stood in front of me, tall and broad as I looked up into his bright blue eyes. 'Were you ever sick as a baby?'

'Um, yes, many times, I think. Apparently, I nearly died. You always said that's why we were close, because I was your firstborn and you were scared of losing me.'

Joseph, Edward, Dad—I wasn't sure what to call him—but he was blinking back tears. 'Because, I can see myself holding you,' he said softly. 'Your little gurgles as you grabbed my finger. You were so perfect ... and you still are.'

I couldn't help myself, I threw my arms around him and he responded, wrapping his arms around me too as I melted into them, tears falling down my face.

'I know this has been difficult for you,' he whispered, wiping my face with his fingers.

I nodded.

'It's hard to explain, but it's not easy for me to get away,' he added, 'but I'd like to meet with Hannah and Gabi too.'

I clung onto him, comforted by the thud of his heartbeat, not wanting to let go. 'Yes, they would love that.'

'In the meantime, let's keep writing to each other, in confidence, just you and me. And we'll arrange something.'

I looked up at him again. 'Thank you, Daddy.'

Reluctantly letting go of him, I waved goodbye. He broke into that grin and blew me a kiss, and buoyant with happiness, I blew him one back.

Heading back to the boutique along the seafront, I wanted to leap into the air as if I were a bird stretching out my mended wings, flying free. Daddy was back after all this time, and yet in so many ways he was a different man. He still had a sparkle in those bloodshot eyes, but he looked so tired and empty as if all his strength had gone just trying to survive. It's not just memories he's lost, I thought. He's lost a little part of his soul too.

Chapter 30

Tuesday, 20th November 1945

E dward was striding along the Brompton Road heading towards Harrods on an impromptu shopping spree when he bumped into the tall and wiry Douglas Hetherington-Jones.

Douglas stopped and placed his glass monocle over his right eye. 'Well, if it isn't the lauded musician, Mr Chopard. How are you on this chilly winter's day, sir?'

'Wonderful, thank you. And how are you and your good lady wife?' said Edward, sensing sarcasm in his compliment.

'In excellent health, thank you for asking,' he replied with a whistling wheeze in his voice. 'So tell me, what were your thoughts on Henry's colleague, the ex-convict?'

Edward stared at him blankly. 'Sorry, I'm not sure what you mean.'

'Oh, so you don't know?' Douglas licked his thin red lips, 'about the dark history behind Archibald Ramsay.'

'No, I only met him briefly. What crime did he commit?'

'Er, let's just say he was an infamous fascist leader. I mean, I understand that we all hate the bloody Jews, but he became far too chummy with the Führer, but perhaps I shouldn't say more.'

Edward felt the colour drain from his face.

216

'I'm surprised you didn't know already, old chap, being a Mayfair Club member, but then you don't attend on a regular basis, do you?' he added with a wry smile, revealing a set of uneven yellowing teeth. 'But I'm sure you can find out more if you want.'

Edward remained silent, responding to Douglas's army salute and then continued his brisk pace, feeling confused. There was something unnerving about Douglas; something unnerving about all of them. A former politician locked away, for what exactly? Were they all part of a bigger conspiracy? And more important, why did Douglas decide to tell him?

Around six that evening, he arrived home laden with gifts that the shop assistant had wrapped beautifully, placing them into a cupboard in his office where he could lock the door. *That's Christmas out of the way,* he thought. So much had transpired recently, he felt emotionally drained, so whilst Connie was out with baby Alfie visiting her mother in Richmond, he decided to take advantage of the quiet time, sit down at his desk and unravel all the events in his diary.

Truly I am blessed. Meeting my daughter, Ruth, and corresponding with her has given me an undeniable healing. Fragmented memories are gradually emerging, which I hope will give me a sense of who I really am. And that brings me peace, when I must hide my true Jewish heritage from my own wife and her bigoted family. Despite my commitment to her and my son, I am destined to live my life in their presence, forever on my guard.

I pray I can make up for my lost time as a father ...

The phone rang out halting the flow of his thoughts. He paused, enjoying his rare moment of privacy, before putting down his pen to answer.

'Evening, Eddie. It's Oli. A bit impromptu, but can you meet for dinner? I've spoken to an old colleague, a journalist … and you might find what he has to say rather interesting.'

Edward swallowed. 'You haven't divulged anything about the letter have you?'

'Divulge that, to a member of the press? Never. I've simply asked him to tell us more about Serpentem Corde.'

'Sounds intriguing, Oli. And, yes, I'd love to. Let's meet at that Greek place, the one in Knightsbridge.'

'Wonderful, see you there in half-an-hour.'

Edward put down the phone, locked his diary and placed it back into his safe.

Arriving at The Brompton Grill, a place favoured by politicians and their mistresses for its discreet booths, an elegant waitress led them to their table through a noisy room full of chattering socialites.

Journalist, Hugh Emmerton awaited them: a stocky, dishevelled man with scruffy blond hair and a wide squashy nose covered in broken red veins from excessive bouts of lunchtime drinking.

'Oliver, hello, and Mr Chopard, it's an absolute pleasure to meet you,' he said, standing up. His shirttails emerged from the waistband of his trousers as he reached across the table to shake both their hands. 'I'm a great admirer of your magnificent talent.'

Edward glanced down at his hands, his face turning red. 'You really are too kind. Please call me, Eddie.'

They all sat down on the velvet-covered chairs as the waitress handed them each a menu.

'A bottle of the 1905 Château Haut-Brion, I think,' said Edward. The brunette waitress smiled and raced off, returning with the French vintage. She offered a sample for Edward to taste, awaiting his nod of approval, before pouring the ruby liquid into their crystal glasses, and taking their food order.

'So Oliver mentioned that you know something about Serpentem Corde?'

Hugh nodded, gulping some red wine. 'Indeed. As a man who believes in justice, it's something I've taken a keen interest in.'

Edward and Oliver remained silent, listening intently.

'Serpentem Corde,' Hugh continued, 'is a secret sect, involving members of Hitler's inner circle. We got wind, several years ago, after an anonymous call to the paper—that it was a splinter group, affiliated to Archibald Ramsay's Right Club.'

Edward put down his glass. 'Oh Lord, he was one of the men mentioned to me today.'

'By whom?' Hugh leant closer, moistening his lips.

'A man called Douglas Hetherington-Jones. I bumped into him earlier and quite out of the blue he asked me what I thought of the former convict, Archibald Ramsay. I was introduced to him at my father-in-law's country estate last month.'

Do excuse me gentleman,' interrupted the waitress. She flambéed their steaks on a pan at the table, throwing in glugs of Cognac and cream and served them up with sautéed potatoes and green beans on white china plates.

Hugh rolled up the sleeves of his white shirt revealing flabby pale arms as he picked up his cutlery ready to eat. 'Still a friend of his, hmm, interesting. And your father-in-law is, of course, the billionaire, Lord Douglas-Scott?'

Edward nodded. 'So when was Ramsay freed?'

'September last year. He was considered dangerous enough to be locked up, along with other key members, for most of the war—suspected of being a Nazi sympathiser.'

Raised glasses, a gamey stench and a shout of "Heil Hitler" flashed through Edward's mind. 'What exactly is this Right Club?' he asked, his fork poised mid-air.

'A secret club held at the Russian Tea Room in Kensington where Ramsay recruited over two hundred members, a motley crew of hardcore fascists, MP's, and some wealthy aristos, all united with the same vision—to rid Britain of any Jewish control. Unfortunately, it turned into something more sinister when they schemed to bring down the British government and forge an alliance with Hitler.' Hugh ate noisily with his mouth open, slurping more wine, his bulbous nose reddening with every sip. 'They all despised Churchill, considering him weak and ineffectual, and plotted to steal classified documents that could discredit him. Fortunately, MI5 sniffed them out, they got caught red-handed and the group was shut down.'

'Christ. Not surprised he was he locked up.' Edward rubbed his forehead, pausing to think. 'You know, the Right Club sounds a lot like the Mayfair Club.'

Hugh's eyes widened with intrigue. 'What's the Mayfair Club?'

'Yes, what is it?' exclaimed Oliver, peering at him, no doubt wondering why he'd withheld information.

Edward let out a long sigh. 'Henry talked me into attending under the guise that it's some kind of gentleman's club, only it was full of vitriolic bullies boasting about being pals with Hitler. They made me feel quite unsettled.'

'Hmm, sounds like Henry has simply formed another Right Club after the old one was abolished, only just for men, but that's probably because he hates women as much as the Jews,' added Hugh with a wink.

'Quite,' said Edward, raising an eyebrow, 'but what's all this got to do with Serpentem Corde?'

Hugh paused, taking a breath. 'Well, select Right Club members took things one step further, mixing Nazi ideologies with the occult.'

'The occult!' Edward gasped.

'That's right. The sect named themselves after an ancient book, *Serpentem Corde*—Latin for *Serpent Heart*—reciting incantations to awaken a dormant reptilian force that they believe resided within the earth's core. When awakened, this energy, it seems, can heal or destroy, depending on how you direct it. They carried out acts of sacrifice ... ceremonies involving chickens, foxes and other wildlife.'

Oliver pulled out a notepad and pen from his jacket pocket and began scribbling furiously.

'Instead of a Pentagram usually associated with the occult, their symbols were more simplistic—a diagonal cross and a circle which they would paint onto their torsos with fresh blood—the cross on one side, the circle on the other, depicting positive and negative energies.'

'But why?' asked Edward, leaning forward as he watched Hugh continue to shovel large mouthfuls of food between words.

'Because they believed the ritual helped harness this supernatural force, giving them the power to manipulate the human mind.' He wiped his mouth on his sleeve. 'Whether truth or myth, this is apparently how Hitler plotted world domination, meeting the sect in secret locations around the globe, visualising his political enemies as dead, and himself as invincible—alongside thirteen other disciples dressed in white cloaks.' He stared unblinkingly at Edward. 'I'm afraid, your father-in-law was rumoured to be one of them.'

Edward exchanged an anxious glance with Oliver. He recalled the words from Hitler's letter to Henry: *You would make a wonderful prime minister. Serpentem Corde will multiply and rise up with mighty fury.*

'Sounds too outlandish to be true,' said Edward, his hands shaking slightly.

'Indeed,' Hugh said reflectively, 'and it's only heresay ... although many of these sects do have bizarre practices, but if their members have faith in their beliefs and act on them ... they're bloody dangerous. One thing is certain, if the group was fixated on amassing personal power, it worked, because Hitler had a magnetism that no one could comprehend, and not just politically—because, trust me, that short, ugly Austrian had a variety of lovers, including many British debutantes. And it's strange.' Hugh paused briefly as if deep in thought, 'bad things seemed to befall the women he bedded as if they were cursed.'

'What do you mean?'

'Well, Unity Mitford, a British socialite, was so desperate to meet the Nazi she travelled to Munich and stalked him, hanging out in his favourite restaurant until he eventually invited her to his table, and soon after she became part of his inner circle. The daft girl grew so besotted, that when Hitler sent her home after Britain declared war on Germany, she used her pearl-handled pistol, given to her by him for protection, and shot herself in the head. She's spent years since being nursed by her mother, unable to walk or talk coherently.'

'That's rather extreme,' exclaimed Edward.

'Yes, and there were many others who suffered depression or took their own lives. Even Eva Braun, Hitler's long-term lover, contemplated suicide. Admittedly Hitler was a bugger, playing her and Unity off against each other and she was driven wild with jealousy, but it's as if engaging in a sexual act with the Führer left them unhinged, and they were damned by the very devil himself.'

Edward looked down at his full plate of food. His appetite was much diminished these days. He took a breath, feeling Hugh's eyes bore into him, awaiting a response. He must know he'd seen evidence to even be asking questions. And God, how he longed to let everything out at the moment, reveal the truth about the red file, and the Nazi donation, but he knew if the press exposed the story, he'd be under suspicion for discovering the letter. He leant forward across the table, his hands clenched together. 'Please, Hugh, what's been said here is confidential, not for public consumption.'

Oliver nodded in agreement. 'If you expose the Mayfair Club or suggest any affiliation to this strange sect, it could affect Eddie detrimentally.'

The journalist slumped back in his chair, rubbed his belly and belched loudly. 'Hmm, you've read my mind. Serpentem Corde needs to be investigated fully, and I could only do that by infiltrating the Mayfair Club first. Which I won't,' he added quickly. 'You do know, though,' he continued, staring at Edward, 'that your father-in-law and his unscrupulous colleagues can't be trusted?'

Edward fiddled nervously with a gold cufflink on his shirt sleeve.

'Just be careful of Henry. If he can't corrupt you, he'll ...'

'He'll what?'

'Look, you're his son-in-law. I don't want to speak out of turn.'

'Please.'

Hugh sighed. 'Well, he's got a temper, a bad temper, and he turns it against anyone who doesn't concur with his views. He's been known to ruin reputations so people never work again. Your saving grace is that you married his daughter and give him kudos with your musical gift, but in his eyes, you're either for him or against him.'

Edward gave an uneasy smile, looked at his watch and saw how late it was. 'We best get going. But thank you, Hugh. You've been immensely helpful.'

Both men stood up and shook hands with the journalist, saying their goodbyes and agreeing to meet soon.

Heading outside back along the Brompton Road, Oliver attempted to tug his woollen blazer around his rotund belly to keep out the chilly night air. 'A rather informative evening,' he said quietly.

Edward trudged wearily beside him, remaining quiet until they reached the street corner ready to go their separate ways. 'Yes, although the occult stuff seems ludicrous. I mean, can we can trust this chap, Hugh? The man eats like an animal.'

Oliver smiled, his plump cheeks bulging above his beard. 'From what I know of him, despite being a bon viveur indulging in whisky and wine, he's a big-hearted man, who loves his family and believes in justice.' He reached out to touch Edward's arm in a gesture of comfort. 'It may well be bunkum. But as Hugh says, be wary of all of them, including that chap you bumped into today. They could have ulterior motives.'

Edward nodded sadly in agreement.

Chapter 31

Tuesday, 18th December 1945

I couldn't believe my eyes when I looked through the window and saw an emerald green Rolls-Royce phantom pull up outside our house. It was eight in the morning and I was on a high of adrenaline about our day ahead.

'Be up and dressed in your finest outfits and bring your coats, gloves, hats and scarves,' I'd told Gabi and Hannah the night before.

'But why?' they'd cried.

'Because we're off on a mystery journey.'

They had no idea where we were going or why. I'd even kept Tommy in the dark and not being able to tell my secret was almost killing me.

I ran outside, feeling rather glitzy in one of Aunt Betty's coats, an ankle length fox fur with matching hat, laughing to myself when I saw some of our neighbour's curtains twitching.

'Whoa,' said Gabi, stepping outside into the wintry chill, looking dashing in a smart tweed suit, 'this is ritzy. At your service Miss Grable and Miss Hayworth,' he joked, taking off his trilby and opening the car door for us as we attempted to climb in demurely.

Noticing the snow start to fall through the windows, I smiled; nature's decorating services and right on cue.

'Where are we going?' asked Hannah. She gazed at me from underneath her black cloche hat, looking so grown up in her fitted 'princess coat' with padded shoulders and lace-up boots.

'To London, Hannah.'

'But why?'

'I told you, it's a surprise.'

'Is this costing us anything?' asked Gabi, ever the cynic.

'It hasn't cost anything, Gabi,' I replied. 'It's a gift!'

'From who?'

'Goodness, you two. Wait and see.'

We finally arrived in Hackney and the roads seemed unusually quiet. The snow now swirling down in great flurries had fallen so much in the last few hours that it had covered all the familiar streets and the demolished buildings in a thick white blanket.

'Everything looks so pretty,' murmured Hannah, and it certainly did. The bare trees bereft of their leaves looked almost haunting, transformed into a mass of spidery white feathers.

Gabi peered through the window. 'Where the hell is this?'

'It's Sandringham Road where we grew up,' I answered cheerfully just as the car pulled up where our old house used to be.

'What!' Gabi craned his neck and stared at me. 'Is this some kind of sick joke? Why would we want to come back to the place where we were bombed and our parents were killed?'

I took a breath. 'Because I wanted you to meet Dad here.'

They both looked at me, their eyes foggy with confusion.

We all clambered out of the Rolls into the bitter cold and I saw Daddy standing there. He was shivering and rubbing his gloved hands together for warmth as snowflakes stuck to his smart overcoat and hat. He waved, shouting hello as Gabi and Hannah stood motionless, numb, no doubt, with disbelief.

'Dad, is that really you?' asked Gabi, his legs trembling as if they might give way.

I felt tearful when he replied, 'Yes, son,' and they wandered towards each other and hugged. It was strange seeing them both together, now Gabi was six feet tall, the same height as Dad.

'I don't understand,' cried Hannah, staring at him, her eyes wide with shock. 'You were supposed to be dead.' Her little face crumpled and she bent over, covering her face with her hands, bursting into wracking sobs.

My instinct was to run to her, give her a comforting hug, but Daddy got there first, pulling her close, holding her until her tears subsided. I knew he might not remember them clearly, but I could see love radiating from him. It was as if his heart recognised what his head hadn't caught up with.

'Your sister and I have been corresponding for months,' he said, stroking Hannah's hair, 'and with her help, I wanted to meet you both here, so I could see where we once lived.'

'Corresponding for months,' spluttered Hannah as she wriggled out of Dad's embrace. She scowled at me. 'How could you keep that a secret? You lied to us.'

'Yes,' said Gabi, gazing at the space where our house once stood. 'You lied to us.'

Daddy raised his eyebrows, looking towards me for guidance.

'Hannah, Gabi,' I said firmly, waiting for them to look at me. 'After we were bombed, everyone thought Dad was a goner, but he was pulled from the rubble with concussion. He couldn't remember anything, not even his name. I stumbled across his photo in the paper, and we met up, and planned this ... to surprise you.'

'Can't remember anything. So what do you call yourself?' asked Gabi.

'Edward!' Daddy replied with a smile. 'Edward Chopard.'

They both stood there staring at him, their bodies rooted to the spot as if they still couldn't believe he was real.

Daddy clenched his hands together. 'Look, I know it's confusing, but I promise I'll explain more. Now who's hungry? Let's go have lunch.'

Thankfully, they both seemed to relax when food was mentioned, their stiffness melting away like defrosting snowmen.

'Right, follow me,' I said, leading the way. I knew where we were going but it was meant to be a secret, so I took them along some unfamiliar routes, and after a twenty-minute trek through an icy flurry, we turned into Old Montague Street. And there it was, over the road, Bloom's kosher restaurant with its big front window. Truth is we'd stopped being kosher long ago, hunger dictating our needs, but we always came here for Sunday lunch to give Mama a break, so I hoped it might trigger old memories for Daddy.

We stepped inside, cold and wet. I don't think any of us had ever been so grateful to warm up.

'I remember this place,' said Hannah. She finally cracked a smile as we all sat down, pulling off our gloves and hats and struggling with frozen fingers to undo our coat buttons.

'You know, where we are right now is only minutes away from where Jack the Ripper's victims were found,' whispered Gabi with a smirk. 'Their bodies were found horrifically mutilated.'

I glared at him. He was seemingly over his sulk and back to his usual brotherly taunting, and I so wanted this place to trigger happy things.

The waiter placed some pickled cucumbers in the middle of the table and by mutual consent, Daddy ordered their chicken soup for starters.

'Joe, where have you been?' asked the owner, Mr Bloom, as he walked over to our table, gazing at Dad with a mystified expression. 'I heard rumours you were dead.'

Daddy jumped up to shake his hand, smiling at the small dark-haired man. 'Good to meet you, sir. And, yes, I admit, the coffin lid gets harder to open.'

Mr Bloom laughed raucously. 'Ah, still the same old rascal. And are these your children?' He looked at us all one by one. 'My, how you've grown.' Before we could even answer, he was distracted and rushed off to serve another customer.

It was obvious from Daddy's face that he didn't remember anything: not the owner, the place, the food, maybe even us. It was like rewriting our family history from scratch.

During our feast of latkes, matzo balls and salt beef sandwiches, I watched Gabi and Hannah's faces as Daddy explained about his severe amnesia and his mastery of the piano. They both leant forward, trying to take everything in, their shiny eyes widening.

'So will you spend Hanukkah with us?' asked Hannah plaintively. She sank her teeth into her rye bread, the salt beef hanging out from between her lips as she stopped for a few moments to lick each one of her fingers in turn, but never once taking her eyes off Daddy.

I dipped my head down, dreading the reply, but watched from the corner of my eye as Dad stroked away some of her hair.

'No, sorry, Hannah, I can't.' He pursed his lips, wondering I'm sure, how best to phrase things. 'Over the years a lot has happened. I didn't know about you three, and, well, I'm married again now with a young son.'

Hannah visibly paled, nearly choking as she tried to swallow. She put down her sandwich, her eyes pleading, reaching out her hands to touch his. 'Pleassse, Daddy, stay with us ... just for Hanukkah.'

Boy did she have that look down to a tee. Mama always said 'those eyes' could make even a devout Rabbi feel guilty.

'I'm sorry, Hannah, I can't,' he replied firmly.

Her obvious heartache spoke for us all. None of us wanted to hear about his new family.

We continued to eat in awkward silence. And Daddy, well, he just sat there fumbling with his cutlery, looking sad. I so wanted to comfort him. He was hiding something, something painful. Even his breathing, those short shallow rasps that got stuck in his chest, showed he was scared ... too scared to let down his guard for even a moment.

He rummaged around inside his jacket pocket and pulled out three small boxes. 'Here's a little something for Christmas or as you call it, Hanukkah.'

We all stared at the Chopard gift boxes as he handed them to each of us.

'Go on,' he urged us with a smile. 'I want to see your faces as you open them.'

Gabi gave his box a good shake trying to guess what it was, whilst Hannah ripped hers open, her eyes dancing. 'Oh, gosh, Daddy, this is bootiful,' she exclaimed, plucking out the gold and sapphire ring and slipping it onto her forefinger. She pushed her hand towards us beaming and then leapt out of her seat, plonking herself on Daddy's knee as if she were a baby instead of a teenager.

Gabi gawped at his diamond cufflinks as he cupped them in his hand. 'Wow, these are proper swanky.'

Mine was a gold ring in the shape of a heart with three diamonds in the centre, and we all had the same tiny inscription inside, *Love Always Dad—1945.*

I reached over to kiss Daddy on the cheek. It was awkward with Hannah still perched on his knee hogging the spotlight, but quick as a flash he pretended to steal both our noses, pinching them playfully with his fingers like he used to when we were little and we both giggled. It was heartening to get a sense of our old fun-loving Dad again.

He looked relieved that we were happy. 'I'm so glad you all like them. I wanted to give a memento of our time together.' He checked his watch. 'Goodness, it's gone four already. We'll need to leave so your chauffeur can get you home in one piece.'

Gabi and Hannah's gloomy faces mirrored what I felt as their head and shoulders drooped like the leaves on a parched plant. The day had sped by too fast.

Dad walked over to a waiter, paid the bill, and then handed me a ten-pound note as Hannah and Gabi stood there open-mouthed.

I stared at it in my hand. It was a huge amount when you're used to ten-bob notes, silver and coppers. 'Dad, what's this for? You've already given us expensive gifts.'

He tugged on his overcoat. 'No, you have it. It's for Yule-tide treats.'

'But this is too much!'

He wagged a gloved finger at me. 'No buts. I want you to have the best holidays ever.'

It was nice of him, of course it was ... but we didn't want his money ... we just wanted him.

'Will we ever see you again?' asked Hannah, looking up at him with a worried frown.

'Yes, Hannah ... and very soon, I promise.'

We all hoped he meant it, reluctantly slipping on our coats, hats and gloves when the door creaked open and a blonde woman wandered in wearing a black cape and beret.

'Joe?' she said, staring at him.

Dad stared back blankly as if he'd seen an apparition.

She walked towards him, still staring. 'Joe, is it really you? I did a double take when I walked past the window.'

'Rachel?'

She took a deep breath, holding onto a nearby chair to steady herself. 'Joe, where have you been? I've missed you.'

I recognised her instantly: that sculpted face and sea blue eyes. She hadn't changed a bit. I'd been in the same class as her son David at school and sometimes went to their house for tea. I knew it was just the two of them. Mrs Morgan was a widow and I often felt sad that David didn't have his dad around.

'Excuse me, aren't you David Morgan's mum?' I blurted out.

'Yes, that's right,' she said studying me. 'Gosh, Ruth, is that you?'

I nodded.

'My, you're looking very sophisticated these days. And this must be Gabi and Hannah?' She smiled at them as they said hello shyly.

'Rachel,' murmured Daddy, 'you've been on my mind for so long.'

All three of us looked at each other realising something odd was going on. Our father was a dithering mess, ushering Mrs Morgan outside as we trailed behind, feeling a gust of cold air in our faces.

I watched Daddy kiss Mrs Morgan's hand whilst he asked her to wait, before beckoning us to him so she couldn't hear. 'Children, today has been very special, but I need you all to keep a secret.'

We all stood there shivering, wondering what it was.

'As you know, I'm now a well-known pianist,' he continued, 'therefore if you want to stay in touch ...'

'We do, we do,' cried Hannah, grabbing onto his arm.

Daddy looked worryingly serious, his eyes dark and intense. 'Then you must never reveal I'm your father to anyone.'

We all nodded in agreement, but when I tried to speak, feeling confused, he put his finger to his lips and whispered, 'One day soon, I'll explain.' He hugged us all in turn and waved goodbye, waiting until we'd all climbed back into the chauffeur-driven Rolls he'd hired for us.

The driver turned on the ignition and I watched him wipe the mist off the windscreen with a cloth as we all peeked out of the frost-covered windows watching Daddy and Mrs Morgan together in their own little bubble, oblivious to the world. And then I gasped when I saw them kiss tenderly and walk off hand-in-hand along the frozen pavements of Old Montague Street.

'So *that's* Mrs Morgan?' said Gabi, his brows knitting together.

'And why did she say she missed him?' said Hannah, voicing what we all were thinking.

I tried to settle my stiff body back into the seat, but I was a mass of jagged edges. The past was all we had to hold onto and it was dawning on me that Daddy wasn't quite the devoted family man we'd always thought. As the driver crawled through traffic, resentment bubbled to the surface. 'Maybe they had an affair,' I said. It was glaringly obvious that they'd once been lovers.

'Don't say that!' shouted Gabi, scowling at me.

Hannah's eyes flashed with anger and her lower lip trembled. 'Yes, don't say that! Daddy loved Mama. He didn't have to see us again, you know. He's got a new family now, but he still spent time with us, bought us presents and gave us a ton of money. He's my daddy and I love him, and all I care about is that he's here and I've seen him again and I never thought I would.'

Hannah's voice was full of hurt outrage. She didn't want to hear anything bad about Daddy. And why would she? She'd only just discovered he was still alive. Tears rolled down her cheeks. I leant over to hug her but she shoved me away.

'Sorry, Gabi. Sorry, Hannah,' I mumbled, feeling a pang of guilt as they both stared out of the window pretending I didn't exist.

That night I lay in bed, turning things over in my mind. Okay, I'd overreacted, but I was hurt—an old love of Daddy's appearing from the past on what should have been *our* special day—a day I so desperately wanted to be perfect. Out of nowhere, the grief came again like a black tidal wave rising within, and I could only breathe and wait, praying it would ebb away, leaving me once more in a numb kind of peace.

I drifted off, waking in the early hours, my head foggy with sleep and strange dreams. I was stuck in a house, a big house, and it had so many rooms, it was like a maze—and I can hear him, Daddy, in the distance, calling my name, and I'm crying, trying to get to him, but I can't, wandering through hallways and rooms, searching endlessly, round and round, until I'm lost.

I felt scared and sat up, but the room's full of shadows snaking the walls and I think someone's there, so I panic and switch on the light, taking a breath, scanning the room—everything's okay—everything's fine—it was just a dream. But I've got the jitters and I'm too scared to be back in the dark, and I definitely don't want to sleep, only Dad's on my mind, so I grabbed some paper and a pen from my bedside cabinet and wrote him a letter.

18th December 1945

Dearest Daddy,

Thank you so much for lunch, our beautiful jewellery and the Christmas money. It was the best day ever, apart from all the times we spent with you and Mama. But I did wonder why you seem so sad. I love you, we all love you, so why do you have to keep us a secret? Would your wife be angry if she knew?

And Daddy, I hope you don't think me rude, but why did Mrs Morgan say she missed you? Did you

once love her? Did you ever love Mama? Be honest,
Daddy. I just want the truth.

Have a blessed Hanukkah and please visit us soon.

Love always,
Ruth

I sealed it inside an envelope, ready for posting, hoping he'd give me some kind of answer. There are only so many people we could share Daddy with, I thought. I couldn't bear to lose him again.

Saturday, 22nd December 1945

E dward sat at his desk going over last minute paperwork
when the phone rang. He barely had time to answer before
Oliver's voice blasted down the receiver. 'Have you seen
the papers, Eddie?'

'No, why?'

'Do you remember that Emmerton fellow, the journalist we
dined with at The Brompton Grill?'

'Yes, of course.'

'Well ... he's dead!'

Edward clenched the phone, pressing it into his cheek.
'What! Where did you hear that?'

'It's headline news. Meet me at The Pavilion as soon as
you can.'

'Okay, will do.' He replaced the receiver and wandered into
the living room feeling shaken, struggling to think of excuses to
get away. 'Connie, my angel,' he said, his voice hoarse. 'I need
to meet Oli about concert schedules. He's been such a support
recently, helping me organise my time.'

Connie turned from talking to one of the maids and stepped
towards him, holding Alfie in her arms. 'Darling, that's fine. All

us gossiping women would only bore you silly anyway, although Lady Dukesbury will miss flirting with you.'

He smiled, thankful for the timing, remembering his wife had invited a gaggle of former debutantes over for afternoon tea. He kissed Connie on the lips and then nuzzled Alfie's soft curls as his son gurgled with delight. 'Well, have fun with the fillies. See you anon.'

'Ciao, darling,' she replied as they touched hands.

Happy that he'd rescued his domestic life, he rushed outside and sprinted five minutes down the road to a local newsagent, grabbing several newspapers, sprinkling coins all over the counter as he apologised to the owner. He raced back, jumped into his Bentley and sped over to the Pavilion tearoom in Kensington Gardens where he could meet Oliver in relative privacy.

Edward sat at a discreet table in the corner waiting for Oliver with a large pot of tea in front of him. Rifling through papers, he stared at the headlines. The *Daily Mail* screamed: **NAZI DEATH OF HORROR**. *The Times*: **DEATH OF A SOCIALIST.** And *The Daily Mirror*: **FIND NAZI MURDERER.** He picked up *The Mirror*, reading avidly, his heart thumping in his chest.

> Divorced Journalist, Hugh Emmerton, forty-two, was found murdered in his two-bedroom apartment in Central London on the evening of December 21st. Blindfolded and suspended by his ankles from the exposed beams of a ceiling rafter, with his hands tied behind his back, the victim's head was shaved and his unlit gas oven left on.
>
> Police believe he had been there for over twelve hours, his body only discovered when the stench of gas seeped into neighbouring apartments.

Mirror Chairman, Guy Bartholomew said, "We hope the killer of this horrific murder will be found quickly. Hugh was a fine journalist with a rare social conscience. He will be sorely missed."

Edward felt nauseous, pushing away his cup of tea. He heard the door squeak open and looked up to see his friend rush in with such speed that his unbuttoned overcoat flapped around him as if he were a bird in flight.

Flushed and sweating, Oliver sat down panting nosily. 'Have you read what happened?'

Edward reached out to touch his arm, attempting to offer some sort of comfort to them both. 'Yes, I feel quite ill. What kind of madman would do this?'

Oliver slouched forward, his breathing still heavy. 'Well, what you read in the papers is, I'm afraid, a watered-down version of what actually transpired. They couldn't report everything, it just wasn't deemed suitable for a family newspaper, but this man was horrifyingly tortured.'

Picking up the white china teapot with trembling hands, Edward poured his friend some tea, pushing the teacup and saucer towards him. 'How do you know?'

Oliver dipped a teaspoon into the sugar bowl, sprinkled three heaped spoonsful into his cup, stirring it quickly, and gulped back some of the sweet black tea. 'Let's just say that two of my colleagues happen to be the forensic pathologist and mortician dealing with the case. They allowed me a private viewing of his corpse this morning. It was a sickening experience and one that will give me nightmares for many a year.'

'So what happened?'

Swallowing hard, Oliver's eyes widened. 'He was lashed so fiercely his back was a mass of welts and torn flesh.'

'Oh God!'

'And far worse,' he continued, his face twisted, as if picturing the gruesome image in his mind. 'His liver and kidneys had been hacked out with some kind of serrated knife. The carpet where he'd been suspended was soaked with blood.' He clenched his hands together. 'It appears the killer wanted him to die in slow and painful agony. Gassed, and then butchered—strung up like meat in an abattoir.'

Edward's head fell forward as he retched, making guttural, strangulated sounds.

'Christ, are you all right, Eddie?'

Edward leapt up and rushed across the room to the lavatories, leaning over the nearest sink to vomit, his head spinning. He kept retching, his stomach churning, not knowing when he'd feel right, when he would function normally.

Staggering back, pale and drained, he slumped back down on his chair. 'I'm so dreadfully sorry,' he mumbled.

Oliver smiled at him sympathetically. 'I understand. It's a deeply disturbing death of a man we'd only recently met. It makes you question your own mortality ... that our lives are held together by such fragile thread.'

'But he was such a nice, friendly chap. What on earth could he have done to warrant this?'

'Well, he wasn't a Jew,' replied Oliver, shaking his head sadly, 'so it's not a racist attack, but I have wondered if it was perhaps political. Hugh had a column in the *Daily Mirror* where he was critical of right wing politics, especially the extremists, which is why he was so knowledgeable about the Right Club.'

'But who would go this far?'

'Somebody with skeletons rattling in a cupboard. Someone scared. I have a hunch.'

'About what?'

'The last time we saw Hugh ... you told him about the Mayfair Club. Do you remember?'

Edward nodded.

'He had a determined glint in his eye, that whatever we said, he intended to infiltrate the group and investigate ... to discover the truth about Serpentem Corde.'

'Oh, yes, that supernatural nonsense,' scoffed Edward. He scanned Oliver's face. 'You think Henry did it!'

'One can only speculate, but remember what Hugh said about Henry—that he had a temper, and he'd turn on anyone who went against him. He wouldn't want the press snooping around ... not with all his crazy secrets.'

Edward sat back in his chair, the chilling image of Emmerton's corpse stamped on his mind. For all Henry's blinkered views, for all his misguided dealings with Hitler, he just didn't believe he could be that evil. He remembered his kind words only a few years ago. *We know you don't have loved ones, so embrace Lizzie and I as your refuge. I've always wanted a son. It's been my dearest wish.* What he'd said had meant so much, he'd often thought of it. 'It's not Henry,' he said, his voice hoarse with emotion.

Oliver tilted his head on one side. 'How can you be so sure?'

'I just know. He's a most generous man and he has a soft side. He might have a temper and he might be guilty of a lot of things, a lot of terrible things, but not this.' He cleared his throat. 'There are other more likely suspects. Ramsay for instance. He's been in the clink so he'd be pretty hard-boiled, and there's also that rather creepy, Douglas Hetherington-Jones.' He twisted his wedding ring with his fingers, not knowing what to do with his hands. 'I can't imagine anyone would do something that depraved, though, and risk being caught.'

'Agreed,' said Oliver, nodding his head. 'No one would be that crazy, but what have they got at their fingertips? Huge amounts of cash that's what—to hire someone if they wanted. There's someone out there, greedy enough to murder someone for money.'

Edward let a long sigh. 'You're right.'

'And I believe, guilty or not, your father-in-law, a man with his finger on the society pulse, has the answers.'

'Hmm,' murmured Edward. 'He must know something.'

Oliver picked up the teapot and poured himself another cup. 'Need a refill, Eddie?'

'No, thanks, I still feel queasy.'

Oliver slurped some tea. 'Perhaps, if we could source more letters from Hitler there may well be clues.'

'Yes, I'll have to get hold of that red file again.' He leant forward, trying to focus. 'And I've got to discover what's in that precious wine cellar of his. There's something strange going on down there. He's so protective of the key and I'm bloody curious.' He drummed his fingers on the table, staring into space.

'What's going on in that head of yours, Eddie?'

'I've had an idea.'

'Go on?'

'There's a New Year masquerade ball being held at Mortis Hall, Henry's country estate. Connie and I will, of course, attend and stay over, but I can invite you as one of my guests. All the Mayfair Club members will be there along with their wives and other elite members of society.'

Oliver peered at him, looking confused. 'And then what? They're hardly going to confess.'

'No, but there'll be hundreds of guests attending, masked up as historical figures. So whilst Henry is holding court, we'll have an opportunity to grab the keys and access his office and cellar.'

'Ah, I see,' said Oliver, his face lighting up. 'And that means alibis when correspondence goes missing.'

'Exactly, it's the perfect opportunity. We just need to count down the days.'

Chapter 33

Tuesday, 25th December 1945

Christmas in Richmond with the Douglas-Scotts was a pleasant affair; the food delicious and plentiful, much vintage wine drunk, and extravagant presents exchanged all round. Edward carefully unwrapped the last gift: a framed drawing by illustrator, C. Allan Gilbert, entitled, *All Is Vanity*.

'Happy Christmas to you both from Lizzy and me,' barked Henry. 'Have you seen the illusion yet?' He leaned back into his red Louis VIII armchair with claw feet, looking like a king holding court on his elaborate throne.

Edward and Connie gazed at the artwork. The illustration portrayed a woman admiring herself in the mirror, but as they studied it, they realised an overlay of shading made the image of the woman appear to be a human skull.

'Ah, yes, I see it now. Why, thank you, Henry, it's, um, remarkable.' Connie smirked. 'Yes, thank you, Daddy.'

Edward and Connie glanced at each other with a bemused expression that revealed they would not be hanging the bizarre piece in the Chopard residence any time soon.

Henry kicked off his embroidered slippers and placed his large broad feet onto the red cushioned footstool in front of him. He reached over, picking up a glass of his favourite malt whisky from the side table and took a swig. 'You're welcome. It's a collector's piece and rather valuable, you know. The visual metaphor meaning that surface beauty can still appear ugly when seen in a different light.'

Edward nodded and smiled out of politeness. *Typical.* The macabre artistry was so characteristic of Henry, always contentious—proffering something he knew would sit uncomfortably with your psyche.

'Come sit,' commanded Henry, signalling to the chairs. The couple did as requested, attempting to relax, exchanging superficial pleasantries and drinking champagne whilst baby Alfie gabbled away happily in his own baby language, making his grandmother, Elizabeth, immensely happy as she bounced him on her knee.

Several hours later, Edward found himself alone. Connie had gone upstairs to rest. Her unexpected second pregnancy had surprised them both and sapped her energy. Little Alfie was sound asleep, Elizabeth was with the butler clarifying details of their New Year's party and Henry had disappeared to take an urgent business call in his office.

Sipping another glass of bubbly, Edward relaxed on a mahogany loveseat by the tiled fireplace full of blazing logs that crackled in the flames. He looked up at the gilt-framed painting above the hearth and shuddered. It was Henry's great grandfather, Lord Angus Douglas-Scott, regally dressed in the black and grey tartan of their Gaelic ancestral clan. His piercing eyes appeared to look right through him, judging him sternly.

He closed his eyes, blocking him out, the warmth of the fire and the champagne soothing him as his thoughts wandered back to his guilty secret, seven days earlier.

As soon as Rachel walked into Bloom's that day, his legs turned to jelly and everything else ceased to exist as electricity surged through him.

He hadn't planned for this. He prided himself on his ethics. He only meant to ask how she was, talk a little, connect the dots of the past—but then there was that one chaste kiss—so innocently lethal, deliciously addictive. Craving more they'd found a darkened doorway, their tongues exploring each other's mouths with passion. Then with urgency as if on a mission, trying not to slip on icy pavements, they walked hand-in-hand back to her house, fifteen minutes away in Farleigh Road.

Rushing upstairs to her bedroom, they pulled apart buttons, tearing off each other's clothes, until they were both naked except for Rachel's nude lace stockings enhancing her honey-coloured skin.

'Stockings,' he gasped, collapsing backwards onto a rocking chair in the corner of the room. He reached out, straddling her across his lap, feeling her moist heat as he lifted his hips and urgently thrust inside her, plunging deeper and deeper as she dug her nails into his back, throwing her head back in ecstasy, the chair rocking back and forth in rhythmic movements.

'I've had these silks since before the war,' she whispered, pressing her full breasts against his chest. 'I wash them gently, dry them away from the sun.'

'You've kept them well,' he murmured. He stood up, staggering a little as she clung onto him, her long legs wrapped around his waist.

'Yes, Joe ... because I can't risk losing something that's so hard to replace.'

He stared into her eyes, desperate to make up for their missing past. Throwing her onto the bed, he spread her thighs apart with his hands and buried his face between them, giving her tiny butterfly kisses as she wriggled against him, moaning with pleasure. They made love for hours, breaking their connection only when thirst took over and he ran down to the kitchen, bringing back a dusty bottle of port she'd had for years, along with two glasses. And with lips tasting of fruity wine they resumed kissing, stroking and licking each other's bodies until they lay back, exhausted, on white linen sheets.

'I could die right now with a contented smile on my face,' she said softly.

He stroked her hair, watching the golden strands fall between his fingers. 'Me too, my love. You are like death to me.'

'Death?' She wrinkled her nose, looking puzzled.

'Surrendering to a force more powerful than my own will. And that is like death ... but a very beautiful one.'

'You were always poetic,' she said, leaning over him, tracing the creases around his eyes with the tip of her finger. 'And you're still the same Joe ... just these lines have appeared. Where have you been hiding these last few years?'

He squirmed, looking away, anywhere but into her eyes. 'One day, my love, I'll tell you my story ... but not now, not when our time together is so precious.'

She smiled at him lovingly, her eyes flicking across his face, as if the truth was there unspoken, as if she understood.

'It's strange, Joe, even when your house was bombed and I couldn't stop crying, I still felt you close ... like a warm breeze on my skin, as if your spirit were walking with me.'

His eyes watered, he felt exactly the same and for the first time in years, he felt a deep sense of peace. 'My spirit is always walking with you, my love.' He pulled her close, their noses touching, their arms and legs entwined.

They fell asleep to the sound of icy sleet clattering against the window until he awoke with a start, feeling disorientated. He looked at his watch. *What!* He sat up in panic. It was 2 a.m. Ten hours had mystifyingly evaporated. She always had that effect, taking him to a sacred place where time ceased to exist.

Carefully disentangling himself from her limbs, he climbed out of bed and pulled on his clothes. Grabbing a pen and some scrap paper out of his jacket pocket he scribbled a note.

I can't believe I've found you again. I promise we will see each other soon.

You made me love you Joe x

He placed it on her bedside table, underneath one of the empty wine glasses and turned to watch her sleeping. She looked so serene, lying against the pillow with a contented smile on her lips. He bent down, kissing her gently on the forehead, not wanting to wake her as she wriggled and murmured in her sleep. 'My beloved Rachel', he whispered, 'I love you so very much.'

Tiptoeing downstairs, he shut the front door quietly, walking out into a stormy night, the wind blowing furiously through the trees. He pulled his coat around him, hailstones whipping against his face as he looked along every side street, trying to remember where he'd parked his Bentley. When he finally climbed into his car soaking wet, and placed his gloved hands on the steering wheel, buried memories flooded back—arriving home late to an angry Rose, because of lost time with Rachel.

He pulled up outside his Knightsbridge residence forty-five minutes later. Walking inside he switched on the lights in the living room to find Connie waiting up for him. Was history repeating itself? Moonlight streamed through the window illuminating her tear-stained face as she sat on the edge of her chair clutching her swollen belly.

'Sorry, darling, long day' he said, dropping down in front of her, holding her tightly. She said nothing and he felt so bad, so sinful. Could she tell, read his mind? This wasn't him. He was a decent man. Why, he asked himself, why did I do that?

'Dreaming of something nice? You'll burn the corneas of your eyes staring into the fire like that.'

Edward jolted, nearly knocking his champagne flying, brought back to reality by Henry's booming voice as he entered the room. 'Oh, just trying to relax. I don't get much time to sit and think.'

Henry sat down on his throne-like chair and opened a small tin, taking out some tobacco and pushing it into the bowl of his pipe using a silver tamper. 'Hmm, know that feeling. You should try smoking one of these. It's a wonderful calming ritual.'

'Perhaps I will,' said Edward, staring at the ornate instrument. 'That's quite a specimen you have there.'

'It certainly is. You need a good tight-grained wood if you want a decent smoke and this old fellow does the job perfectly. It's hand carved from a straight-grained Mediterranean briar, an extreme rarity in nature, and contains 126 grammes of platinum along with a smattering of diamonds placed tastefully around the edge.'

'Goodness, must have cost a fortune.'

'Indeed, but it is all part of the pomp and ceremony. There's a certain satisfaction in taking it out of its padded box, packing the tobacco into the bowl just right,' said Henry with a contented smile. He lit the tobacco, placing the stem of the pipe between his lips and inhaled deeply. 'Ah, lovely,' he groaned, 'that comforting aromatic smell. All I need now is to put my feet up, have another few drams of whisky and I've got the makings of a perfect evening.'

Edward laughed. 'It does sound comforting. I must get myself a pipe one day.'

'Oh, don't worry, Eddie, I've got a few knocking around. I'll find you one later. Are you looking forward to our Masquerade Ball?'

'Very much so.'

'Any ideas on what historical figure you will come as?'

'Oh, I think it has to be Mozart.'

'Fabulous! Perfect choice.'

Edward leant towards him. 'Any idea what you will be wearing?'

Henry vigorously sucked on his pipe before easing it out from between his lips and exhaling a stream of smoke. 'Oh, I will be Henry VIII no less, administrating a good spanking in place of a beheading to anyone who misbehaves,' he added with a roar of laughter.

'Ha-ha, but of course. Speaking about the ball, would you mind if I invited my good friend, Oliver Jungston?'

Henry slurped some whisky. 'Ah, yes, Dr Jungston. I remember him well. He gave that charming speech at your wedding.'

'Yes, he's a good man. In fact, he shares much of your philosophy about the Jews.'

'Does he now?' Henry raised his thick, silver eyebrows, his grey eyes crinkling at the corners.

'Indeed, I've already told him there's an admirable establishment where you can safely vent all your anti-Semitic rage.' He felt a flutter of nerves, sowing new seeds, ploughing dangerous land, wondering if he'd get a confession.

'I wouldn't quite say that,' replied Henry, avoiding eye contact. 'As you already know, Eddie, we're just boys together sharing a drink over mutual causes. You haven't been for a while. I know you're often busy with rehearsals, but now things are calmer, you must come along and bring the good doctor with you.'

'Thank you, Henry, I will. I want to understand more about the basis of your beliefs. We are family after all.'

'Then let's drink to family and mutual crusades,' said Henry, his jowly face ruddy from the warm fire.

And raising up their glasses, they shouted, 'Cheers.'

Chapter 34

Monday, 31st December 1945

Unexpectedly, for all of us, our first gentile Christmas had been truly wonderful. We'd been guests at Tommy's house in Poole sitting around the dining table with his parents, eating tons of delicious treats whilst we pulled noisy crackers and wore silly hats. It was a welcome distraction from work and the frequent nightmares I'd been having about Daddy. They were always ominous and dark as if there was something there … a presence watching and waiting, keeping us apart, but I didn't know who or why. It was just my worries, I guess, trying to work themselves through, but I felt exhausted, waking up through the night. I got so jumpy, I began checking under the bed and inside the wardrobe before I went to sleep.

Thankfully the bond between Tommy and me was stronger than ever. He even, kind of, proposed over dessert, stating, 'With this mince pie I thee wed,' as he attempted to shovel a huge spoonful into my mouth. A ripple of laughter went around the table and everyone clinked their glasses. 'I mean it, though, Ruth Goldberg,' he whispered in my ear, 'one day, I will marry you.' And something inside me exploded like a shooting star, because at long last, I'd found someone who, bizarrely, found me loveable.

He never once mentioned the pianist, so I hadn't had to lie. I'm sure, deep down, he hoped that I'd let go of a grief-fuelled fantasy.

The only problem had been batting off questions from his mother, Frances, her glossy pink lips firing fluffy bullets as I struggled to barricade her from the truth.

'It must be tough not celebrating Hanukkah with your relatives?'

'Do you miss your parents?'

'Where are your aunts and uncles?'

And then Hannah caused a hoo-ha blurting out, 'We can't wait to see Daddy again.'

Tommy's parents glanced at each other in confusion, and I had to invent something fast. 'She means an old neighbour we called Dad,' I'd said, but it was a close shave and one that made my heart race. So before we joined the Joneses for New Year that evening, I called a family meeting over breakfast.

Taking the cosy off the teapot I refilled our cups, trying not to slop tea everywhere. 'Remember, this is serious, both of you. We must do as Daddy asked and not let anything slip. Do we all agree?'

'Okay, sorry I blabbed,' Hannah said, peering at me through blonde curls as she munched on some toast. 'But surely we can trust Tommy and his parents?'

'It's not that I don't trust them, Hannah, but Tommy's father is a journalist who's interviewed Daddy.'

'But why can't we just admit he's our dad? It's not fair.'

Gabi laughed smugly as he rocked backwards on his chair. 'Hannah, you really live up to being a ditzy blonde.'

Hannah's bottom lip trembled and her eyes welled up.

'Gabi, that's hurtful.' I turned to Hannah, trying to be gentle. 'Remember, Daddy's famous now and we are part of a big news story that Tommy and his father might find hard to keep secret. Can you imagine the headlines if the papers got wind of it: **Virtuoso, Edward Chopard, reunited with long-lost children.** It could ruin his life. I mean, his new family don't know anything about us.'

Gabi turned the bottle of ketchup upside down and whacked the bottom with his hand to tip sauce onto his scrambled eggs, making me flinch with every slap. 'Yep, you can't trust any reporter to keep schtum with a story like that. It could skyrocket their careers.'

Hannah wrapped her hands around her teacup as if the warmth gave her comfort. 'But surely that means your relationship with Tommy is based on lies.'

'Honesty isn't always the best policy,' I said, sipping my tea, 'if exposing the truth could hurt people. I would love to shout from the rooftops how proud we are of Daddy, but he's asked us not to, for reasons he best understands.'

'Yeah, so don't gossip, squealer,' snapped Gabi. He nudged her arm with his elbow as he fixed her with a steely look.

Naturally, Hannah burst into tears, leapt up from her chair and raced to the bathroom, slamming the door.

I glared at Gabi, frustrated with his endless sarcasm. 'You could try developing some tact, dear brother.' I jumped up from the table to go and comfort her.

'I'm only teasing. Sorry, Hannah,' he yelled.

Frankly that 'sorry' was amazing. He never apologised for anything these days.

Somehow they got over their spat but part of me understood my little sister only too well. Why should we collude to hide Dad's secrets when he wouldn't confide in us?

Later that day as I helped Hannah go through her wardrobe and choose an outfit for the night ahead, he was there, inside my head constantly, and I wondered who he was with and what he was doing. 'Happy New Year to you, Daddy,' I murmured, hoping somehow he'd hear me. 'I will raise a toast to you tonight wherever you are.'

Chapter 35

Monday, 31ˢᵗ December 1945

E dward climbed out of the red Rolls-Royce, yawned and
stretched. It had been a long four-hour journey. They'd
sat in traffic almost the entire way after being chauffeured
from London in two separate cars so they could bring Oliver, his
valet, and Connie's personal maid. Alfie remained safely at home
with the nanny.

'Welcome to Mortis Hall,' announced the butler grandly as
he opened the imposing double panelled doors.

'Hello, dear Cranford,' replied Connie with a smile as they
all wandered into the marble reception hall. 'Where are Mummy
and Daddy?'

'Good evening, Mr and Mrs Chopard, and Dr Jungston,'
said Cranford before giving a formal bow. He was a tall, thin
man with a shiny, bald head surrounded by a ring of dark hair,
reminiscent of a monk. 'Sincerest apologies sent from Lord
and Lady Douglas-Scott. They are busy getting ready for this
evening's event. Allow me to escort you to your rooms.'

Walking with a stoop, he led them along the labyrinthine
hallways of the rambling mansion. Two young footmen in black

and yellow striped waistcoats and tailcoats trudged behind, weighed down with their vast collection of luggage.

Arriving just after six, they had plenty of time to get ready, with the help of their servants. And two hours later they were attired in their full regalia to attend the Ball.

'Eddie, darling, you do look dashing as Mozart,' exclaimed Connie, clapping her hands together excitedly.

'Do I angel?' Edward strutted up and down the room in his costume: a white ruffled cravat, a blue and gold brocade jacket and breeches, white stockings and black buckled shoes.

'Yes, I particularly love that white wig with the plait at the back. Very sexy,' she said with a wink. 'So what do you think of mine?' She twirled around in her scarlet dress worn over hooped panniers designed to make the skirt stand out in the classic lamp-shade shape, hiding her growing bump.

'You do look rather exotic,' replied Edward with a grin, 'but who are you supposed to be?'

Connie gave him her haughtiest look as she waved a colourful fan. 'Let them eat cake,' she announced, studying Edward's baffled expression. 'Any ideas?'

'Darling, you know my memory is beyond repair.'

'It's Marie Antoinette. She was beheaded after a revolution against her and her husband. Let them eat cake was her famous snipe to the starving population of France.'

'Hmm, interesting.' He pulled her towards him and kissed her gently. 'I do love you. You know that don't you?' He wanted to reassure her, feeling full of remorse about his tryst with Rachel. Her distress was a wake-up call that he mustn't take her for granted.

Connie beamed. 'Yes, I believe you do.' She hooked her arm into his. 'Ready?'

'Absolutely. Let's go find Oli.'

Wandering arm in arm along the corridor they eventually arrived at Oliver's room and knocked on his door. Opening it, he theatrically swirled his black cloak before bowing, and taking off his floppy black hat.

'Goodness, who are you?' asked Connie.

'William Shakespeare, of course. Can you not tell?'

Connie wrinkled her nose with amusement. 'Why him?'

'So I didn't have to shave off my moustache and beard,' he said with a smirk.

They all laughed, pulling their masks down over their faces as they headed towards the spiral staircase, descending down to the grand ballroom with its high ceilings and heavy medieval chandeliers.

'Don't they all look glorious,' murmured Connie, her eyes lingering with intrigue over the many masked figures swirling around in colourful historical outfits, looking from a distance like giant butterflies.

'Oh look, there's Daddy.' She pointed to the other side of the ballroom where they saw Henry holding court, guffawing at full pitch with a glass of champagne in his hand. His burly frame was squashed into an elaborate red and gold doublet with matching breeches, complete with a red velvet robe draped around his broad shoulders. A black, feathered hat perched at an angle on his large, round head.

Edward smirked at Oliver. 'Attired as stated, in kingly fashion.'

'Indeed,' replied Oliver with a wink. 'Am I to presume that's his wife standing next to him with the white powdered face and red wig?'

'Yes, let's go say hello,' said Edward, grabbing Connie's hand.

Henry stood with his legs apart, enjoying playing up to his grandiose character. 'Well, well, don't you all look bloody marvellous,' he bellowed, swaying about, his champagne slopping everywhere.

Oliver took off his hat and bowed. 'Very good to meet you again, sir.'

'Likewise, dear boy, and how do you like my naughty daughter, Elizabeth the 1st?' He pointed to his wife as she curtseyed.

Both Oliver and Edward bowed and kissed Elizabeth's hand in turn as she tilted her head regally.

Edward grabbed a glass of champagne from one of the maids wandering around with a tray as he watched the Douglas-Scotts chattering together. He felt restless, wondering when he should make his move. Taking a deep breath he stroked Connie's shoulder as she spun round. 'Would you mind terribly, angel, if Oli and I go and mingle? I'd like to introduce him to a few people.'

'Not at all, darling. See you both in a bit.' She appeared quite taken aback when Edward leant forward and kissed her sensually on the lips. 'Naughty boy,' she said demurely, looking over her fan at him.

Feeling certain he'd left Connie happy, they both merged into the crowds of nearly two hundred guests making idle chitchat until he tapped Oliver on the arm, signalling that it was time.

'So what now?' asked Oliver, once they'd snuck upstairs and shut the door.

Edward pulled out a suitcase from under his bed, flapped it open and took out two outfits, placing them on the bed. 'We'll get changed into these and I'll grab the keys from Henry's bedroom.'

'Ah, yes, the keys. But how do you know they're in there?'

'Gut feeling and common sense, Oli. Henry has the cellar key glued to him at all times, but I've seen him walk out of there jangling bunches on many occasions, so I'm pretty damn certain—and he's bound to have spares. If I manage to find them, I'll direct you to Henry's office. And remember, if you see any servants and they ask questions, emulate Henry's pompous voice and say you're busy. Do you want to practice again?'

Oliver cleared his throat, staring into a mirror on the wall and pulled a sneering expression. 'Do run along, chop-chop.'

Edward covered his mouth, stifling laughter. 'Excellent, that's not half-bad.'

'Oh God, Eddie, do you think we can pull this off?' His voice was hoarse with nerves.

'Yes, don't worry. All Henry's staff are petrified of him, so they won't speak out of turn.' He held up the gold and red doublet for Oliver to see. 'Look, I wheedled a bit of inside knowledge from Connie and got us identical masks and outfits from Henry's costumier with a bit of internal padding to plump us out. If anyone sees either of us, they'll simply presume it's him and do as they're told.'

Oliver undid his cloak with a frown ready to get changed. 'Hmm, I'll take your word for it.'

Edward now undressed, apart from his silk boxer shorts, placed one leg on the bed as he wriggled into some white tights. 'Meanwhile, I'll endeavour to get into that wine cellar of his and see what the bloody hell is down there that commands such secrecy. We'll lock any evidence in your suitcase and reappear in the ballroom in our original outfits. It's the perfect plan!'

'You make it sound so simple, but my bowels tell a different story,' said Oliver, pulling a sad face.

Edward laughed as he tugged on the red breeches. 'It's good old adrenaline, Oli. Use it to your advantage. That's what I do on stage.' He grabbed the red cloak and threw it around him. 'Now, remember, I've arranged for a chauffeur to take you back to London after seeing in the New Year. Henry already knows you won't be staying over.'

'Thank you, Eddie. You're remarkably organised.'

'Oh, trust me, I've thought of every eventuality.' He pulled down his mask. 'Wait for me here. I'll be back in a tick.'

He slid out of the door, turned right and darted along the corridor towards Henry and Elizabeth's master suite, stopping at an alcove which led up to three carpeted steps with an oak-panelled door at the top.

Turning the knob, he took a breath and crept in, scanning the large opulent room with its imposing mahogany furniture. There was a king size, four-poster bed against the opposite wall, covered with a red and gold brocade bedspread with matching curtains. Bizarrely, two paintings hung on the wall either side of the bed, depicting Henry and Elizabeth dressed in regal finery from the Tudor period. He laughed. Perhaps tonight's fancy dress was a habitual fantasy.

Wondering where to look first, he frantically opened drawers, cupboards and trinket boxes, occasionally looking over his shoulder praying no one would hear and come in. *Where the bloody hell are they?* he thought, his impatience escalating. He scanned the room again, finally spotting a small wooden cabinet in a discreet recess next to an eight-foot-wide wardrobe. He rushed towards it, opening the door and saw numerous keys hanging on hooks, smiling with relief when he could grab the ones tagged 'office' and 'cellar'.

Sprinting back towards their room, he arrived red faced and breathless, handing Oliver the office key.

'You were fast,' said Oliver, his face now a sickly grey hue. 'Right, remind me what I'm looking for again?'

'Focus on his desk,' gasped Edward, still winded. 'Look for the file labelled Serpentem Corde. Grab any documents from inside.'

Oliver nodded, placing the feathered hat on his head and the mask over his face. 'How do I look?'

'Very handsome, with the mask,' teased Edward.

Grabbing a small torch from his suitcase he opened the door and pointed Oliver left, in the direction of Henry's office. 'Good luck, dear friend,' he whispered.

'Likewise,' replied Oliver.

Edward hurried back past Henry's room on a ten-minute hike that took him along the entire outline of the eighty-room mansion before disappearing down a stairway that spiralled to the basement.

He expected it to be deathly quiet as he stepped into the dark corridor, but even here, in the deepest bowels of the building, he could still hear the dull thud of the music from the ballroom above.

Wandering towards the cellar door, he pushed the key into the lock with shaky hands and stepped inside, securing the door behind him. He stood there for a moment in the darkness, a deep sense of shame nudging his conscience. How could he do this yet again, infiltrate his father-in-law's privacy? A man who had taken him to his heart as a son and so generously mentored him? Should he turn back, he wondered, taking a breath. Isn't it best to let some things ride and not look for trouble? He thought of Hitler's letter, the Nazi donation, Hugh's horrific murder and decided for justice alone, he must go on—discover if Henry really was a danger or just a confused, blinkered, old man. He flicked on his torch and cautiously made his way down the steps.

The torchlight illuminated a vast brick room, nearly forty feet in length with row upon row of Henry's prized wine collection stored in long wooden racks. *Nothing unusual here,* he thought. Wandering down the aisle in between the racks he saw a doorway at the end. Should he go and check? It was probably nothing, just a room, but he may as well investigate now he was here.

Pushing open the heavy iron door, an antiseptic aroma enveloped him like a pungent cloud as he coughed, covering his nose with his hands. He looked to the right and saw a clinical-looking room with a black and white tiled floor. A tall stainless-steel medical cabinet stood on one side with a white sink next to it in the corner. Along the opposite wall there was a wooden chair next to a bed on wheels, similar, he thought, to a hospital bed.

What the hell is this place—a cell, a surgery of some kind?

A large rectangular wooden box sat on top of the bed. Edward walked towards it, curious to inspect the contents. He flicked the catch and opened the hinged lid, feeling confused. Before him was a vast array of stainless steel tools set into a purple velvet inlay, everything a surgeon could ever need. A scalpel, pliers, clamps, a hacksaw, scissors and a variety of forked hooks, nuts and bolts.

How odd. Why on earth would he need these? He was about to study them further when the basement door creaked open and the cellar lights flashed on.

Flicking off his torch, he jerked backwards, holding his breath.

Footsteps, slow and heavy, were coming his way.

His stomach lurched as he heard the sound of Henry humming to himself merrily.

The footsteps stopped.

'Another crate of champers, I reckon,' he heard him say, amidst the clanking of bottles.

He seemed to be in there forever, rustling about as Edward stood, rooted to the spot until the lights went off and the cellar door slammed shut.

Close shave, he thought, rasping heavily. He closed the lid of the box, turned the torch back on and made his way out, soaked in sweat.

By the time he got back up the long spiral staircase, relieved that his mission was over, his gut churned with nausea when he saw Cranford heading towards him. He quickly placed both hands behind his back, hiding the torch.

'Good evening, m'lord,' said Cranford, a benign smile on his crumpled face. 'I thought you were in the ballroom.'

'Ah, yes,' he said, talking through his mask in a loud Sgt. Major voice. 'I was just looking for something, a present for my dear Lizzy. So chop-chop make yourself busy, Cranford. We've got lots of guests to take care of.'

Cranford stood motionless, peering at him strangely. 'Are you sure you're okay, m'lord?'

He had to sound confident, pull rank, make him feel awkward. 'Cranford, you're being most improper. I'm fine. Now run along and get on with your work.'

The butler blinked several times as if trying to adjust his vision. 'Cranford, do you want to be fired?'

The old man's eyes widened in a look of horror and he gave a low, deep bow. 'My humble apologies, m'lord. Please, don't hesitate to call for any further assistance.'

Edward nodded in response, his head throbbing as he waited for him to disappear back down the hallway.

'Eddie, Eddie, are you all right, please be all right?' Frantic, Oliver dashed over to the sink in the corner and filled up a glass, throwing the cold water over Edward's face, drenching him as he gasped in shock.

'What the hell's going on?' Edward mumbled, blearily opening his eyes.

'You were out for the count. What the hell happened?'

Edward sat up, water dripping down his cheeks. 'I had the most terrible migraine,' he groaned. 'It was so bad, I thought my head would erupt. And now I'm bloody soaked.'

'Sorry, old chap.' Oliver handed him a towel to dry off. 'Did you go to the cellar?'

He rubbed his eyes. 'Yes, and it's all rather odd.'

'Why?'

'He's got some kind of clinic down there ... a hospital bed and a box of surgical instruments. Can't imagine what he needs them for, unless it was a bomb shelter for wounded aristocrats. Still no idea why he's so protective of the place. It really must be the highly prized vintage.'

Oliver folded his arms and frowned. 'That is odd. Perhaps he has a private physician that attends to him. At least there's no big, sinister secret ... not down there anyway.'

'Indeed,' said Edward, in a weary tone, 'it was a complete waste of time. And I nearly got rumbled twice.'

'Really?'

'Yes, Henry came in to get more booze and I bumped into his butler on the way back. God knows what he'd do if he caught me snooping around dressed like him. Rip my guts out probably.'

'Sounds stressful. No wonder you got a migraine.'

'Quite. Did you get the letters?'

Oliver nodded, pulling out a bundle of envelopes from the front of his breeches.

'Charming.'

'Where else could I have put them?' he replied, throwing his arms up. 'I wasn't exactly carrying a briefcase.'

'Fair point.'

'Come on, let's get changed,' said Oliver, looking at his watch. 'I know you feel ill, but we need to get back and mingle before anyone suspects.' He threw the stolen letters into the suitcase and locked it, and then grabbing Edward's arms, he hauled him up from the floor.

'Right, I'll go first,' said Edward, pulling on his original outfit, 'best not to look conspicuous.'

Edward wandered towards the ballroom still feeling groggy, when he heard a rustling sound. Taking a step back, he stopped by a storage cupboard. The rustling continued. 'Don't tell me there're bloody rats in there,' he muttered. 'A typhus epidemic is all we need.'

Pulling the handle, he jumped back startled when he saw Elizabeth squashed inside with Henry's old school friend, Nicholas Haverton-Jones. They both looked guiltily dishevelled; Elizabeth's brocade dress hitched up around her waist, revealing knee-length pantaloons and her white powdered makeup and lipstick smeared together like a grubby paint palette.

He stared at them trying to stifle laughter. 'Oh! Sorry to disturb you.'

'Please, Eddie, don't say anything to Henry,' stammered Elizabeth, her eyes pleading.

'I wouldn't dream of it, Lizzy.'

'Yes, please don't.' Nicholas gulped, his curly wig hanging lopsided off his balding head. 'Henry will slaughter me.'

'And I believe you, Nicholas. Trust me, my lips are sealed. Would you both like me to close the door again?'

Nicholas gave a sheepish grin. 'Yes, please.'

He continued to head downstairs hoping that Elizabeth might now become an ally, knowing he was witness to her clandestine affair. Manoeuvring his way through the sea of people towards Connie, he tried his best to maintain a calm composure.

'Hello, darling.' Connie pouted as she leant in to kiss him. 'I've missed you. Where have you been?'

'Just socialising, darling. Now come and dance with me. They're playing our song.' She giggled as he pulled her towards him, twirling her around the marble floor to 'Someone to Watch Over Me'. 'How's your father doing?' he asked, nuzzling her neck.

She discreetly pointed to Henry bellowing at a circle of colleagues. 'Daddy often rants when he's had a few.'

Edward laughed and they continued to dance until the song ended when Oliver appeared looking flustered. A maid passed by carrying a tray of Buck's Fizz. He grabbed a glass and eagerly gulped it.

The lights flickered as they all watched Henry drunkenly clamber onto a chair and shakily stand on it. 'Hellooo, Hellooo,' he roared, tapping a microphone, commanding everyone's attention. 'It's nearly midnight, Ladies and Gents. So on behalf of myself and my lovely wife ... God knows where she is, haven't seen her all bloody evening ... I'd like to wish you all a very Happy New Year and a prosperous 1946.'

In the midst of raucous cheering and applauding, Elizabeth reappeared, her makeup once more pristine. She mouthed a silent 'thank you' to Edward and he gave her a wink, sealing their secret.

'So, let's see this bloody New Year in properly,' yelled Henry. He began singing 'Auld Lang Syne', swaying in time to his own tuneless voice as all the guests held hands.

'Should auld acquaintance be forgot
And never brought to mind?
Should auld acquaintance be forgot
For auld lang syne ...'

Edward drifted off, mouthing the words, choked up with nostalgia about Rachel. He'd felt so guilty about his feelings that he'd tried to forget about their rendezvous, tried to forget her almond-shaped eyes and full lips, but it was harder than he thought. Maybe he was weak, but he wondered what she was doing, who she was with, remembering their last sensual kiss.

Oliver nudged him on the arm and he was jolted back, seeing Cranford talking animatedly to Henry, waving his hands around. Henry's face had gone a deep beetroot red and he felt a nervous flutter. 'I think it's best if you leave now, Oli, whilst everyone's distracted. The sooner you're out of here with the letters, the better.'

Oliver nodded in agreement. 'Let's get the case.' He spun round to say goodbye, bowing down to kiss Connie's and then Elizabeth's extended hand.

'Going so soon? But the night is young,' said Elizabeth warmly.

'Yes, sadly I have some urgent work. But thank you for your kind hospitality.'

'You're most welcome,' replied Elizabeth with a curtsey.

Edward called for a footman and they both trailed behind the young boy, watching him like a hawk until he placed the case with all the crucial information outside the front of the house.

'Your car will be here soon, sir,' said the footman.

Edward pressed a five-shilling coin into his hand and the boy's eyes lit up with excitement as he clutched it. 'Thank you, sir.' He took a deep bow, before bouncing back towards the entrance.

Edward and Oliver stood shivering in the darkness, illuminated by the security light on the house. Reaching into his pocket Edward handed Oliver the cellar key. 'Keep this somewhere safe with the other one. It's too risky putting them back. I'll visit as soon as I can get away.'

Oliver nodded, taking a deep breath.

The red Rolls pulled up moments later and as the chauffeur got out to collect Oliver's luggage, they hugged each other and said goodnight, relieved their ordeal was over.

Chapter 36

Tuesday evening, 8th January 1946

Connie lay awkwardly on her side in their Jacobean four-poster with the pillow propped under her hip to support her growing bump. She was already six months gone, much further on than they first thought, and despite concerns over his father-in-law's Nazi leanings, Edward desperately wanted to make his marriage work.

He moved closer, spooning her; the position now favoured for comfortable lovemaking. Nuzzling her neck, he ground his hips against her as she arched her back, falling into a gentle rhythm, gasping with passion as memories of Rachel flooded his mind. Thrusting more deeply, harder and harder, he bit her neck, squeezing her nipples between his fingers, remembering how Rachel moaned with pleasure.

'Ouch' cried Connie pushing him away, 'that hurt! I hate my nipples being pinched. You know that.'

'I'm sorry, darling. I didn't mean to hurt you.' He ran his hands through his hair feeling awkward.

Connie turned over and glared at him, her face drawn. 'It felt like you were making love to someone else. You know the places I like to be touched and the places I don't.'

'Sorry, Connie. I got carried away.' He attempted to kiss her but she shrank back, tugging the bedclothes over herself. Lying back down, he felt lonelier than ever, wishing he was with Rachel, wishing they had wings to fly away.

Wednesday morning, 9th January 1946—9.30 a.m.

Edward sat at the dining table drinking coffee, thinking up myriad excuses so he could drive off and see Rachel when Connie stormed in.

'I'm so angry with Mummy,' she blurted out, her maternity dress billowing around her thin, white legs. 'You know she's been having an affair?'

He stirred his coffee, avoiding eye contact, hoping to plead ignorance.

'Do you know anything about it?' she asked, enunciating every word. She glared at him with her arms folded.

'Um, no nothing. I'm shocked.'

Connie sat down opposite him and leant forward, narrowing her eyes. 'Don't lie to me, Eddie. Mummy confessed that you saw them after I walked in on her kissing that devious scoundrel, Nicholas Haverton-Jones in the powder room. He's Daddy's old school friend, you know.'

He sighed and looked at her. 'Fine, I admit I did see them, Connie. But it's not my place to judge and frankly you shouldn't either.'

'Oh, you, and your righteous views on judgement and prejudice,' screeched Connie, her eyes full of fire. 'It's only natural for me to be upset over my mother having sexual relations with a man who isn't my father. It's disgusting!'

Edward shuddered at the shrillness of her voice. He had never seen her so angry. He stood up and walked around the table to comfort her, wrapping his arms around her shoulders.

She shrugged him off.

'Darling,' he said, pulling up a chair next to her. 'I understand how you feel, but I hope you don't tell your father about this. It would only cause pain for everyone.'

'Oh, don't worry,' she replied with a scornful look. 'I won't tell my poor, cuckold father. I don't want to be responsible for giving him a heart attack. I just cannot understand my mother's sluttish behaviour. Oh God!' she shouted, doubling over, her face contorted.

Edward jumped up, panicking. 'What's wrong, Connie?'

'My belly,' she groaned.

His face blanched as he grabbed her hand, stroking it. 'Darling, you need to calm down, take a deep breath. You know that getting upset like this is no good for you or the baby.'

Connie sniffled as tears rolled down her cheeks. 'But I mean,' she said between sobs, 'why would you say your marital vows in the eyes of God if you're going to commit adultery?'

'I don't know, darling,' he said softly.

He couldn't talk, he was just as culpable. He looked down at the floor. Was it so wrong that he'd made love to Rachel? She had, after all, been his one great passion, and still was, wasn't she? Christ, he was so confused, so torn, between both of them. He recalled Emma from their stroll in the East End. 'You have such a likeness for my Joe. He was the love of my life.' And then her sadness when he denied all knowledge.

What kind of man was I back then ... an adulterous rake jumping from one woman to another? It was evident he'd repeatedly betrayed Rose. And here was Connie, weeping, his wife in the eyes of the church, pregnant with his second child. She'd done nothing wrong. At the very least he owed her his loyalty.

'Is there anything I can do to make you feel better, my love?'

Connie put a hand on each side of the chair and hauled herself up, and then wiped her red-rimmed eyes. 'No, I'm rather tired. I'm going upstairs to lie down.'

'That sounds like a good idea, darling.' He tried yet again to hug her but she turned away.

He felt so lost.

Wednesday morning, 9th January 1946—11.30 a.m.

'Ah, I wasn't expecting you,' said Oliver, opening his front door and staring at Edward blankly. He appeared flustered, panting somewhat as if he'd just thrown on some old clothes and run downstairs.

Edward felt overdressed in comparison, wearing one of his grey tailored suits and a red paisley cravat. 'My apologies, it's been bloody hectic, couldn't get away, but I've managed to snatch some time and thought I'd whizz over.'

'About?'

'About the letters ... I'm desperate to know, old pal.' He waited, shuffling about on the doorstep as Oliver seemed to be looking past him into the distance. 'So, um, are you going to invite me in?'

Oliver smiled, looking sheepish, brushing fluff off his brown sweater. 'Sorry, Eddie, my mind's elsewhere.' He stood to one side. 'Please, come in. I'll make us a coffee.'

He steered Edward into the living room and disappeared towards the kitchen, rather too quickly for Edward's liking. He felt quite unwelcome and wondered if he'd done something to offend his friend in some way.

The sound of the percolator chugged away in the background as Edward tried to distract himself, rifling through the overstuffed bookshelves, grabbing some titles and flicking through the pages, when a book called *The Prophet* leapt out at him. He opened it randomly, transfixed by the words.

It is when your spirit goes wandering upon the wind, that you alone and unguarded commit a wrong upon others and therefore unto yourself. And for that wrong committed you must knock and wait a while unheeded at the gate of the blessed. What judgements pronounce you upon him who though honest in the flesh yet is a thief in spirit? What penalty lay upon him who slays in the flesh yet is himself slain in the spirit.

Kahlil Gibran

He placed the book back on the shelf pondering deeply. The words were a revelation, the catalyst his troubled soul sorely needed. The letters were important, but his conscience more so. He didn't want to commit wrongs and play with love. He had to do something, rectify things once and for all, for everyone's sake, if he ever hoped to find some peace.

Oliver walked in with the rattling tray of cafetiere and cups.

'Oli,' Edward said, pressing his hands together, 'would you mind terribly if we revisit the letters tomorrow? I have some personal business to attend to.'

'Of course not, Eddie.' He murmured a 'Thank God,' under his breath, which Edward couldn't help but notice. *Charming,* he thought.

Placing the tray down on the table, Oliver escorted him back to the front door. 'In fact, Eddie, would you mind if we left it until Wednesday week? I am under the cosh, so to speak.'

Edward nodded in agreement, slightly concerned by his friend's brusque manner. 'Excellent, whenever suits. I hope all is well with you, my friend.' They shook hands and waved goodbye. But he got no answer.

Wednesday afternoon, 9th January 1946

Rachel answered the door wearing a flowery tea dress. She looked pale and fragile as if she'd lost weight, her long hair pinned up loosely making the cheekbones on her chiselled face seem more pronounced.

Edward handed her a bunch of pink lilies which she took with trembling hands. He gazed at her tired turquoise eyes. 'You look lovely,' he said.

'Thank you,' she murmured. She held the flowers as if she might drop them, as if she had no strength in her hands. 'You best come in.'

He followed her down the hallway and into the kitchen carrying a bottle of Moët in his other hand. He placed the champagne onto the kitchen top. 'A belated Christmas present. Shall I open it?'

'Okay,' she said quietly. She took a glass vase out of the cupboard, turned on the taps and filled it with water. Setting it down on the table, she placed the lilies inside.

'Are you all right, darling? You seem a little distant?' He popped the cork open as the fizz overflowed onto the black and white tiled floor.

'I wasn't expecting you, that's all.' She grabbed a cloth from the sink, bent down and began mopping up the liquid.

'Sorry about the mess, darling.' He took some glasses off a shelf nearby and filled them with champagne. 'So did you have a good Christmas?'

'Christmas!' She spun round to look at him. 'You mean Hanukkah! That was weeks ago.'

He wrapped his arms around her as she coldly pushed him away. 'Rachel, I'm confused. Please, my love, tell me what's wrong so I can put it right?'

She sat down at the kitchen table wringing invisible wet washing with her hands. 'You don't get it,' she said, looking up at him. 'You don't understand, do you?'

'Understand what, Rachel?' He stared at her, bewildered.

'That I thought this was over. That you were dead. You did this to me for years,' she screamed, leaping up and slapping him across the face as he recoiled backwards in shock, 'keeping me waiting, promising that you would leave Rose. I never knew when I would see you,' she continued, tears streaming down her face. 'I was constantly left hoping, wondering if we would ever be together. Then I meet you again after years of grieving and I wake up, after an incredible night, only to find you gone from my bed, just like every time before. I promised myself I'd never let this happen again. I hate you!'

'Shhh, please, Rachel,' he put his finger to his lips, 'the neighbours will hear and think something terrible is going on.'

'I don't bloody care who hears,' she shouted as she ran upstairs.

Edward felt stunned, not knowing what to do next. This wasn't the calm, dignified Rachel he remembered. He thought she understood him, with or without explanations, but obviously not.

He sprinted upstairs to her bedroom, feeling his heart thud when he saw her lying on the bed with her back to him, her dress twisted around her legs as she continued to weep. Sitting on the edge of the mattress he reached out his hand and stroked her hair. 'I know I've hurt you, Rachel, but please hear me out. After we were bombed, everything about my life was wiped from my memory ... everything, except you.'

He watched her turn around, tendrils of hair falling over her eyes.

'I've thought about you constantly. It's driven me crazy. You and I are so right for each other, but the timing, the timing is so wrong.'

'The timing was always wrong! Don't you remember, Joe,' she whispered, gazing at him, 'how you pledged to love me forever. And slipped that silly curtain ring on my finger and promised ... promised you'd never leave me.'

He nodded. Yes, he remembered, along with the vision of her so tangible on his wedding day he could almost touch it, knowing his vows were meant for her.

Their bond had always been there from the moment they met; electric sparks dancing between discreet looks and coy smiles, kept contained until her bedridden husband died of cancer. She'd been frightened of being alone, but he'd given her comfort. 'Be brave,' he'd told her, 'every breath is a new start,' and she'd believed him, holding on to all his promises, hoping they'd finally be together. So how could he tell her the truth; that now he couldn't promise anything?

Swallowing hard, his hands began to shake. 'Rachel, I'm so sorry. I have another family now, a young son and a baby on the way.'

Her face turned pale as she stared at him wild-eyed, her bottom lip quivering. 'What! I don't want to hear.' She placed her hands over her ears as if to block out any more words. 'Why? You have always, always been, just out of my reach.'

He reached out, wrapping his arms around her fragile body, hugging her close. 'Please listen,' he said, breathing heavily. 'I realise now how badly I betrayed Rose and I would be doing the same to my new wife, Connie.' He held her face in his hands, looking deeply into her eyes. 'I read something today which had a profound effect on me ... about the emptiness you feel when you commit a wrong.'

Rachel pulled away, her eyes filling with tears once more. 'So, I'm you're undoing am I? The wrong that's been committed.'

'No! But I met Connie at my weakest, when I had nothing to live for. I can't let her down. I would end up hurting you both, as well as my children.'

'So, you came here to tell me this?' Rachel wiped her wet face with her sleeve. 'Thanks.'

'Yes,' he said, trying to hold her gaze, 'even though it breaks my heart. I can't be that weak man again. I've been given a second chance, to live life honourably.'

'And what about me?' she cried, her voice breaking. 'What becomes of me? I'm a widowed woman of thirty-eight with nothing left. You promised me. You promised that one day we'd be together.'

Edward grabbed her hands, wrapping them in his, desperate to comfort her. 'Rachel, you are a beautiful woman with a passionate spirit. You will find love again.'

She covered her face, her chest heaving until she found the strength to speak. 'I think I'd like you to leave now.'

'Leave?' he said, feeling shaken.

'Yes. Leave. Right now!'

He slowly stood up, his face strained. 'Do I have your blessing and forgiveness, Rachel?'

She looked at him sadly. 'No, Joe, you don't have my blessing or my forgiveness.' She jumped off the bed and rushed out of the room, racing downstairs, leaving him trailing behind.

'Rachel, please.' He gazed at her in the hallway, his eyes pleading. He couldn't bear for it to end like this.

'Go,' she cried.

He slumped over, taking small steps through the doorway, solemn, mournful, as if he was in a funeral march. And then she slammed the door shut before he had a chance to turn around and say goodbye.

Chapter 37

Saturday, 12th January 1946

I was still patiently waiting for Dad's return letter in the post. I'd reread the smudged carbon copy I'd sent to him, praying he hadn't taken offence. I had to send it, I kept telling myself— the notion of his possible affair with Mrs Morgan plaguing me like some kind of madness as I lay in bed at night stewing over old times.

I pictured Dad, clear as day at his greengrocer's, wearing his brown cap and long white coat. I'd muck in on a Friday, after school, rewarded with a highly prized shilling for a day's work. Sometimes Mrs Morgan would pass by, smelling sweetly of lavender and dressed all nice with her hair in pin curls, and hand Daddy some fresh pastrami sandwiches for lunch. She would have gone to a lot of trouble, saving up her coupons and queuing at the butchers to get a nice beef joint for that pastrami. Often, I felt like the spare part, looking on awkwardly as Dad leant in close, whispering something funny whilst she'd giggle girlishly. Their eye contact would linger just a bit too long for comfort. As a young girl I put it down to Daddy being friendly, but now I knew he'd been shamelessly flirting.

It was always a mystery where Daddy disappeared to on a Friday night, every week. It went on for several years before we got bombed. His dinner would sit on the table going cold as we all ate in silence. Mama would sigh and put his food on the kitchen top with a plate over it to keep the flies off, and we would all lie in bed listening to her restlessly pace the house, until he'd finally arrive home, sometimes past midnight. As soon as we heard his key in the lock, Gabi and I would sneak out of bed and take turns to peek through the crack of the living room door to snoop on their conversation. And Daddy, well, he always had some feasible excuse.

Mama would stand there with her arms folded. 'Where have you been?' she'd snap.

'Don't give me that old-fashioned look, Rose,' he'd said one night, all smiles. 'I had to do another stock check and then the boys asked me to go to the Black Bull for a pint and said they were buying. "Only one, though", I said, and before you know it they were all buying rounds and I couldn't get away.'

And then he'd sing that favourite song of his, 'You Made Me Love You', and pull her into an embrace for a slow dance around the kitchen. She'd be stiff as a board at first, but he always had a way with her, stroking her hair, kissing parts of her face bit by bit, until she eventually sank into his arms.

I don't think Mama ever believed his stories but how we dreaded those nights. She never argued with him, but we knew we'd get the rough edge of her tongue the next morning.

After Dad left for work, we'd eat our breakfast on tenterhooks, too scared to speak in case we set off her fiery time bomb. Mother with her eyes blazing and spoiling for a fight would stomp about, slamming the kettle down on the stove, making us all jump. I'd often get a clip round the ear for even breathing too loudly. Gabi and Hannah somehow escaped her wrath, but her temper still made them nervous. We all wished that if only Daddy could get home on time, Mama would be happy and smile again. Now, I suspected, it was Mrs Morgan he'd spent our precious family time with.

I'd confided in Gabi and Hannah about my letter, but whatever I felt about the past, Gabi didn't want to hear a word of it.

'Stop fretting over stuff that's not your business,' he snapped, 'or you might find out something you really don't like.'

He'd watch me run downstairs every morning to check the post, and couldn't resist scowling when I came back upstairs empty handed. 'Still checking are you?' he'd say cynically as he'd slouch against the wall, his hazel eyes narrowed, observing me like I was the village idiot.

I'd nod my head feeling dejected.

'What if you've upset Dad and he doesn't want to see us again? Then you'll be sorry.'

I felt hurt that he was being so mean, but determined not to cry. His tongue was so sharp I'm surprised he didn't cut his own throat.

At last, on Wednesday, 16th January at eight o'clock in the morning, there on the doormat was the letter I'd been praying for, distinctively written in black fountain pen.

I carefully opened the white envelope, pulling out the gilt-edged notepaper inside as I ran upstairs brimming with happiness, reading it aloud to Gabi and Hannah.

Dearest Ruth, Gabi and Hannah,

It was wonderful to see you all again. That day was special to me too and I am sorry that it ended with Rachel, or as you know her, Mrs Morgan, walking in and you witnessing my dumbfounded reaction.

I have to be honest if I am to live with my own conscience that, yes, Mrs Morgan and I did once have an affair. Maybe I was weak, but one day you might understand that love can tap you on the shoulder when you least expect it.

I don't recall much about your mother, but I'm certain I did love her in my own way, and besides, she gave me you three amazing children.

As you know, I am married again, and I desperately want to be a committed husband and good father to all of my children. Whoever I was in the past it is not in my nature to be disloyal, I can assure you of that. I pray that you won't judge me for having been close to her. I couldn't bear that if you did. All I want is to feel accepted for who I am with all my strengths and many weaknesses.

Please know that you three are the only ones I can really trust. There are people around me, scary people, that would despise me for my past and who I truly am. And, yes, my wife might be upset too. So that's why I ask you to keep yourselves my secret, for now anyway.

I will visit, I promise, very soon.

Kisses and hugs to you all.
Your father, Joe

I finished reading, feeling shaken. I was grateful for his honesty about Mrs Morgan, but this was worse than I thought. Now, I knew why he looked so sad. He was terrified of the truth coming out, about us.

Gabi collapsed onto a chair, his shirttails hanging out of his trousers. 'Whoa, I wasn't expecting that. Dad's a bit of a rogue.'

'I can't believe it, poor Mummy,' stammered Hannah. She stood by the window in a polka dot dress, her watery eyes gazing through the glass as if in a trance.

I flopped onto the chaise longue in my woollen skirt, pulling my legs underneath me, shocked at their attitude. 'Are you both deaf? Forget Mrs Morgan. Forget their affair. He's surrounded by people he can't trust. He can't let anything slip. It's probably his jealous witch of a wife, who no doubt would hate the very bones of us if she found out. All I know is he's scared, really scared.'

'Sorry,' said Gabi. He looked down at the floor. 'I was thinking back, feeling angry for Mum. All these secrets, this cloak and dagger stuff. It's a lot to take in.'

Hannah ambled over and snuggled in next to me. 'I agree, Ruth. Whatever happened, whatever he did, Daddy needs us.'

I grabbed her hand, putting on a brave face. 'I know he does, Hannah.'

And I desperately wanted to help him, but I felt like Mama must have done, that although he was back in our lives, he still wasn't letting us in, he still wasn't part of our family. He had another bundle of secrets, just like Mrs Morgan.

Chapter 38

Wednesday, 16th January 1946

Oliver wandered around his living room in a restless quandary as he waited on tenterhooks for Edward to arrive. There were so many bombshells. The stolen missives not only revealed the Douglas-Scotts' twenty-year connection with Hitler, but one of them was a lit grenade that could potentially destroy his good friend's marriage. He'd taken some time to think clearly, but there were still no answers. What should he do? What should he say? Did Edward deserve to know the truth or to be protected from it? He flinched when he heard the rat-a-tat-tat knocking.

Rushing to the front door he flung it open, and gave a weary looking Edward a hug. He beckoned him into the living room, and watched him slump into a leather armchair and stare deject-edly at the floor.

'Are you all right, Eddie?' he asked, taking a seat opposite, noting his unkempt hair and thick, dark stubble.

'Let's just say this last week has been complicated,' mumbled Edward, so quietly, Oliver could barely hear him.

'Well, talk to me. You look upset.'

Edward clenched his shaking hands together, making the veins in his arms bulge through his skin. 'Remember when we were in New York and you told me about Jung and his theory on meaningful coincidences?'

'Indeed, I do.'

'Well, I *coincidentally* bumped into the blonde woman.'

'Which blonde woman?'

'The one who's haunted me for years.'

'Ah, you mean, Rachel? The 'vision' you saw at your wedding and believed might be your wife?'

'That's right, the very one. We met just before Christmas, in a restaurant. I'd just finished lunch ... with friends,' he continued, appearing hesitant.

Oliver nodded, signalling for him to continue.

'I finally realised the truth ... that Rachel had been my mistress whilst I was married to Rose, and we rekindled our romance that very night.' He looked away sheepishly. 'When I returned home in the early hours, Connie was understandably distraught wondering where I'd been, and I was forced to confront my own shameful behaviour.'

The doctor ran his fingers over his beard, an instinctive habit when listening. 'So what did you do?'

'I visited Rachel a few days ago and told her it was over. It was obvious I'd hurt her badly in the past, making promises I couldn't keep. So for both our sakes, I felt we needed to say goodbye, once and for all.'

'Hmm, and yet it seems you are still not happy?'

Edward blinked back tears. 'No, if anything I'm in more pain than ever.'

'So are you still in love with her?'

'Yes, and that's the problem, I love her with all my heart ... but the guilt ... that filthy sense of shame ... I can't shake it off.

The truth is, I don't like the man I once was. I don't want to be the same unfaithful husband to Connie as I was to Rose.'

'I understand, Eddie. Stripped bare as you have been of everything you knew, there can be no complacency—and it appears you have developed a deeper sense of integrity, but let me ask you this,' he continued, his voice hoarse with nerves, 'what if your guilt was misplaced?'

'What do you mean?'

Oliver closed his eyes momentarily. Should he reveal what he knew and put his friend out of his misery? 'What if Connie wasn't the person you thought she was?'

Edward fidgeted in his chair. 'Why would you say that?'

'I'm just saying, what if?'

'But she's my wife,' he stammered, 'she's given me a family, our little Alfie, and another one on the way.'

'So tell me … what do you really want right now?'

'To love and cherish my family and to commit to that body and soul.'

Oliver sighed with relief, his conscience appeased. 'Then you have made the right choice for now—and like all wounds, your heartache will heal in time.'

Edward's eyes watered. 'Perhaps it's a good thing we're focusing on the letters. It might take my mind off things.'

'I'm not entirely sure these letters are a remedy,' Oliver replied, raising an eyebrow. 'One of them was sent to your father-in-law only two months ago.'

'Meaning?'

'Meaning a month before Hugh's murder.'

Edward stared at him blankly.

'I best just read it.' He pulled the letter out of his jacket pocket and unfolded it.

25th November 1945

Dear Comrade,

Thank you for asking about my welfare. I am well and enjoying the delights of South American life in a remote village, set amidst a pine forest away from prying eyes. You might say it is the serene calm after the madness, and I count my blessings every day.

The support from US and Russian intelligence officers has been overwhelming and crucial in keeping me away from bounty hunters. Along with a few of the remaining SS, we have been offered protection here in return for military technology, which you so generously funded over the last decade.

It is unfortunate that the plans we envisaged were halted, but there is always a way forward, Heinrich, always a new path. And together we will create a force that can never be beaten: The Fourth Reich—A New World Order. And I will be here waiting, ready to help you lead Germany from afar as we continue working towards our personal Utopia.

In the meantime, I'm comforted that you received my shipped surgical tools and medical research. My investigative procedures on the Jewish race are an essential outcome if we are to know what drives and corrupts these people. Continued elimination of them is the only way to create the pure race we all long for.

Always remember, Heinrich, personification of the devil as the symbol of all evil assumes the living shape of the Jew. And in defending ourselves against them, we are fighting for the work of our Lord.

Yours faithfully,
Josef

Edward slumped forward, his face slick with sweat. 'Christ, this is worse than we thought.' He stared at the floor. 'Those surgical instruments that I saw in the cellar?'

'Yes, I remember,' replied Oliver quietly. He folded up the letter and placed it back in his pocket. 'Looks like your father-in-law plans to use them, if he hasn't already.'

'And there's me thinking it was some kind of innocent bomb shelter instead of a sick laboratory for human guinea pigs. I'm such a fool.' Rocking backwards and forwards, his eyes darted around the room. 'All these years, I've tried to see the good in that man—to see the father, the husband, the human, and where has it got me? Why, why, why has this happened to me?' he yelled, rubbing his hands all over his face, scratching at his skin.

'Eddie, please stop,' said Oliver, lurching forward, 'you'll hurt yourself.'

'Sorry,' he groaned. 'I'm just ... I don't know ... I don't know anything anymore.' He took a deep breath. 'So who is this Josef?'

'He was the chief physician at Auschwitz.'

'Really?'

Oliver arched an eyebrow. 'You've never read about Josef Mengele in the press?'

Edward shook his head. 'I rarely read the rags. The last time was when Hugh was murdered.'

'Well, he's a crazy, crazy man with a Jekyll and Hyde temperament—dubbed 'The Angel of Death', because he'd whistle happily whilst torturing his victims and sympathise with a distraught mother only to send her to the gas chamber moments later.'

'So what procedures did he undertake?'

'Eddie, you're already showing signs of extreme anxiety,' said Oliver, looking at his hands. 'It might be best if you remain oblivious to all this.'

'Oli, please ... if my father-in-law has taken on his mantle, I need to understand what kind of madman we're dealing with.'

Oliver swallowed, wondering where to start. 'He conducted gruesome experiments under the guise of scientific research. His main interest was investigating what caused physical abnormalities, endeavouring, as he said in his letter, to discover the secrets of heredity so they could create the sought-after Aryan race. Many were castrated or sterilised, but others had their organs removed in agonising surgical procedures that he performed without anaesthetic. And some were injected with infections to see how long it would take for them to succumb to various diseases.' He hesitated, watching his friend's face grow paler. 'He was considered a pioneering surgeon, funded by a grant, so his murderous behaviour ran rampant. He also collected trophies of his victims ... organs, fingers, eyeballs. I won't go on.'

A muscle by the side of Edward's mouth twitched and he began breathing rapidly, taking sharp breaths in and out. 'But how could he do that, how could he have such little compassion ... just because they're Jews?'

'Because he was a psychopath, Eddie. Cleansing the world of Jews was just an excuse for sick individuals hell bent on world domination at any cost. But they'd single you out for your race because it's an opportunity to commit all kinds of atrocities. Nazis—they'll stop at nothing—do anything to reach their goals.'

'And Henry has his tools,' he stammered, his rasps getting faster. 'Oh God, poor Hugh was gassed and his organs removed ... horrifically murdered and we'll be next.'

Oliver rushed over and crouched in front of him, his plump thighs bulging through his trousers. 'I knew I shouldn't have told you, now breathe more slowly—inhale, exhale, count to ten or you'll hyperventilate and pass out.' He continued to monitor Edward's face as he closed his eyes, observing the pattern of his breathing, waiting until he appeared calmer.

'Now listen to me, Eddie, if you panic, Henry will smell your fear and you'll get us both killed. Remember, no one has any idea that we are Jews. My documents are housed in Russia and yours are safe. All records before 1912 in the local register office were destroyed by bombing so there is no way of tracing your ancestry.'

'Emmerton wasn't a Jew,' Edward rasped. 'He just stuck his nose into Henry's business like we did.'

'Exactly. They are psychopaths. Any excuse to cause pain—but as I told you before, be the best actor you can. We know that Henry is not rational. And that you can't trust anyone from his circle—but if you pretend everything is fine, your mind will convince your body to remain calm.'

'Easier said than done.'

'What other choice do you have?'

'Yes, you're right.' Edward collapsed back into the armchair, looking drained. 'That reminds me, the psychopath invited us to the Mayfair Club, Friday week. Do we dare attend?'

Oliver stood up and brushed some fluff from his trousers. 'We absolutely must attend. Our absence will only look suspicious. Besides, we must gather a case against him. This letter proves treason, even if we have no evidence to accuse him of murder. And now we know Mengele's in South America, he can be tracked down. He's a wanted war criminal.'

'I'm scared,' said Edward, his face a sickly, pallid hue. 'We've fallen into a vile, festering cesspit. I only hope we can claw our way out.' He took a breath. 'And Connie, my wife ... can I trust her?'

Oliver stared at his good friend, not knowing what to say. He couldn't give him that information, not right now, it would finish him. 'Look, neither of us wants to end up butchered like Emmerton. We just have to play clever—and we can. Trust me, Eddie. You're stronger than you think. Just keep a cool head.'

Chapter 39

Friday evening, 25ᵗʰ January 1946

The usual mix of conservative politicians and the titled elite swirled around like locusts in the smoky panelled room. Edward and Oliver braced themselves, walking straight over to the bar.

'Two double gin and tonics with ice,' said Edward to the barman, who politely obliged with a dimpled grin.

Once their drinks were placed in front of them, both men, almost in unison, raised their glasses and swigged back their drinks in one gulp for Dutch courage. Edward discreetly looked around, praying no one suspected anything.

'Gentleman!' Henry bellowed, from the centre of the room, jarring Edward from his fears. 'A warm welcome to you all. I'd like to announce that we have a new recruit here this evening. The eminent psychologist, Dr Oliver Jungston.' He extended his hand to point in Oliver's direction. 'Some of you will no doubt recognise him from my other soirees, but perhaps not had the opportunity to converse. So now is your chance.'

There was a roar of applause as all eyes swivelled towards Oliver.

Henry clicked his fingers in the air to ensure all eyes were once more on him. 'I'm afraid, I have some rather sad news about one of our own. I'd like to raise a toast to our old comrade, William Joyce, known by many as Lord Haw-Haw. He was executed a few weeks back. Hanged by the neck for treason. Now, I know he ruffled feathers,' he continued, tugging a handkerchief from his jacket pocket and dabbing beads of perspiration off his brow, 'but he had the same vision as the rest of us, for a fascist society in a world without Jews. And for that, we salute him. May God rest his soul.'

'To William,' shouted all the club members, raising their glasses as Edward and Oliver swiftly joined in.

'On to a rather more serious matter,' said Henry, straightening his back. 'It seems, rather unfortunately, that we have an enemy in our midst.' His eyes darted around the club members as everyone squirmed. 'On New Year's Eve at my fabulous ball, when my wife and I welcomed guests into our country home, there was an infiltrator, and confidential documents were stolen from my office!'

A deathly silence cloaked the room.

'My butler was concerned that he'd witnessed an imposter dressed like me hovering around the hallway upstairs, but because of his degenerating eyesight was unsure whether he should risk speaking up. Thankfully, he had the good sense to double-check and on seeing me still joyously entertaining my guests, confirmed his worst fears.'

Edward stuffed his shaking hands into his pockets as he shuffled from one polished brogue to the other, not daring to make eye contact in case Henry sensed his guilt.

Henry sneered, curling back his top lip, exposing his teeth. 'And it appears that this devious braggart,' he swallowed, gasping for air, his jowly face turning red, 'masked up to hide his duplicitous face, retrieved keys from my bedroom and thieved from my office under our very noses. My cellar key is also missing.'

There were audible gasps, raised eyebrows and a solemn shaking of heads from many of the club members.

'Rest assured, the locks have been changed, but this has cut me to the core knowing that someone could betray my trust in this way. I would like everyone here to think carefully if you saw anyone acting strangely, so we can discover the culprit and bring him to justice. And when I say justice,' he snapped, wiping frothing spittle from his lips, 'I mean the Douglas-Scott code for execution where I will personally blast the felon with bullets until his guts are splattered around the grounds of Mortis Hall.'

'Yes, blast him like a pheasant,' shouted Ramsay as a ripple of laughter pealed around the room.

'Anyway, that's the ugly disclosures over with. So let's get blitzed,' Henry roared, the heavy atmosphere transforming back into breezy chatter.

Oliver ambled towards Edward with another round of gins. Edward looked at the tipple with relief needing something to cool down, his white shirt and pinstripe trousers damp with sweat. He swigged his gin back and jumped with nerves when Henry suddenly joined them.

'Well, well. You're downing a fair bit of alcohol tonight, Eddie.'

'Yes, it's been rather a long day.'

''Bout time, you're turning into a man after my own heart. Booze is the best therapy in the world as far as I'm concerned. No offence, Oliver, to your psychological expertise.'

Oliver appeared to give a slight bow, lowering his head. 'None taken, sir.'

'Well, it wouldn't be a bad thing to emulate my wonderful father-in-law,' said Edward with what he hoped was an engaging smile.

'Ha-ha, what you after?' asked Henry. He stared at Edward as if waiting for an answer, and then turned towards Oliver with a smirk. 'No, seriously, what's he after?'

'Nothing, sir, he's just being his usual caring self,' replied Oliver, wrinkling his brow.

Henry stood in his favoured alpha-male pose, his legs slightly apart and his hands on his hips. 'I bloody hope you're looking after that daughter of mine? Don't want her getting upset about anything in her state.'

Edward squirmed, catching a whiff of Henry's unique feral aroma. 'Of course, Henry.'

Henry's head swivelled towards Oliver. 'So, dear boy, Eddie tells me that you share many of my philosophies on the Jewish race, is that right?'

'Yes, that's right,' replied Oliver, the muscles in his face tightening.

Henry bent his statuesque frame, peering down at him. 'In what way exactly?'

Oliver stuffed his hands into his pockets as he wobbled about, appearing unsteady.

'I think you've put Oli on the spot somewhat, Henry,' said Edward.

'What! The man can speak for himself can't he? He managed his speech at your wedding.'

'Yes, just tell us,' commanded Douglas Hetherington-Jones, who appeared from the other side of the room.

Oliver puffed out his cheeks, his brow now furrowed into deep lines. 'Um, well, to quote from Hitler's brilliant memoir, *Mein Kampf*, I do agree, without reservation,' he said with a gulp, 'that Jews are indeed the living form of the devil.'

'Hear, hear,' shouted Henry, slapping him on the back. 'So you've read *Mein Kampf*?'

Oliver squared his shoulders, lifting his chin. 'Indeed, it's my favourite bedtime reading.'

'Ha-ha, if I had known that you were such a neo-Nazi, dear boy, I would have invited you to our club sooner.'

'Well, they say you can never really know anyone,' said Douglas with a throaty croak. His face turned puce as he wheezed, stooping over.

Henry peered at him with distaste. 'You want to get that chest of yours seen to Dougie, terrible cough that.' He extended his arm and whacked him hard on the back as Douglas spluttered, straightening back up.

'Thank you, kindly,' Douglas rasped, still catching his breath. 'It's this damned polluted air.'

Oliver stood by his drinks cabinet and poured them both another gin. 'I've never been so glad for an evening to be over. I felt dynamite crackle with every word. Please God, he doesn't suspect either of us.'

Edward slumped back into a nearby armchair feeling groggy. 'Yes, my nerves are shot trying to stay calm and reasonable in the company of an irrational madman. I'll need to be drip-fed booze after this—but I acted my part as you advised—and we were masked up. Nobody could possibly know it was us.'

'Well done, my friend,' said Oliver, handing him a glass. 'So proud of you tonight. You have a steel core.'

'And you. Nice touch, by the way ... about *Mein Kampf.*'

'I had to think fast,' he replied with a wry smile. 'And a glimpse into their sneering, conniving group ... well, it's made me more determined than ever.'

'To what?'

Oliver reached into his trouser pocket and handed him another letter. 'To ensure that justice is served.'

'What's this?' asked Edward, looking at the envelope in his hand.

'I wasn't sure whether to give you this, but you seem calmer now, and I can't hide the truth any longer. It wouldn't be fair.' He sighed. 'I ask only one thing ... that you read this alone and digest the contents before you decide what you must do, if anything.'

Edward's stomach tightened another notch as he wondered what his friend alluded to. He needed to find out. Swigging back his drink he placed his empty glass down on the side table and jumped up. 'Thank you, Oli. You've made me rather curious. So on that note, I best be off.'

Oliver smiled at him warmly. 'I understand, Eddie. Just remember, take good care of yourself. You are like a brother to me.'

Chapter 40

E dward parked outside his house and turned off the ignition. He looked at his watch. It was 2 a.m. The road had a foggy, ghostlike stillness with not a soul in sight and the Knightsbridge houses were all in darkness. His hands trembled as he slipped the letter out of the torn envelope in the darkness of his Bentley where he knew he had some kind of privacy. He was doing as instructed, but what did Oliver mean by 'Read this alone. Digest the contents?' He unfolded the paper carefully.

4ᵗʰ October 1938

Dear Heinrich,

I have loved playing host to your delightful daughter, Connie. We have been caught up with dining, dancing and talking into the early hours. Entertaining such a beautiful girl for her twenty-first birthday was always my greatest privilege and her grasp of the German language is much improved. Our time together has been like a dream and as you so rightly say, age is not an issue.

She tells me she can't bear for us to be apart, but my divine calling is strong and there is much work to be done on military strategies. I have promised

*that she can return to Munich in the spring of next
year when we can spend quality time together.*

*So for now, I have sent her back in time for the
shooting season in Scotland and then she will have
the hunt balls at Christmas to look forward to.*

Don't let anyone steal her heart away.

Your faithful comrade,
Adolf

Catching his breath, Edward hardly dared believe the scandalous words transcribed from German underneath each sentence, rereading them over and over. His chest felt tight and he wanted to scream with rage. Sickening visions flooded his mind: Hitler and Connie laughing together, dancing slowly, his flabby arms entwined around her tiny waist. Lord knows, nothing with the Douglas-Scott family had ever been straightforward. But this! How on earth did he end up marrying a woman who'd been romanced by a Nazi warlord? He breathed deeply, trying to calm down before furiously screwing the letter into a ball.

Quietly climbing the stairs, he tiptoed into the nursery and leant over the cot to gaze at his son, Alfie, sleeping peacefully with his arms outstretched above his head. 'Alfred Edward Chopard, if you only knew how much I love you,' he whispered. He reached out his hand to stroke his son's cheek as he stirred and murmured, and then stood motionless feeling despair welling up within, wondering what on earth the future held.

Wandering out, he headed into the master bedroom next door, hoping not to wake Connie with the creaking floorboards.

Kneeling by the side of their marital bed as if in prayer, he watched his wife sleep, just as he'd done with his son. She looked so serene laying there, so innocent, her long black eyelashes sweeping across her cheek, her dark hair splayed out on the pillow. How deceptive she was, luring him into her poisonous web. *How could you? How could you?*

He felt completely drained and yet he knew sleep would elude him. He couldn't bear to sleep next to her, not now he knew what she'd done, what she'd been.

Feeling dazed, he staggered upright and drifted out of the room, back along the corridor and into the bathroom, quietly closing the door. Leaning over the sink he splashed his face with cold water and looked in the mirror, reeling backwards, startled by his reflection—the image of a man he didn't recognise—aged, with dark circles under his sunken eyes, his forehead a mass of fine lines and his once thick, dark hair now dappled with flecks of grey. 'What's happening to me?' he gasped.

Saturday morning, 26th January 1946

Dr John Walters, working from his office at the London Hospital, stared at Edward's dishevelled appearance. 'Good God, Eddie, what's wrong? I've never seen you look so ill.'

'I'm really struggling,' Edward mumbled. 'I've barely slept in months.' He sat hunched over on his chair, his hands clenched together. 'I know we haven't spoken in a while, but can I trust you to keep my confidence?'

The doctor pushed his round, tortoiseshell glasses back up his nose. 'Firstly, I consider you a good friend and would always keep your counsel, and secondly, I am legally bound by patient confidentiality. So have no fears.'

'Thank you, good friend. It's just ... well, I've rediscovered some of my past,' he said, hesitantly. 'I have three children whom

I've been in contact with, whom I love desperately. No one knows about them, not even, Oli.'

John sat back in his chair, his eyes widening. 'Goodness, Eddie. Your past has revealed itself and that's fabulous news.'

'Yes, it is, and that's why I'm scared, really scared ... that I won't be around for much longer.' His eyes watered. 'And then there's my adorable little Alfie and another on the way. Family means everything to me. I just don't know what to do.'

John lifted his eyebrows, feeling confused. 'Eddie, it's true that fatherhood is a tremendous blessing and also a tremendous responsibility, but you're a good man, a vibrant man, with a lot of life to live and you mustn't think in such a negative way.'

Edward emitted a long sigh. 'I'm afraid that's easier said than done. My mind is turning, turning, turning, always turning.' He lifted a shaky hand. 'I just need one good night's rest.'

Leaning forward, the doctor inspected the swollen blood vessels scattered across the whites of Edward's eyes. 'Hmm, not surprised, you're exhausted. We all need rest and frankly you look like a broken man.' He paused. 'There's a saying, *The sleep deprived bark at the moon and run with the dogs*, meaning, it tests your sanity and your ability to read people and situations. You might find yourself becoming paranoid, for example, for no good reason.'

Edward stared wistfully into the distance and nodded.

The doctor picked up his prescription pad and scribbled on it. 'I can certainly prescribe you some Veronal. That should help.'

'Veronal?'

'Yes, it's a barbiturate which slows down activity in the brain. I can give you three months' supply, but only take them if you're desperate. They'll mess up your sleeping pattern.'

'Thanks, John. How long does it take to kick in?'

'Within twenty minutes, but don't take more than the advised dosage and don't mix with alcohol. An overdose can cause unconsciousness rather rapidly.' He patted Edward's arm. 'Personally, though, my old chum, I think you just need to escape. Spend some time with your children in the country or get some fresh sea air. Sometimes a change of scene is the best cure of all.'

Chapter 41

Monday morning, 28th January 1946

I wouldn't have believed it was possible; the day our boutique door swung open and my handsome father breezed in.

'Surprise,' he called out with a grin. He took off his Homburg hat in a salutation of gentlemanly courtesy as I stood there speechless.

I raced over to hug him and he held my face in his hands, planting a warm, protective kiss in the centre of my forehead.

'Well, this is unexpected,' I said.

'Are you complaining?'

'No, not at all. I'm happy you're here.'

'Daddy!' cried Hannah. She hurtled towards him like a torpedo, squealing with delight, her skirt flying upwards as he caught her, lifting her off the floor.

'Hannah!' I snapped, 'you're fifteen now—behave!'

Hannah rolled her eyes.

'Aww, Ruth, she's just happy to see me,' said Daddy with a wink.

'It's just not ladylike,' I replied, catching myself turning into Mama, standing there, quite the bossy one with my hands on my hips and my face twisting into that judgemental dark glower. I didn't want to snap, but she was growing up fast and with her hourglass figure and long legs, it seemed improper that she should behave with so little decorum.

Gabi wandered out of the stockroom, clutching a notepad and pen in his hand, his face blank, without even the tiniest twitch of a muscle.

Daddy reached out his arms for a hug. 'Come here, son.'

Gabi stepped forward, shaking hands with him, hesitant, as if they were strangers. I saw Daddy stiffen, so I broke the silence. 'How about I put the kettle on, make us all a cuppa?'

'I've a better idea,' said Dad, 'how about shutting up shop and spending the day with your old man instead?'

'Yes, please,' squealed Hannah, clapping her hands together.

'And before you say anything, Ruth,' he reached into his jacket pocket and pulled out his wallet, 'I'll put five pounds in your cash till so you needn't feel guilty.'

I put my hands up as a barrier. 'Daddy, please, you don't need to keep giving us money.'

'Ah, excuse me, I'll do as I wish,' he insisted.

He handed me the white banknote which I tentatively took.

'Life is short, so I thought, why wait when we could all be snuffed out in an instant.' He snapped his fingers as if to illustrate the point and walked over to our shop counter, picking three apples out of the fruit bowl, feeling their weight and throwing them up in the air, juggling them with rhythmic precision just as he used to.

All three of us stared at him astounded. 'Daddy,' I said, 'I can't believe you just did that.'

'Did what?'

'Juggling those apples ... you did that back in the old days. It was one of your party tricks.'

He grinned. 'Must be a good sign then.' He placed his gloved hands together. 'So anyone up for a walk on the beach so I can take in some of this fresh sea air? Then we can go get some lunch and eat lots of sugary treats.'

'Hooray! Chocolate cake and ice cream, yum,' shrieked Hannah. She bounced up and down doing star jumps.

'That's a lovely idea, Dad, thank you.'

Gabi remained silent, but his beautiful, stubborn eyes glistened.

This meant so much, a chance to have Daddy to ourselves. We grabbed our coats, hats and scarves and followed him out of the shop, pausing only whilst I put the closed sign on the door and locked it.

After ambling down to the beach, we looked out at the sea, watching the waves as they crashed onto the shore, the surf flying up in the air like frothy bubbles. Dad visibly relaxed as he took a deep breath, inhaling the salty air, and we all trudged along the coastline, our shoes sinking into the damp sand leaving a trail of footprints.

I watched Hannah and Daddy walking ahead together whilst she clutched his arm and felt a lump in my throat. It's funny how it's always the simple things that make you nostalgic, especially when Daddy took her hands and twirled her around as they spun, danced and kicked up the sand like dust. She threw her head back and chuckled. Her laughter was contagious and soon Gabi and I were laughing too, skipping past them, our arms stretched out like aeroplanes, whizzing around. I was reminded that when it came to family you were never too old to feel young again.

We spent two hours rambling, stopping to pick up any unusual pebbles, competitively lifting our arms up high to see who could throw them furthest into the sea. Naturally, Gabi won.

'Come on then,' Daddy yelled, 'consolation prize. It's lunchtime, Goldbergs. Follow me.'

We all cheered, sprinting after him. And twenty minutes later we found ourselves standing outside the grand Metropole Hotel.

'Oh,' said Hannah as she stared at the building, 'are we going here?' I saw her glance at Gabi. His face seemed to blanch as he stood there motionless.

'Anything wrong,' said Dad. 'I booked in advance. It's my surprise.'

They both remained silent without even a flicker of a smile.

'Don't be so ungrateful,' I snapped. 'What on earth is wrong with you?' I was shocked at their bad manners.

Dad looked baffled as we all trailed behind him into the plush dining room where a maître d' welcomed us at the door. He took our coats and led us to a large round table with a white table-cloth set out with shiny silverware. We all sat down and looked at our menus. I was amazed; the list of entrees, main courses and desserts, well, it was some of the most exotic food I'd ever heard of. L'escargot, whatever that was, simmered in white wine, braised pigeon in cider apple sauce, and seared duck in raspberry jelly. I wanted to sneak the menu into my bag as a trophy, just to prove that we'd gone somewhere posh to eat top-notch food.

After a lot of curious questions, Daddy asked us what we wanted and ordered us all sorts of delicious delicacies, including champagne! It wasn't long before the waiter brought us a bottle of the chilled fizz in an ice bucket and I felt like a starlet as he poured us all a glass.

'Your first time for champagne?' said the Latin-looking waiter, smiling at me.

'For all of us,' murmured Hannah, fluttering her innocent blue eyes.

He placed the bottle back on the ice with an elegant flourish of his arms, hands flexed as if performing a Spanish dance.

Daddy leant forward and pressed two ten-bob notes into his hand. 'We're celebrating, with no expense spared.'

'Thank you, sir,' replied the waiter, bowing, 'celebrating anything special?'

'Family,' said Daddy raising his glass into the air. 'Ruth, Hannah, Gabi, I'd like to propose a toast.' I felt a bit tearful when he looked at us one by one and said, 'Thank you, all of you, for being back in my life.'

'To family,' we all shouted together, clinking our glasses.

The waiter watched us with a beaming smile. 'Wonderful,' he stated, with an exotic accent, 'the only thing you can never replace,' before he waltzed off to deal with other customers.

'So this is champagne?' stated Hannah, still looking strangely awkward. She lifted up her glass and took a sip. We waited for her verdict as she spluttered, squeezing her eyes shut and then stared glassy-eyed straight ahead. 'Woo, sparkly firework juice. That exploded right inside my brain. Go on taste it, Ruth,' she said goading me with a naughty glint in her eyes.

I picked up my glass, relieved that she seemed more relaxed, and gulped a little too fast. Fizz went up my nose and I sneezed grabbing a napkin, trying to delicately dab my face in a feminine manner. I could see Gabi and Hannah smirking and felt my face grow hot with embarrassment. *Ruth, act like a lady. You're dining out la-de-da style.*

Dad chuckled and raised his glass. 'Here's to sparkly firework juice.'

I was about to say, 'Cheers, Daddy,' when the waiter arrived back with our starters. Feeling starved, I quickly spread thick globs of mushroom pâté onto a hunk of crusty bread. And then I was gone, off in a heavenly delirium, savouring the creamy texture as I bit into it, when a whimpering noise from Hannah interrupted my ecstasy. I turned to my right to see a teardrop falling into her bowl of asparagus soup, and Gabi's head bent over his braised tongue as if he felt sick.

Daddy stopped grinding pepper onto his smoked salmon. 'Is everything all right, you two?' he asked, looking at them, concerned.

Neither of them answered, both their faces contorted in some kind of melancholic torment. Daddy and I glanced at each other not knowing what to say or do.

'Sorry, Daddy,' I whispered, breaking the sounds of Hannah's muffled sobs. I shifted about on my chair. 'I'm not sure what's wrong.'

After a few minutes, Gabi regained some composure, and spoke in broken spurts. 'It's this place ... it's where Aunt Betty got engaged.'

Daddy raised his eyebrows. 'Who's Aunt Betty?'

'She was Mama's sister. She took Hannah and me in when we had nowhere else to go.' Gabi looked back down at his food, not making eye contact. 'Jim was her feller. He proposed to her here.'

Now I realised why they'd been acting so strangely. Father leant forward, his eyes full of warmth as he placed his fork back down by his plate.

'Hannah and I grew to love Jim,' Gabi spluttered. He gazed up at the ceiling, his body tensing as he struggled to stifle his grief.

Hannah's face was damp, covered in endless trickling tears, so I pulled a hankie out of my handbag and handed it to her with a smile, gently nudging her arm. She grabbed it, wiped her face and then noisily blew her nose. 'Jim was like a dad to us,' she said with a sniff.

Daddy's shoulders moved up and down matching the rhythm of his breathing. 'They both sound very special. So where are they now?'

'Nearly three years ago, Bournemouth got bombed. Jim was killed.' Gabi gulped, looking around. 'This place was in ruins. They've repaired most of it since.'

Father looked down at his hands. 'I'm so sorry to hear that. It must have been hard on both of you, losing him.'

'And then Aunt Betty hanged herself, desperate with grief. That's why we run her boutique,' I gabbled on without thinking.

Gabi glared at me with the most evil look I've ever seen, leapt up out of his seat and stomped off with electrifying speed. And before I could think straight, Daddy sprinted after him through the dining hall.

'Did I say the wrong thing?' I crumpled into my seat, feeling like the clumsy dimwit who shouldn't be allowed out into normal society.

'You were a bit brutal,' said Hannah. She was still sniffling and dabbing at her eyes.

'Oh, me, and my stupid, runaway mouth.' I reached out to hold her hand, grateful that she clutched onto mine as a sign of forgiveness.

Twenty minutes sped by as we finished our starters, our eyes scanning the dining room until we saw them both amble in and sit back down as if everything was tickety-boo.

'We were worried about you,' said Hannah. She wrinkled her chaffed nose.

'I just needed some fresh air,' replied Gabi. He picked up his champagne, glugged it straight back, burped, and set the glass back down on the table.

We all looked at each other and a ripple of sniggers grew louder and louder like a happy thunderous roar. I wanted to remember today—these were the good times; our daddy was here, the war was over, and I so wanted my siblings, for perhaps just a little while, to stop mourning the dead and celebrate the living.

Later that day, we all gave Daddy a tour of our home and then went to the park nearby. Hannah and I sat down on a wall to watch 'our boys' play football, cheering them on, just as we used to.

Gabi seemed completely different when we returned a few hours later, his sullen grumpiness transformed into gooey warmth as he relaxed, leaning against the windowsill with a silly grin. It was obvious he needed that bonding time with Dad and I hoped it might soften his spiky attitude.

Daddy didn't leave until eight and before he walked to his car, he turned back, reluctant to go. 'I feel like I'm the luckiest man in the world,' he said hugging each of us in turn, and we all told him how we loved him with all our hearts.

After we watched him drive off, we wandered back inside the house, already missing our day of endless laughter. Hannah ran to the bathroom to brush her teeth before bed and I went back into the living room feeling bereft now he'd gone. I sensed Gabi felt the same and we stood there awkwardly staring at each other.

'Did that really happen?' asked Gabi. 'Was Dad really here?'

'He really was Gabi and you seem much happier.'

'I am.' He let out a long sigh, the angles of his handsome face softening. 'I feel like a ton of bricks have been lifted.'

Catching me unawares, he moved towards me, flinging his arms around my neck in such a rare display of brotherly affection that I was quite taken aback. It was the first time we'd been physically close since our house was bombed. 'I'm sorry if I've been treating you and Hannah badly,' he said, his eyes all runny.

I hugged him back, squeezing him. 'I understand. You must have felt you lost your parents twice over with Aunt Betty and Jim dying. You got some hard edges, little brother, to keep all the hurt away, in case you lost us too.' Gabi nodded and looked down at me tenderly, towering above my five feet three inches. His warm expression spoke all the words needed, as I stretched up and kissed him on the cheek. 'I love you, Gabi ... through good times and bad. We're family, always remember that.'

'I love you too, Ruth,' he said softly.

Hannah ran in yelling, 'Hey, what about me?' and we laughed, pulling her towards us for a warm loving snuggle.

None of us had ever stopped grieving for that day the bombs destroyed our lives. The past was gone, but the pain still cut deep, leaving scars that sometimes tear open. Somehow, spending time with Daddy brought about a deeper healing. *Everything's fine, now, I told myself. We won't lose him again.*

Chapter 42

Saturday evening, 2nd February 1946

Edward sat opposite Connie at their dining table. Their personal chef had prepared their meal of beef fillet with asparagus and boiled new potatoes, whilst Travers their butler poured Edward some white wine and Connie some water from a carafe.

'This is lovely,' said Connie gazing at Edward, breaking the tense atmosphere. Her pregnant belly was now so large that she struggled to pull her chair close to the table. 'It's good to have you all to myself for once. I haven't seen you properly in weeks.'

Avoiding any eye contact, he sipped his glass of Château La Tour Blanche. 'Apologies,' he replied quietly, 'I've been terribly busy with these endless rehearsals.'

'I'm so sorry I couldn't have supported you more, Eddie. I've felt so tired lately. You do realise there's not long to go, don't you?' She patted her stomach.

He glanced at her, fidgeting in his chair. That face he once thought serenely pretty now looked harsh with its angular cheekbones, her lips set in a permanent sulky pout like an ungrateful child. 'Yes, I know, angel. I can't wait.'

He felt so selfish, yet he couldn't reach out to her. It was evident that their marriage was an embarrassing sham with a rotting blackness at the core. And, God, how he wanted to confront her about Hitler, but he daren't. She would undoubtedly burst into tears, rush off to her parents for support and then he'd be linked to the stolen letters.

'Darling, you keep staring at me strangely. Is something wrong?' She looked awkwardly at her plate.

'I'm just exhausted, Connie. Do forgive me if I retire to bed earlier than usual.' He could tell by the look in her eyes that she didn't believe him. He was being too polite, overly stilted, like a bad actor on stage.

'Of course, darling.'

They ate the remainder of their meal in silence with only the grating sound of their knives and forks scraping against their china plates until he excused himself from the table. He pecked his wife on the cheek, barely brushing his lips against her skin before heading off to bed.

It was only 9 p.m. when he swallowed a sleeping tablet with a mouthful of water and lay down on their bed to reflect on the letter. Closing his eyes, he hoped the medication would kick in fast and stop the poisonous thoughts that plagued him. Connie and Hitler kissing and caressing, their naked bodies entwined as they moved into different sexual positions. How could she? Granted the letter was dated 1938, a year before the war began; she could never have known he'd go on to murder millions, but she must have known something of his military plans. What did she see in such an ugly man with such a festering, demonic heart? He remembered what the journalist had told him—that the German leader had taken a variety of lovers, many of them British debutantes, completely addicted to his power.

He was overthinking, he knew it, his brain burning up, his head feeling heavier and heavier, flopping to one side as if filled with liquid lead—until his thoughts scattered and he fell like a stone, dropping into a void of deep, paralysing sleep.

'Darling, are you all right, you're still dressed?' whispered Connie an hour later. She leant over the bed, gently stroking her fingers against his cheek. There was no response as he lay on his back, snoring, his arms and legs spread out. Curious, she picked up the bottle of tablets from the bedside table next to him and looked at the contents. *Sleeping pills?* She placed them back and wandered downstairs, picking up the phone in the hallway, dialling shakily.

'Mummy, I'm desperately upset,' she gasped, the words choking out of her in between sobs.

'Darling, what on earth is wrong?'

'I think ... I think Eddie's having an affair.'

'Oh, don't be silly, darling. He so obviously adores you.'

'You haven't seen how things have been recently.' She wiped away streaming tears with her hand. 'He leaves the house in the early hours and he's often not home till past midnight, knowing I'll already be in bed.'

'That doesn't surprise me, those endless recitals must be exhausting.'

Connie tried to stifle her sobs, holding her hand over her face. 'I know, but tonight over dinner, he barely looked at me. I'm sure he's met someone. I've often wondered about other women, ever since ...'

'Ever since what, darling?'

'Ever since we bumped into a woman years ago. She thought Eddie was her former lover. She even asked if I was one of his floozies. And then one night he came home later than usual. I could smell a woman on him ... her scent was all over his skin.'

'Now, now, Connie, calm down. You don't want to bring the baby on early. Take some deep breaths. Come on, breathe in.'

Connie inhaled deeply and slowly breathed out as her mother waited.

'That's better. I honestly think it's those silly old hormones making you imagine things that aren't true. I remember getting in quite a tizzy when I was pregnant with you.'

'Really!'

'Yes, darling, all ladies get a bout of hormonal madness from time to time. So where's Eddie now?'

'He's in bed, asleep. I found some sleeping pills.'

'Well, at least he's resting that genius mind of his. I tell you what, why don't we meet tomorrow, have a spot of lunch in Harrods?'

'Okay, Mummy, if you say so,' she replied, her voice hoarse.'

'Everything will be fine, darling. Now go to bed and get some rest.'

Connie put down the phone, her hands still shaking. Her mother's words hadn't comforted her. She knew something was wrong. She sensed it in her bones and she would hunt it out, whatever it was, even if it took all night.

Fuelled by fear, she plodded through the house, her bulging tummy along with her swollen legs making her feel like a clumsy mammoth waddling around. She lingered outside Edward's locked office door. *I wonder,* she thought, her paranoia heightening, *if he's hiding something in there.* Slipping her hand into his jacket pocket on the coat stand she fumbled around, finding a key, and quickly looked up and down the long marble hallway to check none of the servants were around.

Opening the office door, she walked inside, quietly shutting it behind her. She turned on a lamp stand, and cast her eyes around the room, smiling at his grand piano with his name engraved on the side. Wandering over to his desk, she noticed a half-written letter with a fountain pen next to it. She picked it up with anticipation, curious if this might be it, the evidence she was looking for.

> *My Dearest Ruth,*
>
> *I miss you too. I feel so lonely back here in London.*

'Dearest Ruth', she read several times, 'I miss you too.' She felt a wave of panic ... was Ruth his mistress, the reason he was always home late? She spun round and looked over to his safe. *That's it! A vault of sin!* Lumbering towards it, her mind raced, wondering what the code might be—twisting the dial with the anniversary of their wedding, her birthday, the date they met. 'This is impossible,' she gasped with frustration, 'nothing works.'

She stewed for nearly an hour, obsessively going over anniversaries, until it flashed into her mind.

Alfie's birthday: 20th February 1944.

She twisted the dial to the numbers 20—02—44.

The steel door clicked open. 'Oh my God, it's worked!' She looked at the bundle of envelopes feeling a sense of dread.

Hearing a floorboard creak, she pushed it shut, panicking that Edward might have awoken. Walking out of the room, she trudged back up the marble staircase, holding onto the wrought iron bannisters, feeling breathless as she reached the top. She tiptoed into their bedroom. She wanted to laugh hysterically when she saw her husband still snoring, spread out like a starfish, sound asleep. *Am I going crazy?* But she couldn't stop, not now. *I'm not a bad wife. I just want the truth,* she told herself.

Once back downstairs, she reopened the safe. 'You are little missiles,' she said, picking up the letters. Could she bear to read them, these passionate musings? She sat down on Edward's black swivel chair, placing them on her lap, her heart hammering in her chest as she pulled out a letter from its envelope and unfolded it, scanning the contents.

1st October 1945

Dear Mr Chopard,

I'm sorry for intruding on your privacy, but I may as well get down to brass tacks. You may recall that I met you backstage after your recent concert along with Mr Gerry Jones and his family. And I have good reason to believe you are my father, Joseph Goldberg, who I thought had died when our house was bombed, four years ago, on April 18th 1941.

Please, Mr Chopard, could we meet? I can tell you more face-to-face. I run a shop in Bournemouth called, Betty's Boutique, and you can contact me via the address or phone number at the top of this notepaper.

Kindest wishes,
Ruth Goldberg

Feeling every muscle in her body tighten, Connie opened up each missive, reading them over and over.

18th December 1945

Dearest Daddy,

Thank you so much for lunch yesterday, our beautiful jewellery and the Christmas money. It was the best day ever, apart from all the times we spent with you and Mama. But I did wonder why you seem so sad. I love you, we all love you, so why do you have to keep us a secret? Would your wife be angry if she knew?

*And Daddy, I hope you don't think me rude, but
why did Mrs Morgan say she missed you? Did you
once love her? Did you ever love Mama? Be honest,
Daddy. I just want the truth.*

Have a blessed Hanukkah and please visit us soon.

Love always,
Ruth

'Scoundrel,' she snapped, anger curdling inside so strong she
felt the baby kick in retaliation. Her eyes darkened as she stared
back at the safe and saw a black diary still sitting there. She
dropped the letters and snatched it up, trying to prise it open. It
was locked. *Only liars lock diaries,* she thought. Slamming it onto
his desk, she picked up a cast iron paperweight and smashed it
down, watching the lock shatter. Struggling to breathe as she
took big gasps of air, she scanned the sickly, sweet drivel about
his three children, his lover Rachel and something else, something far worse than infidelity.

*Truly I am blessed. Meeting my daughter,
Ruth and corresponding with her has given me
an undeniable healing. Fragmented memories
are gradually emerging, which I hope will
give me a sense of who I really am. And that
brings me peace when I must hide my true
Jewish heritage from my own wife and her
bigoted family. Despite my commitment to her
and my son, I am destined to live my life in
their presence, forever on my guard.*

'OH MY GOD!' she cried, clenching the diary in her hands.
'I've been living with a Jew. A dirty, rotten, stinking Jew. He's
deceived me all this time.' Her mouth fell open and she screamed,

louder and louder, until her piercing wail penetrated every corner of the house.

Travers rushed upstairs from the servants' quarters, pushing open the door, aghast when he saw his ladyship hunched over on the chair, her legs splayed out either side of her huge belly, her face a picture of contorted pain. She continued screaming, pulling out tufts of her hair, the diary falling to the floor, the letters scattered everywhere.

'M'lady, what on earth is wrong?' he said, rushing over to her. Soon he was joined by her personal maid, Miss Jackson and Nanny Pickford, along with the wet nurse, Miss Melton, who all bustled into the office to attend to her distress.

'Mistress, please tell us what's wrong?' pleaded Nanny Pickford. She placed her hand on Connie's forehead trying to gauge her temperature.

Connie clutched her swollen bump with both hands. 'I'M HAVING CONTRACTIONS,' she cried, 'SOMEONE HELP!'

With all the noise, baby Alfie awoke, wailing as Nanny Pickford rushed upstairs to see to him.

'I suggest you make some tea, Miss Melton, so we can calm m'lady down,' stated Travers, firmly.

'I DON'T WANT TEA! GET ME TO HOSPITAL!'

Travers bowed. 'Of course, m'lady. Miss Jackson and Miss Melton, please assist her ladyship whilst I speak with the chauffeur.'

The servants eased Connie out of the chair and led her to the waiting Rolls, manoeuvring her into the back seat as Miss Jackson climbed in next to her. Travers then instructed the housekeeper, Miss Benson, to bring down Connie's overnight bag which had been packed in preparation.

Knowing his master would be angry that his wife had been tampering with his private things, Travers saw it as his duty to put everything in order. He quickly went back to the office, collected the letters and the diary and placed them back into the safe as if nothing had been disturbed.

Sprinting back outside, he told the chauffeur to wait, and then raced up the marble staircase, two steps at a time, to wake a sedated Edward, still sleeping through all the turbulence. 'Mr Chopard, please wake up,' he shouted, taking some smelling salts from the drawer of his bedside table and sticking them under his nose.

Edward jerked forward, squinting at Travers, still half-asleep.

'Master, your wife has gone into labour!'

'What?' he said, feeling confused, 'but she's not due for three months!'

'Nature doesn't stick to schedules, sir. Your driver is waiting with the engine running.'

Reality finally appeared to bite. 'Thank you, Travers.' Leaping out of bed he ran downstairs followed by Travers and jumped into the front of the Rolls next to the driver.

The windows of the car were open to give her ladyship some air and Travers watched his master gaze at his wife in the back of the car—her eyes shut tight as she groaned in pain. 'Darling, I'm here?' he said softly, reaching out to touch her hand.

His mistress's eyes opened wide. 'Oh God, not you. GET OUT! GET OUT!' she cried, making grunting noises in between her shallow breathing.

'M'lady, please,' said Miss Jackson, taking her hand, 'you mustn't upset yourself like this.'

'Bloody hormones,' his master muttered. 'Queen Charlotte's Maternity Hospital in Goldhawk Road, please driver. And put your foot down.'

'Yes, sir,' replied the chauffeur, his tyres screeching as he drove off.

Sunday morning, 3rd February 1946

Six hours later, Edward paced the hospital corridors when Mr Walker, the consultant obstetrician appeared. He was still wearing his theatre gown and white slip-on shoes as he peeled off his surgical gloves.

'Mr Chopard,' he said, flashing him a benevolent smile. 'Congratulations. You are now the proud father of a three pound, five ounce, baby boy.'

'Oh,' replied Edward, standing motionless, 'so the birth went okay then?'

'Well, there were some complications as baby was born rather early, but he's a robust little thing—a good weight despite being premature—so both mother and son are doing wonderfully.'

Edward stepped closer. 'A son.' He swallowed, his eyes moistening. 'Can I see him?'

'Not just yet, Mr Chopard. He's being cleaned up and your wife is obviously exhausted. I would give it an hour before visiting.' The consultant smiled again before briskly walking off.

Edward decided he needed some fresh air. He should have felt elated, but he was a bundle of nerves. The birth of his son marred by what Connie's reaction might be, given her earlier unexpected outburst.

An hour later, almost to the second, he walked back into the maternity ward, attempting to politely avert his eyes from any nursing mothers. He shivered when he heard a woman scream, 'TAKE THAT THING AWAY FROM ME!' *What new mother could say that, about her own flesh and blood,* he thought as he arrived outside the private room where Connie had given birth.

'Stop, right there, Mr Chopard. I'm afraid you can't go in!' said the ward sister quickly walking over.

'What do you mean? That's my newborn son in there.'

'We are under strict instructions. Mrs Chopard doesn't wish to see you. She's in a highly emotional state.'

Edward felt his hands go clammy. 'Was that my wife screaming for the baby to be taken away?'

The sister looked sheepish. 'Yes, Mr Chopard. I'm afraid so.'

'But why is she behaving like this? I'm the one who should be angry about things, not her.'

'Your personal affairs are not my business, Mr Chopard,' said the sister brusquely, wiping her forehead with her hand. 'Many women go into shock after giving birth. I'm sure this phase will pass.'

He stumbled backwards, feeling his legs buckle. 'So how is my son being taken care of?'

'Your wife's wet nurse, Miss Melton is here.'

'Is there anyone else with her?'

'Her parents, Lord and Lady Douglas-Scott. They are comforting her.'

In a fit of frustration he tried to push through the door as the sister jumped in front, her plump girth guarding the entrance.

'Mr Chopard!' She glared at him. 'We will call the police if you proceed any further.'

He felt humiliated. How could he be denied access to his own child? 'My humble apologies, Sister,' he said, before drifting back through the ward to wait in the hospital corridor, hoping to get some sort of rational explanation and finally see his own flesh and blood.

He looked up with anticipation when Connie's mother appeared through the swing doors, stretching his arms out to give her a hug. 'Elizabeth, good to see you. Is Connie all right?'

Elizabeth smiled sympathetically. 'Dearest Edward,' she said sadly, 'despite everything, I still feel you are a wonderful man. I'm so very, very sorry.'

'Sorry,' replied Edward, 'for what? How is my son?' He felt confused as she shook her head and walked away.

What's going on? He needed answers, stopping a sneering Henry as he bounded through the doors, his chest heaving, fists clenched by his side.

'You've got a nerve showing your face here.'

'Why won't my wife see me?' Edward blurted out in frustration. 'What have I done?'

'It's over, Edward!'

'What's over?'

'Why your marriage, of course ... or the charade you called a marriage. I thought of you like a son, but you fooled us all, didn't you?' Henry glared at him with a derisory look of contempt and stormed off.

Edward sank onto a chair feeling lost. It was obvious they knew the truth. His secret was out. But how?

Chapter 43

Sunday afternoon, 3rd February 1946

Edward had gone to his local tavern, The Star, for a few snifters. By God, he'd needed a drop of the hard stuff, anything to help wash his troubles away. He wondered if he'd had one too many as he walked unsteadily along his road, passing rows of identical townhouses, when he saw two pheasants bursting upwards in full flight. *Strange*, he thought, hunting season was months away. They must have been startled whilst nesting in the grounds of some rich toff. How he wished he could warn the stupid things, deter them from their undeniable fate.

Stumbling towards his front door, he clutched his set of house keys terrified of what lay in store. Jabbing the key into the lock, he lurched into the marble reception hall and warily looked around. It was evident he was in for it, forbidden from seeing his newborn son. His life, his fame, his marriage, all appeared over. And where was his beloved Travers to greet him? Now, he reflected, after all these years, could he trust him or any of his household staff? He slumped against the wall feeling weary and broken, jerking forward when he heard a voice.

'Welcome home, sir.' His white-haired butler emerged from a door that descended to the servants' quarters. 'I do apologise. I wasn't expecting you back so soon. You've not long missed your father-in-law.'

'Henry!' he gasped, 'but I've just seen him at the hospital. Did he say what he wanted?'

'No, sir, I believe it was a flying visit ... but he let himself into your office.'

Edward's stomach twisted. Blood drenched images flooding his mind: Hugh's corpse, suspended from the ceiling, beaten and mutilated. Was he next?

Travers peered at him sympathetically. 'Can I get you a drink, sir?'

He still felt woozy, but to hell with it. He needed another to numb his fear. 'Er, yes, thank you, Travers. A large scotch might be in order.'

'Very good, sir,' replied Travers with a bow.

He staggered into his office and glanced around, freezing when he saw the safe door wide-open and his letters and diary gone. Of course, just as he suspected: Connie's outbursts and Henry's rage. He was everything they abhorred.

Collapsing into his office chair, he slumped forward onto the desk. Those damn sleeping pills. If he hadn't taken them, Connie could never have got in here. His head reeled as he recalled his wedding vows, *For better, for worse, for richer, for poorer.* Now that sacred pledge seemed nothing more than lines to a ludicrous pantomime. *How shallow her view of love is*, he thought. *Now I'm akin to vermin, no better than dirt on her shoe.* He felt such a fool, believing his wife held different morals from her corrupt father, when in reality their warped beliefs were one and the same.

He glanced at his watch. There wasn't much time. With a thudding heart, he raced upstairs to the nursery wondering what the future held for his two innocent sons.

He opened the door. Nanny Pickford looked up from her kneeling position. 'Good afternoon, Mr Chopard.' She continued picking up Alfie's toys, putting them into a large wooden box.

'Afternoon, Nanny, I wanted to see my gorgeous boy.' Striding across the room, he lifted Alfie out of his cot. Holding his son close, he breathed in his powdery scent as Alfie wriggled about in his arms, grabbing his nose. 'Dada, Dada,' he shouted as Edward laughed and kissed his chubby face.

'Do you think he really is saying 'dada' or just making funny noises, Nanny?'

Nanny Pickford shrugged her fleshy shoulders and laughed. 'I'm sure he *really* has learnt to say 'dada', sir.'

Edward loved his sons so much, he couldn't bear to think of them being raised by servants. He shuddered, knowing Henry would have a sinister plan in store. He didn't know what, but one thing was certain, he wasn't going to wait for a trip to the gallows.

'Goodbye, little fellow,' he whispered in Alfie's ear, trying not to breathe whisky fumes all over his poor little face. 'I hope to see you soon.' He handed his son back to Nanny Pickford knowing he'd be safer with her than anywhere near him.

'Is everything all right, Mr Chopard?' she asked, looking confused. She lifted a squirming Alfie back into his cot. 'Are you going away somewhere?'

'I'm not sure, Nanny, but whatever happens, please look after my boys?' Taking his wallet out from his jacket pocket, he pulled out a crisp ten-pound note and pressed it into her weathered hands.

'Why, Mr Chopard, that's nearly two month's wages,' she said with a look of shock on her doughy face.

'See it as a bonus for all the love you give, Nanny.'

'Thank you, Mr Chopard, and please, don't be concerned. Master Alfred and the new baby will be well looked after.'

Waving goodbye, he looked back at his son with sadness. He felt choked with emotion as Alfie stood in his cot, stretching out his arms towards him, shouting 'Dada' once more.

Stay calm, breathe, he told himself. He walked out of the room, along the corridor and into his bedroom, grabbing some clothes and throwing them into a suitcase.

He had one last thing to do. Running downstairs to his office he dialled Western Union to dictate an urgent telegram. If something happened to him, he had to leave evidence, show his loved ones that they hadn't been abandoned.

Walking out of his office he bumped into his butler, Travers, holding a tray. 'Your scotch, sir.'

'Oh, yes, thank you, Travers.' He picked up the glass and swigged it straight back.

'Going somewhere, sir?'

'Yes, if you could kindly get my coat and hat, Travers.'

Travers nodded as he took the tray away and brought back Edward's black Crombie overcoat. He helped him on with it and then handed him his Homburg hat.

With trembling hands, Edward took the hat and placed it on his head.

'Can we expect you back anytime soon, sir?'

'I pray you will see me again, Travers,' he replied, hoping the bond they'd established wasn't forged on pretence.

Travers bowed with a sad look in his eyes. 'I do hope so, sir.'

Edward saluted him and walked outside, climbing into his Bentley. There was only one place to go, a safe haven where he knew he would never be traced; the home of his beloved Rachel. Turning the ignition key, he started the engine, praying she wouldn't reject him.

Driving through Knightsbridge, he felt lighter, easier about things. The whisky had calmed him, dulled the pain. He headed south towards the East End, relieved there was hardly any traffic that afternoon, although the pavements bustled with all shapes and sizes of human existence. He noticed a group of elegantly attired ladies meandering past, chattering together like clacking birds, and wondered if they had any real concerns within their flamboyant worlds. Naturally, they'd think they did—worrying fretfully about which dress to wear and if some charmless toff had the right kind of gene pool for their future offspring. Existences steeped in pitiful trivia. Thank goodness his Rachel was different. She cared little for the superficial. She would have lived with him in an old shed if it meant being together.

He drove carefully, mindful as usual, building up a little speed, but not taking risks, his stomach flipping as he remembered Rachel's shining eyes and warm smile. Instinctively knowing the route, he sighed, grateful he was heading away from danger. Continuing on through Hyde Park Corner, he smiled at the bronze Angel of Peace on top of the arch, taking a right turn at the crossroads, and cruised for ten minutes, fast approaching Westminster Bridge. Changing gear, he pressed his foot on the brakes to slow down.

The brakes were dead.

It took a while to register, his head feeling muzzy.

He pressed again, harder, his heart pounding as the car gathered speed.

'Oh God!' he shouted, realising the brake line was cut.

He swerved onto the bridge to the bellow of honking horns, his hands slipping from the wheel as he skidded into a stream of oncoming traffic, the sound of screeching brakes and drivers screaming reaching a noisy crescendo. Two cars smashed into him as his head slammed hard into the windscreen with a loud crack, and poured with blood.

He jerked backwards, his head throbbing. Everything around him a blur as he choked on the stench of burning rubber. He tried the door: it was buckled, stuck fast. A rush of adrenaline surged through him. Hurling his weight against it, he somehow forced it open, and jumped out mid-air, just as his car bounced off the bridge and burst into flames.

Suddenly, he was a bird—a shot pheasant falling thirty feet from the sky as everything around him, the sky, the trees, the buildings, the burning dense smoke, became a slow motion whorl of colours and shapes blending into one until he plummeted through the freezing, dark water.

In this silent watery space, an unexpected serenity came over him; the images of mangled metal, toxic fumes and piercing screams ebbing away as his entire memory returned, flashing before him in a lucid sequence of events.

Marrying Rose, playing with his children on the beach, sneaking around with redhead Emma, and that fateful meeting with Rachel at the school gates—all ending in that desperate suffocation under dust and rubble—until he was rescued and breathed in a second chance—the moment he met the bewitching debutante, Connie Douglas-Scott. 'A diamond may dazzle,' his mother once told him, 'but its beauty will never feed your soul.' If only he'd listened.

He felt so weak, treading the cold water, struggling against the current; gasping, spluttering, choking before his lungs filled up with fluid. He pictured Rachel and his children's agonised faces, knowing they may have lost him again, but it was all fading, fading fast as he swirled into darkness, sinking down to the muddy depths below.

Chapter 44

Thursday morning, 7th February 1946

I waited anxiously watching Tommy race past the ice cream kiosk towards me, his face flushed pink from the sea breeze. 'So what's the big emergency?' he said with a grin, 'can't keep your hands off me?'

I ran towards him, wrapping my arms around his chest. 'Tommy. I'm scared. Really scared. I don't know what to do.'

'Blimey,' he replied, hugging me back, 'what's wrong?'

I pulled him over to a wooden bench on the walkway and we sat down—Tommy's lean frame swamped in a white shirt, baggy faded jeans and denim jacket.

'I had another bad dream last night.'

'So what was it this time?' he said, giving me his best 'concerned' look. I knew he was fed up hearing about them.

'I dreamt there was a wolf snarling at my window trying to get in. I'm trapped and can't escape and it's going to get me, rip me in two—punish me, and my Dad. I didn't know how, but I had to stop it ... keep the window closed.' I gulped. 'I woke up with this awful sense of dread, that I mustn't take chances, that I must stay safe.'

Tommy draped an arm around my shoulders, his hair blowing across his face. 'Honey, is this the big urgency, coz there is no wolf and you're not trapped anywhere. It's just a dream, like all the others, nothing more.'

'Except, I got this an hour ago.' Digging my hand into my coat pocket I pulled out the wrinkled telegram and handed it to him to read.

DEAREST RUTH —(STOP)—   03 FEB 1946

MY WIFE DISCOVERED OUR LETTERS —(STOP)— IF YOU DO NOT HEAR FROM ME WITHIN FIVE DAYS I AM IN DANGER —(STOP)— IF YOU NEED HELP CONTACT DR JUNGSTON AT THE LONDON HOSPITAL —(STOP)— FORGIVE ME —(STOP)— MUCH LOVE TO YOU ALL

DADDY   5:14 PM

Chewing on my nails, I waited for his response.

Tommy scratched his head. 'Let's get this straight. This is from your Dad?'

'Yes, Edward Chopard. You never did believe me, did you?'

'Edward Chopard, blimey O'Riley. So you've all met him since the concert?'

I nodded.

He continued to stare at the telegram. 'I guess you didn't trust me then ... to tell me the truth?'

'No, Tommy it's not that.' I threw my arms in the air, feeling frustrated. 'Dad asked us to keep it quiet. He's in terrible danger and it's all my fault. If I hadn't written to him last year, this would never have happened. I'm begging you, Tommy,' I crumpled over about to collapse into tears, 'please help. The post is up the creek since the war ended. This was sent four days ago.'

He pulled me towards him and stroked my cheek. 'Ruthie, don't worry, 'course I'll help, but your dad said if you don't hear from him within five days he might be in danger. Don't you think this is a job for the police?'

'And say what?' My voice sounded strangled. 'We have no proof. I can't say his witchy wife wants to kill him after finding our letters. They'll laugh.'

'Uh, yeah, that's quite an accusation. He hasn't said his wife wants to kill him.'

'He may as well have done. He sent us a letter only last month. There were scary people, he said, who'd despise him if they knew about us. It was obvious he meant her. But I still don't get it, why he's in such big trouble? She must be really mean, just because he had a family before he met her.'

Tommy raised an eyebrow, looking confused. 'There must be more to it than that.'

A memory of creepy Uncle Harry flashed through my mind. 'I dunno, sometimes it's the people closest to you that can be the scariest. And you have to read between the lines.'

'Look, his father-in-law's a good guy,' said Tommy. 'Don't you remember him getting my old man complimentary seats at the Albert Hall and rooms at the Savoy, all because of some press coverage? He adores your dad, took him right under his wing. I'm sure he'd be really upset if he knew about this.'

I felt my brain fire up. 'Yes, that's right and that's why we need to see him, tell him what's going on. I'll explain the letters, why we wrote in secret, how we found each other after so long.' I squeezed his arm. 'So, can you drive me?'

Tommy laughed out loud. 'What in my old jalopy? It might not even get us out of Dorset.'

'Pleeease Tommy,' I pleaded, my eyes filling up. 'I can't bear to lose him again.'

Tommy looked back at the telegram in his hand whilst I waited, my heart thudding in my chest. 'What about Gabi and Hannah?'

'I haven't said a word. I don't want to panic them. I got Dad into this trouble and I'll get him back out.'

I watched Tommy carefully fold up the telegram and place it into his jacket pocket. 'Right, I'll tie things up at work and find out where the top dog is. The hacks at the paper will have his details. Meet me back here at two and we'll set off.'

I almost wept with relief as I wrapped my arms around him. 'Thank you, Tommy. I do love you.'

'You can pay me back with kisses,' he replied with a cheeky grin.

Thursday afternoon, 7th February 1946

I looked around to check no one was watching before climbing into Tommy's battered Morris Minor where he'd parked on the Bath Road. I must have looked ready for the Antarctic, decked out for warmth: black lace-up boots, woolly skirt, jumper, trench coat, scarf, and a beret.

'So what excuse did you give Gabi and Hannah?' asked Tommy, revving up the rattling engine.

'Oh, I blamed you,' I said, peeling off my hat and scarf, 'told them you were whisking me off somewhere romantic. Gabi groaned a bit, but I said they'd get time off too.'

Tommy grinned, the engine making a worrying chugging sound as we set off. 'After this, we'll go away somewhere. Just the two of us,' he continued, glancing at me.

I leant over and kissed him on the cheek. 'I'd love to Tommy.' I pulled out a folded map stuffed inside the car door. 'So where we heading?'

Tommy clutched onto the steering wheel. 'Well, I've done a bit of ringing round, anonymously, of course, and it appears the big man is holding court at Mortis Hall, his Shrewsbury estate.'

'Shrewsbury, where's that?'

'In the quaint county of Shropshire with its famous rolling hills, woods and farmland as befits a lord of the manor.'

'Sounds lovely.'

'Well, get cosy, it's a four-hour drive. There's some snacks and a flask of hot tea on the backseat.'

'Aww, thanks, Tommy. You are thoughtful.' I unbuttoned my coat and spun round, spying a paper carrier bag. Reaching over, I pulled it onto my lap, feeling peckish. Peering inside, I rummaged about, finding a small red torch, the much-needed flask of tea, a huge packet of popcorn and two chocolate bars.

I glanced over at him again. 'We'll be okay, won't we ... going to his house? I mean, he won't be annoyed will he?'

Tommy smiled. 'Nah, don't worry about it. This is about his beloved son-in-law. He'd be worried sick if he knew. And I told you before, he's a good guy, he gives loads to charity.'

'You're right,' I said, relaxing a little. I opened up the packet of popcorn and wriggled into my seat to get comfy.

Thursday evening, 7ᵗʰ February 1946

We drove through many towns that day amidst sporadic bouts of sleety rain, stopping once in Oxford for some orange squash and chocolate cake until we chugged along the A5 into Bicton, the nearest local village. The evening was drawing in and I felt irritable and tired despite drinking the last of the sugary tea. The journey was twice as long as our London trip, and I had to remind myself why we were doing this, but then I thought of Daddy and how he must be frightened and alone. *Don't worry, we'll sort this out,* I said silently, hoping somehow my thoughts could travel and he would hear. I looked at Tommy. He was staring straight ahead as if in a trance.

'We nearly there?' I asked.

'Yep,' he answered, 'thank God. I need to pee.'

Ten minutes later, we arrived. And Tommy parked up on a muddy country path. It was a huge area of wasteland with patches of gravel and weeds, and nothing else around except for some tall, spiky, leafless trees, looming like something deformed in the twilight, and a long ten-foot-high stone wall to our right. The area appeared desolate; the sky a heavy grey after the endless rain, making the landscape appear stark and sinister, and I could hear the wind pick up, whistling through the windows. My stomach turned, but I hadn't come all this way for nothing, so I took a breath and shrugged off my fears, peering at the map. 'Yep, this is perfect, we're right by the country estate. Wait for me here and I'll be straight back.'

'Are you mad?' said Tommy, glaring at me, 'walking up there on your own. I mean, he knows my dad. He won't mind.'

'Tommy, think about it, if the servants see us together, they might think we're riff-raff trespassing before we even get a look in. Besides, I reckon they'll be more welcoming if I turn up alone. A vulnerable girl and all that.'

Tommy narrowed his eyes, peering at me as if I wasn't the full ticket. 'If you're not back in half an hour, I'm coming to find you.'

'Half an hour! Tommy. It will take me a good ten minutes to get up to the house, be reasonable.'

He let out a long sigh. 'Okay. One hour. Tops.'

I grabbed his hand, shaking it. 'Deal, and thank you, honey. You are lovely.' I leant over and kissed him on the cheek.

He pursed his lips, looking less than impressed. 'One hour,' he said again, 'and take the torch, it'll be dark soon.'

Smiling at his protectiveness, I buttoned up my coat and fished out the torch from the paper bag. Jumping out of the car, I gave the door a good slam—because if you didn't, it wouldn't shut properly—and waved goodbye to a grim-faced Tommy. I knew he was worried about me and I loved him for it, but I had to take these steps alone. If this powerful lord could see me as a daughter, just like his, see how vulnerable and scared I was—then everything could be put right.

It was just after six and Tommy was right. This was damp and wintry rural countryside with no street lamps and within minutes, it was rum-black as my grandad would say, not a spark anywhere. I flicked on the torch, grateful that it illuminated the muddy path ahead. Apart from the noise in my head, it was unnervingly quiet, and all I could hear was the sound of my own breathing and the crunch of twigs beneath my feet—until an owl hooted from somewhere in the darkness and I flinched, nearly tripping over.

Thankfully, it wasn't long before I faced the entrance that led up to the house. The wrought iron gates stood open and as I walked up the winding driveway surrounded by the shadowy outlines of trees and bushes, Mortis Hall was straight ahead. Lit up in the darkness, it was just as I imagined a stately mansion would look, colossal, with different shaped buildings, tall and short, appearing to be stuck together. And there were windows everywhere with grids, divided into small square panes. I hated windows like that—they reminded me of a prison with those horrible bars. Maybe I was still foggy from the car journey, but the building was so large, with so many smaller columns and arches, I was unable to see where the main entrance was, until I was right outside, wandering up and down, eventually catching sight of a double-panelled door set back inside two white columns.

I stuffed the torch into my coat pocket and stood still for a few minutes, rehearsing what I would say to Lord Douglas-Scott.

'I'm so terribly sorry. It was all my fault. I made him write to me,' hoping he would understand and talk to his daughter. Finally ready, I grasped the brass door knocker and banged it loudly.

Footsteps echoed against a floor and my heart raced. The door opened a little and an old man with a bald head peered out at me. 'Welcome to the Mortis Hall residence. How may I help you?'

'Um, I'm here to see Lord Douglas-Scott,' I replied, giving him my sweetest smile.

'And do you have a formal appointment?' the old man continued.

'No, um, I happened to be in the area.'

'And your name is?'

'I'm Ruth Goldberg, the daughter of Edward Chopard ... Lord Douglas-Scott's son-in-law.' This was a huge step for me. I felt so brave and strong.

'I see,' said the old man, who I realised must be the butler. 'Then, please, Miss Goldberg, would you kindly wait whilst I enquire if you may come in?'

'Er, yes, okay,' I said.

I shuffled around on the doorstep, wondering if he'd ever let me inside. It was chilly and I couldn't bear to think our long drive had been a waste of time—until the doors swung open. 'Please, Miss Goldberg, do come in. My apologies for keeping you waiting.'

I followed the butler into a marble entrance hall lit up by a dazzling chandelier, my eyes blinking from the brightness. 'Please, allow me to take your coat and hat, Miss Goldberg.'

'Oh, no, I won't be staying long, it's fine,' I muttered.

He nodded. 'Very well, Miss Goldberg, whatever you wish.'

He led me to a large room on the left of the hallway which looked exquisite, like a picture from a magazine: maroon walls, a large oriental rug in swirly browns and creams that covered a wooden floor and two plush brocade sofas in a pale green. 'Please, wait here, Miss Goldberg, in the reception room. May I get you some tea?'

'No, no, that's fine, thank you,' I said, hoping I wouldn't get the sofa mucky by sitting on it. Everything looked so blimmin' expensive.

I waited and waited, watching the big clock on the wall. Fifteen minutes ticked by and I thought of Tommy and how frustrated he'd be if I wasn't back soon. At last, the door opened and a small dark-haired woman walked in wearing black-rimmed glasses.

'Good evening, Miss Goldberg. I'm Anna.'

She spoke with a foreign accent. Maybe she was the house-keeper or the secretary.

'Hello.' I stood up. 'Are you taking me to meet Lord Douglas-Scott? I do need to speak to him urgently and I'm getting pushed for time.' I pointed to my watch to emphasise the point.

She gave a tight half-smile as if I was being impudent. 'Yes, of course, Miss Goldberg. Please, come with me.'

I followed her through the marble reception hall and along a winding hallway that eventually led to some stairs. The stairway was narrow and steep, and each step seemed to go on forever until we came to a dark corridor. There was a flutter in the pit of my stomach. Where on God's earth was she taking me?

Chapter 45

Thursday evening, 7th February 1946

Connie sat on her bed, the strap of her rose silk nightgown sliding off one shoulder as she rocked backwards and forwards, her eyes sleepily half-closed. She'd been locked away in her darkened boudoir since she'd discharged herself from hospital two days ago, grazing on just a few slices of smoked salmon and a large scoop of caviar, along with the occasional glass of champagne to calm her jangled nerves. The doctor insisted she stay longer—'Get your strength up,' he'd said—but she couldn't wait to get out of that awful dump, even if it meant leaving tiny Oscar in an incubator with the nurses.

At night, unable to sleep, she'd wander restlessly into the nursery, staring in a daze as Alfie lay in his cot. She felt as fragile as Dresden china, frightened of her strong emotions when she saw the shadow of Edward's features cast deeply into his genes. How she yearned to pick him up and cradle him, protect him as only a mother can. 'Don't touch them or try to bond,' her father had instructed, 'leave their care to the servants. They are tainted half-breeds now.' His harsh words whirled around her head like razor blades and she'd step backwards out of the room, not wanting to incur his rage.

Curling up on her bed, she switched on the wireless, listening to love songs as a distraction from her muddled thoughts. Picking up a glass of champagne, she held it with shaky hands to her lips, spluttering as the frothy bubbles hit the back of her throat. 'I ain't got nobody, and nobody cares for me,' she sang in rasping tones, thinking of all her lost loves. 'that's why I'm sad and lonely, won't someone take a chance ...' until the phone rang out on the bedside table next to her. 'Oh God, who the bloody hell is this,' she snapped, grabbing the receiver with her free hand.

'Connie,' said the familiar voice, 'It's John, John Walters.'

'Oh, hello, John,' she replied, slurring her words. 'What can I do for you?'

'It's Eddie, he's been in a terrible accident. He was brought into the London Hospital three days ago.'

'What? What do mean? What happened?' She sat up poker straight, slamming down her glass.

'His Bentley careered out of control. I'm so sorry, Connie. He's in a coma.'

Her heartbeat quickened. 'A coma! Oh, gosh. Oh, goodness.'

'That's right, I've been on call day and night, monitoring his progress, but you're welcome to come out of hours. And, erm ...'

'Yes.'

'We've tried to keep this quiet, but it will hit the rags soon. Be prepared.'

'I see. Thank you, John.'

Connie put down the phone and stared into space feeling numb. And then she tapped her bedside table ten times with the index finger of her right hand. She'd been doing this for months, every time things got hairy. She liked tapping—the rhythm and the ritual of it. Somehow it made her feel safe, protected from bad things. She picked up her crystal glass and took another sip, until it fell from her trembling hands, slopping champagne all over the carpet. She left it lying there and grabbed her negligee from the bottom of the bed, draping it around her shoulders. 'Oh God, Eddie, please don't die. I love you. I love you. Oh my, God, I love him,' she cried, astonished by her own feelings.

Travers and Miss Jackson rushed upstairs on hearing her voice, knocking with urgency.

'Are you all right, m'lady?' called Travers.

'Yes,' she replied brusquely, 'don't come in. I'm not decent.'

'Whatever you wish, m'lady. We're here if you need us.'

Biting her lip, she picked up the telephone and dialled, drumming her fingers on the bedside table, her impatience mounting as she waited for someone to answer.

'The Douglas-Scott residence?' answered the Richmond butler.

'It's Mrs Chopard here, Rutherford. Are Mummy and Daddy there, please?'

'Good evening to you, Mrs Chopard. I'm afraid not. Lord and Lady Douglas-Scott have not been here for several days and I'm not sure when they'll return.'

'Oh, I see, thank you,' she replied.

She immediately dialled the Shropshire residence. 'Please, put me through to one of my parents, Cranford, it's urgent.'

'Wonderful to hear from you, Mrs Chopard,' replied Cranford. 'However, I'm afraid her ladyship is not here at present and his lordship is indisposed. I will pass on your message when either of them becomes available.'

She slammed the phone down in temper. 'What's happened? Where has everyone gone?' She felt abandoned, just as she did as a child, left alone with that sour-faced old nanny who refused to play games and constantly scolded her. She pulled on the tasselled servant's bell, hanging by her bed.

'You called, m'lady,' answered her ladies maid a few minutes later as she opened the door and curtseyed.

'Jackson,' Connie glanced up with watery eyes. 'I need you to help me dress and curl my hair. I must look the epitome of glamour.'

'Of course, m'lady.' The maid stared at the empty glass on the floor, quickly walked over and picked it up. 'Are you going somewhere nice this evening?'

'Sadly, no, Jackson.' She dragged her fingers through her tangled dark mane. 'I've just heard the most heartbreaking news. Eddie's in hospital all alone, and I must be with him. He's everything to me!'

Miss Jackson stood motionless by the door in her black dress and white apron, staring at her with wide eyes. She'd no doubt understood from her hysterical outbursts that she'd wanted nothing more to do with her husband, feeling badly let down, but now she was slowly healing.

'Love is a funny thing, Jackson,' said Connie, noting her maid's surprised expression. 'Sometimes it takes losing it, to know its true value.'

She climbed out of bed, wobbling unsteadily and slipped off her negligee and nightgown letting them fall to the floor, leaving her naked, revealing angular ribs and hip bones jutting through her pale skin, along with silvery stretch marks trailing across her slightly flaccid abdomen; the only memento of her pregnancies.

Miss Jackson's face reddened with embarrassment as Connie walked uninhibited over to the mahogany chest of drawers, opened the top drawer and picked out some silk underwear. Connie saw Jackson avert her gaze, looking bewildered, probably considering whether to call a doctor and report her fragile mental state.

Ha, let her, she thought. Standing naked in front of her maid was something she'd normally deem quite improper, but not anymore, not now that she'd born two children and didn't have an ounce of fat on her. The purging during her pregnancies had paid off, and she was proud.

Chapter 46

Thursday evening, 7th February 1946

P lease, have a seat,' said the woman. 'His Lordship will be here shortly.'

I looked around the creepy cell of a room, painted stark white and quite a contrast to the rest of the house. A single light bulb dangled from the centre of the ceiling and two wooden chairs, placed opposite each other, sat near some sort of hospital bed. A steel cabinet stood against the opposite wall next to a small folding table.

I did as she said, but felt confused. Why had she brought me here? And the place smelt odd—there was a strong smell of disinfectant and something else, something rotting, like drains when they're clogged up, or old meat when it's been left out too long and the maggots are on it. I jumped when the door creaked open and a tall, silver-haired man strode in wearing a check suit and a black bow tie, his eyes dancing about as if he was delighted to see me. 'Good evening, Miss Goldberg. How kind of you to come and visit.'

Gulping, I stared back, wondering if I should get up and curtsey to such a respected, wealthy man or if we should simply shake hands, but I was rigid with nerves. 'You can call me Ruth if you like, sir.'

'Why, thank you, Ruth. And you may call me Henry. I hope you don't mind Anna bringing you down to my cellar. There's no privacy these days, you know. Eyes are everywhere.'

I smiled, feeling relieved. Now it made sense. An important man like him certainly needed privacy.

'So my butler, Cranford, tells me that you are Edward's daughter, is that correct?'

I nodded.

'So what brings you here, my dear girl?'

I sensed this Anna woman hovering like a shadow in the background.

'That will be all, Anna, thank you,' he stated firmly, and I saw her nod and briskly leave the room.

We were alone and time was running away. I decided to speak up, however improper. Pulling my shoulders back, I took a breath. 'I received a telegram from my father, and I wanted to talk to you about the letters, the ones exchanged between my father and me.'

Henry peered at me, looking inquisitive.

'Apparently they caused some upset with your daughter, because he had our family first.'

'A telegram, interesting. Is that what it said?'

'Not exactly, but you know, he said the letters had been found and that he was in danger and I felt that might be the issue. I mean, honestly, sir, the letters were never meant to be kept a secret or cause any upset.'

Henry walked over to the wooden chair in front of me and sat down. He crossed his legs and took a cigar and a penknife out of his jacket pocket. Flicking the blade up, he sliced off the end of the cigar and placed it between his pursed lips, and then took out a lighter, igniting it, drawing on it deeply, before pulling it out and exhaling a long stream of pungent smoke.

The air felt stuffy, suffocating, and my eyes watered.

'Ah, my dear,' he replied, 'your naiveté is touching.' He pulled out a wad of papers from inside his jacket. 'Do you mean these letters?'

He handed them to me and I saw a silly drawing on one of the envelopes: a sun with a big smiley face. I smiled and nodded, feeling waves of nostalgia as I flicked through them. 'Yes, that's them.'

He took another puff from his cigar, and I spluttered out a cough, putting a hand over my mouth.

'You know, Ruth, I always warned your dear father to never upset my beloved daughter.'

I leant forward, still clutching the letters. 'But he didn't mean to upset her. He lost his memory. He didn't know about us.'

Henry sat back and laughed, flicking ash onto the floor. 'Yes, and they were delightful musings. I read his precious diary, too. Quite the salacious story with his bit of strumpet.'

I screwed up my forehead, trying to think. Diary, what diary?

Suddenly his voice changed, got a pitch higher. 'So wonderful that my Connie married unknowingly into such a pitiful gene pool ... a Jewish greengrocer from the East End no less. And now, sadly, my family lineage is tainted by half-breeds who must be hidden away from London society.'

I tried to think, my head all foggy. Pitiful gene pool? Half-breeds? Then like a grenade going off, everything Daddy said finally registered: 'There're scary people that would despise me for my past and who I truly am.'

Oh God, what an idiot. I'd completely misread things. This wasn't about his daughter's jealousy, this was about the entire Douglas-Scott family. They all despised Daddy—hated us all for our bloodline. My breath caught in my throat. I was almost too scared to ask, but I had to. 'So, do you know where my father is?'

He shrugged his shoulders. 'No idea, but the farther away from us the better.'

I played with one of the envelopes, bending back a corner into a sharp crease. 'I see, um, well, I think I'd better go. I've taken up enough of your time.'

Henry heaved himself up with a grunt and stubbed out his cigar onto the tiled floor, crushing it with his polished brogue. And then he stared at me with a strange glint in his eyes. 'I'm afraid, my dear, you won't be going anywhere.'

My stomach twisted and a wave of nausea swept over me. 'What do you mean? Surely, I'm free to go. I need to ... someone's waiting.'

He came a step closer, and I could see the pores in his large fleshy face, smell his stale nicotine breath. I knew then they'd be no compassion. There was something about that face: the thinness of his lips, the set of his jaw, that made him look unkind as if cruelty was embedded in his DNA.

'We can't let you loose, have you souring our family name with the press, making up stories that aren't true. That would be yet another Goldberg destroying the Douglas-Scott reputation.'

Gazing up at him, I could barely speak, my throat tight. 'But I won't say anything, I promise. I won't tell anyone.'

His lips stretched into a smirk. 'You know, you're not a bit like your father, Ruth. You must have your mother's looks.' He headed towards the door, breathing heavily, before twisting his head back towards me. 'So glad to make your acquaintance.'

And that was it. The door clicked shut and a key turned in the lock. I was trapped—just like I was in my dream.

Chapter 47

Thursday evening, 7th February 1946

Tommy stood outside the front entrance of Mortis Hall, rubbing his hands together from the cold. Ninety minutes had dragged by. He'd said 'One hour, tops,' so he'd been perfectly reasonable leaving it this long, not acting all possessive and clingy like some blokes. It was probably fine, she might still be having cosy chats with his Lordship—but what if that wasn't the case? What if she'd fallen over and hurt herself in the dark, got lost somehow or even been abducted by a weirdo? So to hell with it—he needed to intervene.

He knocked and waited a few minutes, but no one answered. He knocked again, three hard knocks this time. Muffled voices, several of them, came from within—until the door opened a little and a woman with dark hair and glasses peered out. 'Can I help you?' she asked with a strange accent. Was she Russian, Dutch or German, he couldn't tell?

Tommy shoved his hands into his pockets. 'Apologies for disturbing you, madam. I'm looking for my girlfriend, Ruth. She came here over an hour ago. Have you seen her?'

The woman gave him a blank look and shook her head. 'Sorry, I think you must have the wrong address.'

Tommy frowned, and rubbed his nose. 'My apologies again, madam, but she definitely came here. She's got blonde, bobbed hair. And she's, um,' he used his hands to illustrate her shape and height, 'curvy and about so tall.'

Her eyes narrowed as she looked him up and down. 'No, I don't recall anyone of that description.'

She tried to close the door, but Tommy stuck his foot in the way. 'Look, if you go and find Lord Douglas-Scott and tell him who I am—Tommy Jones, the journalist, Gerry Jones's son—he'll twig the connection and let me in.'

'I doubt that, sir. Private appointments are booked months in advance.' She nudged the door against his foot.

'Look,' he snapped, sweat trickling down his back, 'she headed over here. I know she did.'

'Please leave, sir, or I will be forced to call for assistance.'

He removed his foot and stepped backwards. 'Sorry, madam, I'm just concerned.'

She didn't respond, just slammed the door. *Ignorant cow.* Where the hell was she then? She couldn't just disappear into thin air. Even for a cynical reporter like him, that was a ridiculous notion. There had to be some sensible explanation.

He retreated up the muddy driveway feeling a surge of panic. His instinct was to call the police, report her as a missing person, get a search party out, but he knew that was a waste of time. Someone had to be missing for twenty-four hours before they even registered the call, besides they wouldn't believe him over a rich toff. God, what an idiot, letting her walk off in the dark. Why hadn't he put his foot down like a proper man?

So now what? He was miles from home in a village full of strangers. There was no point contacting his parents or Gabi and Hannah. They'd be worried senseless. What good would that do? Pulling out Edward's telegram from his jacket pocket he read it again.

DEAREST RUTH —(STOP)— 03 FEB 1946

MY WIFE DISCOVERED OUR LETTERS —(STOP)— IF YOU DO NOT HEAR FROM ME WITHIN FIVE DAYS I AM IN DANGER —(STOP)— IF YOU NEED HELP CONTACT DR JUNGSTON AT THE LONDON HOSPI-TAL —(STOP)— FORGIVE ME —(STOP)— MUCH LOVE TO YOU ALL

DADDY 5:14 PM

That's it. He'd go back to his car, drive around and find a phone box, and then he'd call the London Hospital. The doc might not be there at this hour, but hopefully, someone should be able to pass on a message and get him to call back.

Chapter 48

Thursday evening, 7ᵗʰ February 1946

I looked at my watch: eight o'clock. There was so much time on my hands. Too much time to think. Wasted white noise that could have been utilised finding my precious father. I paced up and down, up and down, up and down, my heels clanking on the tiled floor, wondering where he was, what he was doing and if he was travelling from place to place attempting to remain anonymous. No wonder he was scared for his life, now I knew his father-in-law was heartless and cruel.

I loosened the scarf around my neck. It felt so stuffy in this windowless room, but I didn't want to throw off all my clobber because that meant I was here for a while, officially trapped, but the more I paced, the more light-headed I felt, detached from my body somehow as if I was dreaming. Why had I done this to myself, been so stupid? I'd always been too impulsive for my own good. 'Like a bull at a gate,' Mama would say. Why hadn't I learnt after Uncle Harry that there were evil people out there with their own wicked agenda. I thought of Tommy, questioning where I was, worrying himself to death. He would have come looking that was certain. What did the butler say or that Anna with the strange accent? Had they invited him in, pretended to be nice and locked him up too? Was he somewhere in the house?

The stench of something rotting grew stronger. Feeling queasy I wandered over to the sink to splash my face with water, but everything looked so grubby, I didn't want to touch it. The taps were rusty and there was a yellowy brown stain around the bowl, along with a chipped glass and a dried-up piece of soap. Pulling a face, I reluctantly turned on the taps, hearing a chugging noise as a gushing stream spurted through. I felt relieved when the cold water hit my skin, but the chugging echoed around the room like a steam train, and I wondered if the pipes were so old that they'd burst open, fill up the room and I'd be drowned. I turned them off, so jittery I tripped over a bedpan leaning against the sink base. Yuck, was I supposed to use that? God, this was so humiliating. Surely even prisoners in the nick got treated better than this. I flicked my hands around to dry them and scanned the room again.

I stared at the tall, metallic cabinet in front of me. Was there something in there, something I could pick the door lock with? I pulled on the handle, several times, but it wouldn't budge. Groaning in despair I slumped down against the wall. It had been such a long day. The letters were in a heap on the floor, so I scooped them up, stuffing them into my coat pocket. I couldn't read them, not even for something to do. There comes a point when you are so tired, your body shuts down and I could barely keep my eyes open.

And then I noticed something on the opposite side of the room that I hadn't seen before—some kind of square object about four feet high and covered in an old grey blanket, resting against the wall. Crawling towards it, I lifted up the blanket by the corner and tugged it off. My skin bristled with goosebumps as I sat there in silence. A white marble gravestone, engraved with the words:

Edward Chopard, Much Loved Virtuoso
Rest in Peace 1906—1946.

My mouth opened and some weird animalistic sound came
out, a cross between a whimper and a scream. *Oh God! They're
going to kill him.* Or was it too late? Was Daddy already dead?

Chapter 49

Thursday evening, 7th February 1946—8.30 p.m.

Dr John Walters stood by a patient's bed, his pen still in his hand from writing up medical notes. He blinked, trying to adjust his vision, worn out from the late nights, when he heard that familiar clacking of high heels and spun round. Connie wandered towards him, dressed to the nines in a red suit, matching red shoes, a fox stole and a wide-brimmed black hat perched on freshly curled hair. He couldn't stop staring, stunned by her fragility, her suit hanging loosely from her gaunt frame.

'Connie, my dear, how are you?'

'Oh, bearing up, thank you, John.'

He grabbed both her hands, squeezing them gently. 'Congratulations on the birth of your baby son? How is the little fellow?'

She smiled. 'Well, he's, you know, adorable, like all newborn, fresh out of their packaging.' She gave a forced laugh and looked away.

'And goodness you look so slim for a new mother.' He paused, not knowing what to say. 'So terribly sorry not to have congratulated you earlier, my brain is mush at the moment. I feel most ill-mannered.'

She pulled her hands away. 'Don't be silly. You were on red alert after all.'

'Yes, and this must indeed be a very dark time,' he replied warmly. 'Please, come with me.'

Following him to a private room in intensive care, she gasped when he opened the door and she saw Edward lying on a hospital bed attached to a mass of coloured tubes. She walked over to the bedside and stared at her husband. 'Gosh, it's heartbreaking, John. Is this really my Eddie?' She shrank back with distaste. 'He looks like a tramp. Surely the nurses could shave that awful stubble and scrub his nails ... they're filthy,' she added, staring at his hands.

'Your husband's seriously ill,' replied John, taken aback by her response, 'the same as the very first time you saw him, Connie, all those years ago. Only now he's a good stone lighter.'

Scanning her husband's gaunt, pale face, she pursed her lips. 'You're so right, John, and I'm eternally grateful he's under your dutiful care, instead of some anonymous doctor.'

'I'm relieved too, Connie. By the way,' he glanced at her, 'are you going to liaise with your stepchildren?'

'Stepchildren?'

'Yes, I'm sure you know about Eddie's children from his previous marriage. It's early days, but their presence may help his recovery.'

Connie clasped her gloved hands together. 'Of course. I will urge them to come as soon as possible.'

John checked Edward's catheter and IV tubes and then picked up his limp wrist to feel his pulse. 'The three of them will be devastated, bless their souls.'

Connie sucked in her cheeks and raised an eyebrow. 'To be honest, John, hearing of Eddie's accident has been most traumatic and certainly, for now, I'd prefer to spend time with him alone.'

There was an uncomfortable silence. 'Naturally, I understand. And it's wonderful that you came so soon.' He gestured for her to have a seat by the bed. 'The voice of a loved one has been known to trigger a response in a comatose patient. It might just be you that he responds to.'

'I do hope so,' she answered. She sat down, studying Edward's face, looking dazed. 'I don't understand, John. Why has this happened?'

'Well, as you know, Eddie's been in a serious accident that could have killed him. That coupled with old trauma, may have caused severe swelling of the brain. So in many ways, his unconscious state is not a surprise.'

'But how long can he stay like this and survive?'

'Sadly, no one knows. A coma often only lasts a few weeks, but on rare occasions can go on for months, even years, I'm afraid.' He smiled at her sympathetically. 'But he's monitored regularly and rest assured, his IV drip keeps his body healthy and functioning.'

'Thank you, John, you've been so kind.'

'Remember, we're friends, Connie. I must attend to my other patients, but I hope to see you again soon, with much better news.' He walked around the bed and once more picked up her floppy hands in his and squeezed them tenderly. And in his usual flurry, he swept out of the room.

Relieved that she and Edward were now alone, Connie leant over the bed and whispered in his ear, hoping to stir a response. 'Eddie, if there is a part of you that can hear me, I hope you know how much I love you, and how I'll always love you.' She kissed his cheek lightly, barely touching his skin. 'I'll always remember that magical day when I floated down the aisle in that stunning dress—the one that put me on the front cover of *Tatler*.' She smiled to herself. 'We took our marriage vows, bonding for all eternity. And how we laughed and danced the night away—and you made love to me that night, so passionately,' she continued, watching his face closely for a sign, until she turned her head, distracted by something from behind the door.

'Get her by his bedside' said the familiar shrill voice of the ward sister.

Connie stiffened, hearing something being wheeled along the corridor.

'Yes, that grating voice of hers won't rouse him,' added another voice, 'it's like nails down a blackboard.'

'I don't know what he ever saw in her,' replied the sister, 'shallow as ever—she looks as though she's dressed to attend a dinner party rather than visiting her sick husband in hospital.'

'I agree. It's bad form. Although word has it she's gone doolally.'

She heard a cackle of laughter. 'Doesn't surprise me, probably runs in the family, all that inbreeding. Rumour has it, one of her ancestors had kids with his own sister.'

'Noooo.'

She covered her ears with her hands not wanting to hear more. Doolally! Inbreeding! The jealous bitches. How dare they! She felt a lump in her throat at their blatant unkindness at such a difficult time of her life. Those awful nurses always had it in for her.

She tried to block their comments from her mind, continuing to reminisce, but as she stared at her husband's motionless body, waves of anger surged within. 'I know you can hear me, Eddie. How could you mock me like this—telling everyone about your children? How insulting. Yet you refuse to respond to your own wife.' Her green eyes filled with bitter tears as she jumped up from the chair, grabbing hold of the bedrail to steady herself. 'You,' she said, her voice quivering, 'you came to me in disguise as a good man, hiding the truth about being a monstrous Jew.' She wiped her damp face with a gloved hand. 'And yet I've learnt that I still love you. Heavens above, I gave birth to your two sons. Don't I deserve an acknowledgement for that? A flicker of your eyelids? A curl of your lip? ANYTHING?' she shouted with frustration.

As Edward remained unresponsive, oblivious to her pain, something inside her cracked like a rotting lobster leaking poison. 'It's not fair,' she muttered, 'I'm destined to be alone. A mother to two lost boys.' She ripped the necklace from around her neck, each flawless pearl clattering to the floor one by one. 'I need you, Eddie. I need you! And I forgive you, whatever demons infect your blood.'

Feeling faint, she attempted to collect herself, breathing deeply. And then she marched towards the door, tapping on it ten times, slowly and methodically, before heading downstairs to the hospital entrance, ready for her chauffeur to drive her home.

Chapter 50

Thursday evening, 7ᵗʰ February 1946—8.30 p.m.

Tommy stood in a telephone kiosk in a country lane, fifteen minutes' drive from Mortis Hall. He was outside a pub, the old style ones that Ruth loved, painted white with little dolls' house windows and a thatched roof. He waited, willing the phone to ring as he stared out into the darkness. A few tipsy stragglers wandered out of the pub entrance, one singing a raucous song he couldn't decipher, another staggering about, trying to stay upright. He grabbed the phone at the first ring. 'Dr Jungston,' he said.

'Yes, is this Tommy Jones?'

'That's me.'

'So what's all this about? Dr Walters called me saying you needed to speak urgently. Who are you exactly?'

'I'm Ruth's boyfriend.'

'Who?'

'Ruth, Edward Chopard's daughter.'

'What! Is this some kind of sick joke?'

'No! I'm sorry to call you, but I'm at a loss, Edward's disappeared and—'

354

'Stop right there,' replied Oliver. 'Let's get one thing straight. Eddie was brought into hospital three days ago after crashing his car. He's in a coma.'

Tommy paused, numb with shock. 'Oh God, that's awful.'

'Yes, it is. We're just waiting, holding our breath, hoping he might come round.' He swallowed. 'So what do you want to say to me?'

Tommy gabbled out everything he knew: How Edward had sent Ruth a telegram saying he was in danger and how she went to talk to his father-in-law to sort things out.

'So Ruth's now disappeared after heading off to Mortis Hall?'

'That's right,' replied Tommy. The wind rattled the kiosk door and he shivered, looking around, worried that he was being watched. 'But I went to look for her and they said she's not there.'

'This is worse than I thought,' said Oliver, his voice low. He hesitated as if thinking. 'Now, Tommy, you listen to me. Ruth is in danger, terrible danger. I don't have time to explain, but I suspect she's being held in a room in that house, most likely the cellar. And I don't want to panic you, but if we don't find her soon, she might well be—'

'Dead!' replied Tommy, his voice quaking as he gripped the phone.

He heard a 'yes' and his mind went blank.

'Look, Tommy, I'll drive up and meet you. It's a long old way, but I should be there by midnight. How will I recognise you?'

Tommy shuffled about in his baggy jeans, twisting his legs together, trying not to piss himself with fear, which was practically impossible with those ghoulish words rattling around his numskull brain, 'She might be dead soon.' *Dead!* He felt so stupid. She was the love of his life. How could he not have protected her?

'Tommy, Tommy, are you still there?'

A dog barked somewhere in the distance and something rattled, maybe a dustbin lid.

'Sorry, yeah, I'm tall with dark hair and I'm parked outside The Craven Arms on Oaktree Road, opposite the River Severn. I've got a white Morris Minor.'

'Good, I'll be in a black Buick. Have you called the police?'

'And say what, that she's vanished into thin air? They'll think I'm nuts. I'll go back up there, get her out.'

He heard a gasp. 'For God's sake, Tommy, don't do anything rash. Trust me, you're dealing with a lunatic. Wait until I get there. I've got something that might make them jump.'

'Okay, thanks,' said Tommy, his voice breaking. He put the phone down and leant over feeling dizzy, grabbing his legs. *Midnight.* That was over three hours: he couldn't wait that long. When you love someone, you don't sit back and wait for them to die. You do something. Anything. His stomach groaned loudly and then he retched, acid flowing into his throat. *Come on, Tommy, keep it together, don't fuck up.* He didn't know how, but he would find her, bring her back safely, whatever the risk.

He straightened back up and looked towards the pub, his legs like jelly. He wasn't sure when the pubs closed round here, but the lights were still on, and he could still see locals having a snifter. First things first, he'd use their facilities, freshen up and get himself a few stiff ones. Summon up some Dutch nerve.

Chapter 51

Thursday evening, 7th February 1946—9.30 p.m.

Henry sat in the drawing room, dressed in his pyjamas and brocade dressing gown, warming his feet by the crackling fire. This was his favourite time; a quiet house with no irritating wife milling about or demanding business calls. Thank God the old bat was in bed by eight most nights or staying with her incontinent mother. She barely had a kind word to say to him, if she bothered to speak at all.

Cranford arrived with a tray, carrying a large jug of cocoa and a wobbling cup and saucer, placing them all on a nearby coffee table, along with a rolled-up newspaper tied with red ribbon. His butler lifted up the white jug and poured some into the cup, tipping in the standard slug of whisky from a nearby hip-flask.

'Thank you, Cranford,' said Henry. He picked up his warm drink and took a sip, emitting a long sigh. This was just how he liked it: bitter as hell, no milk, no sugar. He grabbed the newspaper. 'What's this? Today's rag?'

'No, it's an early edition of tomorrow's paper, m'lord. It arrived by special courier.'

Henry read the scribbled note clipped to the front.

My Deepest Commiserations,

Clive Bartholomew,

Managing Editor of The Times

He dismissed Cranford with a wave of his hand as he snapped off the ribbon and unfurled the paper, staring at the photograph of Edward's face splashed all over the front page. Feeling a frisson of excitement, he scoured the text, hoping for good news.

> Edward Chopard, the forty-year-old virtuoso pianist has been involved in a terrifying car accident in central London. Chaos reigned when his Bentley careered out of control into oncoming cars on Westminster Bridge exploding in a blaze of flames.
>
> Witnesses say they saw Mr Chopard leap out of the car before landing in the River Thames. He was found floundering in the water by the captain of a passing steamboat who hauled him onboard. Dr Walters of the London Hospital tells us that Mr Chopard is in a coma and they are monitoring him closely.
>
> Mr Chopard is married to the beautiful debutante, Connie, the twenty-nine-year-old daughter of Lord Henry Douglas-Scott. Together they have two young sons.

Fuck, Fuck, Fuck and buggery. He folded the paper back up into sharp creases, still gripping onto it as he stared at the flowery pattern on his china teacup. He didn't understand. Surely he'd done enough to get rid of this piece of shit? He gulped down the rest of the liquid, trying to swallow, feeling his airways tighten. Anxiety always made everything in his body swell. He knew it was no good, he couldn't hold it in any longer, the rage was too strong. He lifted his right arm and threw the cup against the wall, watching it shatter into tiny pieces. 'JUST BLOODY DIE!' he screamed.

Cranford came running into the room. 'Are you all right, m'lord?'

'No, I'm bloody not, Cranford. Now clean this mess up.'

The butler bowed, his face in peaceful repose. 'Yes, m'lord.'

As he watched Cranford scuttle around, picking up the shards of broken china, he ripped the paper into shreds, still raging inside. He'd invested so much in this halfwit, treated him like a son, only to be made a fool of. He wanted to torture him for what he'd done, injecting his filthy scum into his bloodline. And what if he came round from the coma? Without doubt, he'd always be associated with the family name. He'd demand to see his Yiddish brats, expect to take them out in broad daylight, so eventually, someone would see them, know they were related to him.

He slammed his hands onto the chair arms. No, he would not have this eternal damnation. He'd get Anna to sort it. Listed on his staff as 'personal assistant,' she often stayed in one of their many bedrooms upstairs so even the old bat didn't catch a glimpse. A quick visit to intensive care and she'd disconnect his IV tubes and blood supply without anyone noticing; kill him within minutes—please God.

Anna was the perfect spy, or should he say, actress, slipping into traps unseen, working for the gormless psychologist, all because she spoke his precious, native Russian, when really she was a half-French/half-German hybrid and a fascist through and through.

They'd met a decade back, both passionate supporters of Mosley's British Union of Fascists. She was a funny, little thing, he remembered, leaning back in his chair, black-rimmed glasses dominating her small face. A thirty-eight-year-old bookish spinster of aristocratic parentage still seeking her true purpose. And how he helped her find it, recruiting her six months ago to take on the role of her life.

Edward was so touchy about everything, always whining, whining, whining, that he'd wondered for a while if he and his pal might be on to him, conspiring against his cause—he just needed proof. And the doctor gave him just that, allowing Anna to witness some of their most private confidences, including scheming with that nosey hack who was about to expose his mission. There was no way he could allow that, not after years of investment, not after Mengele's genetic research to create a new world, not after they planned a Fourth Reich. This was his life! So he tried to warn them off, tortured the idiot journalist to death, showed them *don't mess with me*. And still they stuck their nosey snouts into his business.

He wiped a slick of sweat from his forehead. His instincts proved right—they always were. 'Should have known, should have known', he muttered repeatedly, clenching his fists, squeezing his nails into his palms. Those pathetic letters were the final death knell, discovering he was the devil's own—his own son-in-law— what a sick joke. If it wasn't for Connie's desperate infatuation, he would have sniffed the creature out—there was always a look about him, something shifty in the eyes. And this was God's blessing, the way the Goldberg brat walked right into his hands. Divine intervention. He rubbed his hands together and moistened his lips. He'd finish her off first thing before the house was up.

He laughed to himself, picking up the medical manual Mengele had sent him that he'd shoved down the side of the chair. It was his big obsession these days and he carried it around constantly, attempting to understand the great man's surgical expertise. Flicking through the pages, he considered which proce- dure would be best: sterilisation, hysterectomy, hmm, that would stop the bitch breeding, but it would be messy and take time. He needed something simpler, having tried out more complex stuff on the family's Welsh Springer. She'd been a working gundog on the Shrewsbury Estate for five years and had been less than useless after giving birth to six puppies. The bitch's womb was removed, along with her stomach and heart and stored in a large tin under the floorboards of his surgical chamber, along with the hack's entrails. He loved knowing they were underneath that floor—a sacrifice to the all-seeing reptilian power—it gave him a sense of omnipotence somehow.

He turned another page, 'That's it, the eyes.' A most straight-forward project. In a few hours, he'd wander along the corridor, wake Anna, and they'd both make their way to the cellar. Then he'd grab the toolkit, now locked in the medicine cabinet after that bloody break in—and together they'd strap the runt to the bed with rope, so the damn thing didn't wriggle. And that would be it. His moment: Enter Henry Douglas-Scott, the righter of wrongs, the king of justice. He'd take out the sharpest scalpel, his sword of truth, and cut around each socket, slicing deep into the sinewy muscle and fat surrounding them and simply dig them out. He smirked. He'd really enjoy that. Edward's firstborn, a souvenir from his precious little girl; poetic justice most sublime.

He felt a rush of emotion as tears welled up. The spirit of his mentor was near. 'This is a new era, a new dawn for us, Mein Führer. We'll complete our mission and eliminate the scum one by one.'

Chapter 52

Thursday evening, 7th February 1946—10 p.m.

Tommy was inside the house, a dining room by the look of it. He couldn't believe he'd done it, found the guts to smash in one of the downstairs windows with his bare knuckles, reach inside and flick the catch so he could climb through. That's what three straight whiskies will do for you—make you fearless or damn stupid. Now his hand was buggered, skin shredded and blood dripping all over. No worries, he thought, I'm not gonna die, and I could care less about the blimmin' carpets.

He eased open the door and looked up and down the corridor. *Now where?* This place was like a rabbit warren and he needed to get down to the cellar, but where were the stairs? He decided to turn right and plodded forward, passing rows of identical white panelled doors, until he heard someone calling out.

'Henry, did you hear that? I think someone's broken in.'

It sounded like an older woman, well spoken, not the foreign bird.

'What!' shouted Henry, 'Where?'

'I don't know. Somewhere in the house. Call the police!'

Tommy opened one of the doors and snuck inside. He crumpled against the wall, his head spinning. That's all he blimmin' needed, the booze hitting his bloodstream. He poked his head out the door and jerked backwards when he saw Henry storming down the corridor in his nightwear, his face red and sweaty.

'I'M NOT CALLING THE RUDDY POLICE,' he shouted.

'Why on earth not?' said the woman, the floorboards creaking as footsteps padded after him.

'Because, my dear, we have important guests staying.'

'What guests?'

'Never mind. I'll wake up the servants. Go back to bed, dear.'

Tommy blinked, trying to steady himself. He felt shivery and hot all at once and there was blood smeared over his shirt. Why did he flippin' drink on an empty belly? Why?

Five or ten minutes passed, maybe longer, he couldn't be sure, until the floorboards creaked right outside the door. Someone was there.

'Henry! Henry! There's blood here—on the paintwork.'

Tommy shuddered. He could hear Henry's angry stomp from a distance and jumped inside an oak wardrobe half-filled with suits, smacking his head against some empty coat hangers.

'Cranford! Anna!' Henry screamed.

He heard a bell being pulled—more footsteps—more voices. God, he'd made a pig's ear of this.

'M'lord, the servants are all up and checking every room. It appears a window has been smashed in the dining room.'

Tommy crouched down, trying to block out the smell of mothballs that appeared to be in bags, hanging down amidst the clothes. He wrinkled his nose. Oh, no, he could feel it coming. He sneezed. The wardrobe doors were flung open. He was hauled out and punched hard in the face.

Chapter 53

Thursday evening, 7th February 1946—11.30 p.m.

I drifted into a weird dream, where the door banged open and someone was thrown inside a cell, someone bruised and battered, someone terrified like me—until I opened my eyes and realised it wasn't a dream, it was real. A figure lay slumped in the corner.

Half-asleep and not quite with it, I screwed up my eyes, trying to see more clearly. The figure groaned and wondering who the hell it was, I clambered off the bed, still in my coat and boots and crept over. 'Oh my God,' I gasped, my heart thumping. 'Tommy! What's happened to you?'

He looked a mess; his mouth taped up, one eye swollen shut and bruised terribly—a weeping, purplish, black mass. A jagged red gash ran across his right cheek all the way up to his ear. He looked like he'd been whacked with a mallet. He made muffled sounds through the masking tape, so I knelt down and peeled it off, as he gulped for breath and asked for water. I grabbed the glass that I'd used earlier and placed it near his lips. He lifted his head, and I heard him swallow, watched a trickle run down his chin.

'My hands,' he mumbled, 'they're tied up.'

364

I fumbled with the thin rope around his wrists which was bound so tightly behind his back I couldn't loosen it. Digging my fingers in, I tried every which way, but it wouldn't budge. 'I can't do this,' I said, feeling frustrated and angry—angry that I couldn't undo a blimmin' knot. I leant over and kissed his forehead. 'Did he do this to you ... Douglas-Scott?'

'Yeah,' he said quietly as if his voice was smashed as well as his body. 'It all happened so fast. He punched me hard ... then I must have blacked out'

'What a bastard,' I snapped, feeling anger rush through me, 'an evil, nasty bastard.' I touched his shoulder and he flinched in pain. Blood seeped through his shirt like smudges of wet paint. What else had he done? Beaten him? Tears slid down my cheeks and I wiped them away with my sleeve. 'I'm so sorry, Tommy. It's all my fault.'

He squirmed, trying to move. 'No, Ruth, I'm sorry. I got drunk, smashed a window, broke in. Not a great plan as it turns out.'

I smiled, stroking his forehead, studying his damaged eye, praying the socket wasn't broken. 'That's not like you, to take dangerous risks.'

He smiled back—that lopsided, cheeky smile that always made me melt. 'Things you do for love, eh.'

I tilted my head, feeling strangely shy. I felt such a warm surge of love for him, more than ever before. He'd nearly lost his life for me. I could have wept for him, for us, for the situation I'd got us both in—but crying wouldn't help us now. I had to stay strong, focus on the positives; after all, we had each other. I leant in and kissed his lips, softly, carefully, so as not to hurt him. 'Will you marry me, Tommy Jones?'

'What now?' He tried to laugh and then retched, screwing up his face. 'What the hell is that stench? Bloody reeks in 'ere.'

'I know, it's proper disgusting. We have to get out of here, Tommy. Find a way.'

'Ruth, there isn't a way,' he said, his voice dropping to a whisper. 'You've seen what he's done to me. We're trapped. But whatever happens, I want you to know ... I'll love you forever. I mean that.'

'And I love you,' I mouthed, feeling desperate. I saw him bite down on his lip, probably in more pain than he'd ever admit and I wanted to do something, anything to make him feel better. Some of the buttons of his shirt hung open so I unbuttoned the rest, hoping to bathe the wounds on his back, face and hands, but there was nothing I could use—no towels, no flannels, no handkerchiefs, nothing in this stupid room. I looked at my scarf draped on the floor. I'd have to wet that, try and clean him up. And then I saw marks on his abdomen—a cross and a circle inked in red on the left and right side. 'What's happened here?' I asked.

'No idea,' said Tommy lifting his head, trying to look. 'Must have been when I was knocked out.'

My body gave an involuntary shiver. How strange, drawing stuff on him like that. What did it mean: a cross and a circle? Were they symbols? I didn't like this. Not one bit. But there was nothing to do but wait.

Chapter 54

Friday morning, 8th February 1946—12.30 a.m.

Oliver bombed along the A5 into Shrewsbury going way over the speed limit, his hands gripping the steering wheel, his face set in a fearful grimace as he focused, almost manically on the road ahead. He'd been so traumatised by his dear friend's accident, he hadn't been able to eat, sleep or work. He was certain that Henry was behind Emmerton's murder and Eddie's crash, yet frustratingly there was no bloody proof for either. And now Eddie's daughter was in danger—a young, innocent girl who didn't know what kind of vicious brute she was dealing with—so he had to do something to help—something to focus his mind, rather than pounding the hospital corridors like a mad man waiting for news.

He'd tried to find reasons for Henry's callous, violent behaviour, reassessing his clinical diagnosis of the ageing aristocrat: He was a textbook narcissist. As Byron once said, 'Self-love for ever creeps out, like a snake, to sting anything which happens to stumble on it.' Whether Henry had psychopathic tendencies, he wasn't so sure. The two mental aberrations were similar; they both lacked empathy and could be sadistic, but the psychopath was unable to control their rage and delay gratification. The grandiose narcissist, however, could—waiting years for the right moment to strike, just like Henry, Hitler, and Mengele. And this was some-one who not only believed he could be the next Nazi leader but who had the patience and arrogance to realise that desire, causing havoc—not just to a few people, but to the world.

He laughed to himself. It was hard to believe such an egocentric idiot, bulldozing his way through life, could get away with such atrocities—but money and power often bought time and privilege, even with the justice system. Now, enough was enough. The lunatic had to be put behind bars, once and for all.

Scanning his scribbled notes taped onto his dashboard he parked up his black Buick on Oaktree Road, next to the Craven Arms. Climbing out of the car, he yawned and stretched out his back, feeling achy from the long journey. He looked around. Everything felt damp and clammy; that sweet, earthy scent in the air, emanating from those annoying erratic downpours. Hmm, he thought, stepping over a muddy puddle, this place is dead, dead as a morgue, with only the sounds of scuffling animals in the bushes—to be expected in a medieval market town at this ungodly hour—but certainly no sign of tall, dark-haired Tommy.

He studied the parked cars on Oaktree road, wandering along each one, checking them closely in the dark night sky. And then he saw it: a white, battered, Morris Minor. That was the boy's car, but where was he?

There was a lurching feeling in his stomach—he'd had it from the moment he'd set out. *He's gone to the house. I know it. He couldn't wait.* Fear for those poor kids coursed through him. So what now? He wanted to rush up there, but if he did, he might not come out alive. He looked over to the phone box opposite the pub. There was nothing else to do but call the police. The problem was, he had no actual crime to report. Would they believe that two missing youngsters had disappeared inside an aristocrat's country manor with no evidence? He had his doubts. Of course, he could show them the letters and they'd be delighted—a war criminal tracked down and Henry arrested for treason—but he could still get away with butchery and murder.

That house was big enough to hide bodies for all eternity.

Chapter 55

Friday morning, 8th February 1946—3.30 a.m.

Rachel lay under her pink candlewick bedspread with a pounding headache, the curtains drawn. She couldn't sleep—it was impossible these days with her mind in constant turmoil, worrying what the future held.

She heard the familiar clatter of the letter box. *Paperboy,* she thought. The lad always came in the early hours.

Jumping out of bed, she pulled her tousled hair out of her eyes and grabbed her gown hanging from the wardrobe door, throwing it over her cotton nightie. Reading might help her nod off, even for a short while.

Running downstairs to the hallway, she snatched the newspaper up from the doormat and padded into the kitchen to make some tea. Tossing it onto the kitchen counter she placed the aluminium kettle onto the stove to boil and then sprinkled some tea leaves into her small yellow teapot.

'So what's news today?' she murmured. She leant against the counter, unfolding the newspaper, staring at the front page?

What! Rigid with shock, she stood dead straight as if voltage had zapped right through her.

This was Joe! Her Joe! His picture splashed all over. Only he was called Edward Chopard and he was a famous pianist.

She held the paper up close with shaky hands, wondering if her tired eyes were playing tricks.

No, she was right ... those were his eyes, his smile.

She read all the details, soaking everything in until it all clicked into place: his more refined voice, his expensively tailored clothes, the reason he gave no current address.

Why did he keep his new life such a secret? Maybe he was too embarrassed to tell a poor commoner like her that he'd finally made it into high society.

The steam pumped out of the kettle as her fingers uncurled and the paper dropped to the floor. She pictured him lying motionless on a hospital bed, her brain a tornado of unarticulated thoughts whirling about chaotically, wanting to obliterate all memories of him one minute and hold him tightly in her arms the next.

Taking a breath, she grabbed the kettle handle, filling up the teapot, her hands still shaking madly as she poured herself the weakest cup of tea ever. Like dishwater, her mother would say, but she didn't care, she just needed some kind of warmth.

She slumped down at the kitchen table, holding the cup between her hands. 'What do I do now?' she stammered. Regardless of his fancy life, she knew her Joe well, and it was obvious he hadn't been happy. And now he was in a coma. Why did fate keep doing this, throwing obstacles across their paths, blocking them from being together? She couldn't let that happen again. She had to take control of her life. He needed her, and she would go to him, hold his hand, sit with him for hours, do whatever it took to bring him round.

Yes, that was it, she *would* go to him, first thing.

Running back upstairs, she threw off her cotton nightie, ready to choose a dress from the rail in her wardrobe. *It has to be this cherry print,* she thought, holding an elegant silk number in her hands, *he loved me in this*—until she froze, imagining his young wife, a mere slip of a thing judging by her age in the paper, loyally waiting by his bedside?

What am I doing? Am I stupid? He's married with two children. He has a rich, beautiful, young wife.

I can't do this. I can't face any more pain.

Chapter 56

Friday, 8th February 1946—5.30 a.m.

Tommy and I sat slumped against the wall, sleepily falling against each other when I heard keys being jangled. My heart jumped and I sat up straight, desperate for help; Tommy was burning up so badly, he barely stirred, his head leaning against my shoulder.

The door creaked open and Henry strode in, looking far too big for this small room, his head almost skimming the ceiling. The small, foreign woman, Anna, trailed in behind carrying a silver tray of what looked like food and drink. A distinct smell of fish mingled with the rot and I wanted to heave. I could almost taste it, the way it lingered. Everything lingered in this stagnant air.

'Good morning, good morning,' he sang out cheerfully, 'are you hungry, you two?' He leaned forward, smiling at us. 'You must be hungry, besides I could hear your rumbling tums from upstairs, so we brought you both some breakfast.' He moistened his lips. 'My absolute favourite, smoked salmon and cucumber, or alternatively, some really delectable liver pate and cress, or plain old ham and tomato—all on freshly baked bread with the crusts cut off.'

Anna placed the tray on the table along with a large urn of tea and two china teacups, and I gazed up at Henry feeling confused, not knowing how to respond. His friendly demeanour, fatherly almost, with those crinkly eyes and wide grin, made it hard to tell whether he was mocking us or actually being nice. I wanted to believe he was being nice so there's a happy ending and we could both go home, but it was there again ... that meanness, like a shadow, flickered across his lips.

'Look at the pair of you,' he said, tilting his head to one side, 'you still in your coat and boots and your young chap lying there with his shirt undone, looking quite unwell. You both seem in dire need of a good strong brew.'

Tommy groaned and shifted his head, seemingly unaware of Henry and his strange accomplice, and I felt uneasy, the way the old man's changed—I can't work him out—but then everything, it all built up, crashing through me like a wave and all my anger and frustration flooded out. 'You hurt him, you know. You're much bigger than him and you really, really hurt him.'

Anna gasped at my outburst, her eyes blazing. 'Miss Goldberg. How dare you speak to Lord Douglas-Scott in this manner, especially after he's been so kind?' Her face twisted with anger and she reminded me of those annoying head prefects at school, the way she peered at me through her glasses with a look of contempt.

Henry touched her shoulder. 'It's fine, Anna. She's from the East End. The girl knows no better.'

He glared at me, his chest puffed out, his hands behind his back. 'Yes, Miss Goldberg, I did hit the boy. What else would I do when someone breaks into my property, offer him tea and crumpets? I mean, he scared us all witless. He's lucky I didn't call the police.' He pursed his lips, placing his hands together as if in prayer. 'But I soon realised he was trying to find you and how much he cared, which is why I put you lovebirds back together.'

I squirmed, glancing at Tommy. I couldn't argue, he had a point—Tommy did break in, but only because that conniving pig had trapped me here. Now, somehow, he'd turned it all around. Now we were the wronguns. I searched for words to try to say things right, make him see reason, looking up at him, my voice hoarse. 'Look, I'm sorry. He did wrong. He broke the law and maybe he deserved his punishment—but I'm worried sick, he's red hot and look at his eye?' I touched Tommy's forehead. 'It's still swollen shut and I think it's infected. He needs medical care.'

Henry studied me with me a sneer, as if I were something that truly disgusted him. He took a step closer and I shrank back, terrified by what he might do next. I saw Anna out of the corner of my eye, smirking, enjoying my weakness.

'Admirable mitigation,' he replied with a laugh, 'but you know, Ruth, you're just like your father, always bleating on, always pointing the finger, when all along you were the miscreants. Remember you came to my door,' he shouted, waving his hand at me, 'and your boy broke into my house.'

'I know, I know,' I stammered. 'I'm sorry ... he needs help, that's all.'

'Well, I'm a charitable fellow,' he said as if collecting his thoughts, 'so he'll get help all right. I'll see to that.' He leant over and whispered in Anna's ear.

She nodded and wandered towards me, crouching down. 'Do you feel tired, headachy and weak?' she said.

The air felt thick and stagnant, making it hard to focus, but her voice sounded warm and calm. I relaxed a little and nodded a yes, feeling my head throb, praying they would show some kindness.

'We need to assess your blood sugar,' she continued, her tone firmer, 'so, please, hold out your hands.'

Blood sugar? Maybe it was the combination of tiredness, shock and hunger but I did as she asked, placing my trembling hands in front of her. Within seconds, she'd whipped some handcuffs out of her trouser pocket and snapped them around my wrists. I reeled back, breathing in sharply. 'Why have you done that?'

'Safety measures,' stated Henry in a robotic tone, 'just in case.'

'In case of what?'

'We need to fix poor Tommy,' Anna continued, a strange glint in her eye as she stood up. You must stay still, very still.' She pulled a ball of rope out of her other pocket and bound my ankles together into an uncomfortably tight knot.

I looked on helplessly, my head in a fog, as Henry lifted Tommy up with a grunt and carried him to the bed, placing him onto his back whilst Anna tied his wrists and ankles to the corners of the bed frame.

'Please, don't hurt him,' I pleaded, trying to make eye contact.

Of course, what did I expect, the bastards ignored me, and Tommy seemed out of it, mumbling incoherently. He looked so vulnerable lying there with his shirt hanging off—and those red marks on his stomach, now smudged with sweat. Why were they there?

Henry appeared to busy himself, unlocking the metal cupboard. He took out some blue gowns hanging inside and threw one on, handing the other to Anna. It looked far too big for her, almost swamping her small frame. She rolled up the sleeves and my heart thumped against my rib cage. They looked like surgical gowns ... surgical gowns for operations.

Henry leant into the cupboard again, rummaging about and then spun round to face me, placing a mask over his forehead, ready to pull down over his nose and mouth. Snapping on a pair of white rubber gloves, he smoothed them deliberately onto each one of his fingers. Anna did the same, her face utterly passive, focused on her hands. It was as if they were both enjoying this, putting on a performance, wanting to draw things out for their own warped entertainment.

'And now for the crown jewels,' Henry said, hauling out a long wooden box and placing it onto the table. He opened the lid and smiled to himself. It's a horrible smile, grim and sneering.

Looking up from the floor, I couldn't see what was inside, but something felt wrong, terribly wrong. 'What are you going to do?' I asked, swallowing my panic.

'Hmm, what am I going to do?' he repeated with a chuckle. 'Remember that old childhood game of noughts and crosses?' He continued to peer into the box.

'Yes,' I replied. My stomach churned.

'Well, I loved it when I was a boy. I was a terror, hounding our dear nanny to play it endlessly. "Come on Nanny," I would say, "one more time"—but instead of pens and pencils—Anna and I are going to play with these.' He pulled out two scalpels and handed one to Anna.

I felt a cold, paralysing swirl of fear. I watched her thank him, her eyes alight as she checked the sharpness of the blade with her gloved finger. The room closed in and I couldn't breathe. My head spun and I lost it, screaming so loudly my lungs felt close to bursting. 'HELP SOMEONE HELP! YOU'RE BOTH EVIL, SO EVIL,' I shouted breathlessly, gulping from the screams, trying to get more air, tears streaming down my face.

Henry waited for me to stop and then stared at me like I was the mad one. 'What do you mean evil?' he said, waving the scalpel around in his hand. 'I give regularly to good causes. I gave my daughter riding lessons from the age of four. I supported your deceitful father with his musical career, even organised a bloody German plane to take him on his tour for Christ's sake. I'm a good person. Always tried my best to be a good man, a good father and I get this close,' he pinched his fingers together, his eyes welling up, 'but it's never enough. All I ever wanted was to belong to something, to give my life meaning.'

'And you do belong. You are a good man with a big heart and you will be a good leader,' Anna reassured him, squeezing his hand. 'We must fight for our cause. And I'll always be here for you, whenever you need me.'

She cocked her head at him, almost flirtatiously and I felt like an intruder, as though I shouldn't be there. My eyelids felt heavy and I blinked, wondering if I'd got things wrong, that my tiredness and panic made me hear and see things that weren't true, because just like my dreams, none of this made sense, none of this was normal. I would wake up soon and find it wasn't real, it couldn't be—people didn't behave like this. And all the while Tommy just lay there in some kind of delirium, occasionally groaning. I feared the worst; that he'd slip away, that he'd soon be dead.

Before I could get my head straight, Anna was in front of me holding some masking tape, biting off a section with her teeth. She leant in close, punching the tape hard onto my mouth before turning back to Henry.

'That's better, dear,' he said, smiling at her. 'So, where were we?' He stared at Tommy's stomach, the sight unbearable—my poor boy, trussed up like raw meat, and soaked in sweat. A wheeze crackled every time he exhaled, and I'm holding my breath, not knowing what to do next.

Tommy squirmed and cried out. A metallic scent mingled with the room's rancid odour, and I knew Henry had cut him. Terror ripped through me and I wriggled about, struggling to free my feet from the rope, making muffled noises through the tape.

A loud knocking broke the tension and I froze. 'M'lord, m'lord, I need to speak with you urgently.'

'What do you want, Cranford?' yelled Henry, sounding irritated, his scalpel poised inches away from Tommy's flesh.

'The police are upstairs, m'lord, wanting to question you.'

Police. Oh God. I felt a rush of adrenaline.

Henry jerked his head towards the door. 'That's fine, Cranford. We just need to finish something. Don't come in.'

I was shocked, he didn't give a stuff, sounding arrogantly unconcerned like only the posh nobs can. But they were up there, the cops, only they can't hear us, they don't know we're here, and if I don't do something, no will ever know ... no one will ever find us down here in this pit.

I studied him and Anna carefully, still holding their scalpels, watching their feet under the bed. They seemed oblivious, chanting something in a language I didn't recognise, engrossed in their own strange world ... only now I can't hear them ... blood pounding in my ears as I steadily shifted my body towards them, bending my knees.

Henry was leaning over the bed, over my Tommy, like a vulture about to feast on its prey, his eyes glinting manically, moving in, taking one step closer.

And I waited, and I waited.

And then I swung out both my legs—kicking his ankles hard.

Henry's eyes widened and his arms flew up in the air as he tripped, falling sideways onto Anna like a felled tree. His scalpel clattered onto the tiles and an unearthly howl went through me.

The door burst open and the butler ran in, his face rigid with shock, taking in the madness of it all.

Henry lay on top of Anna, his legs and arms juddering, until he stopped moving, became completely still.

Anna screamed, her eyes bulging.

A pool of blood seeped onto the floor.

Chapter 57

Friday morning, 8th February 1946—9.30 a.m.

Rachel stood by the doors of Intensive Care wrapped up in a black cloak and red cloche hat, trying to catch the ward sister's attention as she looked at her paperwork. 'Excuse me,' she whispered, 'may I see Mr Goldberg, um, sorry, I mean Mr Chopard. I'm an old friend.'

The nurse carried on flicking through the files she held in her hands without looking up. 'Sorry, dear, family members only.'

'Oh, but please.' She touched the sister's arm, her eyes filling with tears. 'Please ... he's special.'

The sister glanced at her. 'What's your name, dear?'

'It's Rachel. Mrs Rachel Morgan.'

'I see,' she said, 'he must mean a lot to you, Mrs Morgan?'

Rachel stared down at her feet. 'I'm sure you understand what it was like to lose a loved one during the war, how painful it was.'

The sister paused for a moment and then nodded, the hard angles of her face softening. 'Yes, Mrs Morgan, I certainly do.'

'I mean, is this a good time? Is he alone right now?'

'You mean is his wife here?'

'Um, yes.'

'No, the delightful Mrs Chopard isn't here,' she said with a smile, 'so come with me. I won't tell if you don't.'

Rachel touched her chest feeling breathless. She wanted to hug this kind woman, squeeze her tightly. She'd taken a huge risk coming here, but it was worth it. She was going to see her Joe.

The nurse pushed open the swing doors, led her through the ward and into the small private room. 'Here we are, my dear,' she whispered. 'I'll leave you to it.'

'Thank you. Thank you so much,' said Rachel, smiling at her.

She rushed to her former lover's bedside, her heart sinking as she drank in every detail: the gauntness of his face, his jaw now covered with unkempt bristles and his bloodless lips outlined with a blue tinge. He lay there completely still, his eyes closed as if he were frozen in time. Only his chest rising and falling with every breath, proved, thankfully, that he was still alive. 'Joe, Joe can you hear me?' she whispered. 'I hope you can, somewhere in that faraway place you're trapped in.'

She leant over the bed, her fingers tracing his brow, his nose, and around his lips. God, how she'd missed him, the feel of his skin, his strong musky scent. And now she was alone, she couldn't resist any longer. Brushing against his rough stubble, she touched his lips with hers, warming them, hoping passion might stir him. As she pulled away, she felt awkwardly self-conscious. What was she expecting, that he would instantly awaken and kiss her? How silly and naïve. She would have to sit tight as Joe once told her, be patient like she'd always been, and pray.

Sinking down on the chair by his bed, she did just that, mesmerised by his face, so serene in his unconsciousness. It was hard to believe that this was the brilliant, extraordinary man she'd been so deeply in love with. A man so vital and funny, he swept you away with his hungry zest for life. She picked up his limp hand and stroked it gently. 'Remember, Joe, how you waltzed me around the living room, gazing into my eyes as you sang to me, reminding me that life was precious; that we must laugh and dance and sing. I was so lonely and you brought me back to life. And now I want to do the same for you.'

She reminisced for hours, comforted by loving memories, oblivious to time ... until she heard footsteps. She looked up at the wide girth of the sister standing beside her.

'You best go, dear,' she said with a smile, 'in case a certain someone turns up.'

Rachel nodded. 'May I come again tomorrow?'

'Of course. Come as often as you like. But keep to the mornings to be safe. I've heard Mrs Chopard doesn't rise before noon.'

Chapter 58

Monday morning, 11th February 1946

Tommy's asleep, snoring as usual, but I've been awake for hours … my thoughts whirling, too scared to sleep, too scared to let go in case I dreamed.

The slow rattle of a dustcart in the distance and the endless clanking of bins made me think it must be around six. The early morning light filtered through the thin, floral curtains, and there's an icy nip in the air. I shivered, pulling the bed covers up around my chin, still feeling shaky.

There's a clatter from downstairs, someone moving around; Oliver lighting the fire I hoped. His house in Fulham was a lovely place, but lacked a woman's touch—all plain white walls, wooden floors and uncomfortably cold like old properties often are—but he'd taken such good care of us, liaising with the police, keeping us fed and watered and insisting we stayed so we could visit Dad more easily—something I was desperate to do, since we'd sort of recovered.

He'd even said Gabi and Hannah should join us too which was a huge comfort. I'd called them straightaway and they were due to arrive later this afternoon. I couldn't wait. I'd missed them both so much.

The only way I could give thanks for his hospitality was by offering to do some chores. 'Give me some hot suds and a dish-cloth and I'll give the house a good scrub,' I'd said, the morning after we arrived, 'and then I'll cook dinner.'

'No, No,' he'd said, pottering towards the kitchen in his slippers, 'an occasional home-cooked meal is a pleasant idea, but please, nothing more.'

He's a lovely man, so kind and thoughtful and I liked to think we'd know him for years to come.

But I tried not to think of the future, in case Dad's not there.

And I tried not to think of that morning, but it was always there, lingering like a shadow I couldn't shake off.

Those scalpels looming into view, the terrible sharpness of the blades and then the relief when the police piled in, open-mouthed at the strange sight.

It took six of them to lift Henry's hefty corpse off Anna's tiny frame—around seventeen stone of fat and muscle, they reckoned—and she just lay there staring into space, shivering and soaked in his blood. Her knife had pierced right through his heart and he died within minutes.

Tommy and I were taken away in an ambulance, kept in hospital overnight and monitored closely.

A policeman questioned me, but I couldn't focus. I could barely talk, I just kept crying.

I was desperately worried about Tommy but it turned out he had slight concussion, low blood sugar, and too much booze in his bloodstream, which is why he was so disorientated. The cut on his stomach was deep, an awful gaping wound, but it was stitched up and covered with a dressing—and after some food, painkillers and a cold compress, he was back to his old self.

We were both interviewed officially at the police station the following afternoon, put in separate rooms, even fingerprinted. I had to explain everything over and over: Dad's warning in his letters, the telegram, why I visited Mortis Hall alone in the dark. I pulled out all the evidence stuffed in my pockets, and I got a finger-wagging, told I was a silly girl, putting myself in danger like that. And Tommy got an ear bashing for breaking and entering—'Because of the unusual circumstances', to quote the constipated constable, 'you'll be let off with a slapped wrist.' I suppose they had to be seen to cover all corners.

The news about Lord Henry Douglas-Scott filled the newspapers. BIGGEST SCANDAL SINCE THE WAR ENDED, screamed the headlines; how one of Britain's richest aristocrats was Hitler's secret ally and prime suspect in a journalist's murder. The poor man's organs were dug up from beneath his basement floor—the very one we'd sat on. It chilled me to think that Tommy and I were his next victims.

Reporters had dug into the Lord's bizarre past and discovered that he was part of an occult sect, Serpentem Corde, which is why he was chanting those strange words over Tommy's unconscious body. They also discovered that *Mortis* was Latin for *Death*. So the grand sounding 'Mortis Hall' was actually the more sinister 'Hall of Death'. It made me wonder how long Henry had murderous intent to name his mansion that, and if other bodies might be buried in the grounds of that ominous building. It was evident that he was insane; that he'd stop at nothing; that he was behind Dad's accident.

The police had seen the gravestone, freshly engraved, waiting for Dad's body, but with bits of burnt metal at the bottom of the Thames, there was a lack of evidence.

His accomplice Anna proved more of a mystery—described by 'sources' as a lonely spinster, desperate for attention, who lived off an allowance from her wealthy parents. She lived and breathed Nazi ideologies, yearning to be part of a master race, hiding away in the corners of fascist groups, making copious notes and then stalking the speakers wherever they went.

Whether that was true or not we didn't know, but it made sense why she was drawn to the bullish billionaire with his crazy ideals. Two self-obsessed fanatics hell-bent on creating their own warped world.

Oliver was certainly shocked to read about her. We were all in the living room when he threw the newspaper onto the floor, his hands trembling. I think it unnerved him, the betrayal; that he took her into his confidence. 'It makes you wonder,' he said, shaking his head, 'who you can trust?'

Thankfully, she got her comeuppance, already remanded in custody for aiding and abetting, and suspected treason. In a few weeks, she'll go on trial, and word has it she'll get a tough sentence, so she could be banged up for a long old time.

Did all that soothe me? A little. But one thing soothed me more. The very thing I omitted to tell the police—that I had tripped Henry—that I triggered his death. It could have gone wrong, but it didn't—luck, serendipity, or maybe providence lent a hand. And he fell right onto Anna's knife.

It would have been fine if I'd confessed. After all, it was self-defence. But I didn't want to be picked over in the press or declared a hero.

I did it for me. I did it for Tommy. And I did it for Dad. And it will be my special secret for as long as I choose to keep it.

Monday afternoon, 11th February 1946

Gabi and Hannah joined us, having locked up the shop and jumped on a train. I introduced them both to Oliver and we all hugged joyously.

Tommy and I didn't want to talk about what happened or about Dad—we'd done enough of that already, regurgitating events, tormenting ourselves with endless worry. Thankfully, somehow, they both understood as we all tried to stay upbeat, distracting ourselves by playing cribbage, whist, and dominoes, anything, but thinking of sad things.

Dad was mentioned just once, when Gabi and I cooked up some stew and mash in the kitchen. Grabbing my hands he gazed into my eyes. 'Ruth, we nearly lost you and Tommy. So tonight we need to pray for Dad. Maybe five of us can make a difference.'

I nodded in agreement, thinking how sensitive and wise my younger brother was, and after we'd all eaten, I asked everyone around the table if they'd join in. Hannah and Tommy voiced an instant 'Yes' and it was touching the way Oliver stood up, his bloodshot eyes shining as he pressed his hands together. 'What an inspired thought,' he said, 'faith can work miracles.'

It was just after seven and already rum-black, but in the glow of the moon, with the soft patter of rain against the windows, we all knelt on the living room floor, holding hands and recited the Shema. 'Only Tommy stayed quiet, the gentile amongst us, not knowing the words, but mouthing them after.'

And then we did that thing we hadn't done for years—tapped our fingers together seven times for good luck, praying that Daddy would finally wake.

It was strange, but afterwards, a lightness enveloped us, a sense of peace. I felt it, saw it in all their faces, the worry lines melting away—and I hoped that whatever happened, we could catch it like a butterfly and keep it with us forever.

Chapter 59

Tuesday afternoon, 12th February 1946

Fast asleep in her bedroom, Connie was awoken by the incessant ringing of the phone.

'Bloody hell,' she yelled, picking it up with half-closed eyes. 'Yes!'

'Darling, is everything all right? Are you okay?'

Oh God, her mother, yet again, always bloody checking up on her. 'You woke me up. I was asleep.'

'Darling, I'm so terribly sorry, but it is only five o'clock. Have you seen the papers?'

'Papers. You know I don't read that rubbish. Why?'

'Well, darling, I've waited a while to ring because you've been so poorly, but I have some terribly bad news ... um.'

'What!'

'I'm afraid, um ... I'm afraid, your dear father is dead,' she said, taking a breath.

Connie remained silent, her thoughts scattering into dust.

'Darling, are you there? It's so awful what happened. Would you like to—?'

Connie slammed the phone down feeling numb. 'Dead,' she murmured. Her beloved father, dead! Tears ran down her face, and she sobbed, quietly at first, and then uncontrollably, tearing her hands through her hair. She didn't want the details. She couldn't bear to hear the hows and whys. What did it matter anyway? Lord Henry Douglas-Scott, her father, one of the most dynamic, charismatic men she'd ever known, had gone forever, and her own mother didn't sound remotely bothered. Of course, she wouldn't care, the heartless witch, she'd be too busy having it away with his best friend, Nicholas What's-his-name.

She jumped out of bed naked, her hair a mass of tangles. Throwing on her negligee she padded over to the door of her bedroom.

Tapping it fifty times, she turned around once before opening it. She'd increased her taps recently, a compulsion, something she had to do to stop the darkies from getting her. And goodness, weren't they coming thick and fast. The only problem was it took her ages to get around the house. And those bloody servants kept intervening. 'Are you okay, ma'am? Can we help you?' She just wanted to be left alone, to sort herself out.

Wandering into the hallway, she robotically stumbled towards her son's room, pulling the belt around her gown a little tighter.

She tapped on the door another fifty times and spun around again. Twisting the handle, she walked inside.

'Good afternoon, m'lady,' said a strange woman. She was kneeling on an oriental rug and looked up at her with a rather surprised expression. 'Good to see you up and about. Did you want to have a cuddle with Alfie? Oscar's still not home yet, I'm afraid, but the wet nurse is with him. I take Alfie in most days to see him.'

'Who are you?' she asked, stepping forwards, 'and where is my Alfie?'

The strange woman stared at her, her eyes bulging out, big and round. In fact, her entire appearance seemed big and round with that chubby red face and those chunky arms holding armsful of toys. *How very mumsy,* she thought.

'M'lady, I'm Nanny Pickford. I've been in your service for three years.'

'Oh, yes,' she replied, feeling confused, 'that's right.'

'And Alfie's here, look.' She pointed to the thick carpeted floor. And there he was, her little boy, all dark, tousled curls, chattering away happily, playing with his wooden train set. He did so love that train set. Eddie had bought it for him.

She felt a lump in her throat and her eyes moistened. 'Aww, that's nice,' she murmured, 'he does look happy.'

'Yes, m'lady, he is a happy little soul, always laughing. Do you want to know how Oscar's doing? He's put on two more pounds. He's getting much stronger.'

Connie covered her ears with her hands. She thought she might go mad with all this chatter, going around and around in her head. 'No, that's fine, Nanny, thank you. I don't need to know anymore.'

Chapter 60

Wednesday morning, 20th February 1946

Rachel arrived onto the ward first thing, for the last time she decided. She'd tried to stay away until the scandal died down, but it wouldn't die down, not something as shocking as that, not for a long while—so she decided to sneak back in, pretend to visit someone else, holding a huge bunch of pink lilies.

'Oh, now, they're pretty,' said the sister studying the flowers and then her face. 'Nice to see you again, dear. It's been quite the drama here with all his family visiting and those bloomin' reporters sniffing about.'

'Yes, understandably,' replied Rachel, not knowing whether to stay or go. If the press caught wind, she knew it would start a maelstrom.

'Well,' the sister continued, 'we have a rare moment of peace, so do go in.' She reached out her hands. 'Shall I take those from you, dear. Put them in a vase?'

'Thank you,' replied Rachel, recollecting how much Joe loved them, how he'd always turn up with a bunch in his hands. She could only hope their fragrance would somehow trigger something deep within.

She wandered into his room and sat by his bed, just like before, once again reminiscing about the old days, gazing at his blank expression. *Is love always destined to be like this,* she thought, *endless heartbreak and pain?* She ran her hands through her hair, feeling more alone than ever. 'I won't be coming here anymore, Joe,' she murmured, 'not ever again. Of course, I'll miss you, like I've always missed you ... but I need to stay strong, and let you go.'

She sensed someone outside the door and slumped back in her chair, hoping it wasn't his wife or a reporter. Relief washed over her when the sister swept back into the room with the vase of flowers.

'I've been thinking, Mrs Morgan,' she said. 'When Mr Chopard first came into this hospital all those years back, he couldn't recall a thing, except an old tune he used to whistle. Now, what was it?' She placed the lilies on his bedside table, her forehead wrinkling as she tried to think. 'Something like ... I didn't want to do it, I didn't want to do it?'

'You Made Me Love You?' gasped Rachel, her eyes lighting up.

'That's it!' the sister replied, throwing her hands in the air, before breezing back out.

Rachel smiled. *That was our song.* She remembered how he'd sung it to her so many times and how she'd clung onto those words in her darkest moments, questioning if he was up in heaven looking down at her. Was this the answer?

She sat on the edge of his bed and leant in closely. 'You made me love you,' she sang hesitantly, 'I didn't want to do it, I didn't want to do it. You made me want you, and all the time you knew it, I guess you always knew it. Give me, give me, what I cry for—' She paused, choked with emotion, wondering if she saw his eyelashes flicker. She stared at them. They did flicker, she was sure of it, but maybe it was her imagination, maybe it was false hope. She continued to sing, trying to think of the words, until she stopped, feeling tearful. 'What am I doing? I'm so useless. I can't even hold a tune.'

She was about to get up and leave, frustrated with love, frustrated with everything—until his lashes flickered again. And then he blinked several times, before opening his eyes. She held her breath, watching open-mouthed as he stared into space.

'Oh God, Joe,' she said, grasping his hand, 'you're awake.'

He blinked again as if trying to adjust his vision and then looked directly at her. 'Rachel?' he rasped, his voice broken from lack of use. He touched her face with his hands, feeling every contour.

'Joe, thank God.' Her heart swelled and she longed to throw her arms around him, but he was so fragile, so frail. She must contain herself, be practical. She propped a pillow behind him, and grabbed a glass of water from the bedside table. 'You must be thirsty?' She held the glass to his lips as he took a sip.

'Rachel.'

'Yes,' she answered. A tear slid down her cheek. 'Yes, Joe, it's me.'

He moved his head forward. 'I ... smelt ... you.'

'Smelt me.' She wrinkled her brow, feeling confused. 'You mean the lilies?'

'No. You! Your skin ... your hair.'

She blushed, looking away. It was as if they'd only just met, not like strangers, but two renewed lovers, purged by life's traumas, and she felt so stupidly shy.

'And our song,' he said. 'You remembered.' He entwined his fingers around hers, his words slow and laboured. 'I'm grateful ... you're here, that ... you stayed.'

'You heard me?' she said, her eyes shining.

'Yes,' he murmured with a smile, 'everything.' He laid his head back against the pillow. 'I'm so weak.'

She stroked his face, her awkwardness fading. 'You will be, darling. You've been in a coma for weeks.'

'Weeks?' his voice trailed off.

'That's right, but you're awake now.'

He swallowed. 'I have to tell you ...'

Rachel touched his face tenderly, her blonde hair falling over her eyes. 'Yes, Joe.'

'I crashed.'

'I know you did.'

'But I was coming to tell you ...' He took a deep breath, 'that ... I love you.'

She couldn't speak, feeling a huge lump in her throat. Tears gushed down her face—long awaited, happy tears, healing all her years of pain. She brushed his forehead with her lips, and gazed at him. There he was, her Joe, wiping her damp face with his fingers.

The door creaked open, taking them both by surprise, and they both turned to look.

'Good Lord, Eddie,' said John Walters sailing into the room with a startled expression. 'You're back with us. You should have asked the nurse to call me.'

Edward smiled with recognition. 'John.'

John pushed his round tortoiseshell glasses back up his nose. 'And who's this lovely lady?' he said, gesturing towards Rachel. 'I don't believe I've made your acquaintance?' He reached out his hand to shake hers.

'Rachel,' she replied. She stood up, extending her arm, feeling the warmth of his grip.

'So you're the lightning bolt that's sparked our patient back to life?'

'Apparently so,' she said softly.

'Goodness, only Eddie could attract a beautiful woman whilst still in a coma.' He gave a wink and in response Edward's face creased into one of his big magnetic smiles.

'We've known each other for years,' said Rachel. 'I sang him an old familiar song. Or rather tried to ...'

John's eyes crinkled at the corners. 'An old familiar song, hmm, was that the one Eddie used to whistle?'

'Yes,' said Edward with a smile.

'That's wonderful. Songs, smells, unconditional love, they are all potent forces for the subconscious. You must share something very special?'

They both nodded silently, clasping each other's hands. Old soulmates falling into comforting new rhythms.

'And how are you feeling now, old chap?'

Edward rolled his head around, his neck crunching. 'Foggy.'

John chuckled. 'Sounds about right. There's bound to be confusion as your mind adapts. And I'm afraid I need to invade your privacy a little longer, and check you over, if that's okay?'

Edward nodded in agreement as John reached down into his bag.

He wrapped a pressure bandage around Edward's arm and then inserted a needle into his vein, drawing out blood, before sealing it into a tube. 'So my friend. Do you remember who you are—your name, age, where you live?'

'Yes, I remember.'

'Are you sure, old chap?' asked John, pursing his lips. 'Your brain has taken quite a bashing. It wasn't so long ago you couldn't recall a thing.'

Edward's face brightened as he pulled Rachel closer. 'I remember what matters. I'm a father of five children ... who loves a lady called Rachel ... and my name ... my name is Joseph Goldberg.'

Chapter 61

Wednesday afternoon, 20th February 1946

We visited Dad daily whilst reporters camped outside the hospital, cameras flashing. It was scary. They could spot us a mile off. Tommy and I had given tons of interviews, but they wouldn't leave us alone, and now they were after Gabi and Hannah too, so we kept our heads down in the back of Oliver's car, ready to rush into the back entrance with hats pulled down over our faces.

It was another cloudy, drizzly day so Tommy remained in the car with Oliver whilst they figured out where to park as anonymously as possible, agreeing to reconvene inside the hospital lobby. The sister wouldn't let us all in at once, so we always had to stagger the visits.

Trudging through the hospital corridors, we pushed open the swing doors of the intensive care ward, avoiding staring at the rows of seriously ill patients, and stood outside our father's private room.

I glanced at Gabi and Hannah and pushed open the door. My stomach flipped. I had expected to see Dad still unconscious, connected to his drip, but he was a picture of blissful contentment, sitting on the bed, dressed in a crisp grey suit, cuddling Mrs Morgan. We all stared at him, hardly daring to believe our eyes.

'Children, come in,' he said, his voice hoarse. He slowly got up and staggered towards us.

'Daddy, you're awake,' cried Hannah. She bounded over to hug him and he pulled her into an embrace.

I nodded a dazed hello to Mrs Morgan and she smiled back. I don't think any of us knew how to respond, except to take it in turns to hug our father, holding him tight, taking comfort from his heart thumping in his chest. It all seemed so strange, that he was actually back with us, and whatever caused this miracle, I said a silent thank you that our prayers had somehow been answered.

'Ruth, Hannah, Gabi, I have an announcement,' said Daddy. He stood there whip-thin with a proud look on his face as we all waited on pins, wondering what he would say. He reached out his hand and pulled Mrs Morgan towards him as if they were about to dance. 'I know this might come as a surprise, but Rachel and I, well, we're starting a new life together.'

I looked at Mrs Morgan, shimmering in a glow of delirious elation, her arm draped around Daddy's waist. She gave a slow contented smile and said fuzzily in that newly-in-love way, 'and you're all welcome anytime. My home is your home now.'

Of course, we all embraced her. She made him happy, even if we had no idea why she'd suddenly appeared, but then so much of Daddy's life was a riddle and this wasn't the time to grill him for answers.

'Dad, before I forget, I must give you these. The police have finished with them now.' I pulled out the bundle of letters from my pocket and handed them to him.

'Oh those, please, look after them for me, Ruth.'

'Are you sure? Don't you need them for reference ... to jog your memory?'

Daddy seemed to drift off, his eyes all foggy, grasping answers from somewhere in the air. 'You know, children, I've been living my life as if I was still buried beneath rubble, suffocating under lies and loneliness—but after the river claimed me as its own, and I thought my time was over, all my memories came rushing back, and now, thanks to all of you, I can breathe.' He stretched out his arms. 'You all mean the world to me.'

'Oh, Daddy, that's amazing,' I said, overwhelmed with emotion.

No other words were needed, no explanations, clarifications, nothing. We all simply looked at each other and linked hands. And in our silent knowing, it felt as if the wheel of fate had finally turned, the wild monsoon over, and out of the wreckage, like a forest that had been burned to the ground, somehow new growth would come, stronger and greener than ever before.

The next day, around six in the evening, Daddy was discharged from hospital and Mrs Morgan invited us back for a celebration dinner to her home in Hackney, only ten minutes' walk from the empty bomb site where we'd once grown up.

'More sparkly firework juice anyone?' said Dad as we all sat around the table, along with Oliver and Tommy drinking champagne. And we all yelled, 'Yes, please,' our stomachs full to bursting.

This time together meant so much after what we'd gone through, treasuring the simple pleasures of family life: Dad telling silly jokes with mischief in his eyes, whilst Oliver regaled us with stories of their time together, and the rest of us laughed as Rachel—I felt I could finally call her that—served up slices from a huge dish of apple pie.

'To family, friends and loved ones, we have everything, because we have each other,' said Father, raising his glass.

'To family and friends,' we all cheered.

And that was true, despite the past. Even if we couldn't forgive the wrongs, in order to really live, we had to count our blessings, and try to forget, for now anyway.

Chapter 62

Six months later
Saturday, 17th August 1946

Much has happened since then with many landmarks to celebrate the good. We all headed back to Bournemouth, the four of us. Tommy still had his job at the newspaper and us Goldbergs still had a boutique to run—but being so near death focused Tommy's mind and he proposed marriage within the month. We had to start saving, but I accepted with joy as he slipped a ruby engagement ring onto my finger. Becoming Mrs Jones was one of my dearest dreams.

Rachel would never be a replacement mother, but she has become our good friend, and she certainly has her hands full now. Alfie and Oscar went to live with them only weeks after Dad left hospital. Connie was declared an unfit mother after becoming completely unhinged and her servants resigned. Sadly, she was carted off to an asylum, so her mother, Elizabeth, handed the children over, happy, I'm sure, to put her sorrow behind her and start a new life. Although she did ask if she could visit from time to time. And Dad agreed. After all, she was their grandmother, and he felt that both she and Connie were, in their own way, as much victims of Douglas-Scott as all of us.

Their house is bedlam now and Dad said he's never been so tired having a toddler and a baby full-time with no servants in attendance, but he and Rachel make adoring parents, and we often come to visit, along with Oliver and my old childhood chum, David (Rachel's son), always arriving and leaving to the delicious sound of laughter.

Friday, 16th September 1949

It's been two years since my wedding day and I'm five months pregnant with our first child. I gaze at my husband, Tommy, lying fast asleep beside me after a hard day's work, and I silently thank the stars, the moon and God in heaven for him and my wonderful new life.

There's nothing to be scared of anymore, the bad times have gone, and I'm living in a warm, comfortable two-bedroomed terrace looking forward to a glorious future.

But as I lie in the dark, my heart skips a beat when the floorboards creak, and I jolt when the wind rattles the windows. I can't help but worry that something or someone might sneak in and snatch all my happiness away. *There's no one there*, I tell myself, *no one can hurt you.*

But hopes are not enough.

I need to lay my demons to rest—to take control of the past once and for all—so I somehow find the courage to travel back in time to 1941, where it all began.

As a ghost from the future, I'm back in the blitz, watching all three of us, the Goldberg children, standing amidst the rubble of our demolished home. Stumbling over burnt remains, I wander towards my teenage self and my bereft broken family, and with eyes full of love, I give us all a huge hug and a lot of hope. I open up the book that I've written and say, 'Keep strong in this era of bloodshed and pain, for time soon flies and our darkest times will one day bring us all a divine redemption.'